ALSO BY M. G. VASSANJI

The In-Between World of Vikram Lall

When She Was Queen

Amriika

The Book of Secrets

Uhuru Street

No New Land

The Gunny Sack

The Assassin's Song

The Assassin's Song

M. G. Vassanji

DOUBLEDAY CANADA

Doubleday Canada and colophon are trademarks.

LIBRARY AND ARCHIVES CANADA CATALOGUING IN PUBLICATION

Vassanji, M. G.

The assassin's song / M. G. Vassanji.

ISBN 978-0-385-66351-9

I. Title.

PS8593.A87A88 2007   C813'.54   C2007-902329-0

Owing to limitations of space, all acknowledgements to reprint previously published material may be found at the end of the volume.

Printed and bound in the USA

Published in Canada by
Doubleday Canada, a division of
Random House of Canada Limited

Visit Random House of Canada Limited's website: www.randomhouse.ca

10   9   8   7   6   5   4   3   2

And song is *not* desire; so you taught.
Nor is it courtship, nor is it courtship's prize
Song is being.

RILKE

The Assassin's Song

Postmaster Flat, Shimla. April 14, 2002.
After the calamity, a beginning.

One night my father took me out for a stroll. This was a rare treat, for he was a reticent man, a great and divine presence in our village who hardly ever ventured out. But it was my birthday. And so my heart was full to bursting with his tall, looming presence beside me. We walked along the highway away from the village, and when we had gone sufficiently far, to where it was utterly quiet and dark, Bapu-ji stopped and stared momentarily at our broken, grey road blurring ahead into the night, then slowly turned around to go back. He looked up at the sky; I did likewise. "Look, Karsan," said Bapu-ji. He pointed out the bright planets overhead, the speckle that was the North Star, at the constellations connected tenuously by their invisible threads. "When I was young," he said, "I wished only to study the stars . . . But that was a long time ago, and a different world . . .

"But what lies above the stars?" he asked, after the pause, his voice rising a bare nuance above my head. "That is the important question I had to learn. What lies beyond the sky? What do you see when you remove this dark speckled blanket covering our heads? Nothing? But what is nothing?"

I was eleven years old that day. And my father had laid bare for me the essential condition of human existence.

I gaped with my child's eyes at the blackness above my head, imagined it as a dark blanket dotted with little stars, imagined with a shiver what might lie beyond if you suddenly flung this drapery aside. Loneliness, big and terrifying enough to make you want to weep alone in the dark.

We slowly started on our way back home.

"There is no nothing," Bapu-ji continued, as if to assuage my fears, his tremulous voice cutting like a saw the layers of darkness before us, "when you realize that everything is in the One . . ."

My father was the Saheb—the lord and keeper—of Pirbaag, the Shrine of the Wanderer, in our village of Haripir, as was his father before him, as were all our ancestors for many centuries. People came to him for guidance, they put their lives in his hands, they bowed to him with reverence.

As we walked back together towards the few modest lights of Haripir, father and first son, a certain fear, a heaviness of the heart came over me. It never left me, even when I was far away in a world of my own making. But at that time, although I had long suspected it, had received hints of it, I knew for certain that I was the gaadi-varas, the successor and avatar to come at Pirbaag after my father.

I often wished my distinction would simply go away, that I would wake up one morning and it wouldn't be there. I did not want to be God, or His trustee, or His avatar—the distinctions often blurred in the realm of the mystical that was my inheritance. Growing up in the village all I wanted to be was ordinary, my ambition, like that of many another boy, to play cricket and break the world batting record for my country. But I had been chosen.

When we returned home, instead of taking the direct path from the roadside gate to our house, which lay straight ahead across an empty yard, my father took me by the separate doorway on our left into the walled compound that was the shrine. This was Pirbaag: calm and cold as infinity. The night air suffused with a faint glow, and an even fainter trace of rose, all around us the raised graves of the saints and sufis of the past, and our ancestors, and others deserving respect and prayers. They were large and small, these graves, ancient and recent, some well tended and heaped with flowers and coloured cloth, others lying forlorn at the fringes among the thorns, neglected and anonymous. This hallowed ground was our trust; we looked after it for people of any creed from any place to come to be blessed and comforted.

Overlooking everything here, towards the farther side of the compound was the grand mausoleum of a thirteenth-century mystic, a sufi called Nur Fazal, known to us belovedly as Pir Bawa and to the world around us as Mussafar Shah, the Wanderer. One day, centuries ago, he came wandering into our land, Gujarat, like a meteor from beyond, and settled here. He became our guide and guru, he showed us the path to liberation from the bonds of temporal existence. Little was known and few really cared about his historical identity: where exactly he came from, who he was, the name of his people. His mother tongue was Persian, perhaps, but he gave us his teachings in the form of songs he composed in our own language, Gujarati.

He was sometimes called the Gardener, because he loved gardens, and he tended his followers like seedlings. He had yet another, curious name, Kaatil, or Killer, which thrilled us children no end. But its provenance was less exciting: he had a piercing look, it was said, sharp as an arrow, and an intellect keen as the blade of a rapier, using which he won many debates in the great courts of the kings.

I would come to believe that my grandfather had an idea of his identity, and my Bapu-ji too, and that in due course when I took on the mantle I too would learn the secret of the sufi.

But now the shrine lies in ruins, a victim of the violence that so gripped our state recently, an orgy of murder and destruction of the kind we euphemistically call "riots." Only the rats visit the sufi now, to root among the ruins. My father is dead and so is my mother. And my brother militantly calls himself a Muslim and is wanted for questioning regarding a horrific crime. Perhaps such an end was a foregone conclusion—Kali Yuga, the Dark Age, was upon us, as Bapu-ji always warned, quoting our saints and the scriptures: an age when gold became black iron, the ruler betrayed his trust, justice threw aside its blindfold, and the son defied his father. Though Bapu-ji did not expect this last of his favoured first son.

The thought will always remain with me: Was my betrayal a part of the prophecy; or could I have averted the calamity that befell us? My logical mind—our first casualty, according to Bapu-ji—has long refused to put faith in such prophecies. I believe simply that my sin, my abandonment and defiance of my inheritance, was a sign of the times. Call the times Kali Yuga if you like—and we can quibble over the question of whether there ever was a Golden Age in which all was good and the sacrificed horse stood up whole after being ritually quartered and eaten. Whatever the case, I was expected to rise above the dark times and be the new saviour.

This role, which I once spurned, I must now assume. I, the last lord of the shrine of Pirbaag, must pick up the pieces of my trust and tell its story—and defy the destroyers, those who in their hatred would not only erase us from the ground of our forefathers but also attempt to write themselves upon it, make ink from our ashes.

The story begins with the arrival in Gujarat of the sufi Nur Fazal. He was our origin, the word and the song, our mother and father and our lover. Forgive me if I must sing to you. The past was told to me always accompanied by song; and now, when memory falters and the pictures in the mind fade and tear and all seems lost, it is the song that prevails.

2

From western lands to glorious Patan
He came, of moon visage and arrow eyes.

To the lake of a thousand gods he came
Pranam! sang the gods, thirty-three crores of them.

Saraswati, Vishnu, Brahma bade him inside
Shiva Nataraja brought him water to drink.

The god himself washed this Wanderer's feet
How could beloved Patan's sorcerers compete?

You are the true man, said the king, your wisdom great
Be our guest, show us the truth.

c. A.D. 1260.

The arrival of the sufi; the contest of magics.

It used to be said of Patan Anularra in the Gujarat kingdom of medieval India that there was not a city within a thousand miles to match its splendour, not a ruler in that vast region not subject to its king. The wealth of its many bazaars came from all corners of the world through the great ports of Cambay and Broach, and from all across Hindustan over land. It boasted the foremost linguists, mathematicians, philosophers, and poets; thousands of students came to study at the feet of its teachers. When the great scholar and priest Hemachandra completed his grammar of Sanskrit that was also a history of the land, it was launched in a grand procession through the avenues of the city, its pages carried on the backs of elephants and trailed by all the learned men. Great intellectual debates took place in the palace, but with dire consequences for the losers, who often had to seek a new city and another patron. In recent times, though, an uneasy air had come to hang over this capital, riding on rumours of doom and catastrophe that travelled with increasing frequency from the north.

Into this once glorious but now a little nervous city there arrived one morning with the dawn a mysterious visitor. He was a man of such a striking visage that on the highways which he had recently travelled men would avert their faces when they crossed his path, then turned to stare long and hard at his back as he hastened on southward. He was medium in stature and extremely fair; he had an emaciated face with a small pointed goatee, his eyes were green; and he wore the robe and turban of a sufi. His name he gave as Nur Fazal, of no fixed abode. He entered the city's northern gate with a merchant caravan and was duly noted by his attire and language as a wandering Muslim mendicant and scholar originally from Afghanistan or Persia, and possibly a spy of the powerful sultanate of Delhi. Once inside, he put himself up at a small inn near the coppersmiths' market frequented by the lesser of the foreign merchants and travellers. Soon afterwards, one afternoon, in the company of a local follower, he proceeded to the citadel of the raja, Vishal Dev. The time for the raja's daily audience with the public was in the morning, but somehow the sufi, unseen at the gate—such were his powers—gained entrance and made his appearance inside.

He stood with mild amazement beside a pale blue man-made lake, contained by banks of red stone painted with designs in pink and blue; in the middle was an ornate pavilion where played and relaxed royal women in bright clothes and long black hair, the tinkle of their pretty voices echoing off the water like birdsong. All around the water stood three-foot-high carvings that, the sufi confirmed as he approached closer to one, then another, depicted the god Shiva. He was standing on the bank of the sahasralinga talav, tank of a thousand Shiva shrines, whose fame had spread as far away north as Samarkand and Ghazna, whose sultans and generals always kept an eye open for opportunities to foray into Hindustan and plunder its legendary wealth. The mystic stood staring at the closest icon in wonder. Shiva's one leg was bent and raised in a gesture of dance, two hands poised in midair; the smile was mischievous and immediately infectious. Here was a god who liked to play. The sufi had been told during his long voyage, and often with a horrified look on the face of the informer, that the people of Hindustan worshipped not only idols of men and women, but also images of animals and, if that were not strange enough, the human procreative organs as well. ("And may God bring destruction on the infidels!") Some would sacrifice humans and eat the flesh of the head, others mutter nonsense syllables or roar like a bull after bathing in sand. But Nur Fazal himself was an exile for his beliefs and did not take to judging others too easily. There are meanings within meanings, he had always been taught; the truth lies shrouded behind a thousand veils.

He was reminded of a home in the north and west now being ground to dust under the hooves of Mongol horses, and drenched in the blood of his folk and his loved ones. He remembered his spiritual master whom he'd left there, at whose instigation he had taken on this long journey.

He was brought around from his memories by approaching sounds—footsteps and human exclamations, accompanied by a sight that brought him a smile.

A young pandit, a priest in a gleaming white dhoti, a tuft of hair collected into a topknot on his otherwise close-cropped head, was striding towards him with all the exaggerated sense of gravity that seems incumbent to a short stature. His chest was bare, and around one shoulder ran a ceremonial white thread. From the opposite side, the stranger noticed, approached two older, bald-headed priests draped around the whole body in white; a race was on for who would reach the interloper first. It was the young topknot who did so, as he exclaimed, "What are you doing in these premises, you Mleccha, impure Muslim? And you dare to cast eyes on the Lord Shiva himself—out with you!"

The sufi had turned and now smiled at the pandit, as the companion he had brought with him translated the scolding.

"And can't your Lord even speak for himself?" the sufi taunted.

At this, the two white-robed ones, who had come to a stop and were staring, gave off a volley of titters. The topknot turned pink in the face.

"Shiva does not speak to such as you, impure one!" he said angrily. No sooner had he uttered these words than he could have bitten off his tongue.

The sufi threw no more than a casual gaze upon the red statue. To the young pandit's amazement, with a great big thump the Cosmic Dancer raised his already high stone foot, leaned forward, and jumped on the ground. In dancing steps, with the gait of a monkey, Shiva ran to the lake and returned bearing a jug of water. "Jadoo, jadoo!" cried the white-robed ones in a fret, having lost their humour. The young pandit gaped from the ground, where he had tripped himself. The sufi accepted the jug from Lord Shiva and washed his feet. The god meanwhile was back at his place. "There, I have even washed my feet now," said the sufi to the young priest. All who were around noticed that the blue lake had emptied. Fish were wriggling in the mud, and the princesses and their maids were screaming frantically as they scrambled up the shore, their bright wet garments clinging desperately to their voluptuous bodies.

By this time a few more people had appeared, and then some soldiers in armour came, flanking an eminence, at whose commanding sight all the men bowed and the young monks among them cowered but stood watching from a distance. He was a large muscular man, dark as polished blackwood. Unlike the priests and monks, the eminence was elaborately clothed in embroidered short trousers and jacket, the belt at his waist glittering with gold and precious stones; his muscular arms, wearing amulets and rings, were crossed, his legs stood apart. He was the chief minister, Rajpal—the sufi heard it whispered—and he glared at the stranger, pointed at him, then nodded at the soldiers; the visitor was escorted away to face the king.

They approached a large hall open at the sides, its tiled roof supported by gilded posts, and on the top of which banners of various colours flapped in the wind. They passed a gauntlet of cavalry on fine Arabian horses, elephants bearing their mahouts, and a company of soldiers in armour bearing swords and long spears. The entrance doorway was ornately carved; inside, seated on the ground, were perhaps a couple of dozen people. And directly before him, in the distance, prominent like the sun, seated on a gold throne and surrounded by priests and officials, was the king of Gujarat, leaning forward curiously. The sufi bowed. He had still not been touched.

It seemed that a discussion of some importance had been interrupted for his sake. The chief minister gestured, and he stepped forward along a blue runner in the company of his escorts.

His Majesty Vishal Dev, self-styled King of Kings and Siddhraj the Second, then spoke.

"You have performed a feat that has much impressed our priests," said Vishal Dev to the sufi, with an amused, disarming smile. "You seem to have many talents. Tell us your name."

"The feat but performed itself, Great King," said the sufi, through his interpreter. "My name is Nur and in my language it means 'light.' "

"Then tell me, O Light, what brings you to Gujarat? I understand that men of your faith in the north would like nothing better than to break the statues of our gods and force us to worship your one God, who does not show his face yet makes many threats. Have you come to spy, then, on behalf of your Sultana Raziya of Delhi—or is she dead now?"

"No, Great King, I am but a scholar and a man of God. My name means light, Your Majesty," replied the sufi astutely, "but you truly are the sun itself in these realms. Your kingdom is known far and wide outside Hindustan as a haven of tolerance where differences in belief are not persecuted. There is but one Truth, one Universal Soul, of which we all are manifestations and whose mystery can be approached in diverse ways. That is my creed, and if called upon to advise or comfort, this is what I teach."

"You speak with a sweet tongue, like all your compatriots from the west—but they also forge a hard steel where you come from, as my people have learned to their dismay and terror," said the king. "In Patan we have always welcomed poets and philosophers and we encourage conferences and debates. Perhaps during your stay you will grace us with your presence in the afternoons for discussions of a learned nature."

A ripple of excited murmuring ran rapidly through the hall at the king's proposition; for it was the practice in court that the strictest examination be passed in the knowledge of the holy Vedas and the poetics of the sacred language before a scholar could participate in debates and discussions.

Vishal Dev leaned sideways to give ear to his chief priest, Nagada, a tall thin man with an obsequious smile but cold eyes, who had come forward to speak with him.

The raja, having heard the priest out, clapped his hand once, then grinned at the sufi. "My guru Nagada suggests that perhaps you would like

to compare your impressive stuff with the magic of our local practitioners.
What a great opportunity to exchange knowledge! Perhaps you can then
give us your views on how the human mind can affect inanimate matter."

"I am your servant, My Lord."

The assembly stepped outside. The king was seated once more upon
his throne, an attendant holding his royal chhatra over him. On both sides
of him again stood the priests and ministers. The common nobility sat on
the ground as before.

There was a buzz of excited chatter and polite laughter among them, as
though a contest in gymnastics or wrestling were about to take place; a
drink of cold green sherbet was proffered to the king and his advisers, then
to the others. The king put a betel leaf into his red mouth to chew. The sufi
too was proffered the sweet drink, but in a crude earthenware glass, which
he knew would be destroyed, having touched the lips of an impure one, as
he was considered in this country. He refused the betel leaf, finding the
practice—which stained the mouth and lips red—repulsive, even though
his unstained mouth was considered a sign of the vulgar and foreign.

The following three demonstrations then took place.

The pandits had gathered into small clumps grouped according to their
status and denominations; the chief among them, Nagada, stood by himself, as did the minister Rajpal. Nagada gave a nod to the pandits and one
of the Brahmins, as the dhoti-clad topknot priests were called, stepped forward. Crossing his arms, he threw an imperious gaze into the distance,
where children were flying kites in the company of attendants. All eyes
followed that gaze, towards the bright patches playfully riding the air. Suddenly a red kite separated from the rest, flew off arrogantly in the shape of
a hawk, soared high, and described two circles; as a child's cry rose, followed by other similarly pitiful cries, the hawk flew to each of the other
kites and with its sharp beak tore them into pieces; finally it began to fly
higher and higher. The gathering of nobles cheered, "Sadhu! Sadhu!"—
but then immediately fell silent because the bird began to shed its feathers,
as if it were melting, until finally it dropped like a stone to the ground.

The visitor had not said a word, had hardly moved from where he
stood before the throne. His face was serene, as if he might not even have
looked upon the spectacle. But it was conceded that somehow he had won.

All eyes fell on Nagada, and he gave the briefest nod towards a white-robed group. These were the Jain monks, as the sufi had learned by now; the Jains and the Brahmins were always bickering and competing for the attentions of the king.

A fat priest stepped out, eagerly nudged forward by young supporters who could not hold back their excitement.

The priest, who was called Dharmasinha, was well known for the humiliations he had wrought upon unwary foes in just such gatherings. Many a visitor had been shamed out of town by his wiles. Today Dharmasinha was carrying a staff. Casting an angry, disdainful look at the visitor, with a mighty grunt and a heave he threw the staff up. Everyone turned to follow its rise. High above the assembly it hung suspended, awaiting a command. "Beat the impure one!" roared Dharmasinha, pointing a finger at the sufi. "Whip him! Cast him off!" The long stick paused in midair, eager to obey its master's bidding; the crowd held its breath. The king smiled broadly. Then the stick drifted down. It moved a length towards the sufi and paused. Then it turned on one end, approached the startled Dharmasinha, and started beating him on the backside, driving him away. The spectators laughed, even the young monks, even the king.

But not Nagada. He motioned to the young priest who had first accosted the sufi outside. The priest hurried off and after a while, during which more sherbet was passed around, returned followed by a strange, wild-looking woman. She was also dressed in white but her robe was dirty; her hair was dishevelled, her eyes were red, her flabby, grimy face angry and defiant. Her name, whispered around the assembly, was Panuti; and there were two pet snakes around her neck.

Panuti came forward and glared contemptuously around her. Then with quick despatch she took one of her pets, four feet long, by the neck and put its head in her mouth; she pushed the rest of it in, gradually swallowing it until finally the tail disappeared inside her. Her throat stretched, her eyes bulged, her body bent backwards. Finally she became still. The snake seemed to reach the belly, for the woman made a motion in her throat and abdomen that indicated so; then, from behind her, from under the skirt, the black snake appeared and slithered away. There were cries of awe, loud and uninhibited. There were smiles all around, though edged with a tremor of revulsion. Panuti's eyes gleamed pleasure, her eyes sought out the sufi's. This was a match.

Then, and this was her mistake, she took the second snake by its neck and also swallowed it. It disappeared into her mouth, and arrived in her belly. She straightened up, became still, and she waited. The snake did not come out. She coaxed, stroked her belly, it would not eject. She began to writhe and bend, all to no avail. She squatted and strained, and in anger and panic she beat on her stomach. Finally, hopelessly, she started to whimper, then looked up at the stranger and wailed.

"Have no fear," said the sufi to her gently. "The snake only lost its way momentarily—there she comes out to follow her mate."

And out it came.

As the sufi Nur Fazal walked soft-footedly back to the city, the lake was once more full of water, the fish swimming happily; the royal maidens were back in the pavilion, the kites were again flying in the air; on a lawn, young monks were noisily playing with a ball and sticks curved at the lower end, having formed themselves into two opposing teams. The sun was low in the sky and a priest somewhere was chanting Sanskrit slokas, the syllables of the strange tongue rising clearly, churning meaning out of the air, reminding the traveller of his distant homeland where the chantings were as clear but in Arabic. How dissimilar and yet how so completely alike had God made human beings. When the ear-adorned red-lipped Nagada searched his own soul, would he not find the same truth as he, Nur, did when he searched himself for the mystery of his existence?

And, he thought, the world was in turmoil everywhere; how long would it take for that turmoil to reach here, for this world of the moon-faced Gujaratis to drown in blood . . . for that is what he had escaped from, seas and seas of blood.

3

False is the woman in your home, Sir
She will bid you farewell and return
Keep your wits during the journey, Sir
This wisdom spoken by Nur Fazal Pir.

c. A.D. 1260.

The intellectual life; and a query on the souls of women.

Months passed. The visitor was given quarters in a guest bungalow in a green suburb outside the palace gates, an area where many noble families lived. The Wanderer—such he came to be known, even among his followers—was called to the palace frequently to join the assemblies of learned men that gathered to lend prestige and dignity to the royal presence. A disputation on Hemachandra's grammar might take place; a mathematician might recite a new prime number and prove it; there were debates on subjects that philosophers everywhere split hairs over. A commentary on the Artha Shastra might be called for; the great mahakavi Somesvara might recite an elegy on the king, or the chief minister Rajpal, who was his patron. And every once in a while, with much fanfare, a great debate would take place, after which the winner would be paraded throughout the better parts of the city.

The king was much impressed by the sufi, who did not trumpet his skills but carried his knowledge within himself, exposing it only if asked or if he deemed it necessary for the benefit of the audience.

His fame spread, and learned men from other cities too came to hear him and satisfy their curiosity. He had brought rare knowledge with him, from the lands of the Muslims. At first he had been taken as a mere child, an ignorant foreigner, for didn't all knowledge begin and end with the four Vedas? Weren't the secrets of the Atman explained in the Upanishads? Weren't all medicines described by the sages in the Ayurveda? Weren't the laws of behaviour written down by Manu? Wasn't Rama the embodiment of the perfect man, and his bride Sita that of the perfect woman? Wasn't the world completely described in the Puranas? Hadn't the pandits of the land cracked open the secrets of enumeration by their invention of the sacred zero, image of the great Om, the nothingness that was everything? But then as the stranger's foreign terms and ways of argument came to be understood, as his knowledge was realized to coincide with theirs, or supersede it in some matters, or lag behind it in others, he was given grudging respect; just enough, he realized, for his knowledge to be taken and incorporated into theirs. It surprised him that these rigid rule-abiders and fanatics of place and function and classification could also delve so deeply into the mysteries of the universe and develop aesthetics so wonderful, although alien to his eye and ear; and it amused him that they remained so happy in their ignorance of the wide world to the west—of the glories of Cordoba and Cairo, Baghdad and Bukhara; of the works of Avicenna and Galen, Omar Khayyam and Al-Tusi, Aristotle and Plato.

Sometimes in the evening the king would ask the sufi to accompany him on a walk of the palace grounds. The king, tall and lanky in stature, casually wearing a dhoti and a coloured shawl round his shoulders, would at first get ahead of the slower sufi, then pause and wait impatiently; but over time he learned to restrain himself. He was a restless but deeply intelligent man who seemed ever waiting for an omen or a happening in these uncertain times. The sufi walked slowly, as we have said, and he would stare down at the ground before him, until the king's tipped question or excited remark provoked him to look up with a smile and a thoughtful response.

The two of them gazed at the night sky, observed the positions of the planets, and discussed what they portended. How long would he rule, the raja wanted desperately to know; would his dynasty last another hundred years? He was in need, above all, of spiritual solace; but, said he, "I am like a nav in the ocean, buffeted by the forces of different philosophies. The Jain priests debate the Brahmin pandits, each wishing me to choose their path and drive the others away; among the Jains some favour walking about in the nude and some do not; it is sinful, some say, to kill a louse that's made a home in your chest hair and a meal of your blood; and in the villages, oblivious to the learned men, the people go about their own ways with their customs and worship of the gods and goddesses."

The sufi did not reply and the two walked together in silence, past the lake, which was peaceful at this hour, the children and maidens long gone, and the dancing god looked on in dark silence; a few points of yellow light flickered like fallen stars upon the surface of the water, these being candles placed there as supplications by the devoted. A crescent moon shone clear in the sky, sharp as a blade, as the warm air breathed queen-of-the-night and jasmine, though the fastidious and foreign holy man had to remind himself that the whiff of cow dung was but a sign of the closeness of nature, the unity of all life. Somewhere a lamb bleated as if to echo the idea. As they walked there would follow behind them the king's body-guards and the holder of the royal canopy; the chief minister would follow at a greater distance, not to look conspicuous but not to lose sight of his patron either. With him walked a selection of pandits. This was not the first time their restless monarch had attached himself to a wandering ascetic; stories were still told of how, a hundred years before, the great Hemachandra and his monarch Kumarapala had both fallen under the spell of a Muslim magician not unlike this one.

"And the God of the Muslims," went on the king one night, perhaps provoked by the sight of the moon, "is the weirdest and most vain of all. He is unknowable and yet commands you to kneel; with a sword he demands obeisance."

"My Lord," said the mystic, "the Turk general in Delhi or Ghor mouths 'God is great' and holds a sword in his hand. But that is not a man of the Musalman God. He is merely a fighter and a usurper. Of him even the simple Muslim faithful is terrified."

The king smiled. "And what is your way to knowledge, Sufi? What path would you suggest for me?"

"All roads lead to the same destination," advised the sufi, "only some may be longer than others. Stay close hugging the shore, Raja, follow the path you learned on the lap of your mother and at the feet of your teachers."

Nur Fazal, the sufi, like all those who seek that inner truth of existence, had a spiritual guide, his beloved Master, whom he had left behind in his homeland. Every day before sunrise, he would go to the worship room of the house, and there, seated on the floor, meditate on the name of his teacher. Thereafter he would return to this room during the day and, facing west, kneel and prostrate in that humble gesture of prayer to God that bound him to his people. Sometimes, in the courtyard of the house on the other side of his wall, would come a handful of young women to play on the swings that hung from the trees. Singing, laughing, chattering, they swung to and fro, their dainty feet and ankles visible to the kneeling sufi as he looked up and out his window before getting up. He would smile, allowing his eyes to linger for a moment or two upon the sight of so much innocent joy. He learned that the house and the maidens belonged to a famed courtesan named Priyanti. The young women's games consisted of getting each other to utter the names of their husbands—which a woman was never supposed to do—using clever verbal ruses. The husbands, he presumed, were imaginary. Sometimes he heard them running about behind the wall, sounding angry; they were simply pretending to spank their lovers with branches.

One afternoon as he lifted his head from prayer he heard a sound behind him. He turned around to meet the gaze of a short, broad, sinewy fellow, evidently a guard of some sort.

"My mistress next door wishes to consult you," spoke the man.

Warily Nur Fazal stood up and followed. He walked through the gate next door and the garden, where the young women were still about, and was taken inside the house and into an opulent reception room. There he saw, sitting stretched out on a carpet, leaning against a bolster, the most beautiful and sensuous woman. Her hair was long and wavy, her face oval, her eyes the shape of almonds; her glittering bright-coloured clothes clung to her flesh, an ample midriff showed, and the sheer white veil over her head was not there to hide the face.

"Does your lordship attend to the souls of women?" she asked with a smile, then added, "Welcome and sit."

He sat before her utterly mesmerized, as a bolster was brought for him.

He understood roughly what she said, but a young woman came and sat behind him who spoke his language. Feeling nostalgic, he was tempted to ask her where she came from, but that would be impolite, so he desisted.

"What ails you?" he asked when her question was repeated to him.

"Can a woman attain union with the Brahman?" she asked.

A cup of sweet, coloured milk was provided for him, and the young translator came to dab his wrists and forehead with an attar.

Certainly, said the sufi, in answer to the lady's question, a woman could attain union with the Absolute, for which there were many names. In Arabia there had been a woman called Rabbia who had reached the highest spiritual status.

She eyed him a little doubtfully; twitched her bare toes at him. They were delightful mischief-makers. He had not seen a woman as beautiful, as powerful. And she had only begun her gambit. They made some small talk.

"Are the women of your country beautiful?" she asked.

"They are, and so are the women here in Gujarat," he replied.

"You don't find us dark?" asked the dusky lady.

"Dark but beautiful . . ." and sensual enough to tempt the saints, he thought.

Were his senses dulled? Was it Nur who was talking? O My Master, he called out within himself.

"Tell me, Sufi," the lady said, "why, in the stories that are told, are women the cause of temptation and fall of the great men of God?"

"But to reach union with God, a man has to become a woman in his soul," he said.

He recited a poem to her. By this time the young translator had left and now the fan attendant departed softly.

"To be one with God, you have to be one with all his creation," she replied. "That is what our great gurus have said."

"That is also what the great sufis have said."

"Even to love a woman is to love God?"

He agreed. "Some sufis have even said that."

"Love is both art and meditation, wouldn't you agree, Sufi? It annihilates the self in a perfect bliss. What else is God?"

And so she seduced him.

That night he lay in the sweetest embrace in that heavenly abode; all his senses had been roused and satiated. As he awoke, a warm sunshine filtered through the gossamer drapes, a sound of singing came arbitrarily to increase his happiness.

The prayer hour had passed; the auspicious full moon had gone unheeded; the call of his Master, for surely there must have been one, was not heard.

"Come back this evening," the lady Priyanti said softly as he left. And he replied, "But I will!"

As he reached his home, a window seemed to have opened in a corner of his mind to crack his composure. But the thought that lurked behind it he could not entertain. He longed to see her again. Even when he learned from his anxious servants that the previous night a disturbance had taken place in the coppersmiths' bazaar, where his followers lived and where he had boarded upon his arrival in the capital, he could think only of her. He spent an entire day dreaming of her, and waiting.

Finally there came the hour to visit her.

When he arrived at the gate of the house he was let in reluctantly. The young women displayed no familiarity, and even the girl who had spoken to him in his own language failed to acknowledge him. When he asked to see the mistress, the squat middle-aged woman who met him at the door was as different from his houri of the previous night as a hog from an antelope.

He spent the night in an agony of remorse. He had lost his way in this strange land; like the weakest of mortals he had succumbed to the simplest of temptations; his link with his beloved Master was broken. In his meditations he could no longer see or hear him. It was as if a wall had come between them, which he could not surmount; all he could do was to beat his head against it and weep.

The following day he went to the coppersmiths' bazaar and discovered that much of it had been burnt to the ground. There had been a riot, begun apparently during a quarrel over a cockfight or a game of dice, or someone playfully tying a bell to the backside of someone else, these being the pastimes of the humbler folk. But the quarrel had become communal. Some of his followers were killed, including his faithful interpreter and very first follower Arjun Dev.

In despair and sorrow, Nur Fazal left the great metropolis and travelled all across the land, often by himself but also at times in the company of yogis and mendicants who had renounced all their possessions to seek the truth and sing the praises of God. He spent eleven months and eleven days thus, pining for a blessing, filling the folds of his turban with lines describing his pangs of separation from his Master. Finally a sign came in the voice of an ascetic outside the great temple of Dwarka, the birthplace of the god Krishna. The wall of separation came tumbling down as the Master spoke to him. Nur Fazal wept, embraced the feet of the ascetic. He returned to Patan, where he lived in his house and fulfilled his obligations to the court. He gave solace to the monarch, who had been overjoyed to see him again. And he gave solace to his followers, using now the medium of song to impart his spiritual message.

But when he felt he had stayed long enough in the city, he asked for permission to leave.

"My Lord—I have been spoilt by your kindness. The life of a court, gloriously stimulating and fulfilling as it is, is not for me. I must go. Let me take with me those who would follow me."

The raja replied: "Go. My spies tell me that a good number of your followers were killed?"

Nur Fazal did not reply.

"My other spies tell me also that you are a man of secrets. That you have escaped the ravages of the Mongol Hulagu in the west . . ."

"My King, I am a peaceful man, as you must have observed. I have imparted of my knowledge freely; I have also given succour to your troubled mind."

"That you have, my friend."

"My Lord, I seek no worldly glory. You, my King, I wish well. If I can be of service to you or your kin, I shall be flattered and honoured."

The king leaned towards him. "Listen, Sufi. I would like you to read a dream. I am certain my dreams foretell much. I have a particular dream that worries me incessantly."

"Tell me your dream, Raja."

"There is a terrible flood; it washes into Patan, it washes away the streets and the squares, it washes away the works of my forebears, the lake of the thousand Shivas, the temples, it washes away my palace . . ."

"Yes, my King? There is more?"

"Brick by brick the great works of the artisans of the past are washed away. I know this portends the end of my kingdom. Our enemies are already in Malwa and knocking at the eastern gates. Yet, I cannot see more. Perversely, the dream ends there, with the bricks and the lingams washed away. I do not see myself in all that. I do not see my progeny. What can *you* tell me, Sufi? Apply all your powers and tell me."

"My Lord, the sages have warned that the world is but a two-day carnival. The Atman alone lives forever and is indestructible, as Krishna taught the brave Arjuna when he mourned the killing of his kinsfolk on the battlefield of Kurukshetra . . ."

The king stared at the mystic, who he knew had spoken the truth—a truth he had indeed heard countless times but not understood with this same immediacy.

Nur Fazal the mystic then removed a black ring from his finger. He handed it to the king. "My King," he said, "may this token come to the aid of you and yours should you need it. It belonged to my Master in the west . . . who is no more on this earth." For this was the message he had received in Dwarka. He was alone, and he had to forge his own path here in the new land.

The king accepted the token. "Go then," he said. "You have permission to stay in the kingdom. And my mahamatya, the chief minister Rajpal, will draw up a declaration granting you safe passage on this land and permission to set up abode."

And so Nur Fazal the sufi departed the city with his followers, travelling southwards, until he arrived at a peaceful, welcoming place where he chose to settle, which came to be called the Baag, or the garden.

4

Postmaster Flat, Shimla.
My brother's keeper, here in the shadow of the mountains.
All is quiet, unstirring, on this edge of the world as I emerge every night
for my stroll into a lucid, starlit darkness, aware each moment of that terrifying mystery first suggested to me by my father outside Pirbaag the day I
turned eleven. I cannot help but wonder: Is this nightly walk that I take a
mere coincidence, or is it memory's prompt? Is it the same sky here now,
above these foothills, as it was there over the dusty plains that night? It is
comforting to believe in an overarching pattern, an answer to everything,
called the Universal Soul, or Brahman, the Om and Allah of that wanderer
the sufi, our own Pir Bawa; and yet how far did I wander away from this
reassurance.

The air is crisp and cold. Far in the distance rise the shadowy silhouettes of the mighty Himalayas, guardians of this realm for aeons. I try to
imagine the absolute silence in those mountains, amidst a sheer, unprofane
beauty: surely a state to aspire to, free of the clutter and cruelty and delu-
sions of human life? That is what my Bapu seemed to teach. All around me
the ghostly grey buildings of the Institute, currently my refuge and once
the summer residence of the British viceroys of India. Down below, across
the valley forested with pine and rhododendron trees, shine the dimming
pinprick lights of Shimla town.

I have been given for my residence the Postmaster Flat, which stands
like a watchtower at the entrance of the Institute grounds, above the caretaker's office at the head of the long winding driveway uphill. Its two bed-

rooms are actually a luxury for my single needs. The front door opens from the living room and study to a flight of perilously sagging wooden stairs descending to the driveway. The back door faces the Guest House, which is where our former rulers' servants had their rooms, I guess, and in whose dining hall the visiting scholars, of whom I am counted one, eat their meals. My appointment here was sudden, a timely favour granted through the influence of a sympathetic friend. This, and my prize residence, are no doubt the cause of a little resentment among the other scholars. I am regarded by this elite—specialists in the human sciences hailing from across India—as somewhat of a screwball. I catch the occasional amused, if discreet academic smile on a passerby and realize that I have been talking to myself, or worse, humming from my repertoire of the songs of Pirbaag; I know I do this in my anxiety to snatch at the scraps of forgotten melody and verse that still come back to me after so many years' absence.

Sunday morning I took a walk towards the back of the Guest House. It is not on the usual walking or tourist path. The lowlier servants of the Institute live there. As I strolled past the house and into a modest residential area, a few men and women sitting idly around and children playing, I saw one of the kitchen helps from the Guest House. He grinned in a friendly manner and said, "Are you going to the church?"

"What church?" I asked. "Is there a church here?" Let alone Christians.

"There," he pointed to a barnlike building nearby ahead, to which I curiously proceeded.

Outside, under the sloping roof, hung an old sign that announced it as the Anglican church, diocese of Boileau Ganj. Above the door, on a patch of flattened tin containers, was a red Christian cross. I stepped inside and a depressing sight met my eyes. The cement floor was littered and broken, the beams were rotting, the white plaster had peeled off in sections. Two naked bulbs provided dim light from the beams. By way of decor, about twenty potted plants had been placed against one wall; against the opposite wall leaned the remains of the original wooden panelling. Service was in progress and a congregation of three, seated on the floor, were singing devoutly but tunelessly. In front of them was a podium covered by a white cloth with a black cross. The priest stood behind it, and when the occasion demanded, would hit his tambourine. When he saw me, he hesitated, then motioned to someone among the flock, who stood up and brought a chair for me. I sat down. A black Bible and hymn books in Hindi and English were brought for me. The singing had stopped and the priest read from Genesis, the story of Abel and Cain, in Hindi. In English, he translated at the appropriate moment, "Am I my brother's keeper?" and looked, it seemed, for an answer from me.

When the sermon was over, the priest, having explained the story he had read, gave his blessings and came over and shook my hand. He was called Yesudas, he said. Please would I come again to his church? I would do so, I replied. He reminded me very much of a favourite teacher I once had, who was also a Christian. At this moment a few more people arrived, among them two of the servers from the dining room, who looked delighted to see me.

Since then the dining staff has indulged me. Morning chai, which had been irregular, now arrives punctually, brought by a young man called Ajay, and accompanied by a treat. In the dining room I am served first, and if I am disinclined to eat with the others, I am served in the Flat. Ajay is the priest's son.

The phone rang late one night recently. It was Mansoor, my brother; and what a relief it was to hear from him, whatever the nature of our relationship these days. Naturally I was the concerned big brother, and played right into his hands.

"Arré Mansoor, where are you? Do you know how worried I have been?"

"I am well. I need some money urgently, Bhai."

The voice hurried and furtive, not to say dismissive; he could never hide his resentment, even when little. Car horns impatient, incessant in the background. Who was he with? In what city? Always the impetuous one, the dangerous one; sent to test him, Bapu-ji once said.

"What kind of money? And where are you?"

"I'll tell you, but send me some money there."

"I have very little, Mansoor—"

"There must be money that Bapu-ji left behind—and you must have dollars stashed away—"

"Do you think it's easy to send money? The police are looking for you, do you know that? What have you been up to that you have to hide?"

A long, audible breath. What was he thinking? I didn't want him to hang up, didn't want to lose him. The last time I saw him was in Ahmedabad, three weeks ago, when he told me he had become a "proper" Muslim. He had expressed some deeply distressing views, and it seemed he had gone off on a recklessly anarchic path from which he would have to be guided back. Then he had disappeared, taking this number with him where he could reach me.

"Being safe, Bhai. Send me money if you can."

When I said I would try, he gave me an address and signed off, "Salaam alaykum, Bhai."

That Arabic greeting, so foreign to us at Pirbaag, put in to taunt me, perhaps frighten me—in a world where Islam is readily equated to terror and unreason.

A few days later Major Narang of the CBI, who has been assigned to me, came to speak to me. He must have been informed about the late-night telephone call. It was a casual, sympathetic interview like the others, not really an interrogation. I am his link to Mansoor, whom he suspects and I fear is a link to others who may be up to the unspeakable. I told him I hadn't heard from my brother yet. Was he sure he was alive?

We will live with that lie for a while.

5

The Garden of the Pir. My youth. And the world according to Raja Singh.

I recall—fondly, I cannot help but smile—coming home from school in the afternoon, alighting from a rickshaw or a tempo overflowing with children and women, or from the passenger side of a truck in which I would have hitched a ride. Emerging on the road beside the tire-repair shop of my friend Harish's father, I would quickly cross the road, go past the stall where Ramdas, my other friend Utu's father, would throw a quick shy greeting from behind his heaps of red and pink roses and coloured cotton chaddars. As I turned into the grounds of our shrine, past the unhitched brick gateposts and the name board, my heart would lift, my eyes alert to signs of the daily fraternal ambush. Sure enough, out would trot little Mansoor from some hiding place, in dirty shorts and open shirt or singlet, obviously barefoot, chuckling his greeting at the scholar-brother. I would have my embroidered black satchel round my shoulder, and in my hands perhaps some cricket paraphernalia—leg guards, gloves, ball. Cricket was everything.

Little brother would carry and drag my satchel inside the house, where it was always surprisingly cool for the hour; then we would sit down at the table and Ma, beaming her love, not having seen me the whole day, would lay out our snack and join us.

We were the two boys of the shrine. Some would have called us privileged; others, handicapped. It would have been 1961 or '62, Fidel Castro and Cuba were very much in the news. There was talk of the Third World and Panchsheel, the friendship among nonaligned nations that our prime minister Nehru much favoured. Yuri Gagarin, the Russian cosmonaut, had become the first man in space. And so I was eleven or thereabouts; Mansoor was seven years younger.

At the table, the little one, feeling sidelined as I chatted with Ma about my day at school, would start to act up; he would interrupt; he would fuss about his chappati and pickle (he preferred butter); he would kick me under the table—and when I retaliated, she would admonish me, the older one, for not understanding. Mansoor was the darling, her Munu; I called him "guerrilla," a term I had learned from the newspapers. Even then, in those childhood days, my brother did not believe in waiting; he demanded and he took action.

But those quarrels were forgettable. I would soon pick up bat and ball and stroll outside to join my friends, who would already be at play, Mansoor tailing me at a distance, doing his best not to be seen. I was fond of my brother. And now, after my long absence? I still care for him, though I am not able to express this to his satisfaction.

A dusty, broken slip road joining two busy highways serviced our village of Haripir, bisecting it. The shrine stood on this road, at the end of the village closer to the Ahmedabad junction. At the entrance, next to the gateless posts, a wooden signboard fixed on two legs carried a faded legend in roman script: Mussafar Shah Dargah—Pir no baag. The Shrine of the Wanderer—the Garden of the Pir. It was called Pirbaag for short, and also, affectionately, the Baag.

Straight ahead from the gateposts, at the top of a rise, stood our faded old house, attached to the shrine at its farther end, and built around a square courtyard that was mostly open to the sky. The front steps led into a short dim passageway that stepped down into the open square. A side gate here opened directly into the sacred space and was our private entrance into it. A high wall ran from the house to the road, the shrine to one side of it and our front yard to the other, empty except for a swing hanging from a tree. Early in the morning crows would congregate on the tree and create a racket; it was believed that they had been here as long as the shrine. Halfway down the wall was the arched doorway that was the public access to the shrine. Often we used this entrance to go to our house through the shrine and to the back.

. . .

Outside the gateposts at the road where I would emerge after my snack, trailed by little Mansoor, the village would be coming to life as the shopping hour approached. Next to Ramdas's flower and chaddar store, on the right, a peanut seller would have set up; and beside him a row of vegetable vendors; and so on up the hill. Across the street, next to the tire-repair shop, was a bus stand, where a torn Congress party poster staked claim to the area, beside a film poster depicting Raj Kapoor and Nargis in the film *Shri 420*. Chacha Nehru was at the helm of the nation; the country was poor but proudly looking ahead.

The two of us turned left at the entrance into the playground, where Harish, Utu, and others had gathered to play the daily cricket. "Eh Kaniyaa!"—that was my nickname—would come a cry. "Harry! Utu-putu!" I would answer. "I am bowling from yesterday's game, don't you forget! Trueman has arrived!" As I threw off my slippers, to play barefoot, a high ball would come my way, which, laying down my bat, I caught expertly, with precisely the composure required. Losing this challenge would be to court laughter and lose face.

In the farther distance in the cultivated hinterland, a line of camels would stand up and slowly wend its way to wherever it was they retired for the night.

Two crates, stood one atop the other against the low wall that bounded our property on this side, substituted as the stumps for our games; an old monster of a banyan tree, known affectionately as Mister Six, and the radius it described formed the boundary to which a ball had to reach for a score of a four or a six. Some twenty yards beyond the banyan was a small, old, and usually deserted temple dedicated to Rupa Devi, wife of Pir Bawa and beloved to young, unmarried women and transvestites.

Why Rupa Devi's temple was not part of the Baag, no one could quite explain. But it was the women of the Baag who looked after it, and the girls of the town came here to tell the goddess their secrets. Bands of transvestites, the eunuch pavayas who were more alluring than the local women, would stop here periodically on their way to their own Kali shrine of Becharaji up north; and any boy who crossed their path would get teased no end.

The thin but persistent tinkle of a bell was the prelude to dawn in our garden of the saints. It echoed around the shrine as though intending to wake up not only the living but also the dead lying buried under their burdens of draped stone. I would open my eyes in the dark, follow the sound in my mind, as it moved in the aisles between graves, accompanied by a glowing brazier of smoking incense; now the morning azan might rise up from the nearby mosque, a long and sinuous and mysterious call; a cool breeze would waft in through the window beside me, from the open farmland, scented with animal dung and earth. I would shut my eyes again. In the other bed Mansoor would not have stirred. If it was Thursday or Saturday, there would soon come the sounds of singing from the temple, sweet, beautiful, and timeless; intermittently I would follow the tunes of these ginans, as our songs were called, and recall their words, which I had been taught. The percussion would start gently, then increase in its intensity. At some point the singing would have stopped; if I strained my ears perhaps I could hear my father speaking, or perhaps I imagined him, imparting his spiritual teaching to the initiates of the Garden—for it was only they who came to the temple at this hour, to meditate, to sing, and to listen. Some of them were local people, while others had come from various places to show their devotion to the Pir and his Saheb.

There would come the hoots of vehicle horns, people conversing, crows raucously crowing outside.

I would jump up abruptly from bed, immediately wide awake, go and brush my teeth at the kitchen tap, then come to wake up my brother with, "Uth havé nakama, wake up you useless!" The look on the little one's face, the most angelic innocence, the most fragile demeanour. His eyes would open: the most beautiful smile, the body motionless, the full day's energy coiled inside, awaiting release.

At seven o'clock, almost to the dot, after breakfast, I walked out through the side door of the house and into the shrine. Passing the mausoleum, with joined hands I would quickly say my pranaams and salaams to the Pir. I silently prayed to him to bring me success not only in cricket but also in my studies. And as I walked towards the gate and the road, at my own unhurried pace, confident I had time and time, I would be conscious of the gaze of my father upon my back—all his pride and confidence, all his hopes and fears on me.

At the gate, finally, and I would look around, await a ride to school. A rickshaw might be around, having dropped off devotees at the shrine, ready to pick up a paying passenger; but if I was lucky, a truck would stop in a cloud of diesel and dust, in all its garish glory, horn blaring, saving me the fare. The driver might lean out the passenger side and call—"Eh Baba, school time! Let's go, get in." And when I was inside his cabin, the truck picking up speed, he might ask conversationally, "So—did you finish homework? Khub kiriket khela, nai?" Too much cricket—but you must work hard, make Nehru Chacha proud!

One morning as I emerged from our gate into the glare of sun there appeared before me a magical sight.

A green and orange truck, covered all over with pithy sayings—"Jai Mata Di!" "Horn Please OK!" "Oh Evil-Eyed One, Your Face Black with Shame!" "My India Great!"—and Om signs, in gold and silver script of a glittering florid font. It could have dropped from the heavens, a gift from the gods. My face broke into a grin. Leaning stylishly against the door, beaming, arms crossed, stood a short stocky Sikh with a paunch and a bushy unkempt beard. According to the name on the driver's door: Raja Singh of Bhatinda, Punjab.

"School time!" he said, as though he knew me.

He was waiting for me, having just worshipped at the shrine for the first time; in a manner typical of his nature he had chatted up Ma and learned that I went to a Christian school up the road in the town of Goshala. He called his truck Kaleidoscope, but I called it Air India, because he so reminded me of the genial, turbaned maharaja symbol of that airline.

Every two or three weeks he would be waiting for me at the gate, having come from Bombay, Baroda, Ahmedabad, Rajkot—the names of these cities painted clearly on the back of his truck. The passenger door would fly open as I emerged.

"Hop in!"

Saying "Sasrikal, Ji" in the Sikh greeting, I would clamber up, and Raja Singh with a chuckle of approval would race off.

This was my own vahan, and it flew me not only to school and some-times back but also to the greater world out there that I could only imag-ine. Everyone in the village knew that when Raja Singh was stopping over in the area, only he could take the gaadi-varas to his English-medium school in Goshala. In an interior smelling of puri and bhaji, sweat and motor oil, decorated with Ganesh and Guru Nanak on the dashboard and a tiny Sai Baba on his sun visor, I would be regaled with a song or two, hear choice Punjabi curses flung at fellow vehicles or lazy pedestrians or an oblivious cow or dog or pig or camel on the road, and listen to the latest news of the world, with commentary. In Raja Singh's truck I kept up with the latest war in Africa or Asia, what America's Kennedy said and what Russia's Khrushchev replied, what Nehru or Nasser or Sukarno said, India's cricket tour of England, or vice versa. How the godless Russians had sent a satellite to orbit round the earth.

"These Russians, yaar, a dog in the sky . . . going round and round . . . what next? Moon they want to go to, and the stars . . . to the end of the sky . . . is there an end to the sky? Ask your papaji the Saheb to give us his wisdom on this matter."

And if I turned reflective, as we stopped for the camel carts outside the cloth-dyeing factory on the way, Raja would show his concern.

"Ay!—what are you staring like that for? Henh? Fancy going up there yourself in your own *Sputnik*?"

"I would be afraid to go up there, Singh-ji."

"What is there to be afraid of?"

"If an accident were to happen up there, I would be lost in the darkness—and not be able to come back home."

Raja Singh, the man who was always on the roads of Gujarat, who seemed never to have returned to his home in Punjab, stared at me and acknowledged, "Back home to mother and father and your Pir Bawa . . . don't worry, the Americans or the Russians would rescue you." And as if to highlight his own predicament, he launched into his favourite ditty, "My shoes are Japanee / my pantaloons Englistanee / my red topee may be Russee / but fear not, the heart is Hindustanee!"

Raj Kapoor, in the film *Shri 420*, the hero of all nomadic souls.

"No doubt, to Hindustan you must definitely return, wherever you go," Raja Singh concluded, rotating his turbaned head to drive home his point.

I have often wondered about his special attachment to me. He told my parents he saw an aura over me. That pleased my father, especially. But perhaps Raja only felt sorry for me, for the burden I carried, and thought to bring a little of the fun and joy of the world into my life. This much is certain, though: he was the first to know that one day I would leave.

"Raja Singh, tumhara ghar kahan hai?" Where is your home?—my favourite question, a joke between us two, to elicit the expected, the explosive answer: "Bhatinda!"

Smiles and chuckles.

Such a name for a place!

"What do you pray to Jaffar Shah for?" I once asked him.

Jaffar Shah was the patron saint of travellers. He was a son of our Pir Bawa and had the largest grave in the Garden, two feet high and, intriguingly, seven feet long. There were many stories about the journeys of Jaffar Shah, during which he acquired followers to the path of Pirbaag.

Raja Singh would approach the grave with a large basket of flowers, which he spread carefully over its length. Putting aside the empty basket he would lie flat on his stomach in obeisance before it. Asking for what, I now asked.

Red with embarrassment and surprise at my question, he did not say a word at first; then he responded with a smile, "I pray that I win a lottery, so I don't have to drive this laarri around the country any more."

"Tum idhar nahin ayega, phir?" You wouldn't come here, then?

He smiled, sang, cursed at an animate object on the road.

Every time he came he would bring a gift for our family: a specialty item from the town he had last visited—gathia from Bhavnagar, chevdo from Baroda, burfi from Rajkot, a kerchief from Bhuj. And most important, he would drop off for me a bundle of newspapers and magazines he had collected on the road. Sometimes, disappointingly, it would be a small package rolled up, meagre pickings from the world; and then there were the times when to my great joy a large stack would be dropped off with a thump at our doorstep, tied with twine, so heavy that I could not lift it. And thus I found out what they thought and did in Bombay and Madras, Ahmedabad and Delhi, and even in New York and London and Moscow.

6

My princedom before me.

Saturday was moto diwas, the "big day" at our shrine, and people came in droves. I say "our" though it was not really quite so, the shrine had been entrusted to our care, and at some point in the past it had been converted legally into a public trust. An institution does not last seven hundred years without conflict. What these conflicts were perhaps only the Sahebs knew, and so perhaps I would know in due time. But fortunately for our family, the British administration had been friendly to us—ours was the unthreatening world of the spirit, and the freedom we desired was only from the tyranny of the eighty-four hundred rebirths that a careless human has to suffer—and it ensured that the charge of the shrine, which had stayed in our family from the beginning, could not be contested.

People came on foot, and by taxi, rickshaw, and camel or bullock cart, bringing a burst of colour at the gate, for mostly they came dressed respectfully in their better clothes. And when they passed him, Ramdas would greet them from his stall, offering flowers and chaddars; he sold, besides, unauthorized pictures of the Pir, in all sizes, mounted or otherwise; the sufi, presented sideways, was fair and pink with a pointed face and a short, pointed goatee; he wore a green turban and a blue robe; his eyes were a brownish green and gazed into the distance. A radio behind the shopkeeper played the livelier varieties of religious songs. Many of our pilgrims were from away, having been recommended to take their desires to the famous sufi Nur Fazal, the Wanderer of Pirbaag. This would not be their last stop at a holy place, but here they were, their hope, their desperation, their grief written on their faces.

As they entered through the tall archway of the public access way, their eyes would without fail seek out the mausoleum on the right, to which they would drift, before stopping a modest distance away, and then they would say their silent salaams and namaskars to the Pir. Following this they would turn and walk around, pay their respects at the graves of the lesser saints, and hear about a miracle or two relating to the shrine, before slipping off their shoes and venturing up the steps to the verandah of the mausoleum and stepping over the threshold into the inner room that was the sanctuary, to beseech for whatever it was they needed.

The raised grave of the Pir lay in the middle of the sanctuary, surrounded by a low lattice barrier of marble. It had a finish of carved inlaid wood at the top, which was rarely seen because layers of red and green chaddars covered it, the latter embroidered with the Islamic crescent and Arabic text in glittering silver and gold; an abundance of fresh flowers was spread out on the chaddars. At the head of this lush, colourful bed was a kingly crown of dark silver. Behind it stood the eternal lamp shining the light of the sufi. For centuries it had burned there of its own divine energy, consuming neither oil nor wick.

Saturday morning, having played for a while, or read about the world, or studied, or listened on the sly to a cricket commentary on the radio—and consequently with a pang of guilt—I would eventually arrive in the compound, which would be abuzz with the steady, intriguing murmur of worshippers, and sit away in a corner on one of the ancient and less visited graves of some ancestor or holy man, vaguely aware that I was the future master of this place. It took me a couple of minutes, perhaps, to orient myself to the scene before me, and as I continued to observe I would begin to imagine the dramas in the lives of these people that had brought them to seek help. The well-fed man in a suit, looking humbled as he emerged from the mausoleum . . . surely had neglected his parents in pursuit of wealth; the young unhappy woman, avoiding others' eyes as she walked about listlessly . . . Pir Bawa help me . . . what could ail someone like her? Spoilt by a badmaash man, as Ma would say. And the well-dressed city adolescent with his domineering mother could only be on his way overseas . . . to England, where else? Such is sansara, as Bapu would say, life and the endless quest for solutions. The smallpox lady, her dark face covered in pustules, her grey eyes staring vacantly ahead: what could the Pir give her?

She too had come for a miracle. And the man with no legs, his stump of a body tied to a mat, on which he moved about briskly propelling with his hands. A frequent visitor, Pran Nath. The Pir was not helping him, and for good reason, for he was a busybody and gossip, flitting hither and thither like a fly searching for feed.

And there went the thin man from Goshala with the blue handkerchief tied round his head, circumambulating the mausoleum in his rapid, jerky walk, his eyes humbly directed to the ground before him; he came without fail every fourth week, and walked without pause from ten in the morning to two, in a thin, elliptical orbit. And did eight miles, as I once estimated. When he had finished he would step inside the mausoleum, and when he emerged, Ma would have water fetched for him. Another devotee of Pir Bawa. But I knew his story, so I convinced myself; he was a man whose son or daughter had been saved by the Pir from the very jaws of death, and this severe ritual was what he had promised in return. He would continue it till the day he died.

Sometimes Harish or Utu would come over and sit beside me, and I would tell them these stories, with all the authority of someone privy to special knowledge, an inner voice. I sensed the envy in their eyes as I sat there, a prince viewing the domain I would inherit, when their own world was so ordinary, so dreary. What did Harish have to look forward to? A tire-repair shop? And Utu? A flower stall?

Occasionally I would be pressed into service as a sevak, a volunteer to assist the visitors from abroad, to tell them about the history, the miracles.

"At this spot under a neem—no, not this one, forgive me, but its predecessor—sat a group of Lohana farmers from Jamnagar who were on their way to Kashi for pilgrimage and had stopped to rest. Pir Bawa— Mussafar Shah—he has many names, as you know—made them welcome. They were given food. He noticed that they were very tired, and an old woman among them was about to die. Pir Bawa thereupon asked them where they were headed with a dying woman. They gave him their answer, and Pir Bawa replied, 'Do you think this sick woman will make it all the way to Kashi?' 'No, Guru-ji,' they replied. 'We might have to take her ashes only.' And Pir Bawa said, 'I will take all of you to Kashi myself.' And he did, right there. They gathered around him and closed their eyes as bid, and next they were in the holy city, beside the holy river. They bathed in the Ganga, paid their respects at the temples, and when they opened their eyes they were back at Pirbaag. Right here. The halwa they had received from the temples was beside them. And Pir Bawa himself was sitting in their midst. The pilgrims fell at his feet. 'Show us your path, Guru-ji, you are truly the saviour,' they said.

"Now this area with the marble slabs on the ground—you can read the names, sir, and some of the dates are recent, others are ancient. They commemorate the prominent people of the community. That one there says 'Dargawalla,' it is where the ashes of the last Saheb are buried. He was my grandfather . . .

"And this, madam, is where Pir Bawa lay before he died. This here is the gaadi, his throne—this is where he will sit when he returns.

"No, I will not accept money, sir, but you can put a donation in the chest in the Pir Bawa's mausoleum when you go in. And don't forget the eternal flame there, which has been burning by itself for seven centuries, an ongoing miracle in the twentieth century that defies scientists from America itself! And there is also another chest near the entrance for the upkeep of this shrine."

This was the money that fed our family, that sent me to school. I knew it, this basic mundane fact of our existence, how could I not? Yet that knowledge did not properly sink in for many years; the community and history, and the memory of the sufi, were what we lived on.

My English, thus demonstrated, was always a source of admiration. "Arré Kaniya, tari Angrezi kevi sari!" What English! And you learned it at St. Arnold? My friends of course went to the local Gujarati public school down the road, with all the levels, one to seven, packed inside one cacophonous classroom.

Almost unnoticed, my father would have arrived on the pavilion, the cement porch that adjoined our house and faced the graves and the visitors like a stage, sitting on his chair and attended by a handful of volunteers, all attired in spotless white. The women, if there were any, wore saris; the men wore dhotis and the typical two-cornered hat. My father had on his white pugri, or turban. A few people from among the day's pilgrims would be brought to see him. Visitors from overseas were always welcome. At twelve noon, the hour before the communal meal, he would stand up and in a slow procession head for the temple across the grounds. His bearing

upright, his face beaming, his right hand would be raised to confer blessings. As I watched this weekly transformation from the edge of the crowd,
a chill would fall upon me. No longer did my princedom have any appeal
for me. As he moved, people touched the hem of his clothes, they murmured prayers, their eyes filled with the utmost devotion. How could I
possibly become worthy of all that?

The Saheb would go to a cushioned, silk-covered seat in the little temple and sit down facing the congregation that had gathered. He would raise
his right hand in a benediction. And then he would speak, gently, wisely
to an eager audience. He might begin by singing a ginan: "Tell me, soul,
what / brought you to this earth?"

Each time I would realize anew that my father was a part of something bigger than I could comprehend, something that nevertheless I was
required to become.

"Okay, Kaniya, you know a lot, what will become of that stump Pran
Nath?"

A cruel remark, but Harish, who had uttered it, was not one for
niceties. A loudmouth, he had recently begun making vulgar remarks
about women, and had learned a repertoire of hand motions. And so he
exploded with his trademark guffaw when I played along and remarked
sagaciously, "Pran Nath the stump will marry the pox woman." He
stopped laughing to make the inevitable lewd observation.

Pran Nath had caught our attention because a tall, elderly, and
educated-looking woman in a yellow sari had told him off for parking
close to her feet and touching her. Having heard us, with a departing glare
he swung off to the pavilion where, as I watched apprehensively, he
reported me to Bapu-ji.

A minute later a young man came over to tell me, "The Saheb calls
you."

As I went over, pushed on my way by my sniggering friends, my father
said, "What you said was not nice. Ask Pran Nath's pardon."

I looked down at the gloating man and said, "I made an error, Ji, forgive me."

He swung off, satisfied. But the woman with the pocks on her face had come forward, encouraged by onlookers. Her name was Mariam, and Bapu-ji instructed me, "Ask Mariam Bai's forgiveness too." So I asked her forgiveness.

"It's nothing, see?" she cooed, running her hand over the pustules on her face, lovingly, as though caressing a baby. Suddenly, cunningly she grabbed my right hand; I stiffened. Watched by my father and the others, their looks benign but curious, I relented, and next my hand was on her face, guided over each pustule, each revolting clinging larval flab of soft pulpy flesh. She released me with a grin, and I hurried off to our home, barely overhearing someone sing my praise as the true heir of Pirbaag.

I was in tears, my hands trembling. It was as if I had caught the pox myself. Ma had followed me in with concern, and taking me to the bathroom she scrubbed my hands and also my face—for in my grief I had put it in my hands.

For many days I couldn't get the experience out of my head, and even months later the thought of my hand caressing Mariam Bai's pustules made me shudder.

In my humiliation I stayed inside, rested, had my lunch and chatted with my mother. Only much later, when the sounds outside had abated, did I return to the shrine, an exercise book in my hand. My friends had gone; most of the visitors had gone. The pavilion was empty, my father having gone to his library to study and rest.

There came the sound of children playing; then Tarzan's jungle cry, "Aaah-aaah!" as Mansoor, emerging from behind Jaffar Shah's large grave, pounced on an opponent. Other kids arrived, and mock fights broke out among the graves of our ancestors. But Dharmik Master, our religious instructor, was at hand; he had been awaiting me. With a few light cuffs he had the younger boys seated before him, reasonably calm. Lessons began. Except for my mishap, this was the routine every Saturday.

Dharmik Master was actually a printer and binder, bringing in jobs from Goshala and sometimes from Ahmedabad. Bapu-ji used him to repair or reprint old books. When he arrived, all the children who remained in the compound were commanded to sit before him near Jaffar Shah's grave. Master-ji would sing, he would explain; he would call on us to sing. And since I was special, I was the first to be asked and expected to make no mistakes. All eyes would be upon me. But if I faltered, the teacher would smoothly sing along with me, saving me from the pit. After singing period, as he called it, he told stories. How a Pir Shah So-and-so, a descendant of our Pir Bawa, defeated the great guru Shankaracharya in debate; how another Pir Shah So-and-so stepped happily onto a great big tava, a wok filled with scorching sand, which torture the stern and puritanical Emperor Aurangzeb had prescribed to make the blasphemers of his kingdom recant; naturally it had no effect on our man. Jaffar Shah travelled all over India and went all the way to Tibet in a balloon, which was why he brought luck on travellers, and why the truck and bus drivers worshipped him. Stories to recall later, and to retell; but what effect could their magic have on happy creatures whose age itself confers magic? We all believed in miracles; they were all around us, so to speak. But somehow, when Master-ji related them, no one believed them. The kids sniggered. They winked at each other. By the end of the session someone's ear had been pulled, another had received a thuppad on the face; a third one was doing standup-sitdown, holding his ears in humiliation.

Eventually the children would all be chased away, to wreak their mischief outside. The Saheb, my Bapu, having rested, would reappear. He would sit on his chair, ready to give audiences; and if no one else occupied his attention, his devoted followers would sit before him on the floor to receive his teaching.

I thought of him then as Socrates, about whom I had learned in school, or a sage from the Upanishads, which he liked to quote.

7

My hero, my brother—
Kunti kept faith
Prahlada kept faith
. . . .
Dev Arjun kept faith.

c. A.D. 1260.

The Story of Arjun Dev.

In the city of Patan Anularra a certain temple priest resident in the metal
workers' bazaar named Arjun Dev had a strange, persistent dream. In that
dream he saw a lamp suspended in the darkness; every time he saw it it
seemed to have moved closer. Arjun Dev knew that he was expected to
await some momentous event.

Arjun Dev was a member of a community of refugees from Afghanistan, Shiva worshippers who had thrived in that land, especially during the reign of the Shahiyas, the Hindu kings Jayapala, Anandapala, and
others. That reign had ended at the hands of the infamous Sultan Mahmud
of Ghazna, destroyer of temples. More than a century later when the
Mongols began sweeping through Asia, Arjun Dev's father, whose name
is forgotten, decided to join a caravan of refugees headed south. It is said
that the father had received instructions, for the family also took guidance
from a sufi school in Samarkand or Bukhara.

And so Arjun Dev, who had been taught by his elders to expect a
sign, now saw one in his dream. A maha guru, a mighty teacher, was
approaching.

One night Arjun Dev's entire being was suffused with light. He woke up in a sweat, aware that the time was now, he was being beckoned. Exclaiming invocations in Persian and Sanskrit, he left the house and went to the city's north gate to await the arrival of the guru.

When Nur Fazal the sufi came through the gate, and the leader of the caravan unloaded his two packages off a mule, Arjun Dev stepped forward, heading off the porters who began clamouring for custom, and went down on his knees and kissed the ground. "Swamirajo," he said, "Lord, you truly are the saviour." Tum tariye taranahaar. And so he became the sufi's first follower and his interpreter.

Arjun Dev was fortunate among men. He saw Shiva Nataraja step off his pedestal and fetch water for the sufi; he saw the three great miracles performed in Vishal Dev's court; and he became the deputy of the sufi in the new community of followers that began to grow. His karmic debt paid, his time on earth was now over. While the sufi lost his way momentarily, caught in an embrace of carnal bliss when the riot flared up in the metal workers' market of Patan, Arjun Dev was among his followers who was killed.

Nur Fazal nominated Arjun Dev's son Ginanpal as his representative. Then he disappeared for eleven months and eleven days in a self-imposed exile, to do penance.

8

The Garden of the Pir. My family.

Sometimes when I watched him sitting before a bunch of white-clad devotees in the pavilion, imparting spiritual wisdom in his high, tremulous voice, or acting out a ritual as Saheb of the shrine, I would wonder who my father was. And who was I, then? Was I different, deep inside me, from what I seemed to myself?

We were descended, according to legend, from that first disciple of the sufi, his interpreter Arjun Dev of Afghanistan. This was our connection to history, to the larger world in time and space. It gave greater meaning to our life in this little village, and because of this special provenance we believed we had been endowed with the responsibility to give meaning and comfort to other lives.

Bapu-ji's given name was Tejpal. One picture, tucked away inside the family album, revealed him as a teenager, a lanky, athletic youth with slicked hair, a cricket ball gripped in one partly raised hand, wearing the sportsman's light duck trousers and V-neck sweater. The hair had been touched up by some artist to look brown. So he too had been a boy once, with a store of vanity and a winning smile; not the musing, distant look of Bapu, not the kindly, beaming Buddha face of the Saheb, but a humorous demeanour revealing a young man with a precious sense of fun, so that watching that face you too broke into a smile. And you wondered, what is he thinking, standing there at the entrance gate by the road, looking in? For several years after my discovery of it, this photo was my secret friend, confessor to my desires. I would quietly go to our sitting room when no one was around, kneel beside the corner stool at the foot shelf on which the album was kept, and stare at that vision of the father I did not have; search in that sportsman's grin for traces of the Bapu I did have. Sometimes Ma would hover at the edges of my vision, clanking a pan or humming a tune, pretending to ignore me. Where had that boy gone? Where the fun? He had left his childhood behind, buried it like Gautama to become, like his forebears, the Saheb and uphold truth during this trying Kali Yuga, the Dark Age.

There was a time when he had played cricket with me, when I was very young, outside on the pavilion; he would hold my hand and walk with me; he would sing to me. But then the mask had fallen. There were moments of closeness still between us, as when he had taken me out on the walk, or when he explained a problem in geometry to me—a moment that drew a broad smile from Ma and a typical diversionary tactic from Mansoor. But that mask never left him, even then. He belonged to that history, to ancient Pirbaag and all the dead; to Pir Bawa and to the great unknowable Brahman. But not to me as I wanted him.

One day in 1942, the collector of our area, Mr. Andrew Ross, paid a visit to my grandfather. He brought with him a Russian professor, a stocky, bearded man called Ivanow who happened to be travelling in the area, to have a peek at Pirbaag's famous library. But Dada was a crafty man and did not reveal much of the library's contents beyond the obvious. The two white men asked him a lot of questions, and were bold and perhaps concerned enough to ask Dada if he had considered taking up the cause of the Muslim League, the political party led by Muhammadali Jinnah, a fellow Gujarati. Professor Ivanow suggested that Dada steer his people towards the larger Muslim community or, being small and insignificant, they would disappear altogether.

Dada was polite to the two men, whom he had received on the pavilion, which in those days had a pressed earth floor and a ramshackle corrugated roof. My father stood close by, watching and listening, having dutifully brought tea from the kitchen. My grandfather told the visitors that the welfare of the shrine and its devotees were what he lived for. And so he would reflect upon their suggestion. As they were leaving, Mr. Ross suggested that my father find a place in Bombay's St. Xavier's College when he was finished at St. Arnold's in Goshala. My father was overjoyed at the suggestion.

After decades of struggle India had arrived finally at the threshold of independence, yet in a state of turmoil and far from unity, for the unthinkable was about to happen. Unless Mr. Jinnah could be charmed or otherwise placated, it was certain that the nation would be broken, with a separate country called Pakistan carved out up north for Muslims. Although Pirbaag harboured the precious memory and the grave of a Muslim Pir, the question of Hindu or Muslim had never arisen before for its followers. Now they were forced to confront it, but many waited for the Saheb to give the lead. It is said that my Dada spent many hours over several days meditating inside the mausoleum before the grave of the sufi, as was the wont of the Sahebs at moments of crises. Finally he emerged from these consultations with the decision to go and see Mahatma Gandhi in his ashram. Upon his return from this journey Dada made a declaration to a gathering at Pirbaag, reminding those assembled that the path of the Pir was spiritual, it did not give importance to outward forms of worship. Therefore Hindus and Muslims were the same, and the Saheb would not abandon this ancient site, granted to the Wanderer centuries before by the kings of Gujarat, for some place called Pakistan. He was bound to its soil, it was the trust of his family. And so he would put his political faith in the faith of Gandhi and the vision and promise of Nehru.

With great enthusiasm my father Tejpal went to college in Bombay. He stayed two years, studying science, and according to Ma he did remarkably well, winning a silver medal his first year. But after two years, and before finishing his degree, he was abruptly called back by Dada. He was married within weeks to Madhvi, the daughter of a family from Jamnagar.

In Haripir there had recently arrived men in thick black beards, white caps, and long white shirts, clutching copies of the Quran and preaching the tenets of Islam; other men in white homespun cotton and two-cornered pandit caps came, preaching a purer Hinduism. Purity—shuddhi—was the key word. Cease blasphemous cow and idol worship, said the Muslims; abandon carnality and return to the basics of the ancient Vedas, retorted the Hindus. Two fundamentalisms sought the heart of the sufi's followers. Swayed by these imprecations to become part of something bigger, some of them began to call themselves Muslims; they altered their names to sound more Arabic and prepared to go to Pakistan. Others called themselves Hindus, but not many needed to alter their names. In secret, however, when in dire need these purified souls still came to the gates of the Baag, bowed before the Saheb and beseeched Pir Bawa in his tomb to grant them a favour.

Independence came in August 1947; a mass cross-migration of people had already begun between our now two countries, India and Pakistan. For months and into the new year riots and massacres continued wherever the two communities had lived together; there were hate killings in Ahmedabad, Bombay, Baroda, Kalol, even our neighbour Goshala.

My father's younger brother Rajpal now called himself Iqbal after the great Muslim poet. He too had recently got married, and one day he announced his decision to go to Pakistan. Gandhi was on a hunger strike in Delhi to protest against the violence between the communities. Because he also spoke out against the violence against Muslims, there were calls of "Let him die!" and a bomb was thrown in his vicinity.

According to my mother, my uncle was not an overly excitable personality; but having recently declared his faith, he was much affected by the news of the hate killings. His wife Rehana was expecting a child. It was on the pavilion late one afternoon that Rajpal-Iqbal revealed his decision to Dada; there were people with my grandfather, standing or sitting, listening raptly to his every word, as was usual, therefore it was a deeply embarrassing moment. My Dada is said to have taken a long pause, during which no one spoke and there lay the utmost silence upon Pirbaag. Then Dada declared softly, "Very well."

"But you will find arrogance and bigotry wherever you go," my grandfather said to my uncle. "There will be one kind of Musalman against another kind. Our path is spiritual, we do not believe in outward appearance and names. Rajpal, Iqbal, or Birbal, what does it matter? Go and see for yourself, but remember your home is here with Pir Bawa."

One morning a small procession of bullock carts gathered from Haripir and neighbouring villages and headed towards Goshala, from where they would proceed in hired buses to Bombay and thence to Karachi by boat. There were reports of stones thrown and scuffles, but nobody was seriously hurt. It was also said that just as the caravan of new Pakistanis from our village topped the rise on the road, it suddenly halted. A child— or woman—wailed. A little later one of the covered carts returned, bearing three people. A man and a woman first came out and returned to their home. The third person proceeded to the mausoleum of Pir Bawa. Having paid her final respects, she departed once more; but before she left she took a pinch of soil in her mouth and ingested it. This story from the Partition days would be told long afterwards; exactly what point was being made I could never be sure.

In due time a letter arrived from Pakistan with the "khush khabar" that my uncle and his family were safely in Karachi and had been looked after.

A few weeks after my uncle departed, Gandhi-ji was shot dead in Delhi.

My father had an elder sister, Meera, who had died in childbirth in Junagadh. I never saw my grandfather; I knew that he had been a wrestler in his youth, and remember the portrait of a stocky man seated on a chair, with a white flowing beard and a large smile, hanging in our sitting room. There was another photo of him, taken in the pavilion with my father and the two eminent visitors, Mr. Ross and Professor Ivanow, who stood at the two ends in the foursome, one extremely tall, the other stocky. But it was a faded snapshot and the faces were not clear. Dada died soon after my uncle left. Dadi lived a few more years. She was a thin sharp lady with a peculiar smell, and I remember her pouring hot ghee down my nose when it got blocked; and on Sundays, my head in her lap, my mouth firmly pried open with her fingers, administering the repulsive, grainy, laxative mixture called phuki down my throat.

There was a revolution in Zanzibar and a field marshall called John was warning all capitalists in his country to beware; an American spy-plane pilot called Powers was shot down by the Russians; Nehru was in Lagos; and Ken Barrington had saved the English cricket team in their match against South Africa . . .

Thus the world according to Raja Singh, and the newspapers and magazines he brought. It seemed so exciting, exotic, and far far away, would I be able even to touch it? In the central courtyard of our home, under the sky, sitting at a table by the light of a small wick lamp (and the moon, if it was around), I would pore over the news. All would be quiet. At some point Bapu-ji would leave his library to go to the bedroom, telling me to do the same; or the light in the library would go off, and I knew that he had decided to sleep there tonight among his precious books and the past.

There was a place called Nyasaland, and another called Katanga with plenty of gold, where a civil war had erupted; there was a man called Ben Bella in Algeria, another called Hammarskjöld in the United Nations . . .

But the news that seemed to shake the world, though not ours at Pirbaag, was the assassination of President Kennedy.

"The headlines were as big when Gandhi-ji was murdered," Bapu-ji said, having come to stand behind me, and there was a musing, wistful quality in his voice. He read briefly over my shoulder. It was Sunday, we had just eaten.

I turned to look up at him. At this hour his face had lost some of its serenity, his eyes looked shaded. But perhaps it was the lighting here in the dark courtyard; his manner was as controlled as ever.

"Do you think the world war will happen, Bapu-ji?" I anxiously asked before he could quite get started to depart. Anything to detain him, keep my father with me.

He paused, briefly ran a hand over his cropped head, as though contemplating whether I was old enough for his conclusion. Then slowly he nodded: "It surely will, one day."

"And all will be destroyed—this whole world?"

He nodded.

"Isn't that good then, Bapu, Kali Age will end and the gold Krta Age will return?"

My father gave me his musing look. "While we are human, we have human worries," he told me.

He ruffled my hair briefly and left for the sanctuary of his library.

The mask. And my mother coming over sympathetically, as I watched him disappear. Sitting across the table, and saying, "Come on, explain to me: who was this Kennedy?"

To which, perking up, changing the subject to one she liked, I asked: "When will you go see *Mughal-e-Azam*?"

And she, half guilty, totally happy: "Ja-ja havé." Go on now.

She adored the movies like nothing else.

9

My youth, cont'd. The mystic in his library; and the woman in burqa.
My father's library occupied a quiet room in a hallowed corner of our square house. The entrance from the central courtyard he liked to keep closed, but there was a second door which led out into the pavilion that he sometimes kept open.

I remember standing quietly here, watching him seated on the floor on a small red and blue Persian carpet, his portable desk over his lap, a naked light bulb in the ceiling above him. Bursting his eyes, as Ma would put it, poring over some old print or copying away, his old-fashioned nib in its holder scratching at the foolscap paper. Around him, three walls lined with books and manuscripts. Against the fourth stood a throne, an ancient chair of finely wrought black silver, on its seat a red mulmul pillow on which lay a large handwritten book: precious as pearls, the songs of Nur Fazal. On the wall above the throne hung a bright painting of the Pir, copies of which Ramdas sold lucratively in his stall outside the gate. It had been painted early in the century and presented to Dada by an inspired devotee who saw the Pir in a dream. Perched on a stool next to the throne, an oil lamp threw a flickering aura upon all that was represented here. Unlike the eternal lamp in the shrine, this one was lighted every morning and added a sweet smell of oil to the fragrance of incense pervading the room.

Ma would send me with a glass of sweet milk with almonds for him, which were supposed to be good for the brain. And yet, he was the avatar, I would think, with his powers surely he was beyond such elementary aids. Having presented him with the milk, I would withdraw towards the doorway, silent as a shadow, watching him, straining to read the more distant titles on the shelves. A pungent odour of old book dust would drift towards me, stronger than the incense or the oil. I imagined all his books talking at him in his solitude, a cerebral cacophony that only he could pay attention to and make sense of in his inspired wisdom. I admired his utmost concentration, I would unconsciously emulate it in years to come. Glasses on his nose, how vulnerably human he looked, so unlike the beaming Saheb receiving homage on the pavilion. In his books and manuscripts, in history, he seemed to meet his match.

The higher shelves in the room were packed with neat rows of variously titled books. Histories of India; books on science and philosophy— *Nine Scientists Prove the Existence of God* always seemed to stand out; the works of the mystics Kabir, Nanak, Dadu, Mira; stories of the sufis; volumes of Shakespeare; holy books of all the religions; a nurses' handbook on anatomy whose sketchings, as the years proceeded, would have the drawing power to bend the will of any saint, let alone a teenager; and green Penguin editions of crime novels.

In contrast, the lower shelves, filled with long irregular folios lying flat on their sides like basking reptiles, couldn't have looked more drab. But these were the pith of the library, the precious written records of Pirbaag: all our songs and stories, copied and recopied by hand over the years to preserve them from the ravages of time. The pages were stitched and loosely bound into books using smooth dark brown animal hide or snakeskin with raised patterns that felt like goose pimples to the touch. Only my father would know the contents of them all.

Then there was the timeless, hidden treasure, consisting of the oldest remaining manuscripts, some in the Wanderer's own writing—he had touched them with his hands; perhaps he had kissed them, raised them to his brow; shed a tear over them? These and other mementoes were preserved in a trunk covered with red mulmul next to the throne on the other side of the lamp. The trunk could not be opened or moved without the word of the Saheb; stories thrilled us of soldiers and spies who in bygone days had come to remove its secrets, only to fail miserably, foiled by the power and mystery of Pirbaag.

In the past, during Dada's time, foreign scholars would visit the shrine, arriving on bullock cart or muleback, sent by the local British collector in

Ahmedabad or the Oriental Institute in Bombay. And because the collectors had been kind to the reign of the Sahebs of Pirbaag, Dada welcomed these red-faced visitors wiping their dripping brows with handkerchiefs. But he was suspicious of them and did not like them greedily pawing his precious heritage. However, a small brass plate on a doorpost acknowledged gifts from the Royal Asiatic Society and a Mr. Cranston Paul, Collector of Ahmedabad.

One day, sensing my presence at the door, Bapu-ji looked towards me, then gave a rare smile and said, "Come and have a look." He was examining an extraordinary length of paper across his lap and there was a magnifying lens on the portable desk beside him.

I had never been invited inside, except to hand him his glass of milk. If anything, I recalled admonitions from my mother not to enter the library on my own. Therefore no word would escape my lips and I stared in disbelief.

"Come now," he beckoned with a gesture of the head.

Slowly I stepped forward, bent down on my knees in front of his desk, and looked.

On the long sheet of ancient paper danced and skipped a kind of writing in red and black ink that I had never seen before. Not like the stolid Devanagari I had learned in school, dangling from a bar as if from a clothesline, or the slightly less controlled letters of Gujarati; these before me, faded unevenly but still clear, curled and raced crazily, taking their unreadable message across the page as if it had no end, and indeed it did not have one, the lines falling like rain down the side.

My father saw me grappling mentally to read the writing, attempting to steal even a bit of its message, and said, "It's in a secret script—which Master-ji or someone else will teach you one day. It was used to hide our message from our enemies."

"Which enemies, Bapu-ji?"

"Rulers . . . fanatics . . ."

Master-ji had indeed taught us that rulers in the past had persecuted the shrine, sometimes killed our holy men, burnt down precious Pirbaag; in each case through a miracle the tomb with its eternal light had stood intact, resplendent and without a blemish. Sometimes the remorseful persecutor had gone down on his belly before the Pir and become a devotee.

"This page is six feet long," Bapu-ji said, watching me follow the writing down its length. "It contains ginans written both horizontally and vertically—like a crossword."

I was just conscious enough to stare in wonder at the exhibits he was showing me, in this bewildering, unexpected act of confidence. In an open, more modern book beside him was a printed picture of a king seated on a throne under a canopy, surrounded by robed priests and guarded by soldiers in armour. An ordinary-looking dhoti-clad fellow in front of the king was evidently receiving a royal scolding.

"Raja Vishal Dev in his court," Bapu-ji declared, his voice wavering, a thin smile on his lips.

Then he pointed to two coins lying on the desk, black, with glimmers of gold. "Coins," he declared, "bearing the seal of Siddhraj. One day we will have a museum at Pirbaag, where all the artifacts and books from our past can be displayed."

"That's a good idea, Bapu-ji," I said.

"Go now," he said, and shakily I stood up, for I had been on my knees a long time.

"One day I will introduce you to this entire collection," he said with a smile. "It will all be yours to look after."

He was watching me; and I was then looking, I would think later, not at the human father I craved, nor the lofty Saheb of Pirbaag, but a third, different entity altogether. Who was speaking to me then? Pir Bawa himself?

"Can I come and dust your books for you, Bapu-ji?" I asked.

"Yes . . . you could do that once a week."

I nodded. He nodded. I left through the back door into the courtyard, closed it, feeling his eyes all the time upon me.

Ma was sitting on the front step of the house, watching Mansoor playing on the swing outside. She was a plump woman in the way mothers were, and to me beautiful, with creamy skin and long soft hair that was often oiled and smelled of coconut and jasmine, and much given to smiles and giggles and warm fleshy embraces. I went and sat down close beside her. Mansoor was scolding a stray dog that wandered in and out through the gate.

"I don't want to be the Saheb, Ma," I said to her softly. "I just want to be ordinary."

"Ordinary? You are not ordinary. You are the successor, the gaadi-varas. How can you refuse? Can you imagine your brother succeeding your father?"

She giggled briefly. The question did not need an answer, and we both watched my brother imprecating the dog. "Ay—bhaag!"

"You are gifted," she murmured. "You are meant to be gaadi-varas. Everything you touch turns to gold . . . your father is right."

"What do you mean? What has he told you, Ma?"

She said, "When a boy is to become Saheb there are signs he shows."

"What signs? I have not shown any signs! What has he seen?"

"How should I know?"

She blushed and looked away.

Then impulsively, suddenly, she pulled me towards her breast and squeezed me, and I struggled to wipe away a tear.

I released myself from that embrace and asked her mischievously, "How was the filim? You went, didn't you?"

When she smiled her guilty assent, I said, "You saw . . . ?"

Again the smile.

"*Mughal-e-Azam!* You saw it?"

She broke into a peal of laughter.

It was the biggest box office hit ever, advertised screamingly on full pages of the papers. "42nd record-breaking week! Dilip Kumar! Madhubala! A love match made in the heavens, no kingly power can tear asunder!"

"I will tell you the story later," she promised.

But like the rest of the country I already knew it.

How did you marry Bapu, I would ask her. She had replied once, "He won me with his magic!"

"What magic?"

"No magic!"

Then a peal of laughter at my surprised, annoyed face.

The usual story was that she was introduced to my Dada and Dadi and shown a photo of my father. This young man would be her husband, she was told. Bapu was recalled from his studies without explanation, and the wedding was sprung on him as soon as he arrived. She had been afraid of him, she said. He was tall and handsome, but he was the future Saheb. And Sahebs could see through the seven earths and seven heavens into eternity; the thirty-three crore gods bowed before them.

She lived with her fantasies. Sometimes I would see her smiling or chuckling by herself; once I came across her wiping copious tears from her eyes, seated on her bed, and to my anxious inquiry, she simply answered, "I was remembering that filim—bichara Guru Dutt had to die—why did they have to kill him?"

Sitting together at the table in the open courtyard at night, or standing behind her in the cooking area while she prepared something, I would read to her accounts of the films and their stars from the publications dropped off by Raja Singh. She waited breathlessly for every new movie release, kept track of its success or failure, could tell you how many weeks it had played at the Shan in Goshala or the Rex in Bombay. It would not become the Saheb's wife to be seen at the cinema, but she did manage to steal away occasionally on a Wednesday or a Sunday afternoon to a ladies' zenana show in town. Ma had a Muslim friend called Zainab with whom she went, who was from Jamnagar like her and with whom she spoke in Cutchi. Ma took a small package with her every time, which seemed to be the snack they would eat together at the cinema.

One Sunday late afternoon as I returned from playing cricket with my friends, I saw two women in black burqa hurry towards our house and disappear through the front door. As usual I dawdled awhile in the shrine area before going into the house through the side entrance. To my surprise only Ma and Zainab were there, sitting in the kitchen, chatting. Zainab was in her burqa, though the top had fallen off, revealing her thick wavy hair. She quickly returned it to its place. "Where is the other woman who came with Zainab Bai, Ma?" I asked curiously. "My sister left," Zainab explained. "Didn't you see her outside?"

It was some months later when I realized the truth of what I had witnessed that day. It was Sunday again, and I saw Ma leaving the house; I was on the point of asking what was there to eat, when my eye fell on the packet under her arm; this time it didn't look at all like it could contain any snack, bhajia, or ghathia, or whatever. A look of guilt crossed my mother's face, and in that flash she had revealed her secret. Not to be identified as the

Saheb's wife entering the cinema, she would put on a veil beforehand, in Zainab's house, where she would remove it afterwards on her way home. That day when I saw the two veiled women entering our house, for some reason they had come straight from the cinema.

I did not tell anyone about my discovery. It remained an unspoken secret between my mother and me, for we never discussed it either. Every time I saw a veiled woman, a burqa pass by, those deep eyes could be hers, and she could be on her way to somewhere secret.

10

Dear friend
auspicious is the moment
this day when the saint arrives

c. A.D. 1260.

The wedding of the sufi.

The city of Dhara was situated south of Patan, of which it was a tributary,
and was ruled by the good king Devija; he had a wife, Savitri, and a
beloved young daughter, Rupade. The princess was famed for her pre-
cocity, being as unlike other girls her age as a swan is unlike a pigeon. She
was a great soul, it was whispered, who had returned to earth merely to
complete some deed left over from a previous birth and thus pay her final
debt to karma. This was exactly what made the parents fearful: Was the
child fated to leave them soon? When the princess played with her dolls,
she would make them into sages and yogis, gods and goddesses. Here were
Arjun and Krishna on a chariot, the latter reciting the wisdom that became
the Gita; here was Valmiki writing his great book in an ashram by the river.
One particular doll she had clothed in royal garb, though not the familiar one of her father and brothers. She called this doll her guru and her
husband.

Time came for her to get married. She was five years old.

When the royal astrologers were brought to her and a list of prospective suitors proposed, some from as far away as Cutch and Jaipur, the girl
refused to consider them.

"I am already married," she said, clutching her favourite doll close to her. "My groom is far but he has sent this likeness of him. See how handsome he is . . . brave as Arjun and devoted as Harishchandra."

The wedding of their beloved Rupade was awaited with much anticipation by the people of Dhara; neighbouring kingdoms also watched and waited—royal weddings everywhere are always a source of celebration and envy, gossip and speculation. They portend alliances and reflect the prestige of a kingdom. Devija and his queen Savitri tried all manner of tactics to convince the girl to give up her illusion and accept a proposal. Pandits recited mantras over her, gave her potions to ingest. Magicians of the forest tribes came and worked their mysterious crafts. Foreign doctors were brought from the port cities to diagnose her condition, suggest remedies. But the little girl remained adamant. "I am already married," she insisted, "can't you see that?"

The court astrologers who had previously seen nothing but good luck shining on her prospects now proposed to reconsider. She had been born just as dawn had arrived. But now the pandits admitted that at the moment of her birth one of them had as usual gone up to the observatory tower to sight the first sunlight and beat the drum. And so dawn's arrival had been marked a precious moment too soon. Therefore, they now concluded, Rupade had been born at that precise instant when the first rays of surya glanced the earth. And so she was light and dark, grey of eye and brown of body, light of face and dark of hair. She shared the aspects of Kali and Lakshmi; no one knew better than she her purpose and her destiny on earth.

Her mother and father trembled at these pronouncements. They had wished for a daughter who would bring them grandchildren, they had desired her to rule a kingdom as the consort of a prince; they had not wished for a monster or a goddess.

So they decided to wait. Years passed, and the princess grew up into an overaged unmarried teenager. The world was told that she had devoted her life to Krishna. The people rejoiced, but in secret they shook their heads in regret, for who would not prefer a sweet princess and future queen to a freak ascetic?

She stayed close to her quarters, spent much time in prayer and meditation. She undertook frequent fasts. From a plump, strong, energetic child she turned into a thin, emaciated young woman with a long face, but one not averse to occasional playfulness and acting the spoilt child. Every morning a hunter called Mono went to the forest that surrounded Dhara and there killed a deer for her, from whose meat she would taste only a pinch, before the meat was distributed to the poor. One day Mono searched the forest in vain for a deer to kill; he couldn't find any. In fact it appeared that there were no animals in the forest that he could see. After an entire morning spent searching, finally he came upon them all: deep in a thicket, the animals had collected peacefully together in a large circle; in the middle of them sat a mystic. On his lap played a young deer, eating shreds of grass from his hand. Its mother sat a few feet away, trusting and content; two lions paced quietly at the edge of the crowd; a few peacocks and peahens sat next to the doe.

The mystic looked up; the intruder, with his bow and drawn arrow, his spear at his back, trembled.

Asked Nur Fazal the sufi, "What do you seek, O hunter?"

"Master—forgive me for intruding. I seek a deer to hunt for the young princess Rupade of Dhara."

The sufi smiled. Lifting his hand, he released the deer from his embrace; it trotted off to seek its death at the hands of Mono, who took it away. Its mother stood by unperturbed.

The princess tasted the meat; immediately she shouted, "My husband has arrived!" *Vara avijgaya!*

She went running from the women's chambers to the king's hall to make her revelation—which was not appropriate behaviour, for she was no longer the little girl; but for her, no strict rules applied.

"Where is he?" her mother asked her, when she was taken back to the women's quarters and quietened down. "How do you know it is he?"

"He is waiting in the forest outside the city, and I have seen him in a vision. He is fair and he dresses in white. His face is kind and his stature small, like our people's. He has a pointed black beard. Where he sits in the forest, the animals come to sit at his feet and the trees lean towards him to listen to him. I know for certain that he is my groom . . ." *É to amaro varaj chhai.*

. . .

The princess's choice for husband was brought before the king, who looked him over. The visitor was not the desired Rajput prince, even from a distant, less-known kingdom, he was not even a Muslim prince. But then Devija had long ceased to expect royalty to turn up to carry his daughter away to glory. Before him stood a sufi, a foreign ascetic in a white robe and a green turban; he was clean in appearance and wore sandals on his feet; his hair was long and he had a goatee. His look was fearless and penetrating.

"My daughter proposes you for her husband, O Sufi," said the king. "What do you say to that?"

"I too have felt the pull of a kindred spirit, O King," replied the sufi. "I have heard of the princess, Rupade—who has not, in these lands?—and of your sadness; be not sad, Lord, she has only chosen the path of Krishna."

"You will not convert her to your faith," replied the king, "and you will give her a home."

"Our faiths are the same, my King, and I propose to make my home in these parts," the sufi said.

"Good. Then I permit the two of you to marry and stay in this land."

The queen arrived with a servant bearing a tray, and she put a sweet laddoo into the fiancé's mouth; she performed good-luck rites on him and cracked her knuckles against his head. He bent and touched her feet. The scene was grave, there was no singing, and there could have been no more incongruous a site at court than this. In the ladies' quarters there might even have occurred some weeping. To the king and queen, however much they loved her, their daughter was dead.

Nevertheless, a wedding had to be celebrated. The town rejoiced for the princess; streets were festooned with flags and banners; people came out in their best; sweets were distributed, the garba was danced in the evenings; stories of Rama and Sita, Nala and Damayanti, Krishna and Radha were recited in the temples and the homes of the wealthy. At the ceremony, the groom came dressed like a prince, wearing the costume designed for him by the princess herself with the court tailors. The bride was attired in glittering red and gold and green. The two sat and heard out the Sanskrit slokas from the chief pandit; they went seven times round the sacred fire. Finally, the king and queen shedding tears, the princes hiding theirs behind stony faces, the maids and servants openly weeping at the sight of the beloved of the palace finally departing, the groom took away the bride. The palanquins made their way in the direction of the sunset, and it seemed they were swallowed by the sun even as the pale full moon watched the proceedings.

For their dowry the king had presented the couple with land near the forest. On this land was built a modest yet handsome house for them.

"I was brought up next to a beautiful garden," said Nur Fazal to his wife, "far away in the west. We will also have a beautiful garden on our land, and tend it with love and devotion, and in the same manner we will tend to the spiritual needs of our followers, who will be like our seedlings."

The home of the couple came to be called Pirbaag, the garden of the Pir, and it was lovely and peaceful. The earth sent forth a spring among the woods behind the house to nourish the land and its inhabitants.

11

Shimla-Delhi.

My renegade brother.

This journey is for Ma's sake, I tell myself, he was her darling, always took priority.

And to me, always, she'd say: But you are the older one, Karsan, you should take care of him.

He is my kasauti, Bapu-ji would say, Mansoor is truly my test.

Ma: Test is good, na?

Perhaps, Ma, test is good; but what price failure?

Reverend Yesudas: You are your brother's keeper.

And so I go to take him some money. And yes, I admit, it's for my sake too. I do want to see Mansoor.

Major Narang: "You still haven't heard from him?"

This, over the phone, earlier this evening. He knew I was up to something. My visit to the State Bank must have been reported.

"No, Major," I lied, "I haven't heard from him."

The bus is convenient and anonymous; unlike the train, no advance reservation is required, announcing to one and all your impending departure for the big city on the Himalayan Queen. It is faster, too, leaving the darker reaches of the Cart Road at night and arriving at New Delhi's Connaught Place early in the morning. But far from comfortable, it lurches constantly downhill, flinging you from side to side at each hairpin bend, promising sooner or later to crack your skull against the window. My fellow passengers, a grim, bleary-eyed bunch at the end of a working day.

It was not a matter of simply leaving on a jaunt; permission had to be obtained from the Institute director. Forms had to be filled. And therefore an excuse was required.

"And so how are you faring at the Institute?" the director asked when I went to see him with my request. "Everything all right?"

"Yes, thank you, Professor Barua. And thank you for the Postmaster Flat you've kindly allocated me. It's very convenient."

"Yes, you were lucky."

He saw the surprise on my face and smiled indulgently, as if to admit, no, it was not luck but special pleading by a mutual friend. He himself is from the northeast, with that region's typical flat, oriental features; a brilliant but modest man, from what I understand, an analytic philosopher not without a sense of humour.

"I understand you are quite a singer—perhaps you can sing for us—my wife organizes a singing circle on Sundays in the Guest House lounge . . ."

I stared at him, gauging sincerity. "Sometimes I sing to myself—to recall the tunes—"

"You should record them."

"I'm recording the words."

"Record the tunes, the ragas—before we lose these folk melodies. I can make a tape recorder available for you—would you like to have one?"

I said yes. And permission to travel was also granted, fare was given, for the purpose of visiting New Delhi for research. Not that I needed the fare, but it comes with the package of generosity that's been awarded to me. He was being kind, but obviously he would have to inform the major, my guardian angel from the CBI.

"Take care," he said in the western fashion as I left his office. Perhaps he meant more. I nodded.

The bus arrives in Delhi at past six, and stiff and bleary I hop down onto the sidewalk. Public buses are groaning their way round the circus, already full; a newspaper and paperback vendor sets up on the sidewalk; a beggar woman walks by, both arms stretched out before her automaton-like. A chai-wallah is pumping his stove. It feels warm and laden here, after the quick mountain air I've left behind. As soon as life returns to unlock my stiff limbs, I negotiate with an auto-rickshaw to take me to a university guest house recommended to me by the director. It turns out to be a miserable excuse for one (though the grounds are impeccable), dark inside, the room infested with mosquitoes that greet me with vigour as soon as I step in; but the rate is cheap and full breakfast is ten rupees, who is to quibble? The watchman, who checks me in, looks suspicious, what with the recent bombing in one of the city's busiest markets. Kashmiri terrorists are suspected.

After a cold bath and breakfast I walk to Connaught Place, ignoring several autos on the way, perhaps as a paranoid precaution against being followed, until I reach Block C, where I wave down a vehicle.

First stop is the Sahitya Akademi Library. There is material here to look up. The medieval world of Nur Fazal has begun to interest me as never before. I had received it as legend and myth, magic and mystery, all special to us; now I see it more as a real, historical period and myself as a thread in its endless extension. The 1260s or thereabouts—when the sufi arrived in India—what did the world look like then? The Mongols had conquered it from Beijing to Baghdad, for one thing . . . the Crusades had been defeated finally by Saladin, the great universities of Europe had been founded . . . there was the Inca empire in America, the Mali empire in Africa . . . Vast armies moved, peoples perished. What of the individual? Can we really understand the past beyond the facts? When we define the terms, perhaps. I enter the great halls of the library, pay the required fees, and look up the works of the thirteenth-century court poet Amir Khusrau, whose master Alaudin Khilji had sent his generals from Delhi to conquer Gujarat. Thus came the ignoble end of the great city of Patan. Khusrau wrote a narrative poem about the conquest, a tender love story describing how the Gujarati princess Deval became the object of passion of the prince, Alaudin's son Khizr Khan, for whose sake she was captured and taken to Delhi. A tragic story, really, for that was not the end of her fate; Alaudin was killed, Khizr was blinded then killed, and Deval ended her days in the harem of an upstart. But we at Pirbaag, I recall, had a different take on the story of our Gujarati princess.

What's surprising is that, old as it is, and historically vague, the story carries a bitter potency for the nationalist fanatics of today, shames their modern manhood, goads them into states of rage and hatred.

At noon, holding photocopies, I emerge into the now blazing summer heat and take an auto to Old Delhi.

On Chandni Chowk, the main thoroughfare, I thread my way purposefully for a while through the bustle of rickshaws and touts and shoppers and handcarts, before I admit to the uselessness of my solo venture and stop at a sidewalk vendor. Where is Azad Gully, I inquire. Ay!—he asks around, gets a satisfactory answer, then motions to a waiting bicycle rickshaw in what is evidently a prearrangement; a wiry man of about thirty pushes his vehicle towards me. We come to an agreement on the fare, I climb in, and the lean muscles do their job and carry me off among crowds first through one gully, then another, the jeweller's market, the paper market, the perfume market, where finally I am dropped off.

A schoolboy in uniform points to a quiet, narrow alleyway, into whose dark shadows I enter. Inside, a single shopfront is open, a man sitting at a counter observing me as I come along; it's a belt workshop, the showcase under his elbows crammed with buckles of all sorts. Some men or boys work behind him on the floor, sitting in a circle. He directs me to the door of an old-style haveli across the lane. I step in through that door, enter a large courtyard, stop short. All around me the ruins of ancient buildings. Directly in front is a raised platform where perhaps dancing nautch girls performed once upon a time. The great Ghalib could have come to recite his poetry here; he lived not far from where I stand. The courtyard is strewn with rubble; the platform, which has a roof, is stacked with brown boxes containing, according to the description on the sides, computer monitors. A girl stares at me from a doorway to my right; she points to a dilapidated flight of open stairs across the yard, towards which I venture uncertainly. The sky above me is blue as I climb up; in the distance some birds, a couple of kites. The steps are high, and I have to breathe harder as I ascend; the girl down below watches me curiously.

The first-floor landing is abandoned; hardly any structure remains—piles of rubble, a doorway in a fragment of wall; beyond all that, apparently, open air, a sheer fall. There is a second floor, which is less broken; that it is supported at all is a miracle. The landing has no ceiling, but a doorway leads me leftwards to another one and thence around to a set of rooms. On the way, through missing walls I can look down upon the cartons and the girl, still watching me. A woman of about thirty now immediately covers her head upon sighting me, at the same time picking up a wailing baby from the floor.

"Is Mansoor here?" I ask.

She turns a blank stare at me.

"A Gujarati man—" Chhota sa, this height?

"Omar Bhai, from Gujarat—Haripur?" A high voice.

"Hari-*pir*," I correct her, wearily, and she gives me a startled look.

She points me to a door, where someone has already appeared.

I have seen him only once since my return and the sight startles me again—so much ingrained in me is the picture of the little prankster I left behind. He is unshaved, his hair is dishevelled, and he wears a blue dhoti and white singlet.

"You came, Bhai," Mansoor says softly; we embrace awkwardly.

"How are you?"

"Well. Come, Bhai—follow me, to my room."

We climb up a step, walk past more crumbled, incomplete walls, then arrive at a blue oil-painted door. He shoots back the bolt, pushes in the two door panels, and we enter his room: a dark haunting place, the only window small and barred, from which enters a stale, pallid daylight. A naked bulb on a table lamp is the other source of light. There is a chair, a small table, and a bed, upon which we both sit. And look at each other.

"Are you all right?"

"Yes . . . yes, I am all right. As all right as possible."

"Meaning what," I ask desperately. "Mansoor, what are you doing here—in such a place?"

"It's temporary, until I have some money—you brought the money, Bhai?"

"Yes, but it can't last you long, Mansoor."

"I know. But long enough."

He speaks softly, with a smile and what I hope I only imagine is a mad gleam in the eye. There is much I want to ask him—what happened to Pirbaag, to Ma and Bapu, what he's been up to—to continue from where we left off abruptly in Ahmedabad only a few weeks ago. But the time, the place don't seem right. How could the two of us, princes of Pirbaag, have ended up here, of all places—an ancient ruin in a gully in Old Delhi, in an atmosphere of secrecy and fear?

"Come, let's go somewhere and have a meal," I tell him. Perhaps outside in the light we can talk. And he looks starved. He readily agrees. He changes first, into trousers and shirt, and he combs his hair, taking his time, as though waiting for something.

A muezzin's cry finally rises up from the Jama Mosque nearby. My brother throws a glance at the clock. "Come, let's pray," he says.

I look at him, dumbstruck. He picks up a mat from behind the chair, and without a glance at me throws it on the floor, and quickly does the Muslim prayer. A geometric abstraction, symbol of piety, normally I would respect it. But it gives me a shiver of apprehension. When did he become this way? Is it faith or bitter reaction he's expressing?

Downstairs, as we step out of the haveli, the man in the belt store shouts a greeting and Mansoor replies, "Salaam, Mukhtiar!"

It is then that I look at the small rectangular wooden signboard above the store: "Salim Belt and Buckle."

I stop to stare at my brother, a response he seems to expect.

"Mukhtiar from Haripir?" I ask him.

"The same."

Mukhtiar, one of the two sons of Salim Buckle, a man who met a ghastly fate in our village long ago. Hardly a comforting presence here. Two pairs of eyes pin me, as I briefly take in this situation. Then with an awkward smile and a wave at the shopkeeper, saying, "Let's go, Mansoor," I lead my brother away.

At the restaurant in a main street, where it's bright and peopled and cheerful, I watch him polish off his thali with an emotion I can barely suppress. From where we sit, the gold market up the street appears all aglitter with fluorescent light and jewellery, gangs of well-dressed women swarming around the shops, some with cellphones to their ears.

"Since when have you become 'Omar,' " I ask severely, in a low voice.

"I don't want a sufi-pufi name," he answers with an arrogant smile.

"You know who Mansoor was—after whom you were named?"

"He was a crazy guy who let himself be killed."

"Because he believed in the truth—"

"And so do I."

"Why 'Omar'?"

"He was a great fighter."

"And what are you fighting, Bhai? Tell me."

He does not answer.

"And Mukhtiar? What's he up to in Delhi?"

"He has his business. He lives with his family, and he found me that room where I stay."

We order more tea, one more samosa each, and bright orange jelebis from the woks. We sit in silence awhile, look at the human traffic outside, watch the flurry of waiters running hither and thither and shouting their orders. It occurs to me that my brother has not inquired once about how I have fared all these years abroad, about the life I've left behind. To him, I simply abandoned them all. Now he looks up at me and smiles.

"You know they are looking for you?" I tell him. "The police?"

Comes the passionate reply, "They are looking for scapegoats only. Any Muslim will do, to deflect attention from the crimes of Modi's government in Gujarat. They started a genocide there, Bhai, everyone knows it, yet no one is willing to use that word."

He takes a quick breath, we fall into silence. I realize I don't know what to say to my brother because I cannot face his answers, their implications. The killings in Gujarat have taken away my own certainty; I simply cling to my beliefs due to a certain obstinacy, a residual blind faith in our society, that it would never allow premeditated, government-sponsored pogroms.

"Then you are not up to anything silly?" I ask him finally and hopelessly.

He does not answer, busily blows on the steaming tea in his hand, pauses to guide a film of cream to a side of the cup with his little finger.

Having taken his time, he says, "You know, Brother—when we reply sticks for sticks and swords for swords, we are always cut down because we are few and unorganized. It's the big thing that makes the difference—makes them scared."

"What 'big thing'? What are you saying? Are you crazy?"

Again the silence. And I notice we have managed to draw a few stares from the other tables.

"Who's 'we'?" I ask crossly but quietly. "The world does not divide so neatly into 'we' and 'them,' Mansoor, there was no such thing when we were growing up!"

"There is, now."

He accompanies me to the main street. Chandni Chowk is one place that's heavily watched, I tell myself nervously.

He says, "You left a long time ago, Bhai. I grew up in a different India than the one you knew, and I am a Muslim."

I don't know what to say to this, for there is a truth to it. Desperately I plead, "Promise me you will not do anything stupid—"

"Depends on what you mean."

We've reached the end of the road, the Red Fort is before us, the Jain sanctuary for birds on our right. We've just passed the place where the Sikh Guru Tegh Bahadur was martyred by Aurangzeb the Mogul emperor, as the plaque outside informs passersby.

The old wounds, the old battles. They and we, and no place in the middle.

"Try and see sense," I plead as we embrace, then we head off in opposite directions.

12

The garden, cont'd. The war with China, and . . .

A new hatred had set in among us, bitter and poisonous, as expressed by an unforgettable cry.

Chou en Lai, hai! hai! Chou en Lai, hai! hai! Shame on you, Chou!

A procession of boys raging on the road, casting shame on the Chinese premier, among them Harish, Utu, and me. Somehow, in all the excitement Harish had ended up screaming his head off while straddling Utu's and my shoulders, perhaps imagining this was how he would ride that aggressor Chou en Lai, who had lied to Nehru about our two nations' friendship and had now attacked us. Our voices turning hoarser, we jogged from one end of the village to the next, then back.

By which time the invocation had altered, *Chin-chao-mao, hai! hai!*

The nation was at war against a monstrous, cunning enemy. China. We fought the British and threw them out; our ancestors fought sultans and rajas; but what kind of enemy was this? Stories of Chinese devilry threw our hearts into fear. What dharam did they have, they who ate dogs and rats. They had masses of people.

Chin-chao-mao. The evil triplet: China our communist neighbour, Chou the liar, Mao the mastermind.

Nehru was lolloping about in Africa or London conferring about world issues when he was stabbed in the back by Mr. Chou en Lai, who not long ago had professed, "Hindi-Chini bhai-bhai," we are brothers.

"Bhai-bhai shai-shai nothing," said Raja Singh contemptuously. "Chowen Lai threw Chacha Nehru a googly . . . ," and changing metaphors, he added that the Chinese premier had made our Nehru dance the twist.

The year was 1962.

It has been said that everything about our country changed beginning those weeks as the possibility of war teased us and we reassured ourselves it could not happen, we were ready, and then suddenly it was upon us with a full-scale Chinese offensive that frightened us. Can you pin the present to a given event in the past? Memory plays tricks. But so much happened then that pointed indelibly—and in hindsight, yes—to the world that unfolded for us: the country I have returned to, my place in it. Our own fanatics may have killed Gandhi, but the final nail on the coffin of his message was hammered in by the Chinese attack. No more the friendly namasté India of nonviolence and renunciation, of homespun cotton and hunger strikes; we would be serious now.

The previous day, October 20, had been Mansoor's birthday. Normally this would have called for a small domestic event, with a pilau cooked at home, with peas and potatoes, and sweets distributed to our few friends. But this time we outdid ourselves in an excess of worldly joy and celebration. The result, it seemed, was catastrophe.

At Pirbaag, the Saheb's birthday was always an occasion for thanksgiving and a restrained form of ritual celebration by the followers. The urs or death anniversary of Pir Bawa, celebrated as his wedding or union with the Universal Soul, was the greater festival. Visitors came dressed in new clothes and thronged the shrine, with much ceremony the Pir's grave was anointed like a bridegroom, and there was a communal meal. Ginans were sung into the early hours. But this day Mansoor had turned five, and Ma used a sophist's argument to call for a celebration: the Saheb's sons were important too, wouldn't one of them become the next Saheb? There should be a public event, albeit a small one. It turned out to be a large party, in the pavilion, with food and music and such abundant joy that our world had become different and profane for an afternoon. A cake was brought from Ahmedabad by Master-ji, brilliantly decorated with pink and yellow icing, and silver balls, and Mansoor's name in smart blue English script across it. It lay prominently on a stool, a new and alien icon, a subject of profound admiration.

There were the traditional Gujarati songs, of course, celebrating the birth of a son, and his mischievous yet innocent and beloved ways when older, which described Mansoor so well. Someone ventured a film song; someone else performed a skit. A Johnny Walker lookalike appeared and drew laughs with his rascally antics; and the most outré of all, a drunken- and luscious-looking Bollywood Helen in a sinuously seductive slow dance. Mansoor was called from play and the cake was cut, while those who could—even those who couldn't—sang "Happy Birday to You," just as in the films.

Present, too, was my special someone, that very first and secret heart-throb, a nomad girl of the Rabari caste who always wore the same red embroidered head shawl, dozens of plastic bracelets, and a nose stud the size of a small coin. She looked new to the area, must have been a year or so older than I; her face was long and her piercing grey eyes would boldly return my gaze at our shrine, where she came on Saturdays. Try as I might, I couldn't keep my eyes off her for long, all my cockiness turned to sudden ache and vague desire. I was becoming a man. I had already asked Ma, "Is it possible to marry a Rabari girl?" She had answered, "Jah, jah," go away, with a wave of the hand and a gentle shove of dismissal. My question was only rhetorical, the girl belonged to the realm of what was not possible. She was different. Now at the party my mother followed my looks, met my eye briefly, and had the last remaining slice of the precious cake sent to the girl. That earned me a brief smile, I think, of gratitude.

My father meanwhile squirmed in his seat. This was Ma's occasion, she had ambushed him with it. What was there to celebrate in a birth, he would have told her. The message of the shrine was about the punishment that was the cycle of birth and death and the illusion that was the world. But my father bore it, this celebration of a birthday; he smiled, he waved, he clapped as required, all with restraint and embarrassment.

Finally, Mansoor, who was crazy about bows and arrows, and spears and guns and slings, was presented with a dhanush, a bow-and-arrow set of his own, brought from Ahmedabad by Master-ji. The little boys went to fight the bandits on their make-believe rocky terrain of Kathiawad, among the graves. The sacrilege was complete.

On Ma's face, as she watched the proceedings around her, a look of profound happiness, and embarrassment, and, dare I say it, guilt.

Bapu-ji stood up to go and rest. He could have gone from the pavilion directly into his library, then straight into the house; instead he decided to step down and acknowledge the people standing outside among the graves. Having done so, he stopped before the mausoleum, joined his hands to do a pranaam to the Pir. As soon as he turned to proceed towards the side gate of the house, an arrow shot from the new dhanush hit him in the side of the neck.

He gave out a brief but sharp cry, a very human cry, clutched at the wound, and stumbled onto his knees. The turban toppled from his head. His attendants rushed forward to help him up and then walked him into the house.

The neck wound drew a stream of blood; it could have cost him his life, for the boys in their excitement had lost the rubber cup at the tip of the arrow. What would hurt more in the days ahead was the knee that had bumped the pavement. The child who had released the arrow was none other than Mansoor. Having done so, he stood behind the large grave of Jaffar Shah, his kohled black eyes wide open, a nonplussed look upon his face.

That night, while Bapu-ji was in bed, his face drained, his neck bandaged, and running a fever, several of his young followers arrived, having just heard on the radio the news of China's attack in the northeast.

Ma told them the Saheb was tired and needed to sleep. But they had come in the earnest belief that the end of the Kali Age, predicted often enough in the ginans and by the Saheb, might be nigh, and the Saheb had to be informed. The day's events—a blatantly profane celebration in the house of Pir Bawa—had been ominous enough.

My father heard out these earnest young men, smiled indulgently at them, and said, "Let's see." He waved them away, then closed his eyes.

Later that night, fully awake yet weak, Bapu-ji sat up in bed and asked for tea, and when he'd had it with a biscuit, he got up and went to the library.

There, sitting against a cushion on the floor, his desk on his lap, he began to write. A white cap on his head, glasses on his nose.

Ma asked me to go and put a shawl round his back. Silently and with great care I proceeded to do so. I couldn't tell if he noticed me. With a nib, attached to a holder, that he would dip into a bottle of black ink, he was copying onto foolscap paper the contents of a few ancient-looking pages preserved between sheets of glass. I had secretly observed him at work before, but tonight, in this state, his fevered hand scratching on the page, the blotter used sporadically to dry the ink, I sensed the urgency of his mission, his dedication—to preserve our story for posterity.

Ma's night of abandon had ended badly, and she was blaming herself for the double calamity, the wounding of Bapu and the wounding of Mother India. "It went too far," she said, almost in tears. "The variety program was too much. That Helen girl—chi-chi-chi . . ." She shook her head in disgust. "But how could I stop her, or tell all the people to leave?"

"Ma, you brought down the Mahabharat upon us, with your sin," I teased her.

She could have giggled then, but this was a grave matter. What was left unsaid was that she had used up her savings, and perhaps gone into debt, for our afternoon of abandon. What had got into her?

"I am here," Mansoor declared, drawing his bow and arrow. "Why worry? I will destroy those cowardly Kauravas!"

Ma pulled him into an embrace, saying fondly, "My Arjun is here."

How well he fit inside her arms. Usually he was her Munu, today he had graduated into a fighter hero.

In school, no opportunity was missed to speak about the war. Many of us discovered patriotism, as more than words, an urgent feeling. The staff room would echo raucously with argument, our prime minister's name invoked with much anger, for having kept the nation unprepared. In the assemblies, special prayers were said; as the anthem was sung, some pupils and even teachers broke down into tears. One day some army bigwigs came and spoke to us about glorious careers in the military, about patriotism and the need to defend Mother India. They told us about Shaheed Dinoo, who had bravely gone behind enemy lines, walked up to their commander, and said, "I was a Chinese boy who was kidnapped by the Indians. I will take you through the pass." And when the Chinese followed him, thishoom-thishoom, our jawans were waiting for them. And Dinoo? The Chinese commander had his head cut off.

If the ultimate objective in life was to attain moksha, release from the cycle of birth and unity with the Absolute, did the outcome of this war matter? Had it already been settled by karma? On the other hand, the Gita enjoined duty no matter what the result. Thus discussed my father and his close followers. Meanwhile ordinary men and women prayed and sang to the gods; women knitted sweaters, donated their gold.

When our local MP arrived in the back of a pickup, standing beside a large brass tapela in which to collect the gold, it was Mansoor who took the bulkier of Ma's two bangles to add to the collection.

And when in school some of the older boys collected signatures pledging to defend the nation, I too pricked my forearm with a pin and signed my name in blood.

Did our India even have place names like Namka Chu? Or Thagla Ridge? Or Che Dong?

It was at Namka Chu, a gorge high in the Himalayas at the border with Tibet, that the Chinese first attacked, with their AK-47s and large guns, their booted, well-trained soldiers. They came from all directions, surprising the fewer Indians who sat shivering in their cotton clothes and canvas shoes, manning light machine guns. Oh yes, our Punjabis and Gurkhas and Assamese and others were heroic, but they stood no chance. They were outnumbered and outmanoeuvred; Indian regiments were soon in disarray, the platoons fighting to the last man. They were annihilated. Hundreds dead, hundreds wounded and captured.

And the "shameless" Chinese, as Nehru called them, were moving to other positions, threatening an all-out war.

We had been attacked and could not defend ourselves.

In spite of the bile and nervousness which the war produced in us, there was an element of comedy to our exaggerated responses that we would long remember. Ma prepared for the eventuality of the Chinese army reaching as far as Gujarat by having two kitchen knives sharpened; jewellery and other valuables like photographs and a sari had been gathered and packed in a trunk to take with us if we had to leave our home. A blanket, a ladder, and some food and medicine were on standby, in case we had to make a jump and hide in the dry well at the back of the house. A snake had already been forced out of it.

"We are ready," Ma then said, red-faced and huffing from her efforts, a determined look on her chubby features. "Let them come!" Aawé to khari, Chin-chin lok! Beside her, her little Arjun with his bow and arrow.

One late evening after dinner, as I sat at my table in the courtyard poring over newspapers, my father came over from the library and said to me, "Karsan—come with me outside for a moment."

Ma had come out of their room and stood watching as Bapu-ji and I stepped out from the side of the house into the shrine compound. Bapu-ji had in his hands a package wrapped in an old copy of *Samachar*. I followed him to the large grave of Jaffar Shah in front of the mausoleum. My father stopped at the foot of the grave, went down on his knees; I did likewise, and watched with surprise as he pried out a loose brick from the ground. Under it was a piece of damp wood that he also removed to reveal a recess. I peered into it, saw that it was about a foot deep and empty.

"Put this packet in there and close the space," Bapu-ji said, handing it to me, "and do not speak to anyone about this."

"Bapu, can the Chinese attack us all the way here?" I asked.

He thought for a moment. "It's best to be prepared for anything. This has been our hiding place for generations."

The moon had come out and was three-quarters full, casting long shadows in the compound, the silhouettes of trees bearing silent witness to what my father and I had just accomplished, and I also recall a brief scent of flowers blown by an intermittent breeze. There was a slight sound and we both gave a start and looked towards the gate, but there was nothing unusual in sight. I helped Bapu-ji up and we walked back to the house. Mansoor was fast asleep in his bed in our room.

Early the next morning, before school, I again accompanied my father, this time to the old banyan tree outside the main gate that my friends and I had dubbed Mister Six. This old ped had a mangled trunk; a canopy of leaves drooped down from it. At the head of the trunk was a dark shapeless hole, into which Bapu instructed me to drop another wrapped package. I balked. "There may be a cobra inside, Bapu-ji."

"If there is a cobra inside," he murmured, "all the better."

But he took the package from me and inserted it into the recess, pushing his hand completely inside. I gazed at him in admiration.

"This tree is sacred," he said, still in that low voice. "Like the crows, it has borne witness to our history. It will be here when we are gone."

Almost exactly a month after their attack, having occupied some territory, the Chinese declared a ceasefire.

Just as the Kauravas humiliated Draupadi, people said, these Chinese took our shame; our warriors could do nothing. Where was Krishna, where Arjun? But the second inning has yet to be played, the match is not over. Mahabharata is yet to happen. The next time we will match them gun for gun, jawan for jawan. We will have an atom bomb.

Meanwhile we hang our heads in shame. And we blame each other.

⊰⊹⊱

. . . and the outer reaches of communal madness.

Diagonally across the street from us was the local Muslim settlement, behind a gate so immense and strong it could once have belonged to a fort. Here in a mosque was buried the Child-imam Balak Shah, believed to be a grandson of our own Pir Bawa, the Wanderer. The Balakshahis, as his followers were called, awaited the resurrection of their Imam on Judgement Day; meanwhile he performed daily miracles at his shrine. It was from this mosque that the azan would be heard every prayer time; in particular, its singular Arabic call formed a deep, rising counterpoint to the singalong Gujarati ginans of Pirbaag at the dawn hour, when all else was quiet.

Recently, while the rest of the nation was tense with war anxiety, the devotees of the Child had celebrated a thanksgiving, with ceremonies and prayers. Not long ago the papers were full of news about an Italian mystic who had gone up a mountain and brought back news about the impending end of the world. With the Chinese threatening a mighty war in the north, the Kali Yuga seemed to be nearing its predicted demise, and the Balak-shahis thought this might be just the moment for their Child-imam to awake from his grave beside his mother and lead the world to glory. With him would awaken all the illustrious personages from the past, including the Prophet Muhammad, Hazrat Ali, Jesus Christ, Shri Rama, Shri Krishna, and others. The Balakshahis gathered flowers and prepared garlands, they hired musicians, they sang their songs of celebration. When the hostilities ended, denying them the second coming, they quietly heaped their flowers on their few graves and our many.

It was all good fun for the town. "So he's still sleeping?" one might ask playfully, and be rewarded with a smile. No harm was done. And yet, behind this practised communal amity lurked a fire that almost devoured us.

One afternoon, the local school, which stood exactly where the road forked in our village, ended. The Balakshahi children would come down the main trunk of the road; the Hindus lived close to this junction and also up the left branch of the fork, which proceeded to the Baroda highway; and those remaining, mostly the other Muslims and the cattle keepers, went up the right branch and around to the fields behind Pirbaag. Three boys emerged from the school, continuing a lively discussion.

"Ey," says Paado, the shopkeeper Manilal Damani's son, "Pakistan was behind this war, Pakistan. It is our worst enemy, worst . . ."

"There are Chinese in Pakistan?" asks the second boy, a sycophant.

"My father says these Balakshahi people have been praying to their pir to help China! They are Pakistanis themselves only, all their relations live in Pakistan!"

"Saala!" comes the shrill response. The third boy hitches up his shorts, ready for battle. He is the buckle-maker's son, Mukhtiar. "You are calling us Pakistani—"

The two lock in combat—an ungainly embrace, grunts and sniffles—in the middle of which one of the Damani brothers leaps out of the store, separates them and deals a slap at Mukhtiar, throwing him to the ground.

That evening, towards the end of the busy shopping hour, Salim Buckle, the injured boy's father, led a demonstration outside the village shop. The group consisted of a few vendors and their supporters. What they expected from the shopkeepers was not clear. The latter were not from Haripir originally but had come down from the north during the Partition to take up the property of my uncle's in-laws, who had declared themselves Muslims and headed the opposite direction. The Damanis, through their influence on Goshala, had recently made it difficult for the vendors to obtain goods to sell, whether cigarettes, stamps, or bananas, thus stifling their competition. And so there already had been a quarrel brewing between the two parties.

The three Damanis were hefty amateur wrestlers who reportedly ate eggs in secret to build their strength. They were of course confessed vegetarians. As the crowd began to thin at the fork, having had their fill of the word-slinging spectacle, the brothers came out and easily beat off the scrawny vendors; not satisfied by their victory, they called out, "Pakistani cunts!" behind their backs.

The next morning at dawn, as the azan prayer call rose up from the mosque in the distance, and the singing was well under way at our shrine, a short sharp scream cut through the air.

A man soon brought news from the tea stall outside: some unknown person had thrown a piece of meat into the family shrine of the Damanis, an arboreal structure in their backyard housing statues of the gods. The ladies of the family, not to say the gods, had been defiled. And the Damanis were out for blood.

"Now what will happen?" Ma asked softly.

Bapu-ji, my brother, and I were at the table next to the kitchen where we usually ate, and Ma was serving us breakfast.

After a brief pause, Bapu-ji replied slowly, "Even during Partition we didn't experience this sort of thing in our village. Some vile mischief is afoot . . ."

"Who would defile a god's house?" Ma asked. "Hindus would not do this."

"Keep these two inside," Bapu-ji said, indicating Mansoor and me.

She nodded, and as she did so, an involuntary sound escaped from her throat.

Revenge would be certain, they both knew. The only question was what form it would take.

I did not stay indoors for long, of course. Soon enough I ambled my way towards the front gate. Harish was outside his father's tire shed across the road, similarly dawdling, and I waved and went out to meet him. He too had been instructed to stay close to home. His father was a thickset hairy-chested man in a singlet, his hands at his waist now as he stood at the doorway looking out expectantly. Pretending life as usual, the two of us started up the road towards the fork and the school, throwing a cricket ball to each other and making a show of ourselves. The school was closed. Utu, having observed us, came over and together the three of us strolled back towards Pirbaag, hoping to play cricket at our playground. Also in a show of normality, apparently, the barber was setting off on his rounds, swinging his leather bag, calling out his greetings of jovial deference; and a vegetable cart was creaking its way up the hill, in stops and starts. A truck passed.

When suddenly a cold chill had descended upon the street, muting all sound, and a wave of nervous apprehension came trembling through; the shops began to close one by one. The barber stopped and reversed, hurried towards the back of the Hindu quarters; the vegetable hawker pushed his cart to park it outside a shop, adjusted his green dhoti, and scampered off. Harish, Utu, and I parted company without a word, infected now by this new and still incomprehensible fear.

The shrine was absolutely deserted, like the dead of night. Bapu was inside the library. Sensing my presence outside the door on the pavilion, he looked up and said, "Yes, Karsan?"

"Bapu-ji—something's happening—the whole village is closing—"

"Come," he said, "sit down."

I went inside and sat down on the floor beside him. He said nothing more, went about his business. Today he was answering letters.

"Bapu-ji—" I said.

"Yes?"

"Why do Hindus and Muslims hate each other?"

He became quiet, looked away, and for a moment I thought he was going to say, I don't know. Instead, he said, "They don't hate each other. They're only sometimes afraid of each other . . . and there are those among them who exploit that fear."

I did not ask him, Are we Hindus or Muslims, Bapu-ji?—because I knew what he would have said. We are neither and both. We bow neither to Kashi nor to Kaaba, et cetera. And we are respected for that.

It was three o'clock. I had already with some reluctance played Bandits of Kathiawad with my brother Mansoor, in which game at his insistence I was always a hapless sipai, a bumbling cop, so he could be the fierce outlaw who defeated me among the graves that were his fortresses. And I had explored the neglected graves at a far corner of the compound, large and ancient and crumbling, guarded by the thorny scrub and the vicious vicchi-butti plants that could make the skin itch for hours; the broken texts on the stones were unreadable and could well have been in Persian. Among these stone giants stood a small, ornate, and unmarked grave of marble, which I knew Bapu-ji sometimes came to visit. He had said once that it belonged to a princess. Now I sat on the floor, at the edge of the pavilion by myself, intensely tuned to the exhausted stillness all around me. What would happen next, how would the night end?

The answer came with the sudden and various sounds of motor vehicles on the road outside, accompanied by sporadic shouting.

My father's two attendants appeared and woke him up from a nap among his books and told him what was happening. Three pickups had arrived with a load of young men, all wearing red headbands and armed with sticks and swords. Two vans had followed with other young men, wearing green headbands and similarly armed. They had all disappeared into the village.

No sooner had this news come than there arrived a delegation of three men. My father heard them out quietly on the pavilion, after which they left and he turned and entered his library and shut the door behind him. The two attendants and I waited nervously outside, sitting on the floor, arms crossed over our knees. The afternoon was drawing to a close and was still eerily quiet, except for an occasional all-too-human sound: a child at play in a nearby yard, a man's brief, sharp shout. My companions were among the regular stream of volunteers who came to the shrine to serve. They were from the Champaner area, and I heard from their murmurs that they were not entirely new to the situation now gripping us in Haripir. Ma brought tea and bhajias for us, asked me if I did not want to come inside. I said no. Don't go outside, she warned.

Finally Bapu-ji emerged. "Let's go to the Balak Shah place," he told us, looking surprisingly fresh, perhaps having gone inside and had a bath. It was about four o'clock.

The road was deserted, except for the stray dogs quietly trotting about, only too happy to exist without the company of men. In the distance, at the fork, there stood a few young men, some of them swinging staffs in their hands, one of them holding up a transistor radio that crackled. These were the redbands.

The four of us arrived at the massive gate of the Balak Shah shrine. Above the door, in the lookout, there was some movement. Trouble was being anticipated.

Bapu-ji stepped forward and banged on the door with a fist. "Open, this is Tejpal Saheb!"

The small wicket in the lower portion of the great door opened a crack, a face peeped out and withdrew. There was a quick conference on the other side, then the small door opened wider and a voice said, "Come in, Saheb."

Bapu-ji, then I, then the two volunteers went stooping through the wicket. Inside, all was quiet, but on both sides, men and women were sitting outside their shacks, some of them on their haunches, and they stared at us. Not a word was spoken. Our entourage proceeded awkwardly through this gauntlet towards the shrine of the grandson of the Wanderer. These people were related to us in some way, but I was almost completely ignorant about them. This was my first visit to their settlement, yet I knew that they came regularly on Fridays to Pirbaag to pay their respects to our Pir Bawa. Straight ahead stood a group of men waiting for us, it seemed, at yet another gate, which led to the mosque and the shrine of the Child. The sheikh, Sayyed Ahmed, stepped forward and shook hands with my father. He was a short heavy man with a long beard and wore a simple kurta-pyjama and a cap. He patted me on the shoulder and nodded at the two volunteers. Then he led us all in through the gate.

"Sheikh-ji," my father said when we were inside and facing the mosque, which was a tall, domed, whitewashed building with a verandah in front. "What has happened to our village all of a sudden? We must intervene—this is not what we want."

The sheikh looked up above him and said, "Allah-karim knows this is not what we want."

Bapu-ji and the sheikh by themselves walked over to the mosque, climbed up the steps to the verandah, and disappeared into the dark interior to converse in private. I and my two companions from Pirbaag were brought water. Not long afterwards the two elders appeared, solemn as before. They nodded to each other and then we left.

I slept fitfully that night. My mother kept vigil in the courtyard, sitting at my work table, occasionally flipping the pages of a magazine, or napping with her head in the crook of her arm on the table. Bapu-ji was in the library; the two attendants sat outside on the steps of the mausoleum. All was quiet, nothing happened. At four my father went to the temple to meditate. No one from the village attended that morning, and the azan from the mosque did not sound. At five my father came to get me, to perform the ritual of the Ganges water, which involved the pouring of ordinary water from a brass pot into a bowl, into which was mixed blessed water from a small glass bottle. Devotees would be served the sanctified water from the bowl. There had to be at least a second person present for this ancient ritual, and the attendants were not around. While Bapu-ji and I proceeded with the ritual—he let me pour from the bottle—there came a piercing scream from outside.

After the ceremony my father came out to sit on the pavilion. It was still early, the sky was a grey blue, and the air was cool and laced with woodsmoke. Ma brought hot milk for Bapu-ji and told me to come in for breakfast. Suddenly there were sounds of people outside on the road, and at almost that moment the attendants rushed in with the news that Salim Buckle's dead body had been discovered at the fork.

In the village later that morning life had returned to normal; the tire shed was open, a truck stood outside; bhajans were playing in Ramdas's flower shop. The fruit-seller's cart was active, and the barber had resumed his business. The children were in school or at play. And people came to the shrine to beg favours.

Salim Buckle's body was so mutilated it was taken straight to the mosque, washed by the men and kept covered until the funeral that same day. He had been cut up with a sword. Some said his heart had been cut out, others, his liver; a sword had been run through one eye. In the afternoon we boys went and had a nervous look at the spot by the unpaved roadside where he was found; it had been washed with water and swept, but the ground was still dark where the blood had crept through. Dogs were sniffing around.

It was believed that the buckle man had been responsible for the desecration of the Damani family shrine and had paid the price; who exacted it could be surmised; they had gone anyway, and we had been saved devastation.

My father went to the funeral, but not to the burial ground. When he returned, he went not to his library but the sanctum of the mausoleum. There he spent the entire night in communion with the Pir.

By the friendship my brother has kept up, it is evident that the ghost of Salim Buckle still haunts us. What havoc has he planned for his revenge?

13

Negro. The Bible and the pangs of puberty. Isaac didn't matter.

Haripir returned to its normative mode, life proceeded as before. The weekly crowds at Pirbaag, Raja Singh's abrupt arrivals, my mother's furtive escapes to the movies—these highlights continued, inflecting my humdrum existence, marking the fitful passage of time. That day of the near-riot was now a chilly thought, a nightmare remembered. For long afterwards sometimes I would wake up with the clear image in my mind of that dead-still high noon when the knives were drawn. This dream scene became rare but I could never shake it off.

As I passed my fourteenth year, life seemed to bring new possibilities. That year, for one thing, a Christian teacher arrived at our school.

St. Arnold's was an old red-brick building connected by an open corridor to a modern, though already worn complex of classrooms behind. The older portion, some sixty years old, consisted of the principal's office and a storeroom, edged by a narrow verandah and a strip of garden in front. Next door but detached was the chapel, with its high vaulted ceiling and arched door, but it was dingy and neglected and used for nothing but the occasional meeting or by the boys to hide in the back and smoke. The large fenced ground outside was red and barren; it had for long been slated for a hospital construction but meanwhile it was our playground. There were only a handful of Christians in the school, including the principal and some pupils.

Everything about the new teacher, Mr. David, was colourful and unusual; cool, though the term was not in use then. His features immediately garnered him the nickname "Negro" among the boys. He was not darker than most Gujarati men but his hair was a mass of curls and his facial features also seemed to suggest Africa to us; not that we knew much about the continent—except Tarzan of the movies and his jungle cry—or its people. He wore bright shirts, and when he took them off, a finely muscled body was revealed, and chest hair so neat, it could have been curled on purpose. The suggestion of alien savagery had snaked its way into our thoughts perhaps from some orthodox home, or even the school staff room.

Mr. David was in his thirties; he had a high voice, and he spoke Gujarati in the caustic, Kathiawadi way of my mother, besides Urdu and English. His given name was John. He had an easy, friendly manner with us, so different from the bullying ways of the other teachers. He taught us science and PT, and his English was smarter than even that of our haughty principal and senior English master, Mr. Joseph.

Red House had just played Yellow in a match of hutu-tutu on the volleyball court; dripping with sweat and covered with sand, I was walking to the outside tap to clean up before going home. Mr. David had stepped alongside, and I glowed with the privilege.

"Why don't you come to the church in the morning?" Mr. David asked. "I notice you come early to school sometimes. We have a small service every day before bell rings. A smart, intelligent boy like you should come to church."

The church was a block away from the school, a high building of the same red brick, but far tidier, with a beautiful front garden. It seemed almost always deserted.

"I am not a Christian, sir," I said to him, surprised that he shouldn't know that. "Are you a priest, sir?"

"I see," he said, and laughed briefly before replying. "And no, I am the deacon—an assistant. Reverend Norman is the priest. You don't have to be a Christian, Karsan, to come. It's just for comradeship and to think about spiritual matters. What's important in life."

In spite of his friendly manner, he seemed a lonely man. He was not even married, while most of our other teachers had thriving families living in the neighbourhood. Often after school I would see him sitting in a classroom marking exercise books or reading a paper, in no particular hurry to go anywhere.

"I teach the Christian students at noontime every Friday. Come and see if you like it," said Mr. David. "We tell a lot of stories!"

"Do you drink wine, sir?"

His smile broke for an instant, then returned. He said slowly, "Not in the class, Karsan."

To counter the open admiration and awe in which he was held by many students, his presence had also become the occasion for some vile gossip. Christians turned wine into blood, by some magic of the priest, before drinking it up; or, they were really Tantriks and the blood was women's blood; and so on.

I became uncomfortably silent, but much to my pleasure he rescued me in a couple of steps by going on to discuss the upcoming Cassius Clay fight with Floyd Patterson. Mr. David was also the boxing coach. To see him in gloves and shorts, sparring with an imaginary opponent to demonstrate technique, and perhaps to show off, dancing about lightly, throwing a left, then a right, was truly awesome. We would cheer him enthusiastically and mercilessly tease the invisible foe.

Raja Singh was my expert on matters of the world. The Christian wine, said he, became blood in their bodies only. For the rest of us wine was wine. And what was that? He was only too happy to enlighten.

"Wine, young friend, they call 'daughter of the grape.' Beautiful and seductive, this rose-cheeked temptress—many have followed her never to return." A pause, then: "Don't touch it."

"Have you had wine, Raja Singh?"

"Only as medicine, yaar . . ."

"And it gives strength?"

"Whisky, they say, Ji, sometimes does that . . ."

"Johnnie Walker?" A name from the advertisements.

"He is for the rich, yaar." A tone of regret.

What a comfort this friend, with his knowledge about the world; and what a subversive, I now think. It seems to me sometimes that the difference between my raging brother and me was only the presence in my life of this turbaned ferryman, this lorry driver who gave me rides in his smelly truck called the Kaleidoscope and brought me the world in print and talk.

"Singh-ji—are holy people born the same way as others?"

He looked at me, grinned broadly.

"Yaar—everybody is born the same way—gods, rakshasas, people."
Punching a zestful fist into his other palm: "Even pirs!"

"Even pirs?"

"Even pirs."

What I really wanted to know was whether I had come into the world
the same way as other people. Bapu couldn't have done the sex thing with
Ma, surely. He was holy, he was the avatar. Buddha was born in a special
way, so was Jesus. Why not I, and Mansoor? But Ma, who sneaked off to
the cinema wearing a burqa and hid pictures of Dilip Kumar and Sunil
Dutt in her dresser, was hardly Mary.

I was growing up, and I didn't know what I really was.

One day to my amazement I came across two compact black objects inside my desk: they were the two Testaments of the Bible, bound in gleaming leather, adorned with glittering gold text on the front and the spine.
The New Testament had a cross on it. I fingered them guiltily, then quickly
closed the top of my desk. That night, at home in my room, I took the
two books out from my satchel, handling them by the fingertips with reverence and admiration. They were holy books, containing knowledge
and mystery and power. But were they for me? The wrong magic in
the wrong hands could be devastating. These books were brand-new
and illustrated with etchings of tall, solemn men in long beards and
robes. Each book also contained a colour frontispiece. There was a place
in them to write the owner's name, which I did, and to write notes at
the back, which I attempted as I flipped the thin pages and began to
read.

But of the two, the Old (as I called it) was the mesmerizing one, in spite
of the language, because of its language. In the beginning was the Word.
The Word! How beautiful, how profound. And then a multitude of stories, into which I would dip late into the night, reading about Moses and
David; the patient Job, the forbearing Jonah; the strong Samson and the
wily Delilah. And the one that touched me the most, kept me up late into
the night, brooding—the story of the father, Abraham, who was willing
to sacrifice his son, put him to the knife, for a calling . . . Didn't Isaac
matter?—I asked myself. No, because the call of the Almighty had come.

Isaac didn't matter, I wrote in the back of my Bible, and underlined it firmly. *Son didn't matter to father.* God the father and Abraham the father; the Old Testament had many stubborn fathers. They could get angry and they could be kind; the biggest of them all, the God-father, wanted respect. He did not like to be denied. Indian gods were so unlike these overbearing fathers; they were magic and illusion, and they loved to play. Vishnu took nine births; he became a man-lion to fool and slay a demon; he became Buddha and Rama; in the form of Krishna he stole butter and played the flute and teased the gopis. And Shiva the Dancer jumped down from his statue to fetch water for Nur Fazal the sufi in Patan; his son was the smiling, good-luck Ganesh with the elephant face; from his hair flowed the sacred river Ganga . . . So different from God the father, Abraham the father, the Saheb my father.

The Saheb my father? Was I a sacrifice?

I would also read of a passion so tender I trembled and cried out with pain and shuddered and moaned, Pir Bawa forgive me . . . *I am my beloved's, and my beloved is mine,* which could be a line from the aching love songs of our Pir Bawa, which Bapu-ji said were only allegorical; but here in this Bible there was more: *Thy two breasts are like two young roses that are twins, which feed among the lilies—*

"Eh, Karsaniya, what is it?" comes Ma's voice. "Are you still awake?"

Silence; and in the other bed Mansoor breathes deeply on his back, undisturbed, his chest rising up and down in steady waves.

She waits outside, ears cocked; then walks away murmuring.

And I would return to my image of the tall, lithe Shilpa, Bapu-ji's new volunteer; and my Rabari tormenter of the red sari and the extra-large nose stud, whose name I didn't know, whom I had not seen for several months now . . .

I rose up to open to my beloved, please . . . The Song of Solomon was my book of love and lust and longing. I would read and squirm and begged forgiveness for the karmic dirt I accumulated through my imaginings.

With some reservation I resolved to go to Mr. David's Christian class in the science lab one Friday, imposing the condition on myself that if there was wine-blood business or any other nonsense in the session, I would walk out, even if I faced expulsion from this Christian-founded school.

But it turned out to be safe. Mr. David only told stories. There were five of us in his class.

Mr. David could tell movingly the tragic story of Jesus. I had heard it before from Bapu-ji, who called Jesus "Issa"; but Mr. David told it with such animation and feeling that we could imagine vividly the frail figure of Jesus walking barefoot in Galilee. He described the Pharisees and the priests at the temple; he spoke candidly of Jesus' doubts, so that we understood, and his loneliness when he told his disciples they would all betray him; how he waited for Judas to bring the Roman soldiers and betray him with a kiss. Tears formed in Mr. David's eyes, tears formed in our eyes. It was like listening to the story of a film—Nargis in *Mother India*, surely she suffered! Except for the last scene, the crucifixion. That was the problem with the Christian teaching. There was no final joy and triumph when good defeated evil, and Dilip Kumar walked away with song and girl. There was no humour.

Said Mr. David, trying to sound like one of us: "You know how Ganesh is the son of Shiva? In the same way, Jesus is the son of God!"

"How so?" we asked, and were told.

But Ganesh was a happy god; he always smiled. Jesus wept.

When the teacher told us that Jesus had come with his mother to India to learn from its great sages and mystics, that fact made sense. We were a country of sages. They were all over the place, sometimes clogging the streets and roadways.

"Karsan's Bapu-ji is a great guru," said one of the students. "He has disciples."

"Yes?" Mr. David turned to me, disappointment shading his face. "Tell me about your father," he said.

Proudly I told him about Pirbaag, the Garden of the Great Pir, who also had come a long distance into India. How he too and some of his descendants had suffered because of their beliefs.

Mr. David said he very much wished to see the shrine of this great pir.

When Mr. David arrived at Pirbaag one Saturday afternoon, he performed all the rituals—having bought a green and gold Muslim chaddar, a basket of flowers, and a packet of prasad from Ramdas at the gate—and paid his respects at the more prominent graves at the shrine. My father, who was always informed of unusual visitors, was told about this Christian teacher. He had covered his head, he had circumambulated the grave of Pir Bawa, and he had stood before it, holding his two palms open in front of him in prayer. Even as the report was being made, the teacher appeared in the pavilion, having requested to see the Saheb. He came in, bowed respectfully, and sat down before my father. He introduced himself as my teacher and sang my praises.

Ma was delighted to meet him, especially when he praised me and told her that he happened to come from Jamnagar, her hometown. Mr. David was invited to eat with us.

But she couldn't help asking, "What is your naati?"

Ma liked to know people's naati, their community, which term often translated as caste. It helped her to locate people.

Mr. David smiled politely, "Mari naati Issai." It is simply Christian. Then he added quietly, "I am also a Sidi—you must have heard of them."

"Sidi—" Ma shrieked, her hand flying to her open mouth in shock. Mr. David's naati had now been fully revealed.

"The very same. My ancestors came to India from Africa," Mr. David said to her. "They arrived some centuries ago, but no one knows exactly when."

His people, Mr. David said, had been brought to Junagadh by one of the nawabs to work as palace guards. When the last nawab went to Pakistan after independence, many of them were without work, all their prestige gone. Through his father's palace contacts John obtained admission to a mission school in Jamnagar.

Bapu-ji asked him quietly: "Were your people always Christian?"

To my astonishment, Mr. David replied, "My family have always been Muslims. I accepted Yesu at the school."

Mr. David's name at birth had been Yohanna, and his father's name was Dawood.

"Sidis were good soldiers, it used to be said," my father added.

"Are you a soldier? Can you fight?" Mansoor asked, having come over with a few children to gawk at the teacher.

Mr. David grinned and reached out and fondly ran a hand over my brother's hair.

"There was a brave general called Malik Ambar, and another called—"

"You are negro, then?" I asked.

"The term 'negro' is used for Africans of America, Karsan," he said.

"Like Cassius Clay?"

"Yes. Like Cassius Clay. And Patterson, and Liston, and Satchmo . . ."

There came a dreamy wistfulness to his demeanour as we all stared at him.

We sat down in a circle on a mat in the pavilion. In front of Mr. David was placed a shiny new aluminum plate. He looked surprised, then turned it on its edge, watched his reflection in it.

"It's your lucky day, John Bhai," Shilpa, Bapu's new volunteer, who had sat down with us, teased, "you get a shiny new thaali, and the humble folk have to do with these old brass ones."

Bapu-ji looked indulgently at Shilpa.

Mr. David laughed and said, "I will be only too happy to exchange my shiny new one for your old brass one, Shilpa-ji, if you like."

Shilpa agreed; the plates were exchanged. My mother's face turned red.

Shilpa needled Ma. The two were so entirely different. My mother was simple and caring, plump and motherly. Shilpa was the glamorous city girl, the voluptuous torment who haunted my nocturnal readings of the Old Testament. She was a recent widow and a former teacher. While walking along a busy street in Ahmedabad, she said, she had come across a pavement shrine and put a few coins in the donation box. The sadhu in charge had divined her unhappiness and told her to go and serve the Saheb of Pir-baag. And so here she was, devoted to the Saheb. She arrived alternate Fridays, staying at one of the guest rooms, and departed on Sunday. Immediately upon her arrival, she went about sweeping the shrine; to have a sweeper do it was fine, but to do it oneself, lovingly tend the hallowed ground, gave one the humility that was a prerequisite for spiritual advancement. Few women from the higher castes would stoop to such a lowly chore, whatever the rewards. Afterwards she would attend to my father's needs—bring water or milk for him, run any errand he had—then sit moony-eyed at his feet to learn from him. It was enough to make me jealous of my father.

Early mornings, whenever she was around, I woke up to the pure joy of her thin clear voice rising from the temple, giving the devotional shape to a ginan. It was a beautiful sound at the most beautiful, holy hour before dawn, the first sandhya: the air cool and flavoured with incense, trembling ever so slightly with the rhythms of a bell.

That time when Mr. David first visited us, he stayed the night, and the following day he and Shilpa took the bus together. They made a handsome pair, and as Ma and I watched them walk towards the gate, she remarked, "Wouldn't it be wonderful if these two got together." I now know there was only bite to the remark; the two couldn't have been more unsuited to each other.

14

Marching for Mother India; and the facts of life.

Bapu-ji and Pradhan Shastri appeared to be in agreement. But my father was a polite man; he did not believe in unnecessary argument.

Our sanskriti—our traditional ways—were being corrupted, Pradhan Shastri declared, sitting with my father in the pavilion. He listed the evils that had befallen us, one by one. Films and their loose morality; rock 'n' roll, the twist, and Elvis-belvis; immoral books.

"And one more thing." He eyed my father warily.

"Yes?" Bapu-ji inquired.

"Spineless politicians!"

"The Kali Yuga is upon us," my father said noncommittally.

"We have to bring back the Golden Age, Saheb-ji!" exhorted Shastri.

My father of course knew that the golden Krta Yuga would come only after the complete destruction of the present age. Looking at his impassive face from where I sat close by, having served the two men glasses of sweet milk, I could see that Bapu-ji was not ready yet for that great dissolution.

Pradhan Shastri would have been in his late or middle twenties. He was a local man who had disappeared a few years before and now reappeared, reborn as the regional agent of the National Patriotic Youth Party, or NAPYP, which had set itself up in a house at the fork up the road, next to the school and across from the shop. About him was the urgency of a man who would save India from herself, though he spoke with an easy sincerity and deference, the fire in his message revealed only by a glint in his dark black eyes and a slightly heightened tone to his voice.

He was of compact build and wore a crisp orange dhoti round his waist, his bare chest smooth, dusky, and hairless. His hair was cropped short and the tilak on his forehead indicated that he had recently done his devotions to the gods. Ever since his arrival some weeks before, Haripir had become a louder, indeed a little raucous place. At dawn, just as the ultimate notes of the Muslim azan and the Pirbaag ginans had vanished into the thin air, there would come from a crackling loudspeaker the recitation of Sanskrit slokas, as if to welcome by their hard, formal sounds the actual bustle of the day. They were repeated in the evening. During the day passersby might catch parts of a patriotic speech on tape or receive a political pamphlet.

This day Pradhan Shastri had come on a mission. He wanted something from Bapu-ji: an endorsement, in the form of my participation in his pet project.

"Women appear in the filims in knickers," continued Shastri enthusiastically, condemning the west, "and their books are even more dangerous—I know what I am talking about, Saheb-ji, in the cities boys and girls pass them around in secret to each other and learn all sorts of dirty habits. Have you heard of the infamous book *Lady Chatterley's Lover*?"

Bapu-ji: "What does it say?"

"Chi-chi-chi—don't even ask. But everything. What does it not say? The morality of this Lady Chatterley is despicable. Instead of serving her husband, who is wounded in a war, she becomes the whore of a lower caste. What can such a book teach us? And I wonder if it is a mere coincidence that the Britisher author used a Bengali-type name—Chatterley?"

My father did not inquire into what Shastri was implying.

"That is why I need your son—your elder baba—for our NAPYP activities here. We intend to make men out of the boys—by teaching them good sanskriti, good values and discipline, and devotion to our country. We will make them march in uniforms and salute the flag, and we will teach them to use lathis to defend themselves!"

Bapu-ji smiled. "But Pradhan . . . I mean, Shastri-ji," he began, and the man glowed with pleasure at my father's revision, though I gleaned from that slip that Bapu-ji had known Pradhan as a boy. "Shastri-ji," my father continued, "what's the need for martial training in this land of Gandhi-ji?"

Pradhan Shastri's face lost its expression and he briefly cast a cold, hard look at my father. Then he proceeded to explain patiently and sincerely, to reputedly the highest spiritual authority of our parts, that just as the mind needed to be sharp to ward off lazy and corrupt thinking, so did the body need to be in training to protect itself from attack. He concluded, "Saheb-ji, the humiliating war with China—in which we were betrayed by our leaders—I will be open in my condemnation, don't take it badly—showed us that our beloved nation too needs protection. Our soil is our mother."

In the silence that followed, the two men looked at each other, acknowledging the chasm between them. Shastri backed down a little, saying, "But it is only exercise, this martial training, it will keep them fit." And my father met him halfway and said all right, his son would attend; exercise and discipline would do him no harm.

Satisfied, Shastri asked to take a look at Bapu-ji's famed library. He was interested in the English books, and went around reading their titles on the upper shelves, dismissing with a casual wave of the hand all the precious manuscripts that lay bound in leather in piles of twos and threes lower down. "We have to compete against the Americans and Russians, Saheb," he explained. "We must understand them, then using our own ancient science and technology as a ladder or a pole, we must top these westerners."

His eyes fell upon a volume of Wordsworth, whose "Daffodils" he had apparently studied in school. He adored poetry, he said. He asked ijazat, a formal permission, to recite a poem he had written in English. When my father assented with a gesture, Shastri, standing in the middle of the room, solemnly declaimed,

> Mother to tender infant
> Earth to budding peepal
> India my nation pure and simple . . .

At this point he made a discreet personal gesture, not quickly enough, and I broke into a giggle—and earned that cold look from him. My father threw me only the barest glance; it was reprimand enough.

"Very good," Bapu-ji responded to the recitation. "You should consider publishing it."

Shastri blushed deeply, then asked my father if he would consider joining the advisory board of NAPYP; many eminent gurus who were concerned about the nation's sanskriti had joined. Bapu-ji said he would think about it.

Smartly decked out in my NAPYP uniform—khaki shorts, white shirt, red beret, and black shoes—I would depart early Sunday morning through our gate. A few of the faithful would leave the shrine with me, having taken part in the morning rituals at the temple, and chat respectfully with me, not unconscious of my curiously bright appearance. I was learning more about our nation, I would inform them proudly, and training to defend it. I wonder what they made of that; but they simply smiled and nodded and said, "Good!"

My friends and I and other boys, some of them from neighbouring villages, gathered noisily outside Shastri's house at the fork, waiting to be let in. Across the road in the village shop one of the Damanis would be perched at the till, attending to customers, handing out items of morning essentials. At seven thirty sharp the gate of the house would be opened by one of two strong-looking young men in pure white dhotis and smelling faintly of perfumed oil. We would pour in, remove our shoes, and line up in the small front yard to make obeisance to the statue of the monkey god Hanuman, giver of strength and virility, deity of the martial arts, while a hymn on tape extolled the god's virtues. It was Hanuman's army which had carried out the daring raid on Lanka, set that island fortress aflame, and rescued Sita. Some of us would have brought flowers for the god; mine I took surreptitiously from any grave at our shrine that looked especially well endowed that morning, with Ma's permission and no one else looking. After the Hanuman puja, we gave obeisance to our guru, Pradhan Shastri, sitting bare chested and cross-legged on the mat-covered ground, a few feet away from the god. We bowed and touched his feet and he would put a hand on our heads and smile his appreciation. He too gave off a sweet odour. We would then sit before him, the hymn would be turned off, and our lesson would begin.

We learned of our nation's glorious history, which began thousands of years ago, before any of the invaders came. There had been the glorious civilization at Ayodhya; its prince was the perfect man-god Rama, whose wife was the flawlessly virtuous and beautiful Sita, daughter of Janaka. We learned about the great sages of yore and their wisdom. All the science that the western countries now boasted had already been revealed to our sages in the Vedas. China and Iran had received their civilizations from us, when the Europeans were still living in trees. Our civilization had possessed rockets and nuclear bombs thousands of years ago. What was Shiva's trishul but a missile; Vishnu's Garuda but a rocket? That had been our Golden Age. Everything was in equilibrium; dharma meant duty to parents, the law, the guru, the nation, everybody knew his place. But then the Indian man and woman became weak and soft, and the invaders came and raped the nation one by one.

Pradhan Shastri, declaiming in his dry voice, stirred our young blood. How could we Indians have let such glory waste away? How could we have allowed that evil Afghan Mahmoud of Ghazna to destroy and plunder the temple of Somnath not once but several times; or Alaudin Khilji's generals to drag the sacred lingam all the way to Delhi; or the queen and princess of Gujarat to end their lives in his harem? The story of Princess Deval's plight, as she was wrenched away from her father Karan's arms, brought a tear to the eyes of even the most stalwart and rude among us. Yes, we would reply to his rhetorical exhortation, "Taiyar chhie!" We were ready to fight.

Discipline was strict; any chatting or giggling during lessons could result in uth-bess, a painful, humiliating drill in which the "miscreant" had to crouch and stand up in succession fifty or a hundred times, holding his ears; repeated offence earned six cane strokes on the palm or two on the bottom. Further than that was shameful dismissal from this sacred army of Hanuman.

After an hour of heart-stirring history and rousing patriotism, in our shoes again we marched military fashion in twos to a playing field, singing patriotic songs, proudly holding our staves upright, as onlookers on the road watched and cheered. On the field we were put to a military-style drill, calisthenics, and sports. We were taught to wrestle and fight with our hands and with our staves; we crawled on our elbows with our weapons until we bruised and bled and despaired.

But with me Shastri was teasingly, cruelly ambivalent. He never hit me, in deference to my father's position, but he enjoyed humiliating me. He had discovered, somehow, my second name: Nur. I was Nur Karsan, just as my father was Nur Tejpal. I had told no one about my second name, it was never used, was implicit, customary. And so, one day, to call me to attention he deliberately called me by the full name, "Nur Karsan!" totally startling me and drawing upon me a volley of laughter.

"Musalman nu naam laagé chhe," sounds Muslim, he said, distaste all over his face.

"It's the name of our Pir Bawa!" I blurted out, then with presence of mind added, "Hindu-Muslim-Christian-Sikh are all the same to him!"

"That is true," Pradhan Shastri said, startled at my vehemence, and turned away.

He knew I disliked wrestling, hated tangling with another and falling to the ground—even though my Dada had been a good wrestler in his youth. It gave Shastri great satisfaction to see me tumbling to the ground at the hands of his choice pupils, in the grip of a neck hold, my face in the sand. A few times, under the pretext of teaching me a move, he was on top of me, his oil-rubbed body exuding a repulsive sweaty perfume, his red lips emitting the smell of sweet jin-tan, his large eyes digging into mine, terrifying me.

I swore—I wished—then to have my vengeance on him. But like the other boys I also admired him and wanted to be liked by him. His dedication to and enthusiasm for the nation were impressive, and through him we were part of a national army of youthful volunteers ever watchful of our Mother India, who—he had convinced us—was in mortal danger from her enemies.

The world according to Mr. David was a different place from Pradhan Shastri's.

Occasionally during PT lesson on Saturday Mr. David would gather us around on the field and we would have a small picnic and discuss the affairs of the world. He would have sent a peon to bring gathiyas or bhajiyas from down the road and we would share a few bottles of soda. We were flattered to be taken seriously by a teacher. You are the future, he would tell us; let no one convince you otherwise. And we would glance quickly at each other and think, Yes, why not; we are young; the world is ours.

There was much to discuss. Who would win the third world war if it occurred—the godless Russians or the materialistic Americans? Only recently we had been on the brink, with a crisis in Cuba. Would Nehru's policy of nonalignment succeed? Compared to the western countries, India was underdeveloped; Mr. David gave us the statistics to prove this. You could expect to live to be forty-five in India, but seventy if you lived in America. What if you went to live in America when you were forty-four? How old are you, sir? Are the gods real? Are there many—the three hundred and thirty million of mythology—or is there the One? Questions about God could set him off like a rocket. Have you noticed that all the developed countries are Christian, he might say. And when we have a famine in Bihar or Orissa, who sends us wheat? Love thy neighbour is Christ's message, that is why they send us wheat and give us scholarships and help us in our five-year development plans.

"Are you saying, sir, that only Christians can be good?"

"No, I am not saying that . . ."

But his Christian enthusiasm had to be indulged.

It was not always the lofty questions about the world that we tackled; Mr. David also taught us about the facts of life.

"Which of you masturbates?" he asked once with a broad grin, one hand at his waist, a bottle of goli soda in the other. Korn muthiya maré chhé? Hein?

Red faces; twitchy hands.

"All right, which of you doesn't?"

Nervous laughter; shifty looks around.

The reason for the introduction of this subject was that a boy had been caught in the staff bathroom pleasuring himself, as Mr. David put it. He had been suspended.

There is nothing *physically* wrong with "it," our teacher said, waving the soda bottle in his hand. Your bodies are changing; you have fuzz over your lips and chins; your voices are changing—your voice box, Vasudev, cannot decide between a growl and a bilari's meow; and other things are surely happening to you. "It" will not make you blind, as *our* teachers used to say. But it is a waste of energy, mental and physical. You are pouring out your vital fluid, your precious amiras, into the toilet. He poured soda onto the ground. And it gives you dirty, sinful thoughts—in that way it does harm you. It is better to wait until you marry. Meanwhile, you can take a jog; think of Jesus Christ, or whatever god is your favourite. "It" is the devil's enticement, it catches you unaware, it doesn't know night or day. Beware of "it."

But I was tormented by *it* and by *thoughts*. They would not leave me alone.

Oh, *mara angada mahe utthi chhe laher* . . . my body throbs in expectation of you, Nur Fazal wrote. Such potent words, sung by men and women in the prayer hall, rendered so rapturously by Shilpa. *I rose up to open to my beloved* . . . The Bible. If the holy could think such thoughts, what hope had a mere mortal boy? But then, was I a mere mortal boy?

There was a book in Bapu's library, standing innocently between a thin *Hamlet* and a fat Hegel, called *A Handbook for Nurses*. And what a book to hold. In the chapter titled "Reproductive System," there was a full-page drawing of that thing, that monstrous, that mysterious, hairy "female pudenda" as the caption would have it. No entry for "pudenda" in the dictionary. But the boys' lexicography had all kinds of names for this dark terror. I would choke simply staring at its sketch.

Pir Bawa, make this thing, these uncontrollable thoughts, go away from my head . . .

Pir Bawa's answer. One day I found the nurses' handbook missing from its place. Bapu-ji must have noticed that it had been disturbed. It was an old book; had he consulted it too when he was younger? His shelves did not have a copy of *Lady Chatterley,* made noteworthy in my eyes by Shastri's outrage against it.

Another time during Current Affairs, one of the boys picked up courage to ask the teacher, "Sir . . . tell us about pleasuring—"

"What—you want to hear it again?"

Laughter.

"He means—with . . . with the wife." Baidio ne saath.

Laughter, red faces, the most red, however, that of the teacher, even if he was a negro.

Mr. David thought for a long minute, a thin smile on his face. Then he said, "You have a pencil. The wife has a sharpener. You put your pencil into the sharpener . . ."

The boys smiled with relief. Elegantly put. That was exactly what they wanted to hear. And no messy details.

Mr. David was our friend. In response to our open admiration, he confided to us earnestly that his teaching methods were new; he had learned them from an American teacher and American books. One boy in our class became a Christian; his name was Vasudev Sharma, though he was not a Brahmin, as his name implied; he was often teased because of that. He developed a close relationship with Mr. David and was seen running errands for him. Early every morning he would go to the church down the road and sweep it before the service. In this, it was cruelly remarked, he was only performing his caste function.

15

Imagine for a moment that a new destiny has come to call.

Forget the village, it says, and the God-ness, and the soul of the little people; come out into the bright, beautiful world. You can become a Sobers, a Hanif, a Kanhai. A Bradman? That too.

A tempter came and said, Forget everything, come with me and the world could be yours!

And so:

Bapu-ji, please!

Bapu-ji, please!

Bapu-ji, please!

Each time my father replied, No, Karsan, think of who you are.

In the past several months I had played for the Goshala combined schools cricket team in the annual T.T. Rustomji Cup regional junior tournament. All our matches except one we played locally, in Goshala and other towns in the area; the one exception was a match in Baroda, the former Maharaja Sayaji Rao's city. We performed modestly overall, and lost the match in the metropolis to a team from Godhra; but there I had bagged three wickets for thirty-seven runs, and also batted a half century. The pitch was excellent and a treat to play on, the kind I had never trod on in the small towns of my experience. How big a day had dawned for me became evident when the mighty (though physically diminutive) R.D. Patel of the Sayaji Cricket Academy and former captain and all-rounder of the Gujarat Lions came over and spoke to me.

"Come to Sayaji Academy every Saturday and I will coach you. You can spend the night with one of my other pupils or at my house. There will be no charge."

R.D. was a man of few words, but what he spoke that day was abundant enough. I had promise and he could help me. What more could a boy want? This was fate; luck had come knocking. It does not come twice. "I will ask my father," I said.

"We can't afford cricket coaching," was my father's first line of defence against this sweet invitation from the world.

"But it's free!"

"Then think of your position. Cricket for enjoyment is fine. Play all you want and be healthy. But don't take it seriously so it runs your life."

Three days I pleaded, wept, sulked. The news spread in the village: Harish, Utu, and others came to congratulate, eyes wide with admiration, envy. Is it true, Kanya? It's true. All the way in Baroda? Where will you stay? There, itself—in R.D.'s home. And then?—play for Baroda? Gujarat Lions, ey? Maybe. I say, Kanya, you could play for India! Grins all around. If you've come this far, what's impossible? Everything, don't you see, I've already been spoken for.

Bapu-ji could not be moved. "Think of your position. You are the gaadi-varas."

"I don't want to be gaadi-varas!" I finally screamed at him, "Let Mansoor be gaadi-varas!" and ran out of his library.

The shrine of Pirbaag had suddenly become quiet to pay heed to my tantrum. People stared at me where I had come to a halt on the pavilion, grief-stricken, trembling. Finally, Master-ji came up and put his arm around my shoulder.

"Calm, Karsan, be calm . . ."

His hand firm upon me, he walked me up and down the shrine; people staring, moving aside for us. We walked between the larger graves, draped with heaps of flowers and chaddars, and around Pir Bawa's empty throne where he had breathed his last, and past the rows of marble stones laid flat upon the earth, neatly engraved in Gujarati, commemorating my ancestors, the Sahebs of the past. All the while his voice beside me a constant, comforting murmur.

"Look at all this, beta . . . this is your trust; see the looks in the people's eyes, their hopes and fears, their devotion—for generations they've come here and left with solace in their hearts, with guidance and hope. You will give it all up for a bat and ball? Think, Karsan. Your Bapu knows best, he is the Saheb."

We had stopped at the mausoleum, its dark gaping entrance open before us. A worshipper emerged and hurried past us. My anguish was now gone, and I felt free of that possessive illusion. I began to see sense. Master-ji gently pushed me forward. "Go speak to Pir Bawa," he said.

I took off my slippers and went inside, inhaled the incense and perfume and the cotton dust from the chaddars. I looked at the silver crown at the head of the oversized grave.

"I am sorry, Pir Bawa. I will do as you please."

Outside, back in the dry and hot March sunshine, I could see clearly now where my destiny lay. The life of the shrine had resumed. The pilgrim from Goshala went about circumambulating the mausoleum endlessly; the Rabari girl, my secret tormenter whose name I didn't know, smiled slyly at me; she had seen that I was a little boy after all, who could cry up a tantrum; but I couldn't help a sly little smile of my own.

When I returned to the house, Ma was waiting for me. Opening her arms wide with a smile, she folded me in a tight embrace and gently ruffled my hair. But there were tears in her eyes when she released me. "Sometimes it's what's written for us, Karsan," she whispered. "Your Bapu too had no choice."

"I know, Ma."

Mansoor patted me on the small of my back in sympathy, though he seemed to have enjoyed the scene outside.

And so it was back to my world of newspapers and the school, and NAPYP on Sundays. I still had my more modest desire to show up Pradhan Shastri with the boxing prowess I was acquiring in secret from Mr. David.

Mr. David continued to make his occasional forays into our town, where he could depend on the hospitality of our home. Bapu-ji enjoyed talking to him, and Ma's reservations about his caste were gone; his education and status had elevated him. Soon after he had arrived and made his greetings he would take Mansoor's hand and the two would go out for a walk, heading always first for the Balak Shah tomb in the Muslim quarter. It was a quieter and simpler place than ours, without the crowds; perhaps it reminded Mr. David of the faith he had abandoned. When he had spent his moment there, he would walk about town with my brother, buying him a treat before returning to us with some fresh namkeens or sweets.

One Sunday afternoon I went along with them, much to the resentment of Mansoor, who paid me back by trying to trip me all the way. Shastri's training was over and I had changed out of my uniform. Pirbaag was emptying, and Bapu-ji was sitting in the pavilion with someone. Ma, perched on the front stoop of our house, watched the three of us leave through the gate at the road.

I had ventured only once beyond the massive fortified entrance of the Muslim quarter, with my father, on that night more than a year ago when a terror had been threatened on Haripir, and a terrible ransom exacted. This time I discovered that the grave of the Child-imam Balak Shah lay in the verandah of the mosque. Under the peepal tree in the centre of the compound, as we arrived there, sat the old sheikh Sayyed Ahmed, surrounded by a few worshippers. I did my pranam to him with joined hands, which he acknowledged with a quick wave of the hand, and Mr. David said, "Salaam alaykum," which Mansoor echoed to my surprise, and the sheikh replied appropriately. Beside him was the ancient black stone, famous for its prophecies, polished to a shine by age, its bottom surface curved so that it rested on a tangent plane.

In our bare feet we first went up the steps to the verandah to pay respects at the Child-imam's little grave, which rested beside the somewhat bigger one of his mother. Mr. David stood in front of the two graves with his hands raised palms upward before him and his head lowered, his eyelids too. I didn't know how to pray in such a situation and could only imagine the mother and child: Who had died first? Mansoor had however learned the proper way from Mr. David, and he too raised his hands in the posture of prayer. When they had finished, the three of us came down to observe the ritual of the black stone. The procedure was to go and bow before the sheikh, make a silent prayer, then sit in a crouching position upon the curved stone. If it rotated, your prayer would be answered.

A boy of about my age stood up from the stone, looking sheepish and disappointed.

"Go, sir," said a young man to the teacher, speaking familiarly. "Beg with complete faith and Balak Shah will surely give."

"No, Hussein, I am sorry. I am a Christian, I've told you once before, nai," said Mr. David firmly. Then he saw the looks on our faces—Hussein, Mansoor, me—and Sheikh-ji eyeing him sceptically from the ground where he sat.

"Accha, I'll do it," Mr. David relented and stepped forward. Hussein grinned at his success, and the sheikh waved Mr. David over.

The teacher put one foot gingerly on the stone, covering a good part of its length, then he had to be supported as he brought the other foot on and lowered himself into a crouch; he grimaced slightly and adjusted his posture. Finding balance, he closed his eyes.

"Wish, what do you wish?" Sheikh-ji asked. A little smile now played above his white beard as he looked abstractedly towards the mosque and waited.

Mr. David muttered inaudibly, then said, "I have wished." Sheikh-ji said a prayer in Arabic; then in Gujarati he said, "Pir Balak Shah, if you accept this humble man's prayer, please show him your miracle." He lowered his sight to watch the stone.

We all stared breathlessly at the stone, except for Mr. David, who first looked straight ahead, then turned his face to gauge our reactions. Slowly the stone under his feet turned on its axis like a large compass, taking him through almost a quarter circle. Everyone except the sheikh cried out with joy and wonder.

Evidently Mr. David's prayer would be answered.

Next, Mansoor and I each stepped up to have a go with the stone. It did not turn for us.

Hussein told me, "Next time, iman-se karna, do it with faith, and he will surely reward you."

"What did you wish, sir?" we asked Mr. David, as we walked out the mosque enclosure, past the shanties, and onto the road through the massive gate.

Mr. David looked at us both and said with a mischievous smile:

"I'll tell if you tell."

"Kaho né!" Tell us!

"All right. Then it's your turn. I wished that my application to go to America will be successful."

"You are going to America, sir?"

His silence could only mean yes, and it was a sad thought. I didn't know of anyone who had gone away, except for Raja Singh, who disappeared for weeks or months sometimes. But he always returned.

"America? Why so far, sir? Go to England, it is close."

"America is as good . . . even better."

We walked in silence for a while, then Mr. David added slowly, "You are free to be anything you like in America."

"But in India you are also free?"

He did not reply. He asked, "And you, Karsan—what did you wish for?"

"It's a secret, sir."

"But I told you my wish."

We walked a few paces in silence before I could bring myself to speak.

"Actually—to tell you the truth, sir, I wished for nothing."

"Nothing?"

"Nothing, sir."

He turned thoughtful, and just then Mansoor revealed his own wish. "Bapu-ji will buy me a tricycle, Bapu-ji will," he chanted joyfully.

His wish would be granted, even though the stone had not turned for him.

"Why, Karsan?" Mr. David prodded me gently.

"You know the story of Abraham and Isaac, sir—"

"Ye-es . . . ?"

"Isaac didn't matter. He could not wish."

Mr. David put an arm around me, squeezing the sob out of me, and we walked home together.

We had reached the fork in the road, where the shop was quiet, the eldest of the Damani brothers sitting at the till, staring out. He did not greet us; indeed, his manner since the arrival of Pradhan Shastri had become more arrogant than before, and his visits to our shrine, which had been occasional, had ceased altogether. On the street, outside the shop, a vendor was scooping out fresh bhajias from a wok. Diagonally across was Shastri's house, pennants flying, Sanskrit recital blaring over a loudspeaker.

As Mr. David gave our order for the bhajias and we waited, Pradhan Shastri came hurrying out from his open gate. Seeing me, he broke into a grin and complimented, "Ah, Karsan—my messenger!" I had recently been made a delivery boy for his pamphlet, *Hindu Pride*.

Shastri's eye wandered curiously to the man beside me. In all his visits to Haripir, Mr. David had not met Pradhan Shastri. Now they stared at each other momentarily, then each said, "Namasté" in a formal greeting. Shastri went on to chat with the shopkeeper, buying soap or something, and Mr. David, with a sheepish smile at me and my brother, turned to pay the vendor.

It was the strangest incident. Over the years, having recalled it again and again, I became convinced that the two men had known each other before they met that day.

One afternoon after NAPYP exercises, as Harish, Utu, and I hung out on the road, leaning against a truck and sucking on ices, Shastri came out from his house and called out to us from his gate: "Ay Karsan, Harish, Utu—come here, quick!"

We ambled over, and he took us past the yard, where we usually met for our sessions with him, into his living room. We entered with a sense of rare privilege and looked around in curious silence. Shastri's two lieu-tenants, both sitting on floor mats against a wall, smiled coyly at us. One of them, Varun, was stringing together garlands of yellow flowers; the other, Devraj, looked idle. The walls were covered with a deep red cloth and hung with various decorations. The air was musky. From one wall, six eminent-looking men stared out at us from their identically framed photo-graphs. I recognized none of them.

This was when Shastri first gave us his pamphlets to distribute in the village. We left and did as instructed.

It was curious, I observed to myself, not then but gradually over the days and weeks that followed, that neither Nehru nor Gandhi were up on

Pradhan Shastri's wall. Most homes and shops I knew had photos of at least one of them hanging prominently. They were our gods, they had gone to jail for the independence of our country. But I knew that not everybody cared for them. Gandhi had been shot to death a few years before I was born, when Nehru had uttered the famous words, "The light has gone from our lives . . ." When Nehru died, the Damani brothers handed out sweets outside their shop, prompting Ma to utter scornfully, "They're refugees, what do you expect, all refugees hate Nehru and Gandhi."

When Nehru had been sick, prayers were said for him all across the country. Bapu-ji had said a prayer for him on the pavilion. But the inevitable happened; while I was in school, the news came from somewhere—perhaps from the street outside—that Pandit-ji had died. Some of our teachers had wept. Driving me home from school, Raja Singh too shed a tear. "What will happen to us, Kaniya, only Bhagwan knows," he had sighed. "A good man has died and the demons are waiting to pounce upon this land."

Visions of menacing Chinese filled my mind.

So, what did the patriot Pradhan Shastri have against Gandhi-ji and Nehru Chacha? Why did he deny them a place in his pantheon? The answer could be found in the issues of *Hindu Pride:* Gandhi had apparently appeased the Muslims, almost given the country away to them; and Nehru had denied the Hindu nature of our country, opting instead for a secular nation at independence.

I began to feel uneasy about Shastri and NAPYP; their message contained hate and exclusion. Each time we returned from our exercises on the field, marching proudly with our staves, singing patriotic songs, we could hardly be unaware of the poorer boys who had not made it into our corps, staring silently at us. Among them, outside their immense gate, were the Muslims, including the two sons of the murdered Salim Buckle, one of them Mukhtiar.

One morning I brought a few copies of Shastri's pamphlet for Raja Singh. I already knew that the driver of Kaleidoscope had nothing but scorn for Shastri's brand of patriotism, so why would I present him with copies of *Hindu Pride?* Perhaps, perversely, simply to provoke a reaction. It was swift. Exclaiming "Arré," his eyes flashing for an instant, he threw my dubious gift out the window. And then he remained silent and brooding all the way to school.

My father, however, took no stand regarding Shastri and NAPYP's activities in our village. The question only occurs now, Was his the silence of the detached, or the silence of the fearful?

16

Hidden desires.

Shilpa sat with Bapu-ji in the pavilion; she had a copy of the Gita in her hand, from which she read to him from time to time, and he interpreted. It was late afternoon. Another assistant came and sat with them for a while, then left. Soon after, Shilpa stood up from her chair, went to stand behind my father, and tenderly, lovingly massaged his head, her long fingers grasping, caressing the crown, rubbing his scalp end to end, side to side. Her face was flushed from the heat, her parrot-green sari clung to her long, willowy body. Her thick long braid fell in front of her. Leaning against the large Jaffar Shah grave, I watched this intimacy, wondered why I had never seen Ma in such closeness with Bapu-ji. His face, under the ministrations of this devotee, had attained a serene glow. I didn't know he had headaches, for that is what I assumed the massage was for, or that he could even fall sick. The doctor always came for Mansoor or me.

Didn't Bapu-ji see the woman in the devotee, despite his own chaste nature; didn't he smell her perfume, the sweat of her exertion, hear her breath go in and out, her deliciously pointed breasts heave in accompaniment? If Sahebs didn't see the world like weaker mortals, then what of me, who could see nothing else about Shilpa but her womanhood most of the time? Would there come a time when I would become pure like him, unsusceptible to male stirrings and worldly desires?

I knew that even Nur Fazal, our Pir Bawa, had fallen once, given in to the charms of a heavenly temptress; the result had been a calamity for the fledgling community of Patan, in which my ancestor Arjun Dev had been killed; and the sufi had then suffered an agony of separation and confusion, his link with his spiritual master blocked by an implacable wall. That could happen to my father, I thought, watching his head relax to the tender touches of a woman, close to her chest. I should pray for him.

Shilpa gave me a rich smile over my father's head, briefly hummed the song, "Mané chaakar rakho-ji," Make me your servant, Lord, then straightened up to indicate that she had finished. "There, Saheb-ji," she said, giving the tiniest pat to his scalp, and gathering the loose palu of her sari, which must have sent a wave of perfume over him, she drifted off towards the house.

Ma had returned from her zenana show at the cinema and I could hear them exchanging words in the courtyard.

"What could I do," Shilpa said, "if you were not here, Chachi? He had a headache and all afternoon there has been a stream of visitors—"

"Good thing, then, you just happened to be around to put your hands on him," Ma retorted, but the bite was lost on Shilpa, who replied sweetly, "Chachi, I wish only that I could come more frequently to serve my Saheb, but I simply cannot get away enough."

Bapu-ji calm in his chair, eyes closed.

Soon Shilpa came floating out, called me and Mansoor over, and served us tea on the floor at the edge of the pavilion, with dhokla she had brought with her from Ahmedabad. Then she ran back to the house and brought out a glass of sweet milk and biscuits for Bapu-ji. Having served him, she caught my eye, saying, "Karsan, come with me to clean up Rupa Devi's temple."

"But it is for women only," I protested. The only men who went there were the pavayas, the transvestite eunuchs, groups of whom occasionally passed our village on their way to their own shrine to the north. They looked like pretty women and enjoyed teasing the boys, coming on to them and embarrassing them no end.

"As long as you are still a boy and with a woman, that is all right." She smiled. "Wouldn't you like to go with me? Come. And don't worry, the pavayas are not around."

We turned left at the road outside and headed towards the temple with our brooms. On the way we passed my friends, who were playing cricket, and they paused their game to grin and gawk at us. I tried my best to appear to ignore them and not gloat at being seen in the company of a luscious woman.

"Do you know about Rupa Devi?" Shilpa asked.

"She was the wife of Pir Bawa," I explained, sounding a little cocky, and annoyed too that she would ask me such a question. I had used the formal term for "wife," with perhaps some emphasis. Shilpa smiled, ran a hand over my head. "You are such a serious boy," she said, coming very close to me. I almost died there on her breast.

"Rupade Rani was Pir Bawa's wife only in a spiritual sense," I continued, red in the face; "when she tried to be his real wife, she died. She was very young . . ." I stopped because here the story became confusing— Master-ji could never explain it to satisfaction in his Saturday class, becoming progressively uneasy, then finally scanning around for someone to scold, an ear to pull.

We continued to the temple. It was a simple whitewashed structure, with a domed roof topped by a spire on which flew a ragged red flag. It was said that when Rupa Devi died, she had been laid here for the night, but in the morning her body had disappeared and there were flowers in its place. Shilpa and I fell silent, and as we approached, our feet stirring up the fine tannish powder that covered the earth here, we heard murmurs coming from the farther side, where the entrance was. Suddenly a girl of about fourteen appeared, then another, and another, and they trotted off without a word. One of the girls appeared to be pregnant, and Shilpa stared long after them, then stared at me.

I knew how babies were made, Mr. David had told us about it during his sessions, and my friends and I had discussed it. And so I blushed when Shilpa gave me that look.

There was a curtain of old flowers and beads and a bell at the threshold that we both struck as we entered the temple, releasing a tinny sound meant not to travel far but to announce our presence to the goddess. Inside the small, dark room was a gaadi, a throne on which stood the half-profile picture of a beautiful lady in a blue sari, her face made up, her red lips full and smiling. The picture ended at her waist, her two hands raised and joined in a namaskar or prayer. Beside her were three smaller pictures, of the goddesses Durga, Lakshmi, and Saraswati.

One day, so the story went, a painter in Allahabad had a vision of a goddess. The look in her eyes, the shape of her lips and brow, and the dimple on her chin—these gave her a peculiarity he could not forget. He travelled far and wide all across the land in search of the home that must belong to that face. He visited all the famous pilgrimage places, from Kanya Kumari to Kashmir. Finally he met an ascetic on his travels who told him to go to a place called Pirbaag in Gujarat; when the painter arrived and laid his eyes on Rupa Devi's temple he knew at once that this was the place he was looking for, the home of his goddess. He set up his canvas and painted his picture of her, this portrait now in front of us, spending many weeks on the project, paying attention to every detail, the hues on every nail of the hands, the pearls in her earrings, the jewellery round her neck, the folds of her sari. Now here she was, more beautiful than any picture I knew. I had seen her once with Ma when I was little, and then again on my way to pick up a stray cricket ball, when I had been accosted by three pavayas, one of whom had made a grab for my crotch and teased, "Is anyone there? Thief or sipai?"

There were fresh flowers in front of the goddess, on the throne, left presumably by the three young women who had just run off. We added our flowers to the lot, replaced the strings of stale jasmines and marigolds at the doorway, and swept the floor. The dust from the sweepings we daubed piously on our foreheads and lips. This was the same treatment given Pir Bawa's mausoleum in the main shrine.

When we were finished, Shilpa went and stood before the throne, joined her hands and muttered her prayers; then, taking three long steps back, she turned around and we were ready to go.

"It is a rare being who is granted the privilege of serving a god, or an avatar," she said to me in a trembling voice. "Rupa Devi was one of them."

I nodded, dumbstruck, and we walked back.

Her god was my father. Ma disliked her but could not keep her away from the shrine, and besides, she was useful when she came, giving Ma the opportunity to sneak off to the movies. To see Dilip or Sunil Dutt or Rajendra Kumar at the women's zenana show at the cinema she had to leave Bapu to the eager attentions of Shilpa.

When later in the afternoon Shilpa was ready to head back to her home in the city, at her request I escorted her outside to the bus stop. As we stood there waiting together, while I was doing my best to look grave and sound adult to impress her, she suddenly interrupted me: "How is your Mr. David?"

"He is an excellent sir, Shilpa-ji! The best!" I said, dropping my act and only too happy to talk about Mr. David. She had not met him in several weeks now, and it was natural she should ask about him. "Really?" she replied.

"And you know what?" I added, eager for more praise. "He's teaching me to box!"

Assuming my boxing posture, I hopped around to show off, threw a few mock punches in her direction. But she was in no mood for humour then.

"He's different, Karsan," she told me harshly, her face expressing distaste. "You are old enough to know what I mean. You should not get too close to him."

I was old enough but I did not know what she meant. Was it that he was a Sidi—a negro? Or did she believe in caste after all? Did Africans have castes? Nkrumah of Ghana? Nyerere of Tanzania? Sir Abubakar Tafawa Belewa of Nigeria—now there was a Muslim; what caste did he come from?

It all sounded silly; of course I did not heed her admonition, how could I? Mr. David was my hero.

When a few weeks later Mr. David came to Pirbaag, it was the morning of Bakri Idd, the Muslim festival. I discovered that this was in fact a celebration of Abraham's sacrifice, except that to the Muslims the son demanded by God was Ismail, not Isaac; and it was a goat that had saved Ismail, which was why they ate goat that day. Mr. David sat down for a celebratory tea with us in our courtyard. He wore new clothes and his brown shoes gleamed with polish; he had put on cologne. But he was wistfully sad. In the nawab's palace in Junagadh, where he had spent his early years, the Idd celebrations had been glorious, with the slaughter of goats and the communal recital of namaz. The nawab gave generous gifts to his retainers. Mr. David recalled a tricycle, and a toy car in which he could sit inside and drive around. But not very fast, he added, making a face for the benefit of us boys.

Afterwards Mr. David went to the Balak Shah shrine alone. It was the day they would eat meat there. The Balakshahis ate meat only on special occasions. On Bakri Idd a goat was sacrificed in a neighbouring village and two steaming thalis of biriyani were brought to the Child-imam's shrine in a rickshaw to be consumed by anyone inclined to do so.

To my surprise, Mr. David did not return to us later that day but took the bus straight home. That night as I sat with my books at my table in the courtyard, I felt strangely listless. My teacher's visit, instead of uplifting me as it usually did, had depressed me. The day had also reminded me of the story of Abraham, how Isaac—or Ismail—hadn't mattered when the all-important call came. He had not had any say in his fate. Ma brought me my glass of warmed milk, then hovered nearby, something evidently on her mind. She had been this way most of the day; earlier there had been a conference with Bapu, always difficult for her to manage. "What, Ma?" I asked. "Karsan—" she began. "Kaho!" I persisted. She then told me not to become too friendly with Mr. David, people were saying he was a strange one. She would not elaborate.

The next day Raja Singh was at hand, having spent the night in town. The truck was smelly, for he had been transporting sacrificial goats in the area.

"Three Russkies in one rocket," he said with a chuckle, announcing the latest space episode. "What next from those godless ones?"

I sat silent beside him, brooding.

"What's up, friend? Kuch taqlif hai? What is bothering you?"

"Singh-ji, about Mr. David—"

"Arré, that one turned out to be a homo; be careful of him."

"What is a homo, Sirdar-ji?" Of course, I knew, my ears were burning. I only hoped he knew different.

Sirdar-ji was silent, his eyes fixed on the road. A camel cart inching along the road received some choice Punjabi epithets.

"You don't know its meaning, yaar, you boys don't talk about it?" he asked at length.

I shook my head.

"Larkeon ko pasand karté hai," Sirdar-ji said. Someone who likes boys, not girls. "You understand?"

"So what if he likes boys?"

"Ghand marté hai," said Raja Singh, steel in his eyes.

I turned away shocked out of my wits, wanting now only to vomit. He had used the sort of coarse expletive common to the roughest of the older boys, and given it a horrifying reality.

"Sasrikal, Ji," I said finally, as I got off the truck outside the school.

Raja raised a hand in response. "Good luck, Ji," he replied in English, on his face a look of genuine concern for me.

What a horrid place the world was, how graphic and explicit and crude. I found myself, that day and others, avoiding my hero in school. He had become tainted by an innuendo I could neither completely appreciate nor resist in his defence. If I saw him walking towards me, I would rather ineptly pretend not to notice, taking refuge in some boyish mischief to distract me; I would abruptly change my route; I would say, "Good morning, sir," and hasten away, avoiding his eye. I stopped going to his Christian lessons.

I was afraid, I think, of being contaminated and treated as a pariah like him. He was a doomed man, shunned by all but the Christian boys. During PT, when he called us together for a "real-life" session, we were all mostly silent; the snack he ordered was eaten grudgingly.

He seems okay, yaar, but we can't take a chance; people spread rumours . . . He is a Christian, it doesn't matter to him what they say, but we have to bear the repercussions . . . Family to think of . . . My dad is furious, yaar . . .

"Come on now, boys, what is bothering you? Let it out. Be men!"

"What, sir? Everything is fine."

"Anything bothering you, sir?" A smart aleck.

"Me? No. Come on, boys, form your teams! Karsan—boxing practice today?"

"Sir—Ma says I can't come home late."

And that face I loved so much clouding over in disappointment. How is it possible to betray and crush your favourite person?

That weekend, at the NAPYP exercises on the field, I decided to show my stuff as a boxer, taking on first an upstart, a boy from Dholka, a village a few miles away, and to great cheer from my friends I floored him with a left only a couple of minutes into the bout. Drunk with arrogance and the simmering anger and guilt inside me of the miserable week that had just passed, I challenged Varun, Shastri's chela. Built like Johnny Weissmuller but handsomer. He came forward with a smirk that was a mixture of humility and the condescension of a superior person forced to teach an inferior being a lesson. He let me hop around him for a while, his eyes fixed on me, and then, before I knew it, my eye had looked away to some movement behind him and I felt a tremendous pain in my head and blacked out on the ground.

17

To whom shall I bring
this tale of separation
from my beloved?

My friend,
solace of my soul
my body trembles
to be with my love.

c. A.D. 1260.

The lovesick bride.

How do we describe the love life of a spiritual man, a great mystic who can make the trees bend to his will? How does a man such as he make love to a virgin teenage princess? She was devoted to him as a wife, she knew the needs of his body and soul to a nuance; and no skill or understanding or even the roguishness of a younger groom was impossible for him.

He did not visit her in the night, nor allow her to come to him, this pure innocent who had waited for him since childhood, and perhaps from her previous birth; who had declined the pomp and riches of empires for his sake. For the first time now she knew unhappiness. In becoming a bride she had become a woman, though belatedly, with all the desires of a woman. She wanted her man to consume her, wanted to nourish his seed; to this desire he would not yield. Meanwhile a woman named Sarsati attended to the sufi, growing more resplendent in her successive pregnancies. The sufi took interest in her well-being, while Rupade's insides burnt with an envy alien to her being.

"Such is the lot of women," said her mother when Rupade visited her. "They are hostage to their husbands' love. I have asked my Pandit Kamadeva to prepare a potion for you; acting through your skin and odour it will draw your man like a bull to a cow. Meanwhile fatten yourself."

The girl declined potions. "I drew him to me across mountains and valleys, I will win his desire in my own way."

"You drew him not with your body, silly girl, but with your mind and soul," scolded the mother.

Rupade Rani became the virgin mother of Pirbaag. A community of devotees had formed here. Each day at dawn, at the hour called the first sandhya, the most devoted would gather to meditate and recite the ginans the sufi had composed for them. They were songs of love, expressing the desire of the devotee for union with the divine lover, just as Radha had longed for Krishna. And Rupade for her sufi? How precisely did her husband's compositions reflect her own desires! Why had he chosen to ignore her as a woman? Was she too pure? Had she, by her years of spiritual devotions, refined herself out of womanhood, the kind that Sarsati exuded every evening when she sprinkled the Master's bed with flowers and attar? Did Maya's lure finally defeat Nur the Wanderer as he lay on his pallet and that woman came to lie beside him and let him stroke her full belly?

The sufi spent long hours in meditation; he studied and he wrote. He gathered his followers around him to impart his teachings. He received visitors, who came for advice or discussion, for his fame had spread far. And sometimes, by himself, he sang his own devotions to an absent beloved. And the princess would pray, "Is it you I am jealous of, Lord, or is it another woman far away?"

Occasionally, when some voice seemed to call him deep within his soul, he would depart on his own, dressed as a mendicant. No one knew where he went; but after some weeks the followers would pray for his return, and inevitably he came back to them; and to her, but not as she would wish.

What would call Nur Fazal away? We only have hypotheses. But it was believed (and still is) that for those who meditated with complete abandon on his name, he had never departed.

The devotees grew to love Rupade, who tended to them like a spiritual and worldly mother. In time she came to be known as Rupa Devi, the beautiful goddess.

One day a great debate took place in the presence of the king. This debate, on the nature of God, came to be known as the one in which "neither mullah nor pandit had tongue," because the sufi had silenced the mullahs by his defence of the pandits' many gods, and in the process rendered the latter group speechless.

"You have done me proud," his father-in-law the king told him. "You are truly one of my pandits. You have learned the sacred language, though some of my learned men think it is blasphemous and ugly on your tongue; they are only envious. You understand our beliefs. You understand our hearts. But you have failed to be the husband to my daughter that you vowed to be."

"I am devoted to your daughter, my king and father, and we are man and wife; to our people we are mother and father."

"And yet she has not begotten me a grandchild. I have it on good authority that while a certain low-caste in your presence continues to produce babies like a bitch, my daughter pines away for the attention of her husband. Does she repel you, the darling of this court? Admittedly, men's tastes in women are varied; but there are obligations and duties. We Rajputs easily service two or more women, young and not so young; is that beyond you?"

"My Lord, my action or inaction is due only to my love for Rupade. Of that you have my word."

"If in twelve months she has not produced a child, you will not be welcome in this land and your home will be forfeit. Your followers will be outlawed and your name will be anathema."

Spiritual lord to his followers, the "killer" whose mind was his sword, and an unfulfilling husband; a lustful debauchee at night? Definitely a disappointing son-in-law to an indulgent king. A shadow of doom hung over the retreat he had found after years of wandering. Outlawed, neither the pandits and the rajas nor the mullahs and their sultans in Delhi or Sindh or

Multan would accept him. And could he bear to be separated from his Rupade?

Not yet three months after his meeting with the king, a message arrived from the monarch: Remember my warning.

And so finally the sufi began to prepare for that blissful union; he would allow himself the consummation he had long dreaded.

"Rejoice and grieve," he told his followers. "She whose debt was deferred is ready to pay. Kumari kanya, the virgin bride will come to my bed. Rupade, your mother, will enjoy her bliss."

The queen's ladies and Rupade's former maids came to wait on her and to instruct, both from experience and from the sutras of love; silks were brought and perfumes, to render the matrimonial bed soft and fragrant for the happy ordeal. The best, most exotic foods were brought, conducive to endless and repeated couplings, a fruitful union. Wedding songs were sung lustily as if the marriage were new, not years old; not that of a sufi but of a debauched sultan or a merchant of the town.

Rupade became pregnant. Palace doctors, priests, and astrologers were in attendance. The queen came daily. The king came to visit, and he gave Nur Fazal a good, manly thump on the back.

Finally the day of delivery came: Rupade died in childbirth, giving up a dead child, her ultimate debt to the wheel of karma.

"You were right, Sufi," said the king. "Aware of your wisdom and goodness, I misjudged you; aware that her time was short, in all my royal arrogance I forgot and thus hastened her death. Forgive a father his madness."

Nur Fazal married several times in his long life. From these unions came many prominent descendants, including Jaffar Shah, who would become beloved to travellers, and Balak Shah, who would become the Child-imam of the Muslims. But the sufi continued to sing his passionate ginans, in which the lover ceaselessly pines for his beloved.

These love songs no doubt symbolize the longing of the human soul for union with the Universal Brahman, a condition desired by all mystics; some might contend that in these ginans Nur Fazal continued to address his sufi master, as Rumi did Shams Tabriz. But in those turbulent times when Mongol hordes swept through the lands of the north and west where he came from, could he have left a woman behind? We in Gujarat preferred to believe that Nur Fazal had always pined for Rupade Rani, his beloved, both before and after her inevitable death. The sufi had been sent not only to relieve the people of Gujarat from the cycle of endless rebirth but also the princess Rupade of her last remaining debt to karma. And perhaps all these reasons are true.

18

War. Victory. The end of childhood.

September 1965. The Indian Army crossed the Wagah border into Pakistan, reaching almost to the outskirts of Lahore. The previous weeks our neighbour had attacked in the Rann of Cutch and Kashmir, but left its belly exposed between the two fronts. India had pushed through, and now—alarmingly and thrillingly—legendary Lahore lay in sight. A full-scale war was on.

Diminutive, unassuming Lal Bahadur Shastri was prime minister. He was so small that, according to the cartoons, he reached up only to the waist of that giant, the former American ambassador Galbraith. If that were not humbling enough, he wore the plain cotton whites of Gandhian times. Now his stature loomed large and his voice rang clear. Force will be met with force, he said famously, sending the army forth into Pakistan. And the Chinese can make their noises. If each of you forgoes one meal a week, he exhorted in the style of the Mahatma, think how much you will contribute to the nation. Therefore on Tuesdays, after the snack in the afternoon there was no supper at our home. Even the snack was frugal, stale chappati with jaggery or malai; but the milk at night had extra sugar in it, delivered with a conspiratorial smile by Ma, and it couldn't have been more welcome to two hungry mouths. To further assist the national effort, the playground outside Pirbaag became a public vegetable garden, and instead of playing cricket after school, I tended our little portion of it. We grew spinach and eggplant; others grew dhania and methi, doodhi and ghisola. One Sunday a Tata truck came around, preceded by a decorated elephant and a ragtag band, carrying our local politicians, who were out to collect gold and cash for the war. "Mother India needs you, Mother India needs you . . . ," exhorted a woman's shrill voice on a megaphone. "Support our jawans . . . support our jawans . . . fight Pakistani aggression!" Every pause punctuated by patriotic songs by Rafi and Lata, and the little band tried haplessly and tinnily to be heard. "They say one Pakistani soldier is worth four of our Indian jawans . . . let's show them even an Indian woman is worth *ten* of them!" The women brought out their jewellery.

This war was different from the China war, because it was so much closer—in Gujarat, though in the desert mostly, and Punjab—against a sworn enemy that was also related to us, that was a part of us until only twenty years ago. According to an adage that was quoted, your enemy who's your brother is the most dangerous of all. Wasn't the great war of the Mahabharata fought among cousins? This was what had troubled the hero Arjun. Why, he had asked Krishna, should I fight men who are from my family? And Krishna had taught him the meaning of karma yoga. You have to perform your duties, he said; but ultimately nothing matters.

This is what my father would have believed. Ultimately nothing matters. Still, he looked thoughtful.

When your country is at war with its neighbour, which until recently was simply one with it, you don't know exactly what to think, how to respond. You don't have the stock responses of Pradhan Shastri, not the invectives, not the venom and the pure hatred, for you know it to be the country of people who look like you and speak your language, eat what you eat, where Hanif scored his 499 runs, a record you always wished you would break one day when you too played first-class cricket; and you know it to be the country of Iqbal Chacha, your Bapu-ji's brother, and others of the Pirbaag community who decided to leave this India. You feel strangely incomplete; even when you try and cry pure hatred and wish death and destruction on those who live there, you sound false. Are you not patriotic enough?

"They did not emigrate to become our enemies," Bapu-ji said to me. It was evening, and he had paused at my table in the courtyard to answer my question.

"They went to become Muslims and for a better life . . . Though who knows why people decide to pack up and go? It's only themselves they are running from."

"If India defeats Pakistan, they can return, Bapu-ji."

As at all such moments, I wished him only to tarry, to continue talking with me. His face was shaded in the poor light of my table lamp, turned down to conserve fuel, so I could not read his expression as he said slowly and curtly, "Your uncle has repudiated the past. To him our way of life was all lies and superstition. He calls it Hindu."

"Are we more Hindus than Muslims, Bapu-ji? We must choose, no?"

In the current mood in our country, it was clearly better to call yourself a Hindu; and I guessed my uncle would have little scope for ambiguity in his country of adoption.

Ma had come to stand on the corridor outside the bedrooms, and was watching us, arms at her hips. For her the urgency lay somewhere else. Behind her, Mansoor's and my room was wide open, a swathe of pale light falling diagonally across the floor from outside; in the shadow lay my brother, sick with fever. In the past two days Ma had metamorphosed from her usual plump and loving self, the Saheb's good-natured wife who stayed in the background, into a harried demoness who stalked the premises night and day. She looked worn down, her skin pale, her hair bedraggled. On the first day of Mansoor's fever the doctor had not been called, for reasons of economy. Yesterday, the second day, when he was evidently needed, he was out of town. He had arrived this morning and said he would order medication from Ahmedabad; meanwhile the boy was not to eat anything but could drink sugarcane juice. Mansoor could not eat anything anyway. He lay in his bed barely conscious, his body taut with fever, his skin discoloured, and discharging urine terrifyingly dark as tea.

Before, it had been the war up north that had worried Ma, for there were reports of bombing raids close to Jamnagar, where her folks lived. There was no word from them. Now Mansoor's condition overshadowed everything else.

"If my son dies I will walk out from this place," Ma said in a trembling, edgy voice not her own, glaring at the two of us. "What kind of Saheb are you, what kind of foreign pir is this, who doesn't listen to the pleas of a mother? We have not asked for anything. Give, give, all I've done is give—my life, my happiness, *my older son, the first-born of my womb!* Now he wants my Munu too."

My father opened his mouth to chide her; the outrageousness of what she had uttered came from desperation, but surely it had suggested itself from the war-fuelled insecurity and rhetoric that was currently in the wind. This was something I had never heard before, from anyone; perhaps she had. But my father's stern expression had melted no sooner than it had formed, and at the same time Ma broke down into huge sobs and beat her chest a few times, so that it bruised and turned a deep red.

I had never seen her so ravaged; I was shocked and ashamed. The sight of Bapu-ji and me discussing politics had caused her the deepest offence.

There was the utmost silence all around us; it was broken finally by the groaning of a bus on the road outside, the so-called Rajkot Express changing gears, speeding away. As the sound abated, Bapu-ji said, "Let's take a look at him." He turned around and the three of us walked into the room where Mansoor lay.

He had shrivelled into a skeleton, his large yellow eyes with protruding black pupils freaky as a lizard's, his breathing quick and urgent. Beside him on the floor was a barber's brass bowl containing water and a steel needle, left by the crone who was a local healer. Ma must have tried to work whatever magic she could with this rudimentary equipment.

For a while Bapu-ji stood by the bed gazing thoughtfully at Mansoor. He sat down at the edge, put his large hand on the boy's forehead and under one cheek, caressing with his fingertips; he picked up one small limp hand, released it. There had come a tender look on his face. He straightened, then bending forward quickly he picked up my brother, who seemed as light as paper in his arms, his bare feet dangling, and held him close and stood up. He closed his eyes as though in prayer. Ma wept, and I was crying too, I did not want Mansoor to die. However much he annoyed me, he was my little brother, he was a part of my life and I loved him.

To my mother's and my surprise, Bapu-ji carried Mansoor out into the corridor and through his library into the pavilion, which lay clothed in the penumbra of a naked light bulb fixed to the ceiling. The two of us followed him like shadows as he turned and proceeded to the mausoleum, before which he paused, but only for a moment, before climbing the two steps to the verandah and into the inner chamber through its open doorway. Ma and I stood outside waiting, unable to observe or comprehend the encounter between the medieval sufi and his current avatar.

The light of the eternal lamp inside the mausoleum cast a pale yellow glow over the entrance, leaking out over the verandah to the steps where we were standing. It seemed then as though the sufi were with us.

"Pir Bawa, make Mansoor better," I said softly, fervently. One was supposed to offer the Pir something, even the promise of a penance, but I didn't know what to offer. "I'll do anything you ask," I added lamely. Ma looked at me and smiled her appreciation. I wondered what she was thinking then; what prayers she had already uttered here, what promises she had already made.

Bapu-ji came out, carrying his frail bundle that was my brother.

"We'll take him to Balak Shah," he said.

Evidently Pir Bawa was testing the Saheb, telling him to seek help from the Child-imam at the rival, Muslim shrine. Balak Shah, who had died as a child, was reputedly a healer of children.

Ma's face had brightened, for now a real course of action was being taken. She relieved Bapu-ji of his load and carried her sick child in her arms, and our procession of three emerged from Pirbaag in silence, crossed the road past the tire shed, and headed towards the other shrine. A little boy followed us curiously. We went through the massive gate, past the row of single-room shanties, now all quiet save for the tinny transmissions from a radio or two. The mosque lay ahead of us. The last time I had been here was a few weeks before, with Mr. David and Mansoor, when we had all taken our turns on the ancient black stone. Mansoor had been his bouncy self, and Mr. David kind and thoughtful. He had wished to leave for America, and I wondered when he would go. He was still shunned at the school.

We knocked loudly on the gate of the mosque enclosure, for it was late, and minutes later the gate was opened by the short and burly Sheikh-ji, a shawl wrapped tightly around him. We had woken him, but he glanced at the limp form that was Mansoor and wordlessly bade us enter.

"I've brought my child to receive the mercy of Balak Shah," said my father when we were inside.

"Certainly," replied Sheikh-ji. "How can he refuse you, Saheb?"

Bapu-ji took Mansoor from Ma. Holding my near-lifeless brother in his arms as if ready to hand him over, he walked up to the mosque; he climbed the dozen or so steps to the verandah, where he turned left and in slow, deliberate steps approached the little grave of Balak Shah reposing beside his mother's. Through gaps in the ancient stonework balustrade we saw my father kneel and place my brother alongside the little grave. He himself sat down, crossing his legs. We waited.

There followed the unbearable minutes of an oppressive, deathly stillness, until finally I heard Sheikh-ji call, "You will have to go, Saheb. That
is the condition. You have to leave the baba with the Imam for the night."

Bapu-ji slowly came down the steps. His long shirt was crumpled, the
day's stubble partly shaded his face; the thin halo of his hair was dishevelled. Yet he appeared calm. "Come," he said to Ma and me. "We will leave
our Mansoor with Balak Shah." He paused, then added a touch of humour:
"Let the two boys be with each other tonight."

Ma gave a sob. My father patiently waited for her. Finally she nodded;
then she took the shawl from around her shoulders and gave it to the
sheikh. "Put this over him . . ."

"Jaroor," said Sheikh-ji kindly, taking the shawl from her. Certainly.

As we departed, the sheikh was climbing the mosque steps to place the
shawl over Mansoor. It was ten in the evening.

The next morning at around eleven, the sheikh arrived at Pirbaag, in kurta
and pyjama and white cap, his beard gleaming orange, holding Mansoor by
the hand. We had been waiting for them on the pavilion. My brother
looked frail but was all smiles, very much enjoying the attention and concern. He looked washed and smelled of perfume. "I had jelebis to eat!" he
announced.

"Arré! Are you allowed to eat them yet?" Ma exclaimed, her hand leap-
ing to her mouth in that gesture of astonishment. But there had come a
sparkle of joy in her eyes.

"He can eat anything," said Sheikh-ji with a grin, "he's a growing
child!"

Letting go of Mansoor's hand he went and paid his respects to Pir
Bawa, who was after all the grandfather of Balak Shah. And Mansoor,
like a wild buck released, looked around, took his first hesitant steps, then
ran off.

The baby grandson had come to the aid of the grandfather, and the
Balakshahis celebrated this proof of the preeminence of their Imam. Did
we imagine that Sheikh-ji's azan from his mosque sounded a bit louder
now, perhaps too strident at a time of war against Muslim Pakistan? The
Saheb on the other hand had shown a sign of weakness; by seeking help

elsewhere, especially at a mosque, he had revealed a crack in his image. It would come to be used against him.

With the angel of death having come so close to our home, and the dramatic way in which he had been cheated, the war lost some of its edge for us. Reports would come of bombings in Punjab, tanks captured in Cutch, combat in Kashmir; and occasionally, from the fork up the road, outside Pradhan Shastri's house, cheers would erupt and we knew that our troops had won a skirmish if not a battle. Ma's energies now were focussed on fattening her Munu. At the shrine, people poured in as usual, bringing their worldly worries for the Pir Bawa to solve for them. Two weeks after the war began, a ceasefire was declared. Prime Minister Shastri, it was announced, would go to Tashkent in the Soviet Union for a summit with Ayub Khan of Pakistan.

India had won, it seemed—almost. People were relieved it was all over, the killing had stopped. Now there would be room for the better sort of news. Only Pradhan Shastri could be heard regretting the outcome, ranting outside the village store—"We could have crushed them like cockroaches! If our leaders had not been the eunuchs they are, Lahore would be dust! We have been bullied by the world!"

As soon as peace was announced in the media, Ma set off for Jamnagar to see her folks, taking Mansoor with her.

I had been to Jamnagar only once with my mother, years before, when I had met my grandparents. The visit was not a happy one for me, for I had been a village boy in a city, prone to ridicule by my cousins. My status as the son of Pirbaag also put me in an awkward situation, for my mother's family had come under the influence of some purist priests of an orthodox temple. The family never visited us, and my father never spoke of them.

Late in the evening Bapu-ji and I said goodbye to Ma and Mansoor at the gate. Bapu-ji picked up Mansoor and kissed him. Mansoor let me embrace him only after I had let him throw a mock punch at me. Ma shyly touched Bapu-ji's feet in the traditional manner, then looked sadly at him before taking my brother's hand to climb up the steps of the bus. It was the Rajkot Express.

My father and I were now in the care of Shilpa, who had taken a vacation for that purpose. She was in her paradise. Early in the morning would come that sweet rich voice from the temple, stirring the scented air. *Hoon re piyaasi*, she would sing, I thirst for a sight of you; and *swami rajo aave*, when my lord arrives, the jhungi-drum will roll; and *hansapuri nagari mahe*, in the city of Hansapur there will be a fete today . . . She would bring me breakfast and send me off to school. When I returned, she would be at his attendance, song on her lips. Make me your servant, Lord . . . She had the art to give devotion and service with a light and humorous touch, and Bapu-ji became used to her as an indulgence.

Late one night I woke up to hear sounds of conversation in the pavilion. I got up, went out the back door from our courtyard, and stood listening. There came Shilpa's rich voice, then a low murmur that was Bapu-ji, and a couple of male voices. I edged closer to the pavilion until finally I saw shaded in the penumbra Shilpa and two youths sitting intimately with my father. I watched them awhile, unable to hear what was said, then feeling bitter with jealousy turned to go back to sleep. But Bapu-ji had sensed my presence.

"Karsan, come and sit here with us."

Silently I walked in and took the chair one of the volunteers had vacated for me, next to my father. Soon all three stood up to leave, and my father and I sat alone in the half darkness. The trees rustled somewhere as a gust of wind passed.

"The rains will come soon," my father said, "and slake our thirst."

"Bapu-ji," I said.

"Yes, beta."

"Bapu-ji, how does one know one is an avatar?"

I used this term because it implied so much, a direct link with Pir Bawa, and perhaps with God, as many devotees believed.

"It has been said that one knows when one knows."

"Who was Nur Fazal?"

"He was an enlightened soul. When a soul reaches that stage, it becomes one with the Universal Brahman. But out of compassion for humanity he remains in this world to show people the path to liberation."

I sat with him in that rare closeness I had experienced when he had taken me out on that walk on my eleventh birthday, and implicitly confirmed me as his successor. The two of us making small and (to me) big talk, finally I dozed off. When I woke up, still in that chair, the early-morning devotees were arriving, Bapu-ji had gone away, and Shilpa was telling me to go inside, I could catch up on a couple of hours' sleep.

⊰⊹⊱

A victory celebration was organized for our area. It was held on a Saturday in the field outside Haripir, which had been turned gay for the occasion, hung with tricolours and pennants everywhere. A stage had been constructed for speeches. A military band, courtesy of the Indian Army, was at hand, as was the ragtag band from Goshala. Garba dancers were present in their brilliant finery; food stalls and shrines had been set up; and the beggars had arrived in numbers, from where, no one could possibly tell.

The festivities began with a parade of schoolchildren marching in twos, followed by the smartly dressed cadres of NAPYP, four abreast and precisely in step, displaying banners and holding up laathis like rifles; there was enthusiastic applause when we presented arms in front of the leadership, and later when we came to a crisp halt with a silently muttered "Ek-do" as required.

Victory, if that's what it was, was a good excuse for this town fete. The politicians had their chance to shout slogans and praise all levels of government. An army captain thanked the public for their support in the war and said he was looking forward to signing up recruits this very day, especially from Shastri-ji's youth army. Shastri himself spoke last, his message a ringing call for vigilance. "And remember!" he concluded. "It was Ravan's brother who betrayed Ravan! There are Pakistani spies among us, breathing this same air that we breathe!"

A small section of the crowd snickered, apparently provoked by a wisecrack—what air did Shastri-ji expect the spies among us to breathe? The laughter spread, and even the captain broke into a chuckle. Somewhat sheepishly Shastri stepped down, pulling up his dhoti and looking more comical as he did so. But this burlesque was mere prelude; the ugliness waited in the wings.

There was a dance and music show, after which in the sports events Shastri again had a chance to show the mettle of his men. Hutu-tutu drew the crowds; many teams participated, only one of which managed to beat us. Tug-of-war and sack racing were the women's lot that day, while the men enthusiastically gathered to cheer on the wrestling, and then boxing.

The sweet-smelling Johnny Weissmuller lookalike Varun—aka Handsome—had come forward to box and like a pro raised both arms and pranced around an imaginary ring a couple of times to invite applause. Pradhan Shastri called for an opponent for this champion and caught my eye. I made a push to enter the ring. This was my chance for victory—or ignominious, second-time thrashing. My opponent was taller and stronger; he had a longer reach; he had soundly beaten me the last time.

"He'll make laddoo out of you," warned Harish unfeelingly as I stepped forward. He had had a few good rounds of wrestling himself and his athlete's bare torso was covered in sand. He was not the sympathetic sort. But Utu—not much of a show at any sport—said tearfully, "Watch your face, Kanya—he'll break it."

Handsome toyed with me as once before, bouncing around in front of me, just out of reach, his hands at the sides. Cassius Clay–like. Waiting to demolish me, my face.

Remember, there is only you and him, Mr. David had coached, there is nothing else in the entire universe at that moment. Register every motion he makes, even the flicker of an eye. And Bapu-ji's yogic advice: Lose yourself, kill the mind, stop thinking. My hope was to move in closer to my opponent, shield myself against the inevitable barrage of blows, and find that opening quickly. Which I did. For he was quick on his feet but slow with his long arms. He went down in two.

Victory had been sweet, but the next day I felt nervous. What if Shastri expelled me from NAPYP, as he had already done a couple of boys? I was not yet ready to leave the corps, despite my silent doubts about it. The training carried prestige; together with my friends I had fun there most of the time. The next day was Sunday, but training had been cancelled, so I took it upon myself to go flatter Pradhan Shastri. He had borrowed my pocket dictionary recently, I could ask him politely about it; better, I could ask when his "famflats," as he called his copies of *Hindu Pride,* had to be delivered next.

When I reached the fork, his gate was open.

"Boxer avigaya," greeted Devraj sarcastically, the moment I stuck my head in. The boxer has arrived. Handsome was not in sight.

Shastri came over and asked haughtily: "Yes?"

"The famflats, Shastri-ji. When will they be ready?"

"Go," he said. "I gave them to someone else to deliver, didn't you see?"

As I turned around to go, he remarked, "So you think you are a big boxer now—"

"But you told me to fight!" I didn't want to please him any more.

"It was supposed to be a friendly match, you cunt! Not to beat up on each other!"

"But he floored me last time. How about that?"

"Go! Bhosrina, you impure one!" He lifted his hand as if to smack me, and I fled.

Outside the gate of the Balak Shah commune a crowd had gathered. Harish and Utu were at the edge, and to lend a surreal note to the scene, there came the voice of my father behind them.

"What happened?" I whispered.

"They are Pakistanis," Harish said, casually lifting a hand to indicate who. It was holding a sizable stone. He dropped it and looked away somewhat sheepishly.

The massive gate of the shrine was closed, but on the lookout above it were two young men, watching the proceedings below.

In his dry, minimal inflections my father was giving out a piece of his mind. "For centuries we have lived together in this community; now they have become foreigners? Traitors?"

"But Saheb—they didn't come to the celebration—"

"How many of you have gone to Balak Shah to ask for help? Hasn't he cured your children? Those who shout from the rooftops are not always the patriotic ones. Nor are those who try to tear the community apart . . ."

The crowd slowly dispersed.

The recent issue of *Hindu Pride*, which I did not get to distribute, carried a list of enemy agents in Gujarat and the places that harboured them. In his article, the author, one J.M. Lakda, named a madrassah in Godhra, two American missionaries at a local school, and a teacher at the St. Arnold's School in Goshala.

Information had come to light, wrote J.M. Lakda, through the heroic and unflagging vigilance of NAPYP, that Mr. John David of St. Arnold's School had received his education under the sponsorship of a Pakistani benefactor. Mr. David—whose real name was Yohanna Dawood—also had confidantes at the Balak Shah mosque in Haripir. This article had instigated the near riot that I had witnessed, my friends had participated in, and my father had helped to quell.

The next morning, as I arrived at school, a small but angry demonstration against traitors was in progress outside. And a bunch of newspaper reporters were clamouring at the gate to be let in to interview the accused teacher.

The assembly bell rang. Prayers were said, the national anthem was sung loudly, announcements were made, and the boys were told to stay calm, the press would be dealt with. But the press were already in, having squeezed in through gaps in the fence, and no sooner were we dismissed than they surrounded Mr. David.

Of course he had received his education under the sponsorship of a Pakistani, said Mr. David. He had done nothing wrong. And the sponsor in question had been the former nawab of Junagadh, who had moved to Pakistan after independence, and in whose employ Mr. David's grandfather and father had worked as palace guards.

"Were they eunuchs?" queried one reporter.

"Guards," said Mr. David edgily. "Police."

"Then, sir," a man leaned forward, "what about the charges of sodomy—that you have been involved in buggering—"

He did not have a chance to finish, for Mr. David flew at him.

"You shameless man! You haram-zada, you bastard! Who has been saying—"

He ran forward, one hand reaching out with his fingers as if to strangle the accuser. It was a most uncharacteristic display from Mr. David, for we had never seen him lose his composure before. He was soon in the midst of the reporters, some five or six of them. When he emerged from the fracas, his shirt was ripped, his African hair ruffled, his lip bleeding.

Mr. Joseph, our principal, was a pompous man who spoke to us only on what he deemed occasions of great significance. Otherwise he let the vice principal, Mr. Gomes, take the morning assemblies and make the humdrum announcements and threats. But on those special days Mr. Joseph gave rousing speeches, quoting eminent Englishmen, among them Shakespeare and Churchill. We shall fight them on the beaches! he had proclaimed at the start of the recent war, confounding us all.

Now he had called all of Mr. David's favourite students to his office to interrogate them one by one. It was the day following the teacher's encounter with the reporters.

The principal was a portly man with a gruff voice; the vice was tall and thin and fretful. They were known as Laurel and Hardy. When I entered the room, Mr. Joseph was at his desk, and across from him sat Mr. Gomes. With an impatient gesture the principal beckoned me to come in and stand closer to his desk. He came straight to the point.

"One of your fellow students has accused Mr. David of indecent behaviour. Do you have anything to report yourself?"

"No, sir."

"Did Mr. David invite you to go to the church?"

"He told me to go for service—"

"And? Speak up!"

"I went once."

"Only once?" shrieked Mr. Gomes from the side.

"A few times, sir. Four times."

"Who else was present there?"

"Three or four of the others . . . and Mr. Norman. He's the priest!"

"Did you go to Mr. David's flat after school?"

Mr. David had invited me a few times but I had never been able to go. So I answered no to the question; I hadn't been there.

"Were you ever alone with him?"

"Yes, when I had questions, sir. And when he coached me in boxing."

"Did he fondle you?"

I looked at the two men helplessly. What were they up to?

"Did he pat your bottom?" shrieked Mr. Gomes, leaning forward.

"No, sir."

"No? Did he put his finger in your arse—anything dirty like that? Hein?"

I gave an involuntary snort, unable to hold back a fit of the giggles. I could never have imagined a teacher, let alone Mr. Joseph, speaking this way. Tears ran down my face, as I snorted, snickered, snorted, pinched my nose to tell myself to behave.

"What?"

"No, no, sir—he did not!"

I stood up straight, not facing either of them, in case I cracked up again.

"All right," said Mr. Joseph. "You may go. But first—" He motioned to Mr. Gomes. "Six for laughing inappropriately."

I bent, received six stinging strokes of the cane on my backside and hastened out tearfully to the grounds, where recess was not over yet.

Mr. David was not seen in our school again. Vasudev Sharma, son of a low-level civil servant, apparently had confessed to having allowed the teacher to touch him inappropriately. The boys put it more bluntly. Sharma was expelled from our school.

People in the village were generally grateful to my father for averting a possible eruption, though there were the few who sneered, Wasn't it the Muslim saint who cured the Saheb's child? We were aware that the critics had been even fewer in my Dada's time; times had changed.

A few months after the victory celebration, Pradhan Shastri was transferred to another state. By then I had already ceased my activities with NAPYP, for I was certain that it was Shastri who had spread the stories about Mr. David. I recalled the look the two had exchanged when they met at the fork in our village, and my sense then that they had met before.

An aching unease had made a home in me, and a nagging guilt at how I had spurned the teacher whom I had so liked and admired. Whatever he was—and homosexuality was indeed repulsive to my world then—I could not accept that he had deserved his treatment; that he would have taken advantage of a child. I wonder where he went, where he is; years later when I tried to, I could not find him.

19

Postmaster Flat, Shimla.
Major Narang is concerned.
There are worry lines on his forehead.

"You have relations in Pakistan," he says, or rather, asserts.

"Yes," I reply. "I thought you knew that."

The name of our neighbour to the north arouses many emotions, among them raw hatred and contempt. Many would wish they had a device in their hand that they could drop or fling that way and rid us of this nagging problem once and for all. But the major is more sophisticated than average, his tone is neutral, curious. Nevertheless, you don't invoke that name P_____ lightly. I think I know why he is concerned.

Moderately tall and straight backed, the military man that he is, he has a round face, greying hair thinning at the front, where he becomes bald, and he is dark in the way Indians become with age. He tends to smile a lot, and this exaggerates his droopy lower lip.

Since the stated reason for my presence here at the Institute is to research, recall, and write about the famous (the description is the major's) medieval shrine of Pirbaag, it is natural that I be encouraged to speak about it. Recently the Institute director, Professor Barua, called upon me to do so, in one of the weekly seminars. It is Friday; on Wednesday the major (whose visit is never coincidental) and I sat in the director's office, and I gave the two men a spiel on the shrine, as a preamble to my upcoming talk. Barua was intrigued by the more academic question of the sufi's identity, and we agreed to discuss it in detail another time. My interest for now was simply to recapitulate concisely the life of the shrine as I remembered living it. My research notes, transcripts of ginans, etc., would form an appendix. The major thought that was best.

He has nothing on me, of course, couldn't conceivably suspect me—a returning Nonresident Indian—of anything, except possibly shielding my hot-blooded brother, whom he suspects. And so I, the elder brother, am bait.

Yesterday I gave my seminar. There was a large number in attendance, the draw being the freak that I am—the singing, secretive scholar, son or descendant of a pir. The venue for these events is the seminar room with its oval teak table, where perhaps the last viceroy—Lord Mountbatten—met with Nehru, Gandhi, and Jinnah to discuss the future of India; where perhaps the subcontinent was cleaved into India and Pakistan on a map. The scholars positively glow in such an empyreal ambience, where tea in dainty cups and biscuits are individually served by the peons. They are like the poor orphan in the house of a rich auntie, hailing as they do from the deprived small-town colleges of our nation.

I sound bitter; I am. As I sit in on these seminars, of which I have attended only a handful, I cannot help but be struck by this question: Why not a single Muslim presence here, among these scholars? But we are all Indians here, you might say, does one's religion matter? Of course not, especially not here. But with habit one simply notices a trend when it glares at you; and you realize it's been glaring at you for decades. Perhaps I've lived too long in foreign places where such numbers are a matter of concern and debate. And so I cannot help also noticing that there is no one from the so-called lower castes—except the fellow who asks you in hushed tones (you could be Mountbatten's secretary) how much sugar you need. Don't give me that!—you will say; they were given more than fair chance, do you know how many boys from the higher castes set themselves on fire in protest when the Mandal Commission report was put into effect? Lower-caste boys with much lesser grades were given places in universities, while they with excellent grades were denied them. Hard, gruelling work, middle-class sacrifice went unrewarded, futures were destroyed, and mediocrity was promoted. Yes, I know how complex it all gets. And I know of course that India's president is a Muslim.

Caste, class, faith, language. I never gave them much heed as a child. I was tutored by my father in the garden of my ancestors to believe that our differences are superficial; in fact, nonexistent. My brother was less fortunate; and for him life is all division. And so my bitterness is gentle—stereotypically Indian, you might say—compared to the rage he harbours.

Now back to Major Narang and me, as we sit at a table of the Institute's outdoor café, at the edge of a cliff overlooking a deep green valley. Right behind us is the library, in what once was the viceroys' ballroom, with tall windows and high ceilings. Was Gandhi, the half-naked fakir, as Churchill called him once, invited to a dance, one muses. Did he look out the window onto this same view? In the distance, hills falling upon hills, shadows alternate with soft late afternoon light; shades of forest green merging with black. The light blue of the sky has abruptly met the orange glow of the setting sun in a perceptibly sharp line, behind which the peaks of the mighty Himalayas peep out, dim and shadowy. Home of the gods, keeping their own majesty at bay. Shiva resides among them. From the coils of his hair flows the water of the Ganges—which through some mystical magic we drank at Pirbaag every day. A thin haze hangs in the air. In the distance a road curves round the hills and out of town. A train whistle blows somewhere close by, below us, but the train is not visible. Two Tibetan coolies, distinct by their hardened features, their cheeks and eyes, appear from a trail on the cliffside, bearing loads on their heads, heading off perhaps towards the Mall. A whiff of oily smoke—but that's from the kitchen, frying samosas and pakodas.

The major has a style of his own. He gets ignored by the waiters, until he says, "Ay—" and raises a finger. They come scuppering over. When he orders our tea, he instructs, "Chini alag," sugar separate, because otherwise the tea is cloyingly sweet. Though he doesn't ask me if that is how I prefer my tea. It is.

"Karsan-ji—" he says, with a deference ever so slightly spiked with mockery, or perhaps in simple jest.

"Major Sah'b," I return.

He smiles approvingly, continues our conversation.

"It does not look good—it looks suspicious, smuggling a letter to Pakistan."

"Surely not smuggling, Major—how else does one send a letter to Pakistan, except by sending it first to someone in another country to post it?"

I had sent it, sealed and addressed, inside another envelope, to an acquaintance in Canada. Major Narang obviously had intercepted it, read it first before sending it on its way. And I know he's already read the reply that arrived earlier today.

"It looks suspicious—you know we are in a state of hostility."

"I am not quite sure what that means. People do travel there from here? Doesn't a bus run from Delhi to Lahore now?"

"It has been stopped—for the time being."

"I didn't know that."

Suddenly the air has turned cold, a draft blows in, sweeping away a napkin, spreading a thin shower of dust over us. We both turn westwards, whence it came, like a signal. The sun is now a bright yellow disk no bigger than a fat full moon, no harder on the eye, but infinitely more intriguing. And the sky is hued from blue through green and purple to orange in the farthest distance, all in soft tones to gladden the heart. We are both struck speechless.

The major says softly,

"udu tyam jatavedasam devam vahanti ketavah—"

which verse from the Rig Veda I complete,

"drshe vishvaya suryam . . . ,"

for all to see, the sun.

His surprise equals mine. We stop to stare at each other.

"My father used to recite it early in the morning, sometimes," I tell him, "when he looked out the window and the sun shone brilliantly."

The crows cawed in chorus, raucous witnesses to our history, perhaps mocking us, I now think. The last time I was there I did not hear them; perhaps they were driven away by the smell of smoke and burnt flesh.

That was a rare mood for Bapu-ji; it would be a Sunday and we would be awaiting our breakfast of puri and potato; or paratha with methi. Whatever Ma had planned. Always tea for Mansoor and me, milk for Bapu. Perhaps the poison was in the tea, and it was the substance that led me astray?

Major Narang scoops off a handsome dollop of ketchup with a potato pakoda, from which he takes a bite with relish. He has to wipe his mouth.

"I wrote to my uncle," I continue, "for what he may remember and recall about Pirbaag—to inquire if he happens to have any material from it—books and so on." He nods, I continue: "What an irony if the material were preserved in Pakistan. Irony for me, that is, and my family."

"What do you think of the Partition?" he asks.

"It happened," I reply, too quickly. And then, thinking the better of it, I add: "It meant nothing to us at the shrine."

One has to explain, you see. Though what I tell him is a lie. How could the Partition not mean anything when my family was split by its occurrence? And in any case, what Indian or Pakistani or Bangladeshi has not been affected by the politics of its aftermath?

"Have you heard from your brother, Mansoor?"

The repeated question. The same answer, another lie: No. What does he want from Mansoor?

"As you know, he is wanted for questioning regarding the Godhra incident."

The match that set off the violence in Gujarat three months ago. Sixty people, all Hindus, were burnt alive at Godhra station inside a sealed railway bogie that was set on fire. The result was a twenty-fold revenge of rape, murder, and destruction on the Muslims. Pirbaag was one of the casualties. And now Mansoor is on the run.

We both fall silent, perhaps with the same images of grisly death on our minds. In the west the sun has almost gone down, only a red section of a disk now visible between two peaks. Eastwards in the sky, a silver crescent moon slices blithely through the clouds. We stand up together, as if by agreement, and make our way on the gravelled pathway past trimmed green lawns towards the front. The major has put up here in the main building, in a room that once belonged to Lady Curzon, wife of a former viceroy. The room is believed by some of the workers here to be haunted by her ghost, even though she herself died in England.

As we walk together, he says to me: "We have to be vigilant."

I don't quite understand—is he speaking of ghosts?—and so I stare at him.

"Imagine," he says, "nine-eleven happening in our country— Taj Mahal, Puri temple, Mathura, the president's palace. Unimaginable consequences."

"Yes," I agree. "That would be terrible. We have to be vigilant."

I walk back to the Postmaster Flat.

Darkness has fallen, the stars are out; the night is so pure and spare on this hill it is just possible there is no one else left in the world; a perfect place in which to lose the self, contemplate that Oneness. Kill the mind, the sufi sang, in a punning alliterative line: *man-né maaro to mané malo*. I recall my father instructing his devotees, when he gave them a mantra to meditate on. At that time of contemplation of the One, he said, the mind and its thoughts are still, the body is still, like a cat waiting at a mouse hole.

Seated on the sofa with my cup of tea, my only companions two spiders on a wall, waiting. From the centre table that I always draw close to me, I pick up the letter from my uncle Iqbal. It was mailed from Dubai and the envelope was rather flappy at the seal when I got it. It must have steamed open easily enough, I suppose, and then the glue was too scant to reseal.

"My dear farzand Karsan,

". . . We had already heard of the tragedy at Pirbaag, the destruction of property and loss of life. And we gave prayers for the departed. May Allah in His infinite mercy take them into His bosom. Amen.

"We are most delighted however that you and Mansoor are safe, that God saved you from the clutches of the bloodthirsty Hindus.

"Dear Karsan, to answer your question, we have nothing left from Pirbaag save for a photograph of the family—but it is from before your birth. There were a few books, but they rotted over the years and were thrown away. Mashallah, I have been able to bring prosperity to my family. Now what about your future, Karsan? It will please me and my children immensely to offer my brother's sons, you and Mansoor, shelter and livelihood here in Pakistan . . ."

One of his daughters, Shabnam, is younger than me and divorced, he says. It would please him to see her settled with an educated, responsible man. I need to settle down too. The destruction of Pirbaag was a punishment from the Almighty, because idolatry is sin. I should change my name appropriately—he suggests the name Kassim—accept the right faith, and make the move that my Dada should have made fifty years before.

I am beginning to think that writing to my uncle was a bad idea. Major Narang will surely increase his surveillance of me and await the inevitable.

I did not go for dinner to the Guest House, because I did not fancy sitting again so soon with the major, who was bound to be there. And so Ajay from the kitchen arrived at the back door and brought me a tray—tinda and chappati, rice and daal. Later he brought the tea. Ajay is the son of

Reverend Yesudas of the dilapidated Anglican church, who also wants me to make a move and accept the right faith; different from my uncle's, of course.

One night there came a loud crash outside my front door. I got up and shone my torch through the glass pane, expecting a stray langur to have landed. It turned out to be the reverend. As I opened the door a gust of wind almost blew the frail churchman inside. He was a bit drunk.

It seemed that while he was walking outside on the driveway, a revelation had hit him. Why doesn't the unhappy but good Karsan-ji accept Christ, who died for all our sins?

Fortunately for me, Ajay was not far behind his father and took him away, scolding him mercilessly. The reverend left me the cross from his neck. It hangs around a Ganesh.

In the morning, at breakfast, I ask Major Narang if he saw Lady Curzon's ghost in his room.

"Hey—" he begins, with a grin.

This morning in his bathroom he took out his shaving kit and put it on the basin. Going back to the bedroom to get his towel, he returned to find the kit missing, leather case and all, made in England. He couldn't shave (he rubs his chin to show me), but as he came outside the front entrance of the Institute, there on the steps lay his precious equipment. The man at the desk assured him that this was the kind of trick Lady Curzon plays on visitors.

"Think of that," Major Narang concludes.

"Do you think it was really a ghost? Lady Curzon's ghost?"

"The world is full of mysteries that are beyond us," he replies genially, and strides off to his white government Ambassador with its blue curtains and official licence plates. The chauffeur opens the door for him and he goes away, back to Delhi.

20

It is all a lie—or is it? My investiture.

In an ancient ceremonial white and gold robe, I walked in a procession led by my father, the Saheb of the shrine, as the women in white on either side of the red carpet showered jasmines upon us, singing ginans. *Jirewala dhana re ghadi* . . . , Blessed is that moment when the saint arrives. A special criblike chair, a gaadi with a deep seat, had been brought out from storage and placed with cushions on which I was made to sit. This was my throne. It was the same seat on which my father had once been invested, and perhaps his father, just as the robe—a little moth-eaten now—was the same one they had worn. Behind me came and stood the elders, men whose links with Pirbaag went back for generations; on my left sat my father erectly on the edge of his own chair, his own white turban on his head, his face beaming in a rare display of pure joy; on the other side sat Premji, a devotee and trustee from America, also smiling. The photographer came, knelt in front of us, the flashlight exploded.

The pavilion was hot and stuffy and noisy. Before me were faces joyful, emotional, worshipful, receptive of this blessed moment in their lives. He is here, the future avatar has come. They were my people. There were about a hundred of them, a good number having arrived from outside Haripir. The barber had earlier nicked me in the nape and the lime he had stroked forcefully on the wound was now a burning sensation, a sharp little itch so real and mundane compared to the ceremony of which I was the centre. My mother caught my eye from the edge of the pavilion, distinct in her chubbiness, smiling broadly. Mansoor was out somewhere with his cohorts. Even such a momentousness at Pirbaag could not keep him away from them.

The noise—the singing and murmuring—stopped abruptly as my father raised a hand. He stood up and came to me, then turned to face the crowd.

"I proclaim this boy, my older son Nur Karsan, according to the tradition of centuries, as my gaadi-varas, the successor when I am gone." Saying which, he took the ceremonial ancient green turban from the hands of an assistant and put it on my head.

There was a moment of restrained clapping, which my father joined, then the hall exploded into a cheerful, festive buzz as the people resumed their chatter.

A woman came forward and put a garland round my neck; it was Shilpa, tall and lithe. Another woman put a gold chain on me. More gifts were presented in succession. Premji, who wore a white kurta with a red rose at the breast, presented me with a silver pen from the United States, in a case of its own, and a hundred-dollar bill. I received from others a shawl, a shirt, a beautifully illustrated *Alice in Wonderland*.

And then I made my speech, still seated on my throne.

"People," I said, as Premji raised a hand for silence. "Brothers and Sisters, this I vow, that I will serve you and our Pir Bawa faithfully. Even though—even though—though I am young, my soul is exalted, and I am ready to serve you when required. May Pir Bawa bless you."

This is what Bapu-ji had instructed me; what his own father had scripted for him.

"Give us a brief word or two more," said Premji. "Give us your views about the world."

I turned to him in surprise. He was smiling, and I had a distinct feeling that he was testing me. This had not been part of my preparation.

After some hesitation and false starts, I looked up and spoke about science and technology and progress, as Pandit Nehru had so often spoken. I said how with hard work and ingenuity India with its spiritual strength and ancient traditions could reach farther and become a leader in the world.

Perhaps Bapu-ji looked a trifle disappointed, I thought when I was finished, at my regard for material progress. He could hardly have expected me to speak about spiritual matters. My speech would have pleased Raja

Singh, had he been there. But he was on the road. It did impress the people who were present.

They came and shook my hand, the women cracked knuckles against my forehead to ward off evil, some men and women kissed my hand. "He is truly the one," they said, embarrassing me intensely, "he is the successor, the gaadi-varas, can't you see, he is to guide his generation, and how lucky they will be to have him."

Later, my presents and clothes put away, out I went to the playground to resume my normal life. The village garden had long been abandoned there, but the result of that communal venture was now a plot overlaid with ridges and depressions and therefore a menace to the game of cricket. My friends were playing football, which they stopped to surround me and ask me about my investiture, and what I had received as gifts, and if I would talk to them now that I was the actual gaadi-varas. I am here, aren't I, I replied irritably. But could I tell the future now? Could I see through the earth into the regions of hell? Could I cure this bruise? All this partly in jest—but only partly. Rowdily we started going up the road, on the way passing Shilpa, who was waiting for her bus. "See you again, Karsan-ji," she said, in the formal manner she had recently assumed towards me, though still unable to suppress that teasing twinkle in her eyes. The legless Pran was at her feet, pestering her, and was duly teased by some of the boys. He threw a stone at us and we ran, halting at the fork for bhajias. Here Shastri's home had been turned into an extension of the local school, which had consisted of a single classroom before. Now there was also a yard in front. As I was returning to Pirbaag, Pran caught up with me, panting from his exertions. "Karsan-ji, I am going to get married," he said with a grin. "With whom?" I asked, just barely restraining my tone. He dragged himself away on his strong hands, without answering.

My father was sitting on the pavilion with Master-ji, the teacher. Bapu-ji called me over, and when I went to him, he raised a hand to place on my shoulder. Master-ji did likewise. I stooped to let the elders bless me. Bapu-ji kept his hand on me a long time; when he released me, he said, "From now on you must pray every day to Pir Bawa to enlighten you."

"Yes, Bapu-ji," I said, and left.

That evening, when the house had become quiet, I strolled out into the shrine, my domain of the future. It lay in shadows, still as a graveyard, which it was. There was the faintest moonlike glow upon the white walls of the mausoleum, as though charged by the energy enclosed within; further along, the pavilion was lit by its single dim lamp, perhaps the source of that glow. Listlessly I wandered around among the tombs and memorials, numb in the mind from the day's many sensations, unable to hold on to a single one of the numerous thoughts that assailed me.

What had happened to me that day? Who and what was I? What would my life be in the future? Would it include any fun or joy?

Who lay buried in the monument behind me? He had so many names and descriptions. I knew his story well, how he wandered into Patan from war-ravaged Afghanistan or Persia; the miracles he had performed to outwit the king's pandits and magicians and win the king's friendship. But who was he, really? What kind of man? Not an ordinary man but a great soul, I was told, who had come to us bearing the gift of the true, liberating knowledge.

And I was to be his representative.

I stood up on the steps where I had come to sit and turned to face the lit doorway of the mausoleum. Slowly I climbed up and went inside to the inner chamber, where the tomb lay in the centre. Shadows all around me trembled in the light from the eternal lamp that stood in the back left-hand corner, and the air was heady with the perfume of flowers and incense and chaddars, the latter piled up high on the grave. The room seemed occupied by a presence.

Pir Bawa, I said in my mind, looking down at the silver crown at the head of the grave. Please let me be a worthy successor, a good Saheb to your followers. Let your eternal light guide me in my life; let me not disappoint my Bapu.

I stepped out backwards, my hands joined together in a prayer; at the threshold I knelt and touched the floor with my right hand and kissed it before turning around. Back into the night air, with a sense of relief and joy I started heading back to the house. I had walked only a few steps when I saw my mother emerge from our gate. She had something in one arm, held close to her chest; in the other hand she held a torch. She was hurrying in the dark towards the back of the mausoleum. I followed at a distance, attempted to call out to her, but my jaws seemed stuck.

I saw Ma pouring ghee from the urn in her hands into a larger vessel that stood solid behind the mausoleum. She had placed the torch on the ground, its light forming a cone that took in her wide feet. I had seen it, never spared a thought for that vessel, a long, red clay urn of the sort the local potters made. Realization hit me, and I stared, the image clear in my mind, the oil travelling from the urn through an underground channel to feed the eternal lamp of Nur Fazal. The lamp which stood in his stead, its flame supposedly burning and spreading its light through its own mysterious power.

Ma saw me, smiled. She saw the look on my face and lost her smile. She went back inside the house without a word.

The certainty of my realization sat on my heart like stone.

I got into my bed and covered my head with the sheet; and inside my dark tent I silently cried. I did not know what to think. All I heard in my head over and over again were the words: "It is a lie."

I was woken up by the tinkling of a bell, the odour of incense; the singing of ginans. It was dawn.

What is a lie? The meaning of those beautiful songs? Pir Bawa, Nur Fazal? Did he not exist? Is the Saheb—Bapu-ji—a lie? I don't know, I don't know. A flame cannot burn by itself, without fuel, even Pir Bawa's flame, and now this has been proved. Then what about all the miracles of the past . . . and those that occur daily, when people come to the shrine to pray for their difficulties, and their prayers are answered?

In the morning I would not get out of bed. I did not want to face the world.

I was drowning. I was drowning in black space, a thick darkness, and all around me floated clouds, and as I made a grab for them I realized they were only scraps of paper and useless, they couldn't help me; and Bapu-ji was preaching at me in his calm voice, "But all is a lie, Karsan, all is Maya, an illusion. Only the Eternal is real—"

And Ma said, "What are you shivering there for? And don't cover your head in the sheet—some bhut-paret will possess you . . . Kanya!"

Startled, I looked up at her from my bed—she had removed the sheet.

"Arré—you are crying! Why are you crying, beta—what is happening to you?"

"Ma—it is all a lie," I cried out desperately to her.

"Nothing is a lie, we are all here around you. Rest, and I'll bring you breakfast. And don't cover your head!"

I could not touch the food. How could I, my world had fallen off. The puri could not be the puri of old, the potatoes would taste different.

That afternoon Bapu-ji came and sat beside me. He felt my head for fever, ran his hand over my hair. I knew that he truly loved me; and yet why did he not set me free from that burden of the past? *Isaac did not matter . . .*

"What is it, son?"

"It is a lie, isn't it, Bapu-ji? Joothoo chhé."

"What is a lie?"

"Everything."

We both fell silent. In that closeness I could hear him breathing; and I caught a faint whiff of a man's odour from him. I watched his large hands, his long fingers joined lightly together at the tips. At length he said,

"We cannot escape the murkiness of life; if we accept this body, we must accept its dirt. We have to shit and pee, after all. We have to live in our bodies, but we can use them to serve a higher purpose."

"But it's a lie! Bapu-ji, why don't you tell me the truth? The lamp burns because we pour ghee into it—"

"Perhaps . . ." He turned to look at me. "But do we know how the ghee enters the lamp? Have you seen anyone dig up the earth to clean the lamp?"

I could only shake my head, but this sounded like sophistry. He saw the look of doubt on my face and gave a thin smile.

"People need miracles, Karsan. Without miracles they lose their way. The lamp has always been there, it's tradition. Perhaps it needs a little help. That's also tradition. Our message is more subtle—it's about the meaning of existence—but people have a need of miracles. Do you understand now?"

"Yes, Bapu-ji." But I wasn't sure. "Are there no miracles then, Bapu?"

"There are, for those who need them, Karsan."

21

Time passes; the world beckons.

Raja Singh had disappeared for a year; this was the longest he had stayed away, and it seemed as if something essential in the composition of my life had dropped away; still, there would be that quickness of breath on a morning sometimes as I came out the gate, almost expecting to see him standing like the Air India maharaja beside the dazzling Kaleidoscope. Shilpa too had not been seen in a while, having gone to her village to tend to her widowed mother. Her devotion to Pirbaag remained ceaseless; she had even started a women's group of truth-seekers. Occasionally one or two of these would come to spend a few weeks to serve and learn from my father. Her letters to him, robustly announced by the wily postman, brought the expected dark look to Ma's face. I had entered my last year in school and become prey to nagging thoughts about my future. My childhood friends Harish and Utu were already set on their life paths. Harish helped his father in the tire shop; he would soon marry. Utu had found a job in a barbershop in Baroda, and I heard from his father, Ramdas, that he expected to join his maternal uncle in Dar es Salaam, East Africa, where he would drive a taxi. A younger generation of boys were lords of the crumpled playing field beside the shrine. My own dreams of playing for India were long over.

And finally I had learned the name of my Rabari heartthrob: Mallika.

One afternoon upon returning from school, instead of turning into our gate, I walked around to the playing field. I don't know what I expected to see there, the game had not started; was it instinct or prior knowledge, a fleeting glimpse from the tempo, which had brought me home?—but there she was, sitting with her back against the wall fence.

"Ay, chhokra," she called, looking up as I blushed. "What's in your bag?"

"Books," I said. "Do you want to see them?"

"Can you write?"

There was invitation in the voice, and I sat down beside her and showed her my English composition book. "Yes—look."

She looked at the open page, then at me, with a half-smile of grudging respect. She was barefoot, twitching her toes, and her coin-sized nose stud drew my stares; her head was covered loosely; her teeth were white and large; and her eyes . . . they pried into my heart. I showed her a library book about space travel, told her the Americans would soon go to the moon.

"What will they do there? Kick it around like a ball?"

It was then that I asked: "Taru naam shoon chhe?" Her name.

"Mallika," she said slowly in a husky voice.

She moved ever so closer to peek at the book which lay open between our laps; our knees touched, our heads knocked. We looked at each other and smiled.

Voices approached, a few boys appeared, by which time she was up and away. I never spoke to her again. Enough times I came to look for her at the spot where we'd sat together, behind the wall; I had bought two Gujarati readers in Goshala and wanted very much to teach her to read. She was never there, and when I waited it was in vain. A few times I did see her eye me across a distance, once from outside Rupa Devi's temple. Was her reticence due to innate modesty, or had she been warned to stay away from me? The memory of her still catches my breath.

For many months the stacks of newspapers and magazines that Raja brought for me from his sojourns had been my window to a bustling world outside the still point that was Pirbaag; compared to their enchantment, the *Gujarat Times,* which now I read every day, was but a skimpy and dreary local broth that left me craving something more. I was bored. Every afternoon as I got off my ride and turned into that familiar gate, the same oppressive feeling would descend upon me. Was this my future? What could I make of this garden of graves? Wasn't there a way to escape it, find a new destiny? And yet, sometimes, early at dawn, listening first to the rising pure tones of Sheikh-ji's azan from his mosque and then the tinkling of the bell and the beautiful ginans from our temple, I would become aware of the tears streaming down my cheeks. I so belonged here, to this ancient and still mysterious place that spoke to something deep and permanent within the soul. But then that moment would pass and there was still that world outside, beckoning.

That world could be reached from my little garden: I only had to discover the door and walk through it.

On a few occasions during the last holidays three of my school friends and I had stolen away by bus to the big city, Ahmedabad. We idled up and down its busy streets, eyed the girls, window-shopped at the clothing and radio shops, and went to the cinema; then we did our best to beat out the smell of air-conditioned cigarette smoke that clung to our shirts. Ma of course discovered from the residual stink I brought home on my clothes that I had visited the cinema, and I had to swear that I did not smoke, had not taken that first step on the quick road to dissipation.

These adventures inevitably came to an end, once school resumed, but now I felt the urge to set forth on my own, to satisfy which urge I skipped school the occasional Saturday. Was disloyalty also my inheritance? Ma didn't report my jaunts to Bapu-ji, pretended not to know just as I had done about her own escapades to the movies. These had for the most part stopped, it seemed, for Zainab had moved away. But once, however, I had seen a plump woman in burqa all by herself outside our gate, waiting fretfully for a tempo. It must have been a rare, desperate getaway. I quickly walked past her.

The bus stop in Goshala was not far from the school, and as I waited for my conveyance there I had to be careful not to be seen by student or teacher; when the bus passed by the school, where boys would be out at PT, I would duck my head shamelessly, well aware of the amusing sight I presented to my fellow passengers. On my previous visits to the city I had discovered the Daya Punja Library on Relief Road, in the busy Teen Darwaja area, where you could walk in from the street and, if you found a place, sit at the large rectangular table in the long room, under the hanging fluorescent lights, and quietly and importantly flip through a newspaper or magazine. It was bliss to be there, absorbed in, surrounded by pages of print, news about the whole world; every rustle of paper annoying in its mild way and yet so satisfying an accompaniment. I read everything I could lay my hands on, waiting eagerly and sometimes rudely for others to finish. I even read *Filmfare*, from which I would glean tidbits about the movie stars for my mother's delectation. The current favourite among actors was Rajesh Khanna, and anything about him, or a good horoscope, was sure to make Ma's day. After reading for a few hours I would conclude my visit to the old city with an aimless walk along its streets—Gandhi Road, Relief Road, and the little side streets. Invariably I would end up outside the grand Jama Mosque; each time I would hesitate, before finally yielding to its pull and going up the steps, taking off my shoes, and stepping into the vast courtyard. There in fascination I would watch the men wash their hands and feet in the large tank in the centre and then go up to the front—a dark, open hall of numerous pillars—to say their prayers. All this in utter silence; I had never looked upon anything so sheerly Islamic in my life. The people prayed not together but separately, some distance apart. Some would look up at me as I arrived to watch them. My world was so different, so dependent on personality; so closely packed. And yet our founding spirit, our god, if you will, came from a culture that prayed in such mosques. And so I felt connected to this place and these people in some vague, mysterious fashion I could not quite understand or define.

There was a row of bookstores on Relief Road that I would visit one after another. I would stand at the door and look inside longingly, the proverbial beggar outside a sweetmeat shop. Before my time was up I would have dared to venture into one or another of them, well aware that their enticements stood wrapped in cellophane or were kept in cruelly unreachable cabinets. Sometimes, marked as a repeated loiterer, I would briskly be led back out the door. But one secondhand bookstore, owned by a Mr. Hemani, kept its books wonderfully, entirely accessible—on shelves, on carts, on tables—where just anyone could walk in from the street and pick them up, thumb through them. The owner, a tall thin man with a white beard, would discreetly look away as I strolled inside among the shelves, paused to read book titles, picked up one or two to inspect, turned the pages and read a bit. I would ask the price of a book, he would look up and answer with a gentle smile, and I would put it down.

I was aware even then that my love of books reflected my father's devotion to them. I had dreams of possessing my own private library one day. Instead of standing in Mr. Hemani's store I could as well have browsed through Bapu-ji's books. But there was the incomparable thrill of dawdling inside a public book place, on Relief Road in Ahmedabad, smelling the age and dust on them, noticing with a sinking heart how one had suddenly vanished from its place since my last visit, having been purchased by some lucky soul.

One day there was a box of discarded books just inside the door that the owner had put out for passersby to pick up for free and perhaps be enticed to come in. They were all in Gujarati, cheaply made paperbacks—recipe books, joke books, books on ayurvedic medicine—and one whose title leapt at me like a sudden scare: the green text on plain yellow cover read, baldly, in Gujarati, "Pir Mussafar Shah no mrutyu"; Nur Fazal's death. Inside the book, in its curling faded pages, was a poem in couplets describing his final days. Of course I knew about the book, the story it told.

Mr. Hemani, seated behind his little table at the back, must have sensed my excitement. "What have you got there?" he asked. I took the book to him. He glanced at it, returned it, eyeing me curiously, and explained, "They have a dargah somewhere here, where the pir is buried." I nodded dumbly. "Here," he said, getting up, and I followed him to a shelf against the back wall. "All kinds of books on sufism . . ." He picked out a paperback and handed it to me. "You should start with this." I took it, looked at it, then handed it back. "I'll buy it when I have saved some money." "Keep it," he said. "My present to you." The book was *A Conference of the Birds*, a canonical title, as I would learn in due time.

That was the most I had spoken with Mr. Hemani. Did he realize that I was from Pirbaag? How little it meant to him—"a dargah somewhere here." I knew that in spite of the thousands who came to visit us every year, to most people outside Haripir, Pirbaag meant very little. And now this book, discarded, of so little value here.

I did not carry much money on me. When I bought my daily newspaper after school, I would keep back what change I received, with Ma's knowledge. The meagre hoard I collected was pocket money, from which came the luxury of my bus fares to visit the big city; there remained then usually a pittance to spare. I would sometimes eat a snack from a street vendor, or, sitting on the steps of the great mosque, eat a packet of peanuts. One day, however, I had enough to go to the tea shop standing prominently at the hectic Teen Darwaja intersection, across the road from the library. It turned out to be a marvellously bizarre place, for it was also a cemetery. The eating tables were spread among a dozen or more old unmarked graves, which were built up with cement and painted olive green. Upon each grave had been placed a fresh red rose towards the head; waiters raced past the buried dead, balancing trays of tea, bhajias, idlies, paying them not the slightest heed. Most customers too seemed quite used to sitting and eating among graves. I was directed to a table next to a baby's grave where a well-dressed boy of about my age was already seated. I had seen him a few times at the library, noted that he always seemed rather too confident of himself. We nodded, then after a while, noticing that I had ordered nothing to eat, he pushed his plate of bhajias towards me. His name was George Elias, he said, but I should call him Elias or Eliahu. Are you Christian, I asked. No, Yahudi—Jew. His family ran a chemist shop nearby, but they lived in the Astodia area. He wanted to be a scientist and planned to go to the IIT or to America. That day he was filling an application form for an American university.

"What course do you want to study in college?" he asked.

"I don't know," I replied, embarrassed that I was sounding like the rustic that I was. "I want to learn everything . . . history, philosophy, science . . ."

"Don't you have to choose between arts and science in your school?"

"No," I replied.

"Strange school. Why don't you go to America, then?" he said.

"Is it possible? To America?"

"Just write to them. It's easy. They want people like us. One of my uncles is already there." He gave me what seemed like a purposeless wink.

As I stared at him, excited, uncertain, suddenly the world had altered. To go away from here? Thousands of miles away? Into the beating heart of the world? It was possible. But over there the illusions of Maya ruled supreme, and Kali Yuga was way advanced . . . But that was also where Mr. David had wanted to go, what Balak Shah the Child-imam had promised him on the miraculous grey stone. You can be anything you want in America, Mr. David had said, that was why he had wanted to go there. Perhaps he was there already. But what about me, I was the future Saheb of Pirbaag. I could still go, couldn't I?

"I will bring my book which has a list of all the universities in America—the top ones only," Elias said, "and you can pick one from there."

I nodded dumbly, only half believing him.

But the following Saturday he had brought the book, which apparently his uncle had sent from America. It was a large-sized volume with pictures and was titled *The University or College of Your Choice.* We sat together on the steps of the Daya Punja Library and pored over the luxurious, glossy pages, each of us supporting on his thigh one half of the massive tome. It was a confusing catalogue of wonderland, everything inside exciting and beautiful. Elias showed me a list of institutions at the back, with their addresses. He had circled one of them for me: Harvard University. That same day, with his assistance, and as instructed by the book, I wrote a letter to the university inquiring about admissions and posted it.

When the application forms came for me some six weeks later, I was surprised, thrilled, frightened. I had not expected them; the prospect of applying to a university in America had looked more and more ridiculous as the days had passed. Now I mulled long and hard over them. How attractive, how impossible—even the quality of their paper intimated wealth and power. Why should those people who sent men into space and educated presidents be interested in me? I filled in the blanks as best as possible, expecting to complete the rest with the benefit of Elias's guidance. But Elias did not come to the library when next I visited, so I completed the form on my own. I had already written the required essay, which I had not intended to show my friend, for it described my life and heritage. A fee was required to be sent with the application that amounted to about a hundred rupees, an astronomical sum. In my letter to the university I said I had no money; if I could find it, I would send it to them. Meanwhile, please, could they still consider me. I also had no money to take the tests they had recommended. With my application in my hand, on my way to the post office

I saw Elias behind the front counter of Samuel Chemists, assisting the customers who were clamouring for attention from the sidewalk. I told him I was going to post my application.

"Wait—" he said, and hurried out. "Show me." And then: "Yaar, you should have typed it!"

"Where would I have found a typewriter, tell me?"

"And how did you make it look so crumpled?"

He looked genuinely concerned.

"I won't send it, then. What's the point of wasting postage money?"

"No—send it. They know we are poor in this country. Are you sending it by registered post? You should. Or these post-wallahs—you never know with them, they will copy your application for their own children and throw away yours into the dustbin."

"Yaar, even if I send it by ordinary post, I will have to beg the bus conductor to take me home for free."

I could have cried; clearly I was out of my league. My friend looked at me sympathetically. He glanced quickly over his shoulder into the shop; then he casually went inside, hands in his pockets, and stood at the till. He chatted up an elderly man with a black cap, who I presumed was his grandfather, then slyly opened the cashbox unseen and slipped a note into his pocket. He hung around some moments, then cheerfully strolled out.

We had to stand in a long queue to get my letter registered.

On the way back, I ran into Mr. Hemani standing at the door of his shop, sipping from a cup of tea and contemplating the busy street. How he made a living was a mystery, there was hardly ever anybody in his shop.

"Ay Karsan, where have you been? You haven't come to visit for some time," he said. "Busy, eh? Exams?"

"Yes, Hemani Sah'b, very busy."

Struck by a moment of inspiration, I shot my hand into the envelope I was holding and brought out a recommendation form. "Hemani Sah'b—I am applying to university—will you write a letter of recommendation for me?"

Startled by my abrupt gesture, he took the form and stared at it, his eyes going up and down. "Impressive . . . ," he said. "Very impressive, Karsan." He gave a grin. "I will write the very best reference letter for you, Karsan, don't worry."

And that was that.

One Saturday, as I came out of our gate, there stood Raja Singh like an apparition, grinning broadly, leaning against the passenger door of that old truck, the Kaleidoscope I knew so well. Nothing could have pleased me more than seeing this familiar figure again, whose absence had left a hole in my life. I kept shaking his hand, not wanting to let it go. "But where were you, Sirdar-ji? Where did you go off to, forgetting all about us?"

"Arré sorry, Kanya . . . elder brother died and mother needed support."

Pulling me towards him, he embraced me. "Jeet raho, putar. Arré what a man you've become . . ."

To be closer to his mother, he had been doing the Delhi-Punjab routes, he explained. Bodywise he had evidently done well with her stuffed parathas and butter, his bush shirt stretching desperately to cover the hairy potbelly. Following my eye he patted it solidly. "Khub khilaya," he said, she fed me a lot. I asked him where he was off to now. "Umdavad," he said. Ahmedabad.

"Take me there, Sirdar-ji," I said, then in a low voice: "I'm going there too."

He glared at me. "We have grown up, have we? And school?"

I did not reply.

"Permission from Mai-Baap?"

I pursed my lips.

"What do you do in Ahmedabad? Smoke? Visit whores?" Randiyon ki pas jaté ho?

"I only go to the library, Sirdar-ji. To read. And I go to the book-stores!" Parné ke liyé!

"Chhotu, get permission from them, then Raja will take you. Don't do it behind your parents' backs. They have put their trust in you. You will be a Saheb one day."

There was nothing to say to that. He dropped me off at the school.

When I returned home that afternoon, several bulky stacks of news-papers and magazines were waiting for me beside my table in the court-yard. Practically a library. Raja must have been collecting them for months. I choked back my emotion at this thoughtfulness that sought no reward. For all the responsibility I had been burdened with, this driver of the Kaleidoscope was surely my compensation.

"Happy at last?" Ma said, coming over as I stood staring at my gift from the roads.

"Yes, Ma. Happy."

"Now you won't be bored."

And she was happy. She went to the kitchen to get my snack.

Mansoor, already there and nibbling something, called out across the courtyard, "Why bother to read all that, Bhai? You'll forget it anyway!" and Ma affectionately reprimanded him with a light smack on the back of his head.

That night I dragged the stacks into my room, cut open the strings around them, painstakingly reordered them according to my own system. Finally I picked up something to read. Perhaps a copy of *Time* with a story on the Vietnam war; or the *Pioneer* from Chandigarh, the *Statesman* from Calcutta. Yet as I flipped the pages, I knew there was just a little something missing from this experience, reading about the world by the light of a wick lamp, in my own courtyard in the confines of the family home, in this sanctuary garden of which my father was lord.

I sneaked off to the city only once after that, when I spent several hours dusting Mr. Hemani's books and reshelving them, for which he was immensely grateful. I didn't see Elias anywhere, but I left word at the chemist's that I had looked for him.

Months passed, I had almost forgotten about my application to go to America; it had been a wild and impossible idea, I did not expect anything to come out of it, and with time even George Elias began to take on the aspect of a flake. But from time to time the tantalizing thought would steal in, What if? What if the impossible happened? My shell would crack, my world would come apart, I would fly . . . Really? A good thing then, all that was in the realm of fantasy. Meanwhile, after consulting with Bapu I had applied to go to the MS University in Baroda. It was less than a hundred miles away, and I could be home during the holidays.

And then it happened. The impossible.

It was Saturday afternoon, I was returning home after time spent with Harish and Utu, who was visiting that day. We had stopped for tea at the new chai shop up the road; sitting on the bench outside, mangy dogs busy around us among the refuse, we talked cricket (the West Indies were in India) and girls (there were lots of pretty ones in Baroda) and joshed each other, attempting to maintain that old relationship. The recently engaged Harish was prone to teasing now. He had retaliated with typical brazenness, bringing up Mallika, and since her family delivered milk in the area the double entendres came tripping out with raucous laughter. Happily, Utu's occupation was not mentioned. We had always been an unlikely troika, but in a village, as they said, anything that moves is a carriage. Now things were decidedly different.

As I passed through the shrine and reached our back gate, Ma suddenly popped up before me. "Go see your Bapu in the lai-beri," she said.

"What's up, Ma?"

Her large wide eyes signalled a warning and she waved me to go on. Warily I turned around and went to the pavilion and thence into the library.

My father was sitting as usual on the floor. In one hand was a clean, white foreign-looking paper, a letter. On his portable desk beside him was a large white envelope of similar superiority with foreign stamps on it. He looked up at me, and his face seemed rather small.

"Bapu?" I ventured from the doorway.

"You . . . you applied to go to university in America—"

"Yes, Bapu-ji."

"Without telling us—or does your mother know?"

"No, Bapu-ji."

"I am very disappointed."

Plain words; coming from him, sharp as a dagger. Bapu-ji, my father, with all his hopes and his faith and his pride in me, disappointed in me. This was it, the full sentence. Disappointment. The last time I had disappointed my father was when I wanted to join the cricket academy in Baroda and had thrown a public tantrum. That was nothing compared to this double-cross, this act of filial betrayal.

Ma had come to stand at the other entrance, her round figure filling its width.

"Your son wants to go to America," Bapu-ji said in a flat tone to my mother.

Her mouth fell open; she gaped at me.

"Yes, Ma," I said uncomfortably.

There followed a moment of silence, all her response on her guileless face, her hand at her mouth in that typical gesture of shock or surprise. In this case, both. And then, "Arré Karsan," she said finally, and tears fell down her cheeks.

The large white foreign envelope had arrived with much fanfare in my absence and my father had signed for it. Ma had seen the expression on Bapu's face after he'd opened it and called for me, and she had had time to speculate and worry. Now this.

Bapu-ji handed me the letter of admission and the envelope, looking away to avoid my eyes. As I read it, I could hear him speaking sternly and without emotion: "You are the successor to a line. People expect from us, they rely on us—we are not free from obligations and duties—"

Not only was I admitted, with many congratulations, there was also a full scholarship.

"You are the future Saheb of Pirbaag, Karsan . . . you will be the light of our Pir Bawa, the father of our people—"

That was when I said in frustration, "But I don't want to be God, Bapu-ji!"

I was weeping too. For I knew in my heart the import of what he said, already felt the guilt it implied, and that in spite of everything I would go.

In the next few days Ma tried to cajole and plead with me. "So far away? . . . who will look after you . . . aeroplanes can fall, nai? . . . what will you eat?" My mother's sadness seemed mundane and small and manageable to me; I grieve now to recall this. She knew too well that first and foremost I was my father's son and successor. That is where the battle was. Try as she might, she could not budge me from my resolve. I told her I would come home for holidays, and in a few years would be back for good. Soon she would even forget that I had been away. That seemed to mollify her somewhat.

Bapu-ji simply said, "You have taken your own decision. A Saheb is not supposed to have a heart. But you have broken this father's heart."

If he had simply said, No, I refuse you permission to go, I would have complied. He was my Bapu and the Saheb. But he didn't refuse; he expressed his displeasure and gave me the choice. I would go, but our fight was not over.

I did not feel as cocky and resolute as I appeared to my parents. I was scared and nervous and uncertain. Did I really want to go away so far from the certitude of everything I knew? What for? Exactly the words of Raja Singh when I told him what had happened.

"Arré yaar-ji, what for? Life is short, but. Why give up all this?" He spread out his arms to indicate my world, but dropped them abruptly. Wasn't he the one who had enticed me with that bigger world?

And Mansoor, admiration on his face: "How did you make him agree, Bhai? You will be free now—Bapu-ji won't be able to make you do anything he wants."

"That's not why I am going, Mansoor. And I will be writing regularly. You be good when I am away."

My fare was part of the scholarship. All I had to do was board a plane with my passport. Raja Singh was entrusted to take me to Bombay and seat me on the plane.

Early on a Sunday morning in August, I was ready to depart; Raja carried my bags from the house to his truck, and I began my farewells.

First I went to pay homage to our shrine, the beloved garden of my people. The mausoleum of the sufi reposed in silence, overlooking all its domain through a shroud of mist bequeathed by the recent rains. With some trepidation I took the three steps up and entered the inner room. There, joining my trembling hands before the tomb with its crown, I prayed, "Pir Bawa, I thank you for letting me go. Bless me and guide me in all my endeavours. And bring me back home safely to you." I stepped back, then turned around to leave, after a brief glance at the eternal lamp whose secret had once caused me so much anguish. Outside I joined my hands to Jaffar Shah, patron saint of travellers, then to all the other personages and ancestors.

Bapu-ji was waiting for me at the entrance. I bent and touched his feet. As I stood up he took my face in both his hands with an urgency and looked at me, into my eyes, intensely. He kissed me on the mouth and slowly uttered a string of syllables. "This is your bol," he said. "Always remember it." He paused, then said, "Repeat it to me." Slowly and almost in a whisper and meeting his eyes I repeated the syllables back to him. He continued, "This bol comes to you from Pir Bawa through the line of your ancestors. It will bring you comfort and assist you. It is your special mantra. Do not abuse it. Do not repeat it to anyone but to your successor—when the time comes."

Together we walked towards the front gate. My family and well-wishers were waiting for me. Harish walked over from his store across the road to say goodbye; he was a married man now. We shook hands. Good luck, dost, come back safe. I will; and you keep well, friend. Utu's father, Ramdas, who sold flowers and chaddars to worshippers, and also the gaudy clandestine pictures of the Pir, put a garland over me. So did several women, faithful devotees of Pir Bawa, whose history and mine were inter-twined through the generations. Ma wept, tears streamed down her face as she hugged me tight to her bosom, and she cracked her knuckles against my head. Releasing myself from her grip, I went to shake hands with my brother and embraced him. "Be good and take care," I said. "I will, Bhai," he replied, nodding seriously. "Don't worry."

Finally I went to my father, my hands joined in a farewell. He pulled me almost fiercely into an embrace and said, "Pir Bawa be with you."

"Goodbye, Bapu-ji," I whispered.

They all waved as Raja Singh held the door open for me, saying jocu-larly, "He'll be back in a jiffy, won't you, Karsan—the months and years will fly . . ."

What broke my heart was to leave Mansoor behind; to see his face sad yet defiant, accusing: You who had everything had everything to leave and spurn. Look after him, I prayed to Pir Bawa. Turning to face the road, I realized that one of the faces I had seen this morning had been Mallika's; she had stared but kept her distance at the back. There had been more finality to the farewell than I had expected.

My flight was still a few days away, so my parents had permitted Raja Singh to take me on a detour before seeing me safely off at Bombay air-port. During those days the two of us traversed the length and breadth of Gujarat. "You should see your Mother India before you leave her," Raja said with satisfaction. He was a happy man on the road, as I had always known, his face a catalogue of expressions, mouthing invective and opinion, as he pounded his fist on his horn and the cassette player endlessly dribbled out tunes new and old. We ate and rested at roadside dhabas, where we also checked our conveyance for possible problems. The food was coarse, the spicy, oily curries burning all the way down my gullet like acid. At night we would lie down under the sky on the string cots placed outside these establishments, and early in the morning wash ourselves at a standpipe or a well, and after a breakfast of parathas, dahi, and steaming tea, off we'd go—to the sound of pious Sikh kirtans on the tape.

I appreciated those carefree days on the road, for they numbed my sadness at leaving; by prolonging my stay on the land and saying my gradual farewell to it, I was soothing my guilt. At night I would lie awake missing home and composing letters in my head to Ma, Mansoor, and Bapu-ji; and even to Raja, who was in the cot beside me, snoring deeply. Occasionally he would startle violently, when a mosquito landed on his face or when he broke wind.

Our first morning out we travelled north to Patan, the ancient capital of Gujarat, now—to my utter amazement—a small and flat dusty town, a few isolated ruins serving as reminders of its past glory. There was a large spice market nearby, from which we picked up goods to take to Junagadh in the west; on our way there we stopped at the temple of the goddess Becharaji, patroness of the eunuch transvestites, the pavayas, who as always were impossible to tell apart from pretty women, except when they suddenly smacked their palms together in their characteristic manner to tease and embarrass you. It was appropriate that we stop at their shrine, for the pavayas often stopped at the temple of our Rupa Devi on their way here. Past Jamnagar we went to Dwarka, Shri Krishna's birthplace, and stood in a long queue of pilgrims for a turn to go inside his temple; thence past the ancient town of Somnath to Junagadh and the Jain shrine on Girnar, where we saw some very ancient monks, stark naked, looking like skeletons. The truck broke down only once, between Jamnagar and Junagadh, costing us half a day. Close by was the town where Jinnah, the founder of Pakistan, was born, Raja said; also proximate was the city where Gandhi was born. Junagadh of course was where Mr. David was born, as was my cricket hero Hanif, but it was a dusty, smoggy city. Picking up vegetables and cloth from Junagadh, we raced to Bhavnagar, then to Navsari, home to a famous sufi shrine. Throughout our journey we had stopped, or slowed down out of respect, at shrines and temples, even the small roadside ones where according to legend some miracle had taken place. Sometimes the miracle was simply the discovery of a preserved corpse. It seemed that once upon a time the highways of Gujarat had been traversed by legions of holy men, and now no town or village seemed complete without its own little shrine to a saint. Finally we entered the territory of Daman on the Arabian Sea. It had been a Portuguese colony until recently, and its attraction was the hotels on the beach and access to alcohol. I could have a bath and eat a decent meal at a guest house; and Raja could guzzle down a few cold beers in private, while advising me to keep away from alcohol at all cost. The next day he took me to Bombay and the airport.

"Chhotu, look after yourself," he said, giving me a tight embrace, and kissed me on both cheeks. He stood outside as I—full of apprehension but in the friendly company of a businessman also travelling abroad—entered the departures area, and he was still waving at me as I lost sight of him.

22

The two came to the door of our Pir
bleeding beggar, angelic child.

"Walking, running, Patan's enemies pursuant
we have now reached the end of our road,"

the beggar said; "My child is precious,
more precious is her honour and the word."

c. A.D. 1300.

Death of the sufi; fall of a kingdom.

Forty years before, the wandering sufi Nur Fazal had departed Gujarat's
capital, Patan, with the goodwill of its ruler, Vishal Dev—vainly styled
King of Kings and Siddhraj II, titles that already rang hollow in the face of
a bitter reality, the threat from a powerful army rattling its steel in the
north. Vishal Dev was succeeded in time by the tragic prince known to
the generations to follow by the unhappy title Crazy Karan.

The heedless devastations of war in his homeland had brought the
Wanderer to the friendly gates of Patan. By a strange reversal, the conquest of Patan brought its last king, Karan, to the door of Pirbaag seeking
protection for life and honour. It has been said that in the latter case the
hand of fate was tempted by the lust and arrogance of Patan's king.

Raja Karan had long lusted after his able minister Madhav's beautiful
wife, a padmini and a Brahmin; he managed to steal her. The minister, to revenge himself upon his king, did the unthinkable. He went
to Delhi, capital of the dreaded Afghan ruler, and invited him to invade

Gujarat. Gujarat of the glorious Patan, city of poets, philosophers, and princes, known to Arab travellers as Anularra; of the bustling wealthy ports Khambayat and Bharuch trading cotton and spices, horses and slaves with the entire world, from Africa to Arabia to China; of Somnath and its temple of untold riches; Gujarat with its handsome moon-faced people and beautiful women. Come to Gujarat, said Madhav to the sultan, there is much that awaits you there; the king is ineffectual and ill prepared to fight. The pass at Abu, where two of your illustrious brethren were defeated in the past, is not defended.

The sultan in Delhi was Alaudin Khilji, self-styled Alexander the Second, who had only three years before assumed the throne, having put to death his uncle, the previous sultan. Khilji sent two generals to conquer Gujarat. From the Banas River in the east to the ocean in the west, the earth trembled under Delhi's might, and Gujarat's cities and towns fell one after another: Patan, the capital; Khambayat and Bharuch, the ports; Somnath, Diu, Junagadh, Surat. Blood flowed in torrents, the dead littered the landscapes; chestfuls of gold, pearls, diamonds, and rubies, thousands of elephants, frightened boys and weeping women trailed behind the victorious armies as the added spoils of war. The temple at Somnath, destroyed before by another ferocious Afghan and subsequently rebuilt, was destroyed again; the sacred lingam was dragged all the way to Delhi to be stepped upon. The Queen of Patan, Karan's wife Kawal Devi, was taken away to the harem in Delhi, there to become a wife of the sultan; the unfortunate Karan, losing a decisive battle, hid himself in a fortress with his daughter, Deval Devi, then fled disguised as a beggar. On his way he arrived at Pirbaag.

The sufi Nur Fazal was old, his hair and beard had turned white, and his mortal body had wasted with age. His face shone with wisdom, but his eyes had softened; the arrow of his stare had been put away. He was awaiting now his term on earth to expire; but one job remained, one debt to be paid in the karmic ledger before his soul bid farewell to the world.

He looked at his visitor. The man before him was not a beggar; he was supple in body, his strength largely untested; under the grime his skin was smooth; his fingers looked delicate, as did his feet, bleeding, not used to bare ground; his cheeks were flushed and his eyebrows were shaped.

The girl beside him was angelic. Dust could not hide the full cheeks, the silken hair. She came in peasant clothes, but the anklet, overlooked round her leg by one who had disguised her, was as exquisite as only the finest craftsman at Patan could have turned. And there were the two gleaming conceits fixed on her ears, the studs which she must have insisted on keeping. Her wide black eyes beseeched the sufi: Help me live.

"Royalty shines through the grime and tatters of your disguise, Raja, as the sun does through clouds and dust," said the sufi, looking up with a smile after kindly perusing the princess. "This house is your house, in your honour lies ours. Your ancestor gave me opulence and justice as hospitality; I can only offer a poor house."

Forty years ago the sufi had offered his protection to the house of Vishal Dev were it needed; now Karan called upon that word, and returned to the sufi his ring.

"Give Deval Devi my daughter your sanctuary, Guru," said Karan. "Make her well. I will call for her when I return to win back my kingdom. If not, another will come to take her to a safe royal house."

"You must hurry," said the Wanderer, "for Munip Khan the lieutenant of Alap is in the vicinity and searching."

Karan with a few attendants disappeared into the darkness. The girl began to sob, and the pir took her by the hand.

Deval became Fatima Devi; her hair was braided and her head covered; she attended at the kitchen and served the pilgrims. When Munip Khan's soldiers arrived at the sanctuary, they noticed her extraordinary beauty and were tempted to abduct her; but they were on the lookout for Karan and his men, and she was under the protection of a sufi, who could have cursed not only them but also their progeny for generations. So they left empty-handed.

But some weeks later they returned, loud and determined. "Bring forth the Hindu princess!" they demanded.

Deval Devi had been betrayed.

It was a day when many pilgrims and refugees from the war had arrived at the holy place. The soldiers came in through the gate, tramped past the people resting on the ground, and headed for the open kitchen at the back. Deval, who was chaffing wheat, saw Munip Khan's soldiers coming towards her. She stood up in fear, looked around helplessly, and ran straight into an open fire nearby, which quickly consumed her.

When the girl was no more, a garland of flowers lay among the ashes of a dead fire. The sufi picked them up, crumpled them in his hands, and let the petals drift away in the wind. "Go, Deval, go to your beloved father," he said.

All his composure was gone, his heart was filled with rage, and in a harsh voice he pronounced a curse: "Deval will seek her reckoning one day."

He had preserved one flower in his hand, which he buried in a corner of the ground of Pirbaag.

The people wept. Forgive us, Father. Forgive us, Baba. Give us penance, Guru-ji. But not all had sinned. Among them there was a girl, a kitchen help grown envious of the beautiful Fatima. On her hands and her tongue thorns could now be seen growing, as on the leaves of the prickly pear. And there was a boy whose hands and tongue had also sprouted thorns. The spiteful girl had whispered her secret to the boy, who had gone and reported it to the camp of Munip Khan.

"Forgive us," the two of them begged.

"Go," said the Pir, for once without mercy.

He was tired now and his spirit was ready to depart. "Ginanpal," he said, turning to his deputy. "The call has come for me. Gather my people."

The sufi sat at his favourite spot, surrounded by his followers. He thanked them for their support and instructed them to abide by the spiritual path, the satpanth, which he had taught them. Through that path he had brought them Kashi and Mecca; he had bathed them in the Ganges; he had given them the key to escaping the cycle of 8,400,000 repeated rebirths into this unhappy world. In the Kali Yuga, the path of righteousness was a hard one, he told them. But he was leaving them the ginans to sing and learn from, and he was leaving behind his successor, Ginanpal. He assured them finally that one day he would return.

Ginanpal said, "Please don't go, Pir Bawa. The people will miss you."

"You will take my place, Ginanpal," the Pir told him. "But I will always be with you. Now lean forward and bring your ear close and let me whisper to you something." Ginanpal did as instructed and the sufi whispered the sacred syllables of the bol to him. Speaking aloud, he added, "Let this bol be the chain that links you and your successors to your Pir. One day its secret will be known to all." Then the sufi said to all those gathered,

"Look at that spot." His eye fell on a place some twenty feet away. "Place a lamp there," he instructed. They obeyed. And then, sighing, the Pir released his spirit. At that instant the lamp lit up and became a symbol of his presence.

And Ginanpal became the Saheb of Pirbaag.

23

Then felt I like some watcher of the skies
When a new planet swims into his ken;
Or like stout Cortez—when with eagle eyes
He star'd at the Pacific . . .

John Keats

Cambridge, Mass. c. 1970.
Free at last, and one among many.
To walk the giddy streets of Boston-Cambridge, breathe deeply each morning the sheer exhilaration of freedom. Freedom from the iron bonds of history; freedom from the little shrine by the dusty roadside with its rituals and songs, in a little village in which my father was avatar, guru, and god; freedom from a country constantly lacerating itself, digging old wounds until the pus-blood stench was so overwhelming. The freedom, simply, to be and to become anew—among people your age, who would dare the old and cynical, to whom nothing was impossible and no thought inconceivable.

Don't trust anyone over thirty, they told you when you arrived. And would that I never got to that accursed age! Bapu-ji was old, old; Ma was a dear but old. India was a doddering ancient-old with confused memories.

Oh to be away! To be independent, to have fun; to brush aside all those restraints of the past and think clearly, for the first time, about your own life; to search for knowledge—naively and from the beginning, without presupposition; and at last, to be simply one among many, an ordinary mortal, in this world clamouring all around you, with real people and their real concerns.

I let myself go.

I had come to the legendary city of knowledge and punditry; to its legendary ivy-covered university. For my American classmates, every moment of their existence was to be conscious of and exult in the fact that they were at Harvard. Unlike them I had arrived almost by accident; my friend Elias could well have pointed out Oklahoma in his guide to universities and that's where I would have applied. And so I had to learn, if not to exult in, at least to appreciate the glory and prestige of the place, and thank my sponsors, whose representatives I had had a chance to meet at a reception.

But I had arrived at a tumultuous period, a time of levity on one hand and rage on the other, at least among the young. True to its other tradition (the Tea Party), Boston-Cambridge (it's hard to think of one without the other) was once more a city of rebellion. Prophets, seekers, revolutionaries, anarchists exhorted from street and podia, with messages of political and spiritual malaise and a call to action: engage, seize the day, challenge and overturn the status quo in this mighty, materialistic, but blind America. It was a time like never before, so my generation said, and would continue to echo well into their middle age.

The Vietnam war ground on far away, but at home it was a throbbing open wound on the nation, hundreds of boys coming back dead every day; Richard Nixon, the president, seeking peace with honour, in those memorable words, had ordered the secret bombing of Cambodia. B-52s pummelled the forests. Protests erupted on campuses across America, there were riots in the cultured streets of Boston-Cambridge.

But this innocent abroad, unlike other foreigners, was unmoved by the protests, the daily flyers and teach-ins and marches; the excitement could not lure me; this rage of my age group left me curious, a little alienated, and even nervous. I did not understand their politics, I could not feel it with their passion. And it didn't become a guest to throw his opinions around, did it—or even to form them so quickly. How could I—trained in the distant school of Raja Singh's Kaleidoscope—tell the socialist-workers apart from the pacifists, the committed intellectual from the anarchist seeking any cause, and any of these from a rich boy or girl seeking guilt or thrills or both? I was ignorant about the world. I was so far behind the times I had to catch up starting from the Mesopotamians.

I had quickly made one enemy: Time. There were clocks everywhere in this fast culture, mocking, teasing, reminding, admonishing, their two hands raised like whips to goad you. Run, run, you are late. I learned relativity in a way to make Einstein proud: not only were there too many clocks, they moved differently here than they did back home. In those first weeks I would be seen rushing down corridors, from class to class, dropping books, running into people, only to arrive late or at the wrong destination. Appointments were torment. Why did they have to be so exact, made in advance, written in stone? So used was I to a leisurely passage of time, proceeding not in irreversible minutes but from age to age in circles. What was the hurry? Cornered by a news vendor on the street or a panhandler inquiring casually where I came from, I would stop, to inform, to chat. Time ceased, when all around me was the frenzy of Harvard Square in perpetual motion. I come from a village called Haripir . . . my father is a guru, actually an avatar of a pir who himself was an avatar . . . The face before me would turn blank, the indulgent smile fade; I would walk away, reluctant Mariner. Professors had to gently show me the door—drop-in-anytime-for-a-chat wasn't to be taken literally either. (If you could, you wouldn't have to be told.) This wasn't India. Time ruled.

To my collegemates I was the genuine article, a prize asset—an absent-minded, soft-spoken son of a guru with a delightful accent copyrighted recently by Peter Sellers and the Maharishi Mahesh Yogi. I was to show off; they took me around.

One day I saw a girl.

I had gone with my roommates to MIT, the other university down Mass Ave, on a Friday night to see a movie. If Harvard was ivy, MIT was shadowy grey stone, large columns. This was my first sight of that science mecca, its forbidding grey features partly covered by the shadows in the sinisterly quiet, windy side streets. All kinds of stories were told about this place: its denizens walked about with woolly strings of mathematical formulas growing out of their heads instead of normal hair; they walked about twirling bombs and missiles round their fingers; they slept with moon rocks; they had developed radar, which had won the last war—well, almost. They were modelling human brains. They were weird, which did not mean they did not party.

The movie was *2001: A Space Odyssey*, a futuristic science-fiction adventure in which the heavens and the humans performed a dance to a waltzy music, to which the science geniuses of the Institute had come prepared to be stoned. The auditorium was packed up to the crowded aisle floors, and the audience was raucous as it settled down; they had seen the movie before, tonight was merely a repeated ritual. Suddenly a streaker ran down an aisle and across the front, female parts jiggling; laughter, and pray nobody looks at my red face. Lights went out in the midst of all this excitement, the crowd went still, the intergalactic waltz began. Furtive, twitchy glows in the dark, an odour of marijuana in the air. Sin. As the show progressed the fumes grew stronger, sweetly acrid; the audience lay back; laughed a lot. Halfway through, a bomb scare—a common occurrence—put a stop to the proceedings, and the lights came on. A move began for the doors, not too rushed, considering the scare. That was when I saw the girl. She had brown hair, large eyes, an almond face; she was fair but could have passed for an Indian. Was that what was so attractive, combined with her loose-limbed American mannerisms? She had turned to look behind her, and our eyes met. She made a face, to show her annoyance at the situation, then got up; the big guy beside her, in a laughable white afro, also stood up. And I quickly looked away. Too late. In that one momentary exchange, I had been struck, as though by a laser; life could not be the same again.

When I came out I noticed that I was alone; I had lost my friends, or maybe they had abandoned me. There had been talk of partying at a fraternity on Mem Drive by the river, and seeing girls, for which I was evidently unsuited. What experience did I have with girls? Shilpa, much older than I, had aroused in me a shame-filled lust; and there was Mallika, the girl whose presence at Pirbaag had tormented me for so long, who finally had spoken to me that once . . . and told me her name. I preferred to be alone now anyway, and I started walking along Mass Ave back to the heart of my new world, the Square.

That face . . . the girl's image from the auditorium haunted my long walk that night. Was she Indian? Spanish? What an apparition; what a diversity of people here. All sorts. But it would be nice to meet her . . . For what? To say what? Silly thought. To be friends, what was wrong with that? Some experience you have, talking to girls.

On the way, at Draper Labs, a dingy yellow-brick corner building, a night vigil was in progress to protest the research of missiles at these premises; some forty people standing or sitting quietly by the dim porch light, sporadically raising placards or calling out to passersby; beyond this, after the grimy, gothic chocolate factory silently pouring out enticing sweet vapours from its tall chimneys, the street became dark, cold, and deserted; empty buses waiting outside a moribund supermarket; then suddenly a flurry of lights, and Central Square with Dunkin' Donuts, more enticing aromas. I fought off the temptation, promising myself a hazelnut muffin and tea at Pewter Pot later. I began luxuriating in a kind of silence I had only lately discovered; the kind that my father would experience, perhaps, in his library or when he came out late at night among the graves and perused the sky. Pinpricks of light in a deep, mysterious blackness that he had once likened to a blanket covering the universe. What lay beyond it? he had asked. Here the stars were visible only if you squinted through the perpetual haze that seemed to veil them. I thought about my next letter to Bapu-ji. Thank you, Bapu-ji—I would tell him—for letting me come here. He had been wounded by my decision, his face had soured when he handed me my letter of admission, having read it first; but here I was, a few months later, dreamily walking along a street in Boston-Cambridge. I was happy, immensely so. What did he expect from me now? What did I expect from myself? Did I want to return and be a Saheb to my people? (But I must.) Silence . . . *like a cancer grows,* as the popular song on the radio said . . . so much, so much to learn and find out. Oh, where was I buried all these years?

I had crossed Central Square, into another dark patch of street across from the post office, when I was stopped by two rough-looking men my age.

"What money do you have?"

"What? Money?"

"What money you got, man, hand it over, quick."

"I have seventy-five dollars . . . with which to buy books tomorrow."

"You kiddin'?"

"I beg your pardon?"

"You from India, right? You from India."

"Yes. From the state of Gujarat."

"Right. No kiddin'. Good night. Take care."

"I will. Good night."

Only when they were out of earshot and I was alone did I realize that I had escaped getting "mugged." A crazy word. I was learning a new English. I started hurrying, my heart beating fast, thanking my luck for seventy-five precious dollars saved.

When I told my friends about this adventure I became a day's celebrity. I had survived a mugging. At dinner the next evening in the dining hall a wild cheer went up for me as I entered. A cartoon appeared in the *Crimson* that week, titled, "From Gujarat, You Kiddin'? Welcome to America!"

A bitterly cold winter, the mercury in the nether regions of the scale, in the *teens,* they said; the nights, especially on weekends, bleak and desolate. Often by myself, I would stroll around the Square, visit the bookstore, which was, quite wonderfully, open late into the night, one person sitting at the cash register, looking quizzically up from his reading, recognizing perhaps a kindred soul—a fellow mystic of the book world. The basement was devoted entirely to philosophy, mysticism; Bapu would have loved it. And Pewter Pot, a tea shop on Mass Ave the other side of the Square that sold varieties of teas and muffins, where you could sit and read until past midnight and they actually left you alone. What a haven this city was, what a refuge, how accepting of the oddball. So your father is a guru?—a god-man? Jeez, mine is a senator—from New York? I am Russell. How do you do? And I am Bob—from Ottawa. And I am Dick. Hi. These three were my suite mates at Philpotts House, and they easily took me, differences and all, as one of them.

And the girl? I hadn't seen her again, had no hopes of doing so; she remained a sweet thought as Mallika had once been.

. . .

I dreamed I saw Dada. I had been brought forward to be blessed by the stocky old former wrestler, who was seated on his gaadi, hunched forward, in the pavilion of the shrine. I knelt before Dada, kissed his hand. Dada, chubby in face, a halo of white hair on his head, put his hand on my shoulder.

"Beta, I free you from responsibility . . . you are absolutely free—"

"I don't want to be free, Dada, I will always do as you say!"

"I have freed you, Karsan, to seek out all the corners of the world."

"I am here for you, Dada."

As I turned to depart, he said, "Beta, can you spare five rupees?"

"Rupees or dollars, Dada?"

"Five . . ."

"Rupees or dollars, Dada?"

My mother believed that a dead person came in your dream because he (or she) wanted something—if not you (thank God for that), then some tribute. And even if he wanted you, the tribute might just do the trick.

I opened my eyes to the sight of a strange bright room, warm sunshine pouring through the glass and curtains of a large shut window. A male orderly was silently sweeping near the door. The metal bed was high and firm, the sheets crisp and white. I was evidently an inmate of the infirmary.

A nurse breezed in, a stout middle-aged woman grinning friendly concern in answer to my bewilderment.

"Hi! You're awake. Nice morning out there, isn't it? Do you recall what happened last night—how you got here?" She helped me to sit up.

"Yes, I think so . . ."

"Good, tell me."

I couldn't, actually, but she helped me. I had gotten off the subway at the Square. And then, blank. With patient prompting I recalled briefly Moses the panhandler at the Yard gate. "Hey bro, will you spare a quarter?" I slipped, reached out for a hand. Not Moses, somebody else . . .

"It was your friend Russell," the nurse said. "He was with you. And did you give him a fright!"

"Did he bring me here?"

"With some help."

Thus my winter experience, a common enough initiation to the icy season, though not always to the extent of being knocked out on the road and seeing your grandfather in a dream. I was allowed to go to my room later that afternoon.

What did the dream mean? Going along with Ma's explanation, Dada desired something from me. Usually the dead asked for a favourite food, and that could be arranged by feeding it to a priest or a beggar. But Dada, leaning forward on his throne, had asked for cash. Five rupees, not much. What would he do with money, where he was, I asked myself sardonically, he being a spiritual man. Well, if he demanded cash, he would get it. The next time I saw old Moses at the gate, hand stretched out, "Buddy, can you spare—" I presented him with an extravagant five-dollar bill that drew a howl of pleasure. He disappeared for a few days.

Ma would have gone to a temple and fed the priests. She would have pestered Bapu-ji for a prognosis; and for a second or third opinion she would have cornered some other pandit, paid out more of our precious rupees.

When I saw the girl again, it was early spring, and she was part of a large antiwar protest march that had come to a raucous stop outside the Coop on Harvard Square. The police came, hulking, frightening aliens in riot gear, and my friends and I disappeared. We were not political. We watched from our windows, towels to our faces, as tear gas filled the Square, and the screaming protesters dispersed in all directions. A week later, there she was again, in another demo, this one on the front steps of MIT, with her friend the blond afro. There was a group of about forty, going around in a circle, chanting slogans, handing out leaflets. I had come to listen to a lecture by the physicist Dirac, knowing that I would understand nothing; but for the senior science students at Philpotts, a god had arrived, and so I decided to go for the darshana as well.

On the steps, I tried to get a flyer from her, but it was someone else who put it in my hand.

"No to the War in Vietnam!" "No to the Military Industrial Complex!" "No to Weapons Research on Campus!"

She was among the loudest there, thrusting out flyers at the steady stream of passersby, most of whom would politely take one, smile at her pleadings, and walk on. A few jeered; the odd one joined the group. But she did not convince, she did not belong here, as I stared wistfully at her, having missed her attention. She was too pretty, she looked too clean. Her clothes were intact, their dishevelment too mannered. The hair seemed only loosened somewhat. The peace patch on the full right bum I could have sworn was new. And those shoes and socks! Beside her walked pants worn to shreds; shoes probably stinking; eyes bloodshot; and—I would have added, with more experience, something I could only sense—bodies wasted by LSD and sex.

I was right about Dirac's lecture, though; I understood nothing, except that he had predicted the antiparticle of the electron while not much older than me, and now in old age was searching for the source of life. I saw adulation among the audience of the kind I had only known at our shrine back home, directed at my father or the grave of Pir Bawa. Men like that had altered the course of the world, and how little did we know about them in the part I came from. How could I spurn knowledge and education the way those radicals on the steps of MIT demanded?

Some weeks later, one drizzly Saturday morning at eleven, while I was having breakfast at Pewter Pot—hazelnut muffin was my favourite, with plenty of butter, and tea—and somewhat idly perusing the pages of the weekly *Phoenix,* a shadow swept across my page. A cartoon was on it, I must have been smiling. When I looked up, there she stood before me in a green army jacket too big for her, too attractive on her; and a red beret, for my benefit, so I have always believed. Both the jacket and the beret were wet with rain. She took them off and sat down across the wobbly oak table as my face reddened, my bladder called.

The Girl. Ask and you shall receive. Was I dreaming yet again? I stared.

Her arms crossed in front of her, she demanded, with a nod at my reading, "Funny?"

There was a surprising soft edge to the voice that rather took me aback. It was the first time I'd heard her up close, not shouting a slogan or a chant on the street.

"Oh . . . yes." I didn't offer to show her the page. But I introduced myself: "I'm Karsan Dargawalla—I've seen you around."

"You sure have. I'm Marge."

Marge *kewa,* the thought came naturally—Marge *what?*—and even as I opened my mouth to inquire after the surname, she came out brusquely with:

"Why've you been gawking at me?"

I gaped, like a guilty child, and she glared back. "You have been staring at me. There—outside—on the street. Why? It's embarrassing."

How I came out with what I did, I could hardly believe afterwards.

"I am so sorry . . . You are so beautiful, your good self."

Inept, surely; yet how authentic and innocent. How could it go wrong?

A delicious giggle burst forth from her lips as two dimples made their appearance on her cheeks. She stifled the laugh, and I looked away in a hurry.

" 'Your good self'!" she exclaimed. "Far out!" She laughed again, then abruptly stopped, blushed profusely, and said sharply, "You keep your eyes to yourself! My boyfriend played football in high school, I'll have you know."

I was not sure what that was supposed to mean. But to my relief she did not seem *very* angry. "I will, I promise. I'm very sorry. I did not mean to offend you."

She nodded and ordered coffee.

"What are you doing tonight?" she demanded over her mug and to my astonishment.

A lonely evening at the library was what I looked forward to; an assignment on Plato was due anyway, and some Keats had to be scanned, a daunting task not helped at all by the odd rhythms of my accent. But I was alert. I did not want to sound like a loser. And so: "I may go out with my friends."

She sniffed. "Why don't you come out to the coffeehouse at MIT—you'll meet better types than your millionaire preppy friends."

She told me exactly where to go.

It was a dimly lit room on the third floor of the MIT Student Center on Mass Ave; you could find it from outside simply by following the music, a solo voice accompanied by the strum of a guitar. There was free coffee, cider, and doughnuts; what more could a poor student want. A girlfriend—most of the audience were couples—but I had come to meet a girl I had promised not to harass; to be precise, not to stare at. The lights were dim, the music was enjoyable, the singer improvising on Beatles songs and other current tunes. I sat down at the only vacant table, at the very front. Would Marge come, or had she made a fool of me? It appeared that the singer was explaining his improvisations only to me, and I would nod, pretending to understand, and shoot my eye towards the door. Finally she appeared, wove herself in between tables and sat beside me.

Afterwards we strolled outside on the lawn, the walkways lit by large spherical lamps on posts, and finally we sat down on a stone bench. Her full name was Marge Thompson, she told me. "In case you are wondering about my dark features, I have Scottish as well as Spanish blood. I am American. You too can become American, you know."

She paused for me to acknowledge, and I nodded humbly.

She had gone to MIT intending to study chemical engineering, but she wasn't sure any more. She was an atheist and a Marxist, she said proudly. "And what are you?" she asked. "What kind of Indian are you—or is there only one variety? You worship cows, don't you? I must say all you Indians here sound the same."

Not discouraged, and not quite catching at once all the profusion of her words, I told her as much about myself as I could. Later I often asked myself, Why? Couldn't I tell that *that* would be a sure turnoff? Perhaps there was the need to explain myself, bring my world out as just another experience. How wrong I was.

We both fell silent and watched the student traffic go by. Even at this hour on a weekend, they still scurried about with their books in their hands.

At long last she said, "You are a very complicated guy. You frighten me, you know. You scare the shit out of me."

"Why—what? I mean—" I spluttered, utterly crushed.

She looked at me wide-eyed. "Why? . . . Why? It's like . . . wow! . . . You stare into a well and you don't know what mysterious thing lies at the bottom waiting to jump out and pounce on you?"

What did she know of wells? *I* came from rural India. We had a well at the back of our house . . . at the bottom of which, to be honest, a cobra had lived. I looked sheepish.

How uncanny of her to have seen something dangerous deep inside me. The dark stain of history.

We parted, she to the main building of the Institute, I to wait for the bus to Harvard Square—the Dudley bus, Marlboro Man on the side, telling me from his horse that I was in America.

I saw Marge Thompson again a couple of times before the summer break. She was always with people, and usually with the blond afro, her boyfriend, who—as she had warned me—had played high school football. I understood now what she had meant.

I wished I could take her aside and tell her, "Trust me, please. I am not a complicated person. I am ordinary. Give me a chance to be ordinary. Just be my friend."

⤛⤜••⤛⤜

America of those days is a blurry experience now; it's narratives interweaving, shifting perspectives. So much happened so fast. It's a complex painting that invites you to look close and relate the parts, make out the stories—all about me, Karsan Dargawalla, God-designate from an Indian village, struggling to be just ordinary.

24

Epistles.

"Dear Bapu-ji,

"Pir Bawa protect your health and well-being, and that of Ma and my brother Mansoor, with which blessing I write that I am settling down here in Cambridge . . ."

[The form of address was a formality, it was our way to begin a letter. This always nagged me a little: since my father was an avatar of the Pir, I was calling on him to bless or protect himself. But of course he was to me first a father, for whom I asked protection. And so perhaps there was a logic there somewhere.]

". . . Everything is new to me but the people here are very friendly and kind. I eat at the college so you should not worry whether I am fed well or not. It is not hard to be a vegetarian here. There is a thing called 'pizza' which is a naan with cheese and tomato sauce on top and can be completely veg. And tell Ma that in Amriika (as she calls it) it is impossible to starve, even if you tried! There are mountains of food and people eat all the time. They eat even while walking, or when they are in a class and the professor is speaking! You may find it hard to believe this, but some of them walk barefoot!—when they can so easily afford shoes. Even when they come from a good home, their manners sometimes seem very crude and they appear to revel in filth. Often they express themselves by swearing. But Bapu-ji, I seriously believe that this is a free society and forward-looking; perhaps freedom comes with the choice to be crude.

"As to Godlessness, which you warned me against, believe me when I tell you that there seem to be too many faiths around. This is a religious country! Even gurus and pirs from India have a following here; they go around teaching, though I believe many of them to be fakes. Sometimes I warn the people I know here about fake gurus. Spirituality and the meaning of life seem to be on many people's minds. This should please you!

"As to morality: here, Bapu, you were right. One has to watch out, and believe me I do watch out. Boys and girls freely express their feelings for each other; they touch, and so on, quite openly, in the most rude ways, just as in American films. But this is not something for you or Ma to worry about, I am not an American after all.

"Still, there is a lot to learn here; I know that you wanted me to study science—physics and astronomy; but I am looking around before I decide my course (they call it 'major' here); this is what my adviser has suggested to me. There is all the world's knowledge here, Bapu-ji.

"I miss you and Ma, and of course dear Mansoor, very much and think about you all every night when I go to bed; our home is most vivid in my mind and I remember every corner in it. Tell Ma not to shed too many tears for me, and Mansoor, I hope, is behaving himself now that he is the eldest and the only boy at home.

"I touch your feet. Bless me, Bapu-ji.

"Your loving son,

"Karsan."

⊰⊱

My father wrote,

"May Pir Bawa preserve son Karsan, his successor at Pirbaag, with good health and always keep him resolute on his path . . .

"In the world in which you find yourself, there will be many temptations, both of the spirit and of the body. Those of the body will be easier to fight than you may think at first. Those of the spirit you must especially beware of. They are the slow-working poisons that eat your insides and leave you bereft of your soul and empty of your purpose.

"The ginan says,

Kesri sinha, swarupa bhulayo
Aja kero sangha, aja hoi rahiyo.

Saffron Lion forgot his true self
Living with goats, he became a goat.

"Never forget yourself and your mission in life. You are special.

"Your mother and brother have read your letters and rejoiced. They should write to you in due course. Meanwhile accept their greetings and prayers.

"Remember to give me the details of all the subjects you are studying there—I can advise you on their value to you. Physically I may be far from you, but in spirit I am as close to you as your breath.

"With all my blessings,

"Your Bapu-ji."

⊰⊱

The story of Saffron Lion. A handsome lion cub once strayed from his kin and was lost in the forest. He found himself among a herd of goats, and he grew up with them. They were generous to him and he learned their ways and came to think of himself as one of them. He ate leaves and thorns, he bleated. When danger threatened, in the form of lions and foxes, he ran away with them.

One day a pride of lions attacked, having stalked the goats and surrounded the herd. The poor goats ran blindly all together, seeing no possibility of escape. Saffron, too, was terrified. As he ran behind the others, he saw a lioness come bounding after him, determined—it seemed to him—to tear his heart out. But something inside Saffron this time made him stand his ground; he stopped to face the enemy and gave a mighty roar. At that moment, the lions all stopped in their tracks, they slunk away.

Saffron was disturbed. Why had his friends not stood up to the lions as he had? They, on their part, began to shun him. He was left to trot along after them. The other animals jeered at him, though when he attempted to speak to them, they ran away. One day a wise old tortoise took pity on him and told him, "Young sir, take a good look at yourself when next you drink at the river."

Thus Saffron Lion discovered his true self.

Karsan Dargawalla a lion among guileless goats? It seemed more the other way round, so naive and nervous I often felt. And yes, at times I was lonely and terrified. That after all was the flip side to the joy and exhilaration of freedom. Even my American friends had their blue moments sometimes, missed their moms and dads, little brothers and sisters.

A letter to Pirbaag took three weeks to get there; I received one after the same interval, always on a Monday. And so weeks passed, time measured in postal deliveries.

Bapu-ji's epistles were guidance from a distance, pointing out the hazards of my journey out here alone; he had let me go, and awaited my safe return back to the fold. Each time, though, having waited until noon to pounce upon my sky-blue air letter in the mailbox, as I read it over once and then more carefully again, I would feel that pull of the heart at the absence of any intimacy in his words; a single sentence from my father to say that he missed having his eldest son around. I wanted dearly to be missed; I was certain they missed me at home—how could they not? If I could recall my home so minutely, how could they have forgotten their Karsan? But Bapu-ji was not the one to say how fondly he remembered pulling my cheek, or playing cricket with me when I was very young; or even just seeing me around with a cricket bat or poring over the papers at my table in the open courtyard. In the final analysis, family and relationships were mere sansara—a cage keeping you in this world, chained to the cycle of births. This he had always taught, as the Saheb of Pirbaag. All his worry and concern, his love for me, he kept restrained within him, with that detachment he had cultivated and believed to be essential towards the objects of the world, while he waited for me to return and take up my duties as his successor.

But I recalled, felt in every bone of my body the very fatherly embrace he had given me when I left. It was that rare instance when that reserve had broken.

And Ma? She who had been all tender emotion—tears and laughter—sent her regards and love but would not write. The thought would cut woundingly through any understanding I tried to compose on her behalf. I would recall that it was Mansoor who had been her favourite. But then, I chided myself, Don't be a baby. She *had* loved me. Didn't we sit outside on the steps of the house, just she and I, when with a naughty smile she would confess to me about a visit to the movies? Didn't she trust me with the unspoken secret of her disguise? Then why no word from her?

How happy must Mansoor be to have seen the back of me, the much-praised and favoured successor to the throne. He had always been jealous, creating ways to divert attention from me. He would now have the run of the house, and access to my things—my bat and gloves, my tall, gold pencil cane that I had won as a prize, the V-neck cricket sweater I could not find when packing.

⊶⊷

"Dear Mansoor,

"Even though you don't reply to my letters, Bapu tells me you like receiving them. So here is another one and I hope you do reply this time. I cannot imagine what keeps you so busy that you cannot reply to your brother who is so far away and remembers you all the time.

"You are free to use my cricket bat, the one with the autograph of Garfield Sobers, but please, please don't be careless with it. Remember to treat it with linseed oil once a month—but not more; don't leave it lying carelessly in the sunlight. It can break.

"Did you or Ma find my cricket sweater?

"Harish has not replied to my letter. Nor have Raja Singh or Ma. What is wrong?—have you people given up on me so soon? And what news of Utu? Is he in Dar es Salaam yet?

"But tell me how you are doing. I am happy for you that you will be attending St. Arnold's. You will not regret it. How do you get to school? How are your studies? How are you at badminton now? Now there you picked a game I simply cannot play!

"I have sent you a shirt by parcel post. I bought it at discount but in rupees it still cost a lot. Don't worry, I could afford it!—and I know you will like it. Ask Ma what happened to the théplas she promised to cook and send me. No sooner the son is out of sight than he is forgotten—tell her I said that!

"Love from your brother,

"Karsan."

⤜⤛⤙⤚⤚⤜

I couldn't help the feeling sometimes that I had stepped onto a tiny island, and no sooner had I done that than it had started to drift away. I was terrified, then, of drifting into nothingness, into an endless darkness, anchorless; without belief, without love; without a people or nation to go home to. Is that what freedom was?

But my father kept his sight on me, he would help me chart my course in this perilous sea. Did I want that? A long breath. I could not say it yet, but I was beginning to know in these silences that no, I did not want that long-distance navigator, I would take the terror of the unknown with the thrill of discovering myself and the world.

⤜⤛⤙⤚⤚⤜

"Dear Ma:

"May Pir Bawa bless you and keep you in the best of health, with which blessing I write that I am fine and hope and pray you are the same. I am eating well and have not fallen sick even once. I did fall down once, but I am all right now. I miss your cooking—your chevda and seviya and kadhi and fried bhindi. But most of all I miss talking to you and hearing the stories you told from the filims . . .

"I touch your feet, Ma. You are my goddess.

"Your son,

"Karsan."

⤜⤛⤙⤚⤚⤜

"Dear friend Elias!

"How wonderful to hear from you! And what a surprise to learn that you are in Israel. For how long? Didn't IIT work out? And why Israel, why not America?

"I am sorry for not having written first. I had been meaning to write but I kept putting it off, waiting for just the right moment to write all about my life here. And what a life! But first, before I start and bore you to death, I would like to thank you from the bottom of my heart for giving me the idea to apply here and helping me with the application. It is all due to you that I am here and I never forget that for a moment.

"I was sad to read about the riots in Ahmedabad. They must have happened soon after I left. I wonder why my Bapu did not write to me about them. I guess India is India, eh? Such things keep happening there.

"I wrote to Mr. Hemani but never heard from him. I wonder how he is. I remember so well that bookstore. If you have news of him from your folks, please let me know.

"Keep well, Elias, and write to me soon!

"Your friend and jigri-dost,

"Karsan."

⊰⟨⋅⋅⟩⊱

I never heard from him again, often wondered what happened to him.

⊰⟨⋅⋅⟩⊱

"Dear Bapu-ji,

"I wish the blessings of God upon you and Pir Bawa's protection in your health and well-being, with which I write that I am well here, don't worry about me. I slipped on a stretch of ice once, but that was nothing serious.

"What I sent you was a list of only the required books. There are many, many recommended texts also—stacks of them. If you want I can send you a list of them, but the postage will increase.

"Bapu-ji, I have discovered that I love poetry. Yes, English poetry! I find the English rhythms rather difficult sometimes, because of my dési accent, and I even cause laughter in my class sometimes, but I think I understand the meanings and symbolism very well. And, Bapu-ji, I have also made an interesting discovery through my readings. It is this: there were poets in English who wrote devotional poems using 'extended metaphors,' which lasted over several verses. They are called the 'Metaphysical Poets.' I like especially John Donne's *Holy Sonnets*. I had to write an essay for my course, and I recalled how you would explain some of our ginans, which also had long metaphors that developed over several verses; sometimes the whole ginan was based on a single image. But my professor wasn't impressed, and I had rather a quarrel with him. He said Donne had used worldly and scientific metaphors and wrote for a sophisticated reader, whereas Indian devotional poetry was written for simple, uneducated folk using folkloric mythology. I argued that you can use metaphors from any realm and our ginans too needed sophisticated interpreters sometimes. But he did not change my grade from a B+. He is rather a chauvinist.

"I have many questions, Bapu-ji, I am buzzing with ideas. Please don't think ill of me, or that, like Saffron Lion, I will go astray. I am only trying to understand myself, which I am sure you will approve of. Life here, among so many different kinds of people, is challenging, and exciting, because every moment I am compelled to ask questions of myself and compare myself with others. How different are they from me? To tell you the truth, talking and discussing and arguing about life with them, I find that we are not so very different!

"Bless me, Bapu-ji.

"Your loving Karsan."

-<-(-->->-

"You should be careful on ice, beta. Have you bought the right kind of shoes for winter, with rough soles to prevent slipping? If not, buy a good pair. It is false economy to skimp on the essentials. You have not gone to America to fall and break your bones.

"You are right, there is no need to waste postage to send me long lists of recommended books.

"Your thoughts are interesting. I am proud of you, my son, that you take your lessons seriously and are trying to understand yourself. That, after all, is the message of Pir Bawa, and all the sages of the past. Understand yourself. You are the truth. *Tat tvam asi,* say the Upanishads.

"But remember, the search for knowledge is a difficult one; it is like walking through a forest. You can easily lose yourself. That is why there are gurus in the world. Even our Pir Bawa had a guru, whom he left far away in the north. Your guru is your father and Saheb. You should never hesitate to ask him for guidance whenever you are confused or in doubt.

And so I am happy that you wrote to me about this John Donne and his metaphysics. But no need to quarrel with your teachers.

"Raja Singh the lorry driver was here and remembers you fondly. As do your mother and brother, and Shilpa, who again comes regularly and continues her devoted service to the shrine of Pirbaag . . ."

⊰⊰••⊱⊱

[Shilpa the luscious. It is Shilpa I've always wanted to ask you about, Bapu-ji, my guru and Saheb. Yet how can I? Shilpa whom Ma hated, I know that; Shilpa who would dig her long shapely fingers through your hair, massaging your head with oil, and at no other time did I see that look on your face that I saw then. Ma watching from the distance. And others staring enviously, your women devotees. There was pleasure on your face, Bapu-ji. What is it like when a Saheb experiences pleasure or pain? The question is this, Bapu-ji: What is the relationship between the body and the soul of the Saheb (or Pir Bawa)? It is only now I can begin to articulate these thoughts, my father, when I am so far away, on my own. But I dare not write them to you; not yet.]

⊰⊰••⊱⊱

". . . Tell me, Bapu-ji, why are we special? Why these few people in this particular part of India? Couldn't other people, whoever they are, in whatever part of the world, be as blessed? Is it possible that we are the ones who are ignorant and less fortunate? I don't believe this of course, but these are just some of the thoughts that come to me.

"Recently in class we read a poem by John Keats, who is considered a 'Romantic Poet.' He writes:

> That I might drink, and leave the world unseen,
> And with thee fade away into the forest dim:
> Fade far away, dissolve, and quite forget
> What thou among the leaves hast never known,
> The weariness, the fever, and the fret
> Here, where men sit and hear each other groan . . .

"It is addressed to a nightingale. Isn't that beautiful, Bapu-ji? It leaves me breathless, expressing as it does the same thoughts as our ginans, all about the futility of the world and the temptation to escape from it. What do you think, Bapu-ji?

"Sometimes, I think, living in a small place like Haripir we tend to forget that the world out there is much bigger and there is nothing special about us. Or that all peoples are special in their own way. Or that we are all the same. And it seems that I had to come to America to learn about myself!

"As always, I think of you and Ma and Mansoor, to all of whom my prayers and well wishes.

"Bless me, Bapu-ji.

"Your loving son,

"Karsan."

That was the start of my undoing. Teaching Keats to my father. This naive but honest, irrepressible exhibition of a budding intellectualism, an opening of mind and personality. "I had to come all the way to America to learn about myself." How true, how dangerous. This was exactly my father's fear—that I would begin to see myself from an "*outside*" perspective: a distorted, irrelevant image from the other end of the telescope. Yet it was impossible to hide my excitement—one might as well have asked Columbus, or more appropriately Archimedes, to keep quiet.

Archimedes of course paid for his folly with his head.

⤙⤚⤛⤜

My father wrote,

"May Pir Bawa preserve son Karsan, his beloved successor at Pirbaag, in excellent health and keep him resolute and wise in his ways . . .

"Learning is a wonderful thing, my son; this is why you were sent to the better school in our area, all the way to completion, and why your Dada also sent me to the same school and to the university in Bombay. But learning can also bring arrogance and blind you to the facts of life.

"You may remember that the Quran and the Bible tell the story of

Azazel, the best and cleverest of God's angels, who possessed the knowledge of 360 million books but did not understand his true essence. In his arrogance he disobeyed God; he did not bow to the clay statue God placed before him. He asked the question: Why? And so Azazel lost all, became a denizen of hell.

"Book knowledge is not everything. It is good that university makes you think and reflect on our path. We may not be special, my son, but we must keep with what we know and are certain of. It is true that all people are special to themselves. Your destiny is at Pirbaag, never forget that. A great soul came among us and gave us his wisdom and our key to the secret of life. You were born to continue that guidance among our people and to care for this tradition.

"Our friend Premji does not live far from you, I understand. He will contact you to help you keep in touch with our ways. Meanwhile, pray to Pir Bawa constantly. Recall the wisdom of the ginans. Remember your bol every day. It ties you to your guru and the line of gurus that goes straight back to Pir Bawa.

"Your mother and brother send 'lots of love.' And accept plenty of the same from

"Your father and Saheb,

"Tejpal."

⊰⊰⊱⊱

[How can I continue the line of the gurus, Bapu-ji? I don't feel spiritual or powerful, I feel just ordinary. I have always felt ordinary. I cannot be like you; I cannot guide people, or give them a mantra that will show them enlightenment. I would be a hypocrite and only confuse them if I tried. What do you want me to do then, Bapu-ji?]

[And also, Bapu-ji, tell me, was our Pir Bawa an avatar of God or God? And if so, are you an avatar of God? Do you expect me to become one? This also I dare not ask you, for I may not be able to bear the answer.]

. . .

[You say that knowledge is not everything; or that it is a forest of illusions and I will only get lost. Why? Knowledge excites me, Bapu-ji, I am not afraid of it. I need a guru, you say. But actually I need more than one guru; aren't the wise men I read—philosophers and poets and scientists—also my gurus, besides you? They have given their lives seeking enlightenment. You must trust me not to go astray, Father. After all, who guides you?]

-≺-≺--≻-≻-

"Dear Mansoor and Beloved Ma,

"The first snow can be beautiful, did I ever tell you? And sometimes, when you look out the window you see white flakes and streams going on forever, it seems, and you are in a cocoon in its midst; and you walk to the window and see the trees hanging with white wool, and the ground too is soft and white; this vision I saw a few days after Christmas. Afterwards, though, when it warms up the snow turns to black water on the streets; there are puddles and pools everywhere and passing cars splash dirty water on you. And it is as if something clean and white had been dirtied and spoiled.

"But now it is spring, the beginning, and little buds of green or yellow sprout on the trees. The sun is warm but tender and the earth seems clean. And you appreciate the wonder of nature. In spring also there are more people on the streets and everyone looks cheerful; music seems to be playing everywhere.

"I received the chevdo and the thépla; just as I like them, Ma. So you do remember your Karsan! And thank you for wrapping them in the sports page of the *Samachar*. How I miss playing cricket! How I miss *seeing* people playing cricket!

"I will not remind you to write to me. I know you will, one day, when you feel like it.

"Yours affectionately,

"Karsan."

25

"Hey, don't you find me attractive any more?"
she said, and my face burned red.

Russell was with me, and Bob and Dick, the four of us having set out on a mission to the Square to look for lunch on a hectic, cold, and windy Saturday. At the traffic island, teeming with pedestrians, where the news-stand famously sold papers from all over the world (except India and such places), I had caught a fleeting glimpse of her, also waiting to cross, and quickly looked away to avoid possibly embarrassing myself. But she had seen me, and the next thing I heard her sharp, excited voice shouting in my ear. "Hi!—how are you?" She had pushed her way through the throng and was tugging at my sleeve with a mitted hand. I turned around, pretending surprise. "Why, hello!" We stared at each other. Smiled. She wore a red jacket, the hood flapping over her hair, and she looked beautiful. The boyfriend Steve now caught up with her, grinning and looking rather silly to my jaundiced eye. The six of us crossed the road and huddled apart from the crush of people to finish our greetings. That was when she came out with her mischievous remark, accusing me of avoiding her. And so as repartee I tried my best to sound cool. When you are a foreigner you have all the courage in the world, what do you have to lose? In this case, plenty.

"I am complicated, you know," I said, giving her a mysterious-Indian smile and a nod of the head.

A look of confusion clouded her face, but only for an instant. Recovered, she turned to the restless giant hovering possessively a head above her and said: "This is the guy from India I was telling you about—remember? With the funny accent—and he's as complicated as Jesus. I told him that."

Bob and Russell exploded with laughter, and Steve growled, "Aw, what d'you know of Jesus—"

"He's son of a god, that's not far off the mark," Russell replied.

I joined in the laughter this time, red face and all, regretting that virgin day when in a spell of alien earnestness I had revealed the details of my background to my new friends. Happily the spotlight shifted and we exchanged other pleasantries before saying goodbyes, though Bob, the Canadian among us, lingered to chat with the twosome before rejoining us.

"You know Marge?" I asked suspiciously.

He nodded. "Sure. A bit. She's from Canada."

And she had told me she was American; and that I could become one too. What a backward fool I must have seemed to her. How positively clubfooted I had sounded back there.

What did I want from this girl? She had caught my fascination the moment I had glimpsed her at the theatre. I found her hauntingly attractive, with her dark brown long hair (not visible today), her olive skin, her oval face; that sassy manner of hers, instead of deterring me, only provoked me further. It seemed as if we had known each other in our previous births; such an instant attraction could only be explained this way, where I came from. And so I wanted to be with her and get to know her; I wanted to gain her respect, as someone interesting and intelligent, not some mixed-up complicated and crude fellow from a backwater of the world. She attracted me sexually, too, and came into my thoughts at night in bed, so that I would toss about in discomfort, sleepless; but I would not allow these thoughts to become explicit and taint the purity of my feelings. I wanted to win her in a noble way; what I meant by winning I did not quite know. She had a boyfriend, after all. But it was she who had taken the initiative again and come to speak to me. I must mean something to her, despite my complications, as she put it. Did I expect to take her home with me? My models of man and wife had been Rama and Sita—hopelessly idealistic and traditional. I did not know how to approach her. It embarrassed me that I did not have—could not even muster if I tried—the hip, male predatorial language and attitude of conquest that were common around me in that permissive age. She was no virgin. How did I know? I was naive but not a total dolt. I would get so anxious with my slippery thoughts, trying to shape and rule them according to the values I had brought with me, there would come tears of frustration in my eyes.

One night, at the instigation of Russell and Bob, I called her up. They came to my room, sat on my bed, and ordered me to pick up the phone. "Enough pining away after the fair maiden. Now take action," Bob said. After some argument, I agreed and told them to wait outside. I dialled.

"Hi . . . Can I speak to Marge please? This is—"

"Karsan from India, I know. Hi!"

"Could you tell so easily?"

"There is only one person in Cambridge who speaks like you, and that's you," she said.

"That bad?"

"That bad. How are you?" she asked.

"I am very well, thank you. Listen—would you like to go out with me . . . on Friday, if you are free?"

"You met my boyfriend—"

"Steve. The football player."

She laughed. Delightfully, the gloriously soft giggle of the morning she had sat across from me at Pewter Pot. "Yes. Anyway, I don't think it's a good idea. I am sorry. And I apologize if—"

"Yes?"

"If I misled you into believing—"

I did not let her finish. "No—no need to apologize. You didn't mislead me—you were simply you. You know, I am convinced that we have known each other in our previous births—"

She laughed. "Nice try. Well, bye."

"Bye."

That was that. A heavy heart, but I was happy, in a way, with that sense of finality. A door had closed on the impossible, there was no point to further anxiety. So I told myself. To which Russell added his reassuring note, "At least now you know. You tried. Now you can move on. There's plenty of fish in the sea."

And Bob the big Ottawan: "She's harder to hit on than most girls I know." That raised eyebrows, and he quickly put in, "You'll find someone, don't worry."

As if that's all there was to it, finding someone.

I hoped I wouldn't see her, but of course I did, from a distance, for about a year. She must have seen me too on those occasions, but happily she let me avoid her. And then she disappeared.

My friends fixed me up occasionally with other girls. They were good company mostly, and we were matched only to satisfy the requirement of symmetry among the sexes that was so important in this culture. Girls whose boyfriends had gone away; girls who were not very attractive or not really interested in relationships with guys. Nothing foolish happened, nothing was expected to, I didn't know how; and I had been cured of the disease of love, at least for the time being.

But one girl I was set up with was a fellow Indian called Neeta. She was from a well-placed family in Delhi, and if that were not enough, alarmingly attractive and sophisticated. She was studying economics and had ambitions of going into politics. An uncle was the current governor of Kerala. She had met Nehru as a child. Her family members had marched with Gandhi during the struggle for independence. I learned all this soon after I had picked her up outside her residence, as we walked across the Yard and introduced ourselves. I couldn't help feeling embarrassed about myself, in a manner I had never felt with my American friends, alien and strange though I was to them. It seemed to me that this girl must see through me, and find behind my new facade the genuine rustic from a backward Indian "gaamda," as she might put it to her cosmopolitan Indian friends and family back home. Nevertheless we managed to engage each other, discovering to our surprise, past the first awkward hour, that we shared sensibilities. We had dinner and saw a political thriller at the Orson Welles, the South American context of which she took pains to explain to me. After the films, we talked earnestly and idealistically about "home," late into the night, first over tea in a café, then in my room. She was so much more aware than I about conditions back home, and taught me things about our country that I didn't know. Finally—at whose suggestion I cannot recall—she spent the night in my room, taking my bed while I threw a blanket on the floor for myself. This seemed neither unusual nor discomforting then, all around us was the casualness of student life. However, the next morning we both were embarrassed. With hardly a word exchanged, she quickly dressed and departed. And my friends, grinning from ear to ear, would not believe nothing had happened, the hormones had not kicked in, or I had not scored, as they vulgarly put it.

We never dated each other again. I mention her here only because she did come back into my life, so many years later.

But why did she sleep in my room that night? As a dare to her friends, I always thought, and to herself; and perhaps also because one of her friends needed her bed for some reason. And I too, I suppose, had dared myself. (I could easily have gone to a friend's room, as could she.) I had added to my store of experiences that were unthinkable in the world I came from. I had skirted closer to the edge and come out none the worse for that.

My father would have differed from that verdict.

26

The call of the shrine.

The phone rang.

It had been a quiet evening, this last Friday of March break, most of the students and all of my friends having gone away; an occasional jingle from the radio, turned down low, surfacing like an odd bubble to break through the room's stillness. Come tomorrow and the academic life cycle would resume, through to the climax of final exams, which prospect loomed like the Damoclean sword over our daily joys. Outside the window, sporadic student calls, sharp and clear and far; in the farther distance, somewhere, the familiar whine of the Dudley bus, the odd car or two.

And Karsan Dargawalla, budding intellectual (it was hard not to observe oneself thus, sometimes), bent over a Keatsian ode, Plato's allegory of the Cave, Camus's *L'Etranger*.

And then the phone, drilling a hole into that repose, that thought, that world. My life.

"Karsan-ji?" the voice at the other end spoke softly. "I want to speak to Karsan Dargawalla, please." A very Indian voice.

"I am Karsan. Hello?"

"Karsan-ji, how are you, beta; this is Premji from Worcester; you may remember me from Pirbaag, where I come to visit every year."

This was the call I had been dreading, which Bapu-ji had promised, to remind me of my vocation in life. I had never had any intention of contacting Premji or any of the other devotees of Pirbaag in America; I had never even inquired where exactly Worcester was.

"Yes, Premji Chacha, kem-chho?" How are you? I asked respectfully.

"Arré you should have called me before, beta! You've been here so long now, and I am right here in the neighbourhood!"

"I have been very busy."

"Yes, yes of course. I realized that. That is why I did not myself call you. But your Bapu-ji has requested that I look after you. I hope you are free tomorrow. I want to come and meet you. We will have lunch and then I will show you around!"

The next morning at nine there duly came his knock on my door. Premji was a well-built man of medium height, with close-cropped hair. He wore a windbreaker and scarf, a man armed against the weather, so unlike himself when he appeared in milk-white dhoti in Pirbaag and spent so much time near my father that Bapu-ji once had to tell him to please take his leave, he was tired. Premji was beaming broadly, and he gave me a warm embrace.

"You're a man, now. Wah! And Harvard! You are our pride and joy, Karsan-ji. Come, let's go."

We had breakfast nearby, when Premji reminded me that this was the time of year when he went to India, specifically to visit the shrine. "I would like to send some things home," I told him. Premji was happy to be of service. And so we went to Filene's basement store in downtown Boston where I bought a shirt each for my father and brother; for my father it had to be large enough to wear like a kameez over pyjamas. Upstairs, I looked for perfume for my mother, and despaired over the prices. Once I had bought attar for Ma from outside the mosque in Ahmedabad, and it had cost a mere few rupees. Premji came to my rescue, however, assured me he would buy a bottle duty-free from the airport and present it to Ma on my behalf. Afterwards we did some sightseeing. We walked the Freedom Trail, which I had already walked once before with my friends, starting from the house of Paul Revere, who had rode at midnight to warn John Hancock of the coming of British troops to arrest him. Premji was in excellent physical condition, leading on with a spring in his step and not a trace of fatigue or boredom. He did yoga every day, he informed me, immediately after his meditation at the hour before dawn, on the mantra he had received from the Saheb at Pirbaag. Thus the spectre of the shrine was with us, thanks to these constant promptings from him.

In the afternoon, after a late lunch we drove to Worcester. Premji was divorced, I had learned by now, and his house did look somewhat messy. There was a rank odour of unwashed dishes coming from the open kitchen. We both took a nap, then had tea with Sara Lee cake and watched a basketball game on TV; partway through he went to the kitchen to attend to the dishes. The game was not quite over when we departed for the prayer meeting, which was held in a second-floor suite of a modern office building.

Having taken my shoes off in a foyer, I stepped into a brightly lit broadloomed inner sanctuary. Then paused, took a long breath. Where was I? Staring up from a low table in the front was a large, framed portrait of my father waist up in the formal costume of the Saheb of the Pirbaag shrine, turban and all. He was smiling openly, rather uncharacteristically, with a warm permanent glow on his face; the close-up revealed details—light eyebrows, dimpled chin, large flat ears on the long face—in a manner I had never noticed on him before. It gave me an uneasy feeling, this image of my father; it seemed threatening, and yet it seemed so false.

There were about fifteen people in the room, mostly men and only two women, sitting quietly on the floor. I was invited to sit beside my father's portrait, facing the congregation, and beside me came to sit a suitably sombre and officious Premji. To one side, on a separate table, had been placed some offerings—flowers, coins, and a bowl of fruit—together with a book of ginans. This represented the gaadi, the throne of Pir Bawa. Premji, having sat down, gave a nod, and a young man recited a ginan. He was followed by another. Then Premji gave a small talk, relating an exemplary episode from the life of Nur Fazal, the Wanderer, our Pir Bawa. The proceedings were closed with a prayer, which I the designated successor had to recite from what I could recall.

Afterwards, when we stood up, the devotees all came and bowed humbly before me and warmly shook my hand. Some of them kissed my hand. Unlike Premji, these were simple folk, working at low wages, clothed awkwardly even to my eyes. They loved the Saheb, and they loved me, the son. I was deeply touched; these were my people, and I felt a pang of guilt at having ignored them and dreaded the thought of being with them. I promised I would come again, insisting I had to return to my room that night to study. But I agreed to have dinner with some of them, and so we drove in two cars to an eatery downtown where we shared a large vegetarian lasagna.

We emerged from the restaurant into a dimly lit, deserted street, ready to part ways, when a strange incident happened. A man called Dervesh ran over to a convenience store across the street and returned with a bag of apples, which he held up for me. "Bless this offering, Karsan-ji," he pleaded in a trembling voice, his eyes liquid with emotion. "My wife cannot bear children . . . when she eats these apples blessed by you she will surely conceive."

I was dumbfounded, came out only with "Arré . . . but . . . ," aware though that my father blessed offerings of this sort quite regularly. I had seen him do it in the temple and on the pavilion.

Premji, who stood beside me, firmly picked up my hand and placed it on the paper bag. Instinctively, I muttered, "Let your wife conceive, then . . . Pir Bawa bless her . . . her womb."

"Thank you, Karsan-ji," Dervesh said, and to add to my amazement he pressed into my hands a hundred-dollar bill and one apple.

Before I could even begin to refuse this astronomical sum, Premji again intervened, stepping between us. He put his hand on the man's shoulder and said, "Pir Bawa blesses you, go now. She will conceive."

Dervesh joined his hands in farewell and left.

I still recall him, looking somewhat comical, in brown checkered pants and blue windbreaker, his thin hair pasted down with gel, and bearing the recently put on flab of the new immigrant. He would have been from the potmakers' community behind the shrine, people who had worshipped there for centuries and—from the stories I had been told—bore persecution for their beliefs.

Premji explained to me, "If he didn't pay, he wouldn't believe your prayer would work for him." He smiled and added, "You have to get used to your status, Karsan-ji."

"We meet every Saturday, all of us who live in the area," Premji informed me in the car on the way back. "But it is all right for you to come once a month, to the big gatherings. At those times we get people from as far as New York. You are your father's successor, now is the time to begin your calling!"

I couldn't reply. Bapu-ji had without fail mentioned this calling of mine in his letters; but far away from Pirbaag his reminders had seemed abstract and dutiful, and neither urgent nor demanding. I had felt grateful for that. My succession to the throne was a distant eventuality, and I had time enough in America, so I had led myself to believe, to reflect further upon it. Now suddenly here I was almost conscripted as viceroy to a small overseas community. This was his doing.

My head felt heavy and my stomach queasy; I opened the window and let a rush of cool air pummel my face. Premji threw a glance in my direction. I loved my people, this I had affirmed today. They were, mostly, simple people. Tonight I had been reminded in the starkest terms of where I came from, and I was touched. But I couldn't help a feeling of my world closing in on me to suffocate me. My father catching up with me. I had to be careful, I told myself in that speeding car on the highway, I should make my position very clear very soon. I would not be anybody's godman in America. The experience with Dervesh had already tainted my newfound independence, my growing sense of my world.

More and more I had begun to entertain the thought, the suspicion, that the ways of Pirbaag might be mere superstition, based on an historical episode become vague and coloured with mythology. I dared not let my father in on this speculation, of course. Perhaps he had had his doubts when he was younger and been cured of them, as I might be in due time. But for now the golden apple of fertility which Dervesh had pressed into my hand felt awkward and sticky to my touch. I needed time to reflect on my destiny, I wanted to be left alone. How to do that, when they all respected and loved me as a young god and expected me to behave a certain way? I mumbled that I would try to do as asked. Premji gave me another quick look in response.

When we arrived on campus, Premji parked and took me to have tea, after which he walked with me inside the Yard, towards my residence. It was late.

"Can I also give you a book to take for my father?" I asked him on a whim.

"Certainly," the man replied, and we went up to my room. I opened the door, proudly turned on the light to reveal my domain. There was my table with my papers and assignments awaiting me; and there stood beside it the bookshelf that was my pride, containing the book I had just thought of sending to Bapu-ji, the Norton edition of the poems of John Donne, replete with critical essays. And there was my chair, on the back of which was strung, to my anger and utmost embarrassment, a black brassiere. "These guys," I muttered, in a hopeless bid to explain to the elder that I was merely the victim of a prank, and threw the object into my trash can. Outside, I could hear my friends tittering. Evidently they had returned from their holidays.

Taking the book, Premji, red in the face, went on his way, saying he would take my well wishes and prayers for the Saheb and his family and Master-ji the teacher and everybody else at Pirbaag. He would take my respects to the mausoleum and to the patron saint of travellers, Jaffar Shah. He gave me a long, sad look as we parted, and I had a distinct sense that something had broken that could not be fixed.

⋖⋪⋯⋫⋗

Premji returned two months later.

It was late spring and festive in spite of the ongoing war and the protests against it. This was the season of shorts and T-shirts, loud happy music blaring out from the windows of student houses, entertainers vying with protesters for attention from the crowds in the Square. Prospective students were taking their tours of the campus, led by student guides, among whom was one Karsan Dargawalla of India, pleased to meet you, and alumni strolled about nostalgically, held parties, bought souvenirs. With much fanfare and laughter I popped open my first champagne bottle as an attendant at the president's reception for the alumni in the Yard.

"I will pick you up and bring you to the prayers," Premji said to me over the phone one night, having conveyed all the good wishes and blessings he had brought. "But this time you must spend the night in Worcester!"

India had raised his spirits, he sounded cheerful. And so I was loath to bring them down.

"Premji Chacha, I don't wish to come for the prayers—"

"Why ever not?" Shock, the words ending almost in a yell.

"I want to . . . I really have to be alone these years in my life. I need to be alone, Premji Chacha."

"Alone with your American friends. I see. Well, if you need anything, call me. Goodbye."

"Thank you. Goodbye."

A few days later a package was dropped off for me at residence. There was no message with it and no letter inside, but it was obviously from Ma, delivered by Premji. She had sent varieties of Gujarati snacks, and to my intense delight also included a copy of the movie magazine *Filmfare*. The feel of that magazine in my hand, its pages against my cheeks, with a faint aroma of spices, was like being touched by her, so many memories it carried of our moments together. She had gazed at the same photos of the stars, run her hands over their glossy feel, held them to her cheeks. But the world of Hindi cinema was now far from my mind, though I was not averse to watching a Bollywood (a term not in use then) movie once in a while when shown by Indian student groups. I was not familiar with the recent hit movies, or the current favourites among the actors and actresses. And, much more grievously, I had lost touch with the world of cricket, which came represented in the newsprint she must deliberately have chosen to wrap the foods.

During the first week of the new academic year, in September, a box of savouries was waiting for me one day outside my room. It was gift-wrapped in beautiful red, green, and silver paper and bore the name of a store in New Delhi. There was no sender's name, but I could guess from whom it had come. I saw Neeta on campus only once after that, from afar, and wisely we avoided each other.

27

The call of the shrine, cont'd.

"Once more I remind you, my son, of the story of Azazel, who had the knowledge of books but failed to understand the meaning of his life."

My father thanked me for my gift of a shirt; but this maxim about the fallen angel was his only nod towards my other gift, the Donne book. Books are not everything, remember Azazel from the Bible and the Quran. He did not understand what was truly important; he lost all.

But for me books opened the hidden doors to my mind; they were everything.

I had come to the university to learn about everything I possibly could. That is what I had very blithely written in the application for admission that I had mailed from Ahmedabad; and that is what, flashing a cheerful smile, my big, lanky academic adviser had confronted me with in his office soon after I arrived.

"Everything, eh?" he said. "We wondered who this applicant was with a fantastic appetite for learning. But your Mr. Hemani convinced us you were genuine! A good friend you have in him."

I described to him at perhaps too great length the kindly bookseller in his shop, whom I would visit during my stolen bus journeys to the city, to which he listened patiently and with bemusement.

"Well, we've had sons of rajas and presidents here but never an heir to a medieval saint!" he said. "Let's see what Harvard can teach you!"

The two of us bent over the catalogue, he guided me through the plethora—his word—of choices that were available to me. The courses we selected required vast quantities of reading, and I complied voraciously. Over the months every book and every subject became a thrilling voyage of discovery; every author, every professor a guide into the unknown. Where others complained about assignments, did them at the very last moment and forgot Dante or Homer the moment they handed in their papers, this boy from a village in India revelled in the new knowledge. With a deep breath of excitement I would pick up a fresh book, read the blurb at the back, leaf through the preliminary pages; savour the moment, before I plunged in and spent a good part of my evening. Outside, the streets were in turmoil; incessantly, the media discussed the war in Asia; its unpopularity on campus was evident everywhere, from flyers and picket lines and teach-ins to the heckling of unpopular professors and stormings of unpopular departments. There were bombings of public places; there were shootings by police. All these were but a mere curiosity to me.

I was called a nerd, though not offensively; I was an alien after all, and due certain allowances. But I was not bothered by the description. You are a book jock, they said in exasperation, as I walked down the corridor with more books from the library or the bookstores on the Square. I would grin, I would smile my Indian signature smile. Yes, I am that, I would say. Shiva has opened his eye and revealed the light of a thousand suns . . . and I am going to soak it up. In my culture we respect knowledge and learning, we worship our teachers.

Do you know what Thucydides says about the writing of history? Or Ibn Khaldun? Have you felt the excitement of reading "Gerontion" aloud, or the Chandogya Upanishad, or the Rig Veda? Have Freud and Jung kept you up at night? Or Dostoevsky? Camus and Nietzsche? Heisenberg and Bohr? You cannot deny that the plight of Hector in the *Iliad* doesn't absolutely move you to tears.

How could such a clamorous, exciting universe of the mind, how could so much of the world have been hidden from me previously?

But according to my father, all this was illusion, a fever of the brain, because all true knowledge lay within oneself. It came from meditation and introspection; the germ of truth was awakened inside you when you went to your guru, touched his feet, and he bent and whispered a mantra in your ear. Bapu-ji had all sorts of books in his famous library, but the only ones I had known him to care about were those relating to Pirbaag, especially the leather-covered manuscripts that he constantly read and copied and preserved—because they contained our sacred knowledge, our special history. The rest stood quiet and dormant on his shelves. He must have loved them once, paid heed to them. And later rejected them.

How much did my hunger for all the knowledge in the world mean to me—what price would I pay for it? To bring Azazel down from his high horse, to teach him humility and the proper perspective, God his father made a statue of dirt and asked the arrogant scholar to bow down in the dust before it. Azazel refused, "Why should the son of fire fall down before a son of clay?" and Azazel was exiled from heaven, bitter, angry, and vengeful.

My father had his own way of bringing me down to earth, showing me the steep price of freedom.

Almost to the year after I met Premji, a telegram arrived for me, read over the phone by an exquisitely neutral voice belonging to Western Union. "Your mother gravely sick; return immediately; ticket will be sent. Bapu-ji."

I had been sitting on the edge of my bed when I heard this news. The phone returned to its cradle, I found myself having shifted back towards the cold hard comfort of the brick wall behind me, my feet drawn up close, staring ahead; a stone in the pit of my stomach. Gravely sick, your mother gravely sick, your mother . . . A self-contained world suddenly shattered to reveal its illusion. And tender memory among the ruins.

Plump and fair, nose stud glittering, and always that wan smile of greeting as I came in the back gate after school. A smile to say, All is well, then. And the wonderfully warm mother smell of her embrace, partly the coconut oil and jasmine of her hair, partly the chappati she baked; it was the smell on her pillow, which I liked periodically to exchange with mine. When Mansoor grew older we would fight over who got to take Ma's pillow. She was our busy quartermaster of the courtyard who kept us fed and clothed on our meagre budget. And she had that private existence outside of the spiritual world of Pirbaag—the magical movies. The two of us sitting on the front step of the house on a Sunday evening, she would relate a story from one of them; she would wipe back a tear, a flood of tears might then burst out, for the best movies were invariably the tragic sagas. I would squeeze her fat arm. I loved her intensely. I kept her secret, understood the need that made her sneak away to the cinema disguised in a burqa. Then why did I leave her? Would my brother have done the same?

Early the next morning a travel agent at the Square called, asking me to pick up my ticket.

"So you are not planning to return, Mr. Darga—" he said, looking it over before handing it to me later that day.

"Of course I am returning," I replied, but unable to control the tapering confidence in my voice. Something was wrong.

"Your ticket is not negotiable, Mr. Darga," the man challenged, ready to take on an argument. Business was slow.

"We'll see," I smiled, and hurried out of his shop.

At Pewter Pot, where I was so known by now that my tea arrived immediately I was seated and a fresh hazelnut muffin placed before me, I read the ticket carefully. It was for a one-way fare to Bombay.

He did not want me to return to America. My life of freedom and learning was to be aborted. This was what his own father had done to him when he recalled him from the University of Bombay, St. Xavier's College, and got him married. He had acquiesced; he expected me to do the same. Did he actually think he could erase the last two years of my life and lead me to walk another path? Did he not realize that I was not quite the same Karsan he had known?

It was what he feared, of course.

But I should be beside my mother, whatever else may be true. Had I become so callous and selfish as to need convincing of that duty? "Gravely sick": how ominous that sounded; my family cremated their dead and then buried them. Your world lies at the feet of your mother, every boy is taught that. Nothing is as precious, nothing deserving more respect, not even the gods. You can have a second of anything else, but there is only one mother who bore you in her womb and gave you birth. Ma. Like Kunti: to whom all her five boys meant so much that she asked them to share everything, including a wife. Like Yashoda: to whom her beloved Krishna, her Karsan—our names were the same—could do no wrong.

I had to go to Ma . . . and not return?

Bapu-ji from his little shrine in the middle of nowhere in the world had with one stroke, one telegram, checkmated me. Whichever way I turned, I would lose.

There was one tiny recourse left. I tried that.

"Send return ticket," I cabled twice that same day.

There was no reply, and that was that. Sickening silence; contemptuous, cruel disregard. My own father? Meanwhile the departure date was approaching. Five days to takeoff. Why, Bapu-ji, why do you do this to me? Don't you trust your own Karsan—your gaadi-varas? I would sit up nights, stare at my room by the light outside the window, take in the sight, wall to wall, corner to corner—my bookshelf, my desk and my telephone, my cheeky posters; my own little kingdom. I would go outside and walk about the Yard, sit at the foot of the Puritan's statue, contemplate the hushed intellectuality that lay draped over the scene with so much delicacy . . . broken occasionally, aesthetically, by a string of tentative piano notes, a riff from a saxophone. And then, outside, the Square thrumming with activity, the inexhaustible heart of Cambridge.

How could I give all this up? I had become a part of it now.

"I cannot come unless by return ticket. Please."

Ma, don't die.

I did something I hadn't done since my arrival: I prayed to Pir Bawa. And I repeated my secret bol countless times. It will come to your aid during difficulty, Bapu-ji had said. But don't abuse it. It did nothing for me.

On the night of my scheduled departure I lay in my bed in darkness, quietly crying. The phone rang several times; I didn't pick it up, knowing it could be Premji calling to remind me to be on my way. It was even likely that he was booked on the same flight. I was aware of every airplane flying overhead then . . . east towards the Atlantic, to London, to Paris, south to Rio; one of them passed over me at 9:25 by my watch . . . the PanAm I had missed, surely, droning away angry and disappointed, Premji looking out the cabin window, devising sentences to say to my father.

Ma, don't die.

Was there a greater sin than not going to a mother's deathbed?

"Please keep me informed of Ma's health."

I would no doubt hear the news if the unthinkable happened. But there was nothing, no cable, no letter for a whole month. I called Premji's number in Worcester, but it was out of service.

Six more weeks passed. Should I go to Worcester to look for Premji, or the devotees I had met there on a Saturday last spring? They might have news from home. Premji lived in a bungalow off Pleasant Street, and the meeting to which he had taken me had been in a building not far from there; it had housed the offices of a company called Engineers Mutual. That shouldn't be too hard to find, I figured.

Early on a Saturday morning I took a Greyhound bus for the town of Worcester. I had twenty dollars with me, not insubstantial, but still too little for my adventure, as I was to discover. It was bright but cold, the wind biting as I stepped off the bus at the depot and started walking. I had come expecting to identify Premji's quiet suburban street soon enough once I was on Pleasant Street. But the road was long and the side streets all looked similar; I was the only person on foot. Fortunately a taxi stopped for me and I got in. The driver was kindly and drove me into a couple of neighbourhoods, where I came out and asked people if they knew a Mr. Premji, or if there lived any Indians in the area, dark-haired people who looked like me. No luck.

"Where next?" the driver asked. "You know anyone else?"

I told him I wanted to find the offices of a company called Engineers Mutual.

The man shook his head. "Tell you what, I'll drop you off downtown, you ask around or find a phone book there."

An hour later, the address of Engineers Mutual tucked inside my pocket, I sat at a restaurant in the downtown square, looking out the window, sipping a soda, and contemplating my next move. The Pirbaag faithful had gathered at six thirty for their devotions, it was eleven in the morning now; what to do in the meanwhile? I walked around, had a soup and sandwich, for which I spent more than I anticipated; I browsed in a bookstore, then found the library, where I had a nap until closing, when I was turned out. Finally, at six o'clock I caught a taxi for the offices of Engineers Mutual.

The building was new and stood alone at a distance away from the main road; it had a glass exterior and was brightly lit. These details I had hardly noticed before. At this grey hour all looked quiet for miles around except for the gusting wind. I had never come across a bleaker scene in my life. When I tried the entrance door, it was solidly locked. My depression was complete. I was at my wits' end. With Premji beside me the previous time, how easily the door had swung open. Everything was different today. I decided to wait, standing close to the door and facing inside, desperate to shield myself from the cold. A police cruiser came whining up the long driveway, and when the window rolled down I explained my purpose; the cops checked my identification and reluctantly drove away, maintaining a crawling speed until they disappeared. Six thirty came and went, nothing happened. Finally at seven I started walking back to town, bitterly disheartened, realizing how ill-conceived my plan had been. Of course, if the devotions had taken place, everything would have turned out all right. It hadn't, and I had this long walk back to the station. I was hungry; my fingertips, my toes, my ears all stung from exposure. I had no choice but to take the taxi that stopped for me.

At the bus stop I had a dollar bill left on me, and assorted loose change. The bus ticket to Boston was well over that amount. I was stuck.

"What shall I do?" I asked the clerk at the counter, expecting perhaps a kindness.

The man shrugged.

I walked to the convenience store at the station's other end, explained my predicament. The man grinned. "Tough luck."

I came out of the store in absolute despair. Where to go? I was frightened. The ticket clerk had his sights on me; what did he think I would do? No doubt the store man was watching my back. A woman sat down on one of the linked plastic waiting seats attached with coin-operated TVs; she must have arrived recently, was waiting to be picked up. She looked miserable and gave me a red-eyed glare, pulled her suitcase closer. A drunk had retched near the end of the row, where I decided to sit, away from the woman. There was no one else around. This is what the world is like, outside of my books, I thought. This is what it can be like to be alone. Most of the world does not live on Harvard scholarships.

A while later, having composed myself, I tried calling up my friends at residence. They were not in but I found another lonely soul next door with whom I left the number of the pay phone where I could be reached. It was eleven o'clock when the phone rang. "Wait there till morning, I'll come and pick you up," Russell said. "Don't worry, nothing will happen to you."

Someone came and sat close to me in the middle of the night, perhaps seeking warmth, but otherwise I was not accosted. Russell arrived at nine thirty in the morning in a borrowed car and we drove back to Cambridge.

Exams came, summer approached. Still no message from home; not one line, to say: Your mother is well. Guilt gnawed at me, quietly and persistently, with the thought that I would not have been asked to return if Ma's condition had not been serious. The Saheb did not lie. I had been heartless, a selfish obstinate son who had put himself before his mother. My first and my only thought should have been of her. But there had been an alternative, a two-way ticket, which my father in his godly wisdom and his own obstinacy had denied to me.

Someone suggested I look for a person who would be travelling to my part of India over the holidays. Through an ad on a notice board, therefore, I met a student called Ramesh who kindly agreed to attempt to look up the shrine at Haripir during his visit home. He was from Rajasthan and his mother enjoyed no outing more than a visit to a holy place or shrine. During the summer a letter arrived from Ramesh in India telling me briefly that he had gone to Haripir and met my mother, Shrimati Dargawalla. She was as well as could be, and so were my brother and father. They all sent me their love. His own mother had benefited from the visit too. My hands trembled as I read the letter, and read it again. My fears were over. "Thank you, Pir Bawa," I said. "And thank you, Ramesh."

Early in September I met Ramesh over bagels and flavoured tea at the MIT Student Center, when he gave me a package of food from my mother. Tell him not to worry, Ma had said, tell him I am well. With the food was a copy of a cricket magazine.

But what had been wrong with her?

28

The price of freedom.

The winter looked bleak as it had not done before, the ground hard, the trees bare, the evenings long and empty. My friends had steady girlfriends now, all very upper class and levelheaded. Suddenly their penchant for horseplay and games was gone, and they were conscious of the future. You are not going to spend all your life clowning around at Harvard, after all, the four years will soon be up, the reckoning is close. They prepared to enter law and business and politics, and the tenor on our floor at Philpotts House was often hushed and academic.

Alone in my room at night, hopelessly I would look up from a book and let out a quiet howl of despair. My mind had begun to wander and worry. No longer was there the charge, the tension to it. Gone, that excitement of before, that burning driving thirst for all the knowledge of the world; gone and turned to ash. Everything seemed *okay* now, whatever I read; not banal, just, So-what? or worse, Big-deal. What had my rebellion been about, what had I cried tears for; how could the one thing that had come to mean my very existence suddenly abandon me now, leaving me with nothing—just a flaccid brain, an unbearable emptiness.

Help me, Bapu-ji; help me, Ma. Help me, Pir Bawa, you who also travelled so far away from home . . . You surely must know what this is about. I am alone now, totally absolutely alone.

To my friends' horror, I had transformed myself from the friendly Indian with the Maharishi smile into an irate alien; if they unthinkingly kept the volume on their stereos loud when I tried uselessly to concentrate, the next time someone was huddled with his girlfriend or frantically finishing an assignment I would sing—sing those ginans I knew so well; their alienness of melody and language driving them up the wall, as they described it. Or recalling Raja Singh I would hurl out choice Punjabi expletives, swear at imaginary stragglers on the road, the camels, the Rabari women, the kids. Or declaim in the grossest form of my funny accent (as it had been called) pieces of pure nonsense composed from remembered readings: *Hail, Banquo, let us go then you and I, to your beginning and your end! If you prick us with a pin, don't we bleed? No, but we are God! Then on thy belly shalt thy crawl!* And when one of them banged on my door in sheer frustration, out from my room I would emerge like Hamlet's ghost, so I thought, but more a belligerent Mr. Hyde. The prim girlfriends would flee.

Finally, my revenge for all the times they had laughed at me, treated me like a yahoo.

One day I got drunk on bourbon; another day I stayed over at a student house in BU and got stoned. I pinched a book from the Coop; it was called *Steal This Book,* a radical primer by Abbie Hoffman. How clever. My friends began to fear for me. During my saner moments I spoke with them, listened, apologized. We made up. A round of pizza from me. Croissants at the Blue Parrot. They suggested that perhaps I needed to go home for a while. *Go home? For a while? Go home and become God? You've got to be kidding! I'm all right, Jack!*

Then once again, those empty soul-sucking moments in the night, silent vampires . . . and the crescendo of the uncontrollable despair in the privacy of my room. The lack of all will and confidence, any interest in anything. The feeling of Alone. Of groping for something to cling to. For dear life. Crying to the dark. *Someone somehow tell me what to do, someone please help me . . . someone set it straight, this tormenting mind! It's come off, it's twisted . . . it's whirling round and round inside me . . .*

A dream. An excavation site, muddy, wet, deep, and craggy; people digging strenuously with spades . . . in, out. Cut, and I am alone, and a voice says above me, Come out now! Wait! I shout desperately, I'm still digging! I continue digging in the twilight . . . in, out . . . as black lumps of brain come flying out of the ground.

Another dream. Bapu-ji walks among his followers in Pirbaag (it must be), waving his blessings at them; but look—all is silent, and they don't respond to him, they turn away. And someone cries out desperately, But he is the Saheb! Why is no one greeting the Saheb?

What was happening to my father, to Pirbaag?

Karsan, the destroyer.

My father's letters had resumed, though they were much less frequent than before, and they were heartbreakingly brief; there was no advice in them. "My dear son Karsan, Accept our greetings for your birthday. Yesterday we celebrated your day by cutting a cake. I hope you were able to celebrate with your friends there. We are all well and Ma's health is improving. Your father Tejpal."

Where is the love, Bapu-ji? *Kem, tamaro dikro mati gayo?* Am I no longer your son, even a disobedient one?

Yes, the snow looks beautiful now, after the blizzard; soft white clumps balanced on the tree branches like pearls or tears, lights reflecting off the white crystals so that the night has the magical glow of fairy land; snowball fights, and Bob the burly Canadian is out showing off on his skis. I too should be out there among the brightly clothed boisterous fellows, this is the only way to beat the winter; only it's one of those days and the heart feels heavy, wants to drag me screaming into the darkness, though I won't let it, no I won't let you do that today, heart, it's lightness and freedom I want. It looks so good outside, I know that if I only let some of that cold air enter the lungs and clean out the old, poisoned blood inside me I'd be a new man. Perhaps I will go out, take in a deep breath of that bracing cold . . . it's what I need . . . why not? Indeed, why not . . . I can step out . . . it's soft as pillows out there . . .

I was rescued within minutes of falling on the cushion of fresh snow on the ground, someone having seen me tumbling past his window. I sprained my wrist and was blue in the bum. I had a bad dream, I explained to the doctors, and to the two cops who came by to the infirmary. I had been having nightmares recently, I said. My friends concurred, but not without giving me an ultimatum: Behave, or else.

. . .

Dr. Julius Goldstein was a small balding man with round glasses, looking more like a graduate student than someone who would heal me. He was the psychiatrist at Health Services, and I had gone to see him, upon advice, convinced that I was mentally sick, unable to come to grips with the processes of my mind. He was kind, with a soft but clear voice and a mannerism in which he would lean searchingly towards me when he spoke. I had lost him within the first few minutes of our first encounter, with the exotica of my life, and we both seemed to sense a hopelessness in the situation; he couldn't go where I came from. Still, he convinced me to lie down ("I don't like losing control of myself . . ." "Don't worry, you won't lose control, nothing will happen to you. It's normal.") and encouraged me to talk, and not looking at him but at a small landscape painting up on the wall before me, I unburdened myself to myself. Only rarely would he prompt. I told my stories, collecting them under different headings. My fears, my strong memories, my jealousies, my contradictions. At the end of each hour, then, I felt I had unwound a tangled strain of thought in my mind, experienced a limited clarity. Sometimes I came out with a heavier heart and more depressed than before, and if at the end I believed I had not been cured, then I had also to admit that I did not know what I meant by a cure. Perhaps all I needed was a chance to talk clearly to myself and thus let in some light of day into my benighted soul. Dr. Goldstein brought our few sessions to a close with one piece of advice.

"Have you spoken to your father—or written to him—about what you want from your life?"

"No . . . actually not."

"Well, that might not be a bad place to start, would it? Remember, he doesn't know what you want."

He doesn't? He is the Saheb, isn't he?

"Your father may be better disposed to your wishes than you give him credit for."

My wishes? What I want from my life? I had not even articulated to myself what the meaning was of the freedom I had craved so much, for which I had gone away to America, and then disobeyed my father, committed a cosmic offence. Freedom, and then what? What life did I have in mind to lead in my freedom? Like a child I had wanted to have my cake and eat it too. But as a child I had known I didn't want to be Saheb; I had wanted to be a great cricketer. That is what I would tell Ma as we sat together on the steps of the front porch, it was what R.D. Patel of the cricket academy and the Gujarat Lions might have made possible. That had been my wish, my desperate desire, to which Bapu-ji had said, No. It was too late for cricket now. But not for my freedom.

Yes, Dr. Goldstein's searching look seemed to say to me, as though he had followed my reasoning. He was a man in his late thirties, and I imagined him to have fought battles of his own. He sat back; he smiled at me. For the first time I saw sympathy in his eyes.

This was a time in the seventies when many people, involved in a currently trendy form of group therapy, went about revealing to their friends and acquaintances exactly what they thought of them and why they had been troubled or offended by them for these many months or years, as the case may be. One day my friend Russell came back from a weekend spent at a retreat. He cornered me in my room in the evening, and as I sat crosslegged on my bed with a book on my lap, he told me rather brashly how he had always hated my supercilious Maharishi smile and my ego and my bookishness; and how one day he had seen me picking my crotch and could not, for many months whenever he peed, get the image out of his mind; and so on, a litany of irritations he had detailed in a long letter addressed to me, which he now put in my hands without a care for my feelings.

I let Russell have his say, while keeping my composure, because he was so desperately sincere, and I agreed to consider for myself the crash therapy he had undergone. Of course I had no intention of following that fad. If anything, I had to convince him at some point to come to his senses and stop going about offending his friends. But this incident prompted me finally to follow Dr. Goldstein's advice to write frankly to my father and tell him what I wanted for myself.

29

"*Dear Bapu-ji,*

"[How many times have I begun this letter, Father, attempting to tell you the simple truth about myself, without offending or hurting you, and asking your forgiveness, your indulgence, your understanding—for you are wise and thoughtful, and above all my father. But all my attempts at niceties have failed, sounding hypocritical, if not false. In the end, all I can come out with is this blunt declaration.]

"I herewith renounce my status as gaadi-varas of Pirbaag, successor to the Saheb-ship of the shrine. I no longer believe in our path, the sat-panth as you called it, the true-path of the ancient sufi; to me it is nothing but a faith and blind like all the other faiths. By this I mean no disrespect to those who believe in it; I accept that to them and to you I have simply lost my way. They are my people, I cannot deny that, just as you are my father and elder. If I have a say, I would like the successorship to go to my brother, Mansoor, who deserves it more than I do, because he is still there with you. But you know better, Bapu-ji.

"I never wanted this status, as Ma will surely tell you if you were to ask her. It always terrified me to think of such a responsibility on my head; to be God to my people (at least to some of them), a keeper of souls, guardian of graves, preserver of the past; to always think of Brahman and Atman and the terrifying eternity behind the dark sky at night. I was not made for that. Where was the joy in it? But I could not tell you this, I was afraid to disappoint you because I respected you and loved you. I always wanted to be an ordinary Indian boy, Bapu. My ambition was to play first-class cricket, you will recall that. I might not have succeeded at it, but I never had a chance to give it a try. Bapu-ji, forgive me for being honest, you were never there to listen to or notice what your children or even your wife desired. You lived in your own world. Did you know that Ma went to see films in secret for fear of offending you? That she had to wear a burqa to disguise herself? Perhaps you did; but why did she have to do things in secret? You made plans for me and Mansoor without taking into account what we wanted. So rarely did you pause to speak to me like a father that when you did so, it was a Diwali for me. I would revel in that moment for days. How I missed having a real father!

"And finally, Bapu-ji, how can I ever forget—or forgive—how you tried to coerce and mislead me into returning to Pirbaag. Why? Because you were afraid of all the things I would learn that would make me see things in perspective, including our own backward, primitive tradition— yes, I do believe that!—in which a mere man is treated like God and even believes himself to be an avatar of God. I still don't know if Ma was really sick. If she was sick, wasn't it your duty to tell me what she suffered from? Did you realize how much you hurt me, what suffering you caused me? For I love Ma, like any son loves his mother, but you put an inhuman price on my being able to come and see her.

"What do I desire from life? Simply to be an ordinary person. Can you understand that, Bapu? Someone who likes to find out about new things, marry the girl he wants, follow cricket and baseball. (Yes, I do like baseball now, and occasionally even American football.) Someone who likes to read for pleasure; for whom this world is not a miserable prison but a place in which to seek personal fulfillment and happiness, full of other ordinary people like me.

"I have told you in all honesty, Bapu-ji, what I have become; what I think of my life and what I desire from it. Pirbaag is not for me. There must have been someone called Nur Fazal, the Wanderer and sufi. But he lived hundreds of years ago and was a mere mortal. I am simply an ordinary, secular Indian studying in America. Please forgive me, Bapu-ji, if I have offended you, but this is my truth.

"Your loving son,

"Karsan."

. . .

Truth as it was then; in some respects unfair and naive—what is an ordinary, secular Indian, after all? Is such an entity possible? Haven't recent events in my home state disproved even the ideal of such a notion? And harsh, too, my judgement of my father—how much choice did he have in his life?

I realized only gradually that I had in effect banished myself from home.

30

March 15, 2002.
Kali Yuga. The Destruction. Pirbaag, Gujarat.
I had called him preserver of the past, almost in contempt; and now it was
gone.

Thirty years later I was back in the old grounds, the prodigal returned.
I would have wanted to cremate my father, but he was gone and cremated
days before; and I stood in the midst of a destruction so absolute—result
of the recent communal riot or pogrom or mass revenge, call it what you
will—a catastrophe so complete, I could only gasp, and then gasp, and
staggered towards the edge of the old pavilion and sat down.

The smell of burnt flesh and bone and garbage; filth desecrating the
graves, stray dogs rooting in the periphery, two bullocks carelessly feeding off the overgrowth; the marble mausoleum—once the centre of my
existence—grey with dust, pockmarked by the impact of angry missiles.
Dare I go inside? I must pay my respects. Here I am, Pir Bawa. I stood up
and walked wearily towards it; went up the steps and over the threshold, to
be greeted by a sharp dusty wind from the darkness. Gradually my eyes
began to see in the dark. An angry storm had passed here: shreds of cotton
chaddar, dry petals in the dust, the lattice barrier broken and fallen, the
grave naked and soiled, bereft of its crown . . . the tang of ammonia . . .
and two rats scurrying about in the corners, among the rags.

Back outside, the glare of destruction. The clamour of disbelief. This
could still be a dream, this wrecking ground. Visions swimming before me
of the heyday that had passed . . . the hopes and prayers brought here by
the hundreds on Saturdays, the music of the ginans, the whiff of incense

early at dawn, and the tinkle of bells . . . and all the history and legend and permanence of Pirbaag. I had denied its charge, but surely not to see it thus, pulverized, testimony only to the death and agony of those who had come to hide in it, or to protect it from the havocking mobs.

I sat down on the steps, before me this ruined kingdom that I had once rejected. It was too late for tears, for by now I had lived and lost already, far away in a life of my own devising, and wrought a stoic armour around me that gave me my semblance of composure. But to see *this*? So grotesquely complete in its destruction as only my native land could make it. So beyond the redemption and forgiveness that I thought I had earned as the privilege of my age and its experience, the reward of its mellowness and moderation. Was I being laughed at or only being commanded to laugh?

Pir Bawa, is this your final lesson. The impermanence of everything. Do I see here the stamp of Kali Yuga, the Dark Age that Bapu often described, and awaited? Or is this a symbol of a cynical political system that seasonally lubricates itself with the blood of victims?

"Karsan Saheb . . ."

I came to with a start. A boy stood shyly before me, barefoot, grimy. I gaped at him, astonished.

"Karsan Saheb . . ."

This form of address . . . so unequivocal, from this stripling in singlet and shorts born years after I left here. How does he know me, does he know what he's saying? I have not even announced myself in this town. Can the face reveal so much?

"Your Bapu said he left instructions for you."

"Instructions? Where?"

"He left them with Pir Jaffar Shah."

"Jaffar Shah?"

He ran off to his mother waiting in the distance, and the two stood staring at me.

And I couldn't help but smile, just a trace. Jaffar Shah was often the gateway to the heart of Pir Bawa. I remembered. The kindly saint of the sojourner, beloved to truck and bus drivers. Under the curious gaze of boy and mother, I stood up and went to his grave, its massiveness having stood up to the attacks. Here, seated beside it, Master-ji had taught us lessons in the tradition; and Bapu-ji had a hiding place in the ground known only to the two of us. Except for stains on the sides and a few chips off its concrete, the grave lay clean and calm, with already a cheery aspect from the few red flowers upon it.

The boy returned curiously to watch. I knelt down at the foot of the grave, swept off with one hand the sand on the warm paving, looked for the loose stone I knew must be there. A faint reek came off the ground. The boy's small fingers helped me to find a gap, and together we prised the brick out to reveal a brown envelope, intact and still glossy; below it, scraps of paper and cardboard apparently hidden long ago, perhaps the same ones Bapu-ji and I had buried here, against the eventuality of a Chinese invasion.

The envelope was addressed:

> *For my son, gaadi-varas Karsan Dargawalla*
> *to be opened upon recitation of his bol.*

How determined, how uncompromising, even in desperation. He would not let me off easily.

I went back to sit on the steps. There would be the business aspects to attend to, regarding the property. I had no interest in it. And this envelope: should I open it? I blanked my mind, willed the syllables of the bol to appear; they wouldn't, of course. Over the years I had willed myself to forget them, breaking off my sacred connection to the shrine, to my father and the succession.

A ginan came to mind instead, a song of destruction: *Be aware, my brothers, the Daitya will come and destroy the world* . . .

And then another, a song of death: *You hero, going after "me" and "mine," your life was wasted* . . .

A group of men and women approached respectfully, joined their hands in greeting. "Saheb, allow us to clean this place up."

I gazed up at them in absolute wonderment. I was touched too by this show of loyalty. The humility, the respect and sympathy. Why? What did they seek here now, from this place of the saviour who could not save himself?

"But that is impossible now, it is all gone . . . Go to the temple next door—it's all right to do so . . . it is open, after all."

While on my way here in the car, fearful expectations in my head, though what I imagined was nothing compared to what I later saw, and speculation about time's inevitable toll on the old home, and nostalgia the bittersweet palliative lulling the mind, the driver proudly pointed out on my right the new temple of Haripur. It was an impressive white structure, walled and gated, standing on the site of the old temple to Rupa Devi and covering the old ground where I used to play cricket. There was a dome from which pennants of various colours flew. A little further up came a dilapidated wooden gate, almost at the edge of the road, between a tea and a flower stall. "Pirbaag," announced the driver, and stopped. "Nothing there now." This was not the gate I had known, and in my anxiety I ran inside to look at the place which had been my childhood home.

"No, Saheb," the people before me replied to my advice that they should go to somewhere less defunct. "Allow us to clean this place."

They brought out brooms, covered their mouths and noses with rags, guided me out of the compound so I wouldn't breathe in the dust they would raise. I came to stand out on the road. Saddhus in orange robes waited outside the gates of the new temple, partly inside the area which had been our front yard. Across the road, the old tire shop had become a full garage; the man inside was sizing me up—was that Harish? I took a step forward, stopped. No longer could I dare to presume, so much had changed. And to its left, further up, the Muslim shrine and settlement, also utterly destroyed; only a gaping hole where once stood the massive door. Who remained to tell its tale?

A white Ambassador drove up and parked sharply a short distance down the road. Before the dust had settled, the driver had jumped out and opened a passenger door, to let out a graceful sari-clad woman as out of place on this wasted road as a mermaid. She looked around briefly and started walking purposefully in my direction, avoiding roadside debris, perhaps on her way to the temple. It seemed the car had driven past its objective.

The lady saw me staring, paused and smiled briefly, then turned towards the gate behind me.

"Hello—namasté," I said instinctively. "This is the wrong gate—the temple is further down."

"No, this is the right one."

She had joined her hands in greeting, and for a moment we peered at each other almost indiscreetly.

"Saheb?" she said.

"I am sorry—" I attempted to deny the title that I had rejected once, then stopped, frozen by her look.

"Karsan Dargawalla?" she asked.

"It can't be—"

But it was she. The name had escaped me, but not the memory.

"Neeta—Neeta Kapur," she offered. "Boston?"

Of course. That long face, the cheekbones. Only older, leaner. It was hard not to stare, recall through a haze what she had been. Beautiful. Enough to intimidate. And wise. But now here, in the sticks? It seemed incredible.

"Yes, I remember," I said in English. "At least I think I do."

There was a quiver of a smile on her lips. It was only a single evening we had spent together, ultimately embarrassing, but the memory surely brought back in her a warm feeling for those youthful times, as it did in me, despite my condition.

"Do you come to this temple regularly?" I asked, though she had already told me she had come to the old shrine.

"No, I come to Pirbaag—your place. I used to come from Ahmedabad when your father was alive. I would bring my son here, when he was sick and there was no hope."

"What happened?"

"He died. But I was comforted."

"But Pirbaag is no more now, it is finished," I told her.

Two chairs had been brought for us to sit on the pavilion, which had been made passably clean, though the stench lingered; shit and carnage. Across from me the mausoleum, distinct only in its deprivation; in front of it the Jaffar Shah grave. A memory returned, nagged at the mind's edges . . . Mansoor playing the bandit among the graves, bow and arrow in hand, Ma's little Arjun. Nobody I had asked seemed to know where he was now, or whether he was alive. That was one matter I had to attend to.

But who would come to this place now? What miracle or solace could it offer?

"But you can keep it alive," the woman beside me said with a soft emphasis.

I shook my head. "It's gone." The body destroyed, the heart cut out, I said to myself, though that sounded too purple, I thought, aware of the sophisticate before me.

"Do you know what happened here?"

She nodded. "Nobody could stop the madness."

"Nobody wanted to."

She nodded again, abstractly. We had been served steaming hot sweet tea from the stall outside, and she balanced her cup and saucer on her lap.

"Why don't you stay in Ahmedabad for a few days?" she asked after a while. "You can't sleep here—there's no place to—and you need time to collect yourself. And you can come to Pirbaag when you want to."

Our eyes met, and she blushed profusely.

"There are decent hotels close to where I live," she added.

She had a house in the city, from the period when her husband was governor of the state. She saw me glance at her forehead, without a bindi, and gave the slightest nod. Her husband had died. She lived in Delhi now but came to Ahmedabad occasionally, when she would visit Pirbaag.

It seemed a reasonable suggestion. Pirbaag, what was left of it, was safe for the time being, there was a police guard on constant duty. I could stay in the city while I decided on a course of action and waited for Mansoor to contact me.

I hoped he was all right. From him I expected to find out what had happened here, why this ancient place that was a neutral haven got attacked, how our father died. Nobody here had the heart to tell me that.

Meanwhile, another brainwave:

"Why don't you spend a few weeks in Shimla afterwards, at the Advanced Studies Institute? My sister is married to the director there, Professor Barua—I could talk to him about you. It would be an excellent place to gather yourself—that is, if you are not planning on returning to America immediately."

"Canada . . . I come from there."

"Oh. Well? . . ."

I had heard of the Institute in Shimla, reputedly a perfect retreat for study and research, with an excellent library. I said I would think about her suggestion. To myself I had to admit that the idea seemed attractive, though I would be putting myself further into her hands, and I hardly knew her. Her being a widow made the situation more awkward. But I needed time to recover and to think. Whether I liked it or not, and whatever I decided to do with the status, I was now the inheritor of this ancient refuge, its Saheb. By now a defiance had also welled up in me, a strong desire to gather something from the debris and ashes, and construct a monument to Pirbaag. The precious library was gone, with the Saheb who had embodied its tradition, who had painstakingly and often in his own hand preserved its records, but I still carried some of that heritage in my memory, and on my tongue.

And so, yes, I decided right there, I would stay awhile in this retreat in the hills. And sing and recall. Sing and recall.

⤙⤙⤚⤚

I would like to say then that Pirbaag never left me; and I, it. There is a partial truth to that; I only wish it were the entire truth, for it would pull the curtain over my personal life, obliterate its ache. But the truth is that I did find another life there, in North America, one of personal happiness and freedom; a second birth in which I managed to leave behind the manacle that had been Pirbaag, forget the sacred bol given to me by my father that tied me to my heritage and succession. But what did the Pir say, and my father reiterate?—every flower withers; and where's the cheek that does not fade, says the poet. It seems that Bapu-ji always won; but his was the cosmic truth of transience, therefore a truism, mine that of the small and personal joys that defy the grand design, but inevitably must confirm it.

31

c. 1970s.

The joys, the love. Cambridge, Mass., to begin with.

English became my field of specialization in university. It seemed the obvious choice, given my enthusiasm for its poetry, which had begun with the Metaphysicals of seventeenth-century England and not abated. Vainly for a mere freshman, though not without a little validity, I believed that I had fully grasped the much-trumpeted concept of the "undissociated sensibility," how through clever, extended use of imagery a poet like John Donne could compose a poem that was simultaneously a spiritual idea. Poetry and philosophy had coincided, in one Metaphysical sensibility. I then asked, brashly to some, didn't the ginans of my childhood achieve the same? To my disappointment, neither my father nor my teacher had been impressed by this immodest proposal, for their own reasons. I was not discouraged, but I had to admit with humility that the poets of my interest were steeped in a tradition of European and Christian learning, while the ginans of my childhood were written mainly for simple folk. Nevertheless the similarities were there, and I was convinced that the best of the ginans were as beautiful and satisfying as the best of Keats, who had become, for a while, my passion. Thus I had discovered for myself a mystical strain in English poetry that seemed amazingly familiar to my Indian mind. The dying young Keats wrote of death and transience in the same unflinching manner as I had heard from my elders, and which from my own mouth now so often shocked my American friends.

How similar was the well-known line of William Blake, "To see a world in a grain of sand," to the one in the *Bhagavad Gita*, enjoining Arjuna to see the One "in all beings, undivided in the divided"; and how close the lines "I saw Him, and sought Him, I had Him and I wanted Him," of the medieval anchorite Lady Julian to the erotic mysticism of Mira or Kabir or Nur Fazal? The conceits of Donne's *Holy Sonnets*, the thoughts of Keats or Blake, lay scattered throughout the songs of my childhood. Were the connections historical or psychological? What would a map of influences look like? And so on.

I was well immersed in my subject, then. I had discovered a vein that I could mine to my heart's content through the long process of a doctoral thesis. Of course, this choice of specialization and career was inspired by the spirit of the world I grew up in, the spiritual sensibility that had formed me. I could hardly deny its presence in my life; it was a given, like DNA, and both my strength and my limitation, and I had to make of it what I could. What I had rejected was the expectation and demand that world placed on me, and its fear—and perhaps contempt—of the larger world of which I felt so much a part now. My father had seen immediately the implications of my new enthusiasm: in reading the poetry I did not become the poet but the critic, one remove from the mystical experience and devotion that produced the thrill, the union with the Divine. Saffron Lion was not a mere conceit to him but his own son and successor straying away.

A Ph.D., I was happy to discover, was a convenient shelter for the alien who knew not the ropes of living in the new country, providing him a world within a world in which to function, to be acceptably eccentric. It was an exhilarating existence of the mind in an elite university where my physical needs were modest but taken care of, in an era of intellectual freedom and experimentation. I had an apartment now in a converted house on Banks Street, close to the university, and I had an assorted group of acquaintances, none very close. Of my undergraduate friends, only Russell remained in Cambridge, at law school; Bob and Dick had gone away to other professional schools.

My father continued to write his brief, dutiful missives, and I could not but reply in kind. There ran a silent current of mutual hurt in our muted correspondence, filling the spaces between words with a tension I could almost touch in the crispness of the paper I held within my fingers. What I heard from Ma was through him; Mansoor wrote occasional notes to request jeans, shirts, and the like, nothing else. There was no news as such from home, and after my loud assertion of freedom I could not even pick up the requisite tone to inquire of my father about matters relating to the minutiae of life at home. I felt shut out. And yet, what did I expect from him?

My grievance was based on a contradiction, a double vision of myself. I imagined for myself a life free of the burden and expectation of tradition, to be and think as I wished without my father's advice or admonition; and at the same time, in some vague, illogical, and dreamlike manner, I saw myself at "home" with my family. It was as though I had let go of Pirbaag, but not home. This illusion had to find a resolution, and it did, but not in a manner I could have expected.

There came a prolonged period of weeks without any correspondence from Bapu-ji. This is it, I thought, he has finally cut me off completely. Then one day, two years after that season of my filial rebellion, my declaration of independence from him, Bapu-ji wrote to me that Ma had died a few months before. I had never previously been told what she had suffered from, and he told me nothing about her illness now. She had been cremated without notice to me; I had not been given the option of a visit home. I felt terribly wounded and angry. He had no right to deny me my mother yet again.

Without Ma, I thought cruelly but not unreasonably, Bapu-ji would continue to live in his arrogant God-hood. And he at least had Shilpa, and all the other volunteer devotees who came to sit at his feet and administer to his needs. But I felt sorry for Mansoor. He had been so close to her. I still thought of him as my little brother, though he was a teenager now and I hardly knew anything about him, what he thought and felt, what he wanted to become. He had never replied to my queries, never asked for advice.

I was sad at my own loss, but I had lost the right to feel sorry for myself, for I had truly abandoned Ma. If she had only written to me. In standing my ground against my father I had taken the chance that I might never see her again; the gamble was called, and the price exacted. Along with the letter with his news about her death, Bapu-ji sent me a picture of

Ma, which I always put in a prominent place wherever I moved. I did not possess a picture of Bapu.

A few months after that news, Marge Thompson reentered my life. There was no reason to look back now.

When the student radicals rejoined mainstream society, older and subdued, how ordinary they looked: clean, middle class, and well mannered. And so did Marge, except that her given name was Mira, her father was Indian, and she was brought up a Canadian. I ran into her outside the English department late one morning, just as I entered the front hall, when she turned around abruptly after a fruitless scan of the jobs board. For a moment we stood gaping at each other, until she broke the silence with a soft "Still staring, I see." There was a twinkle in her eyes, and we both laughed. And I knew this would be a different relationship from before. Expressing my surprise at seeing her, I took her to the Greenhouse Café, which stood on the site of the memorable Pewter Pot, where we had first met, and which had sadly been gutted by a fire. It was here during our long catching up that she made her confession.

"Canada?" I pretended surprise, for I had been told already by Bob long ago where she was from.

"Where all those cold fronts come from—in the weather forecasts," she said, echoing exactly my thoughts. "Watch out for this cold front— brrr!"

"You are hardly a cold front," I added unnecessarily, with an uncertain laugh, ready to add much more flattery in my excitement (for example, that her namesake was a medieval mystic much admired in the parts I hailed from), but I wisely held my peace. I recalled too well that time in the past when I had let out too much.

It was five years since I last saw her, so we couldn't help exchanging glances of renewed surprise at each other, for this was such a fantastic, unexpected reunion. I couldn't help but recall how poorly I had fared during our previous encounters, and was thrilled at this new beginning. We spoke as equals now. I had always imagined a fragility beneath that brashness she had presented as her personality; her shabby dressing had not convinced either; now there was not even a pretence of far-outness. Here she was in a tan skirt and blue shirt, her brown hair parted and tied casually on either side, such a beautiful girl. There was a new, calm sensibleness to her. She had become what I had wished her to be. And I? I had a greater facility with the culture and had lost much of my awkwardness; and my accent, I believe, had lost its worst abominations—though there were instances still when I opened my mouth only to draw a smile from my friends. She told me she had taken a leave of absence from MIT to volunteer for Senator McGovern's presidential campaign, and after the disappointment of that 1972 election she had gone to finish her studies in Montreal. She was back in Cambridge, had moved in with a friend, and was looking for a job and hoping to go to graduate school. She had broken up with Steve not long after I had last seen her; he was in California studying mathematics at Berkeley. A slob he had been, but also, apparently, a genius. But to get back to Marge. She was brought up in Winnipeg, she said. Her mother was Cathy Thompson, born and bred in Iowa, and her father was Amrit Pad-manabh, a Buddhist and medical doctor, and a poet and musician in his spare time.

Perhaps it was these enigmatic origins that had called out to me so urgently the moment I first laid eyes on her. I observed to her something to that effect, and she was embarrassed, flattered, and quite moved. On an impulse, she took my hand and squeezed it, then dropped it.

I was in love. Years before, a simpleton foreigner, I had been in thrall to the wonderful tease and radical Marge Thompson and had desired her as my special friend in a vaguely pure way. I had even thought I was in love. But now my feelings for her were profoundly certain, as I sat across from her and watched her tell me about herself, and as I in turn confessed to her about my recent life, though cautiously, all the while staring at her and admiring her and smiling inanely, my insides in an awful clutch, my head dizzy with unspoken thoughts and this single refrain: I love this girl. She's come back, unattached, and I must not let her go.

We agreed to meet later that day, ended up having an early dinner together, agreed further to meet again soon, which quickly—and much too slowly—became the following morning. Soon we began to see each other frequently.

But she had to discover me anew, and be convinced that this time I was safe, no longer the complicated Indian dragging behind him miles of background. There was so much we had to talk about and learn from each other. Now my attachment to my home was slender and I had no intention of going back to live in India. I was just another graduate student, an aesthete and an intellectual, a little vain perhaps, with hopes of one day teaching my pet theories at some college. And she was no longer the posturing loudmouth radical, hustling revolution on the streets, but a beautiful, sensitive girl who needed attention and devotion; I had all of that to give her.

Those initial days of our courtship were as sweet and tender as they were anxious and uncertain. I would wake up joyfully every morning, thankful for another day; a nervous tingle worrying my spine as I showered and brushed and tortured myself: what if this was all a dream; what if she had changed her mind, having realized her folly, and mocked me when we met again. I would hasten to our meeting place. And no, every time, no: she was real and she was there for me as promised.

We usually met first thing in the morning, had coffee in a restaurant, or out in the sun on the steps of my department building or a bench in the Yard. I would head off for a class or a teaching duty or to the library, and she would wander off to the jobs boards, where she was not having much luck. Spring was not the time to look for campus employment. There was a certain shyness in our manner, a modicum of edginess; a decision was pending: to commit or not. And so although we always parted reluctantly every time, the absence also gave us a respite in which to recompose. We met again in the late afternoon, by arrangement or on a pretext. Evenings she preferred to spend with her friend, and I had my own work to do; they were not to be toyed with, anyway. But there was one day when we did not meet at all; I spent that evening in an agony of anxiety close to the phone, yet afraid to pick it up lest I seemed pushy and drove her away. Had my dream ended, was she, after all we had recently said to each other, the same tease she had once been? But the next morning she was again waiting for me at the corner where I emerged on Harvard Square. Big smiles of relief. We went to have our coffee and did not discuss the previous day but had a long, drawn-out parting; after a few steps on our separate ways we both turned to wave again at each other. I think of that day as the turning point in our new relationship.

Why do I go into these details, so trivial in retrospect? To remind myself that I lived—"became of the world," as my father would have said.

This was what I had desired, to be a thinking, feeling person like anyone else, for which I had spurned my calling.

Marge Thompson with Karsan Dargawalla: I recall repeating the names, getting a thrill from their unlikely, gobbledygook togetherness. What did she see in me, this gawky village cartoon from India with a name to match?

She liked my naivety and honesty, she said. She had seen enough of the cynicism, the bitterness. It was as if I were new to the world, I was like a *poem . . .*

"Stop BS-ing me!"

"There, you can't even swear properly, QED—" she teased, and gave me a push and ran, and I gave chase and brought her down. But what do you do then, Karsan Dargawalla, you clumsy oaf? And so she taught me how to kiss—in public, in full view of picnickers, on the banks of the Charles River. Applause. A public blessing by the water. It was done.

Her past—to use a euphemism for her previous intimacies—caused me no anxiety; whatever its details, she had found her destiny in me; and, paradoxically, I was swept away by her. She would confess to me, years later, what I should have long guessed even if only to flatter myself: that my running into her outside my department had not been a complete accident. She had inquired about me. All the better for my fragile self-respect, of course.

That night we had dinner at my place, to which she arrived dressed as for a formal occasion, bringing paraphernalia with which to decorate our evening. While I cooked, a skill I had taught myself, she busied herself with the table and setting up a suitably romantic ambience. And later that evening as we relaxed on the cushioned, carpeted floor (such was student living), I discovered the wonder of female closeness, the terrifying tastes of tender intimacy. We had became lovers, certain and complete together.

The following month I visited Winnipeg with her.

After the hubbub of Boston and its blithely chaotic streets, Winnipeg seemed destitute and bleak, in its flatness, its spareness, seeming more like a town from the old Wild West of the movies. And yet the prairie held its mystery and beauty, its clinging flatness suggestive of the infinitude of earth and sky; and the people, as though always aware of the modest human circumstance, had a refreshing openness about them. Dr. Padma-nabh was waiting for us outside the suburban family home when we arrived on a Saturday afternoon, straight from Boston, having hitched a two-day ride. He was a small man with a ready smile, wearing shorts that day, and he took me straight inside, Marge and her mother following. As soon as I had sat down on a living room couch, he handed me two slim volumes of his poetry, as though he had been waiting all morning to do just that, and then began plying me with questions about myself, not interrogatively but apparently out of genuine curiosity. The fact that I was a student of poetry at a prestigious university had won me over long before I arrived; what I replied about my background was neutral and safe, nothing to bewilder. His wife, Cathy, a fleshy woman with yellow hair, brought us lemonade and stood at the doorway. It was she who rescued me, as I wondered how to respond to the books in my hands, saying, "Let him freshen up first, Paddy. Then I'll make you some tea. I know how much all you Indians like tea!"

She showed me to the guest room and as she left me at the door, she gave me a hard look that said she wondered exactly what type of relation-ship I had going on with her daughter in these permissive times. I had come as the boyfriend, and Marge had thrown in, with her description of me, just the hint of an impending engagement.

"Thank you, Mrs. Padmanabh," I said, and she replied quickly with a smile, "Call me Cathy. We'll get to know each other a lot, won't we?"

"I hope so," I said, elated.

That night after dinner we all sat in the living room for tea and dessert and the doctor entertained us with his saxophone, cutting a droll figure, the instrument coming down almost to his knees. But he was a good player, and I was told to my surprise that he sometimes played in clubs. He sat down and a family moment followed, touching in its togetherness, espe-cially when I recalled my own circumstance. Before we retired Paddy was convinced, without much difficulty, to read from his poetry, which he did briefly in a dry and mildly expressive voice. It was the kind of confessional poetry of alienation that I was still unfamiliar with, clashing images from the East and West, and I made comments that I later thought were silly if not quite insulting to him. This was all the more galling to me when I real-ized that the doctor too had sought approval during my visit.

Marge—as I continued to call her—had a ten-year-old brother, an impish, fleeting presence in the house, called Gautam; he was present only for a part of that first evening, after which he disappeared into his room, from which we heard the dim but distinct thumping from his own brand of music. Cathy was a devout Christian; therefore to compensate for the large black wooden statue of the sitting Buddha in the living room there were many images of Jesus in the house, including a reproduction of the Last Supper that hung prominently on a wall in the dining room. In time I would become aware of the religious tension that existed between the couple. Gautam's other name was George.

"Do you like my family?" Marge asked.

"Very much," I replied.

It was late the following evening, the summer sun was on the horizon across the flat landscape, and we were out on a walk in the neighbourhood, hand in hand. My answer was the one she expected, of course, and she looked happy and contented. And it pleased me to see her thus; I felt I had achieved that. It was a balmy evening with just a trace of coolness blowing in with the dark. The silent soft-lighted bungalows on either side of the street, set amidst their broad, rich lawns perforated by the occasional flower bed, composed a picture of sublime beauty and perfection. Marge hopped around naming flowers for me, and some varieties of maple. A few walkers with dogs passed us, then a couple of cyclists, an adult and a child; a lawn mower sputtered off somewhere, and we skipped past a couple of sprinklers. The whiff from a barbecue at the back of a house added surprise to the odour of earth and grass. I was moved enough to tell her I could easily live in a place such as this, be part of this serene suburban existence and raise a family. She squeezed my hand.

"And my father?" she asked. "What do you think of him?"

"He's a truly wonderful guy," I replied. "Not my idea of a jazz musician and poet, though . . ."

One of the poems he had read was called "Red River Buddha"—an evocation of India in Manitoba that was far in spirit from the poets I studied and admired. I had quibbles about it, yet it was memorable.

"What do you know of jazz anyway," she said.

"Nothing. And your mother is nice too."

We stopped to turn back; we looked at each other and smiled shyly. Spontaneously we gathered each other in a deep embrace, then walked back together holding hands, with the unspoken knowledge that we truly belonged together and would spend our lives as one. When we left, it was with the understanding that I could now be considered a part of the family. Marge had told her parents what I said during the walk. ("You know what he told me on our walk? You want to know? He said that he could live in a place like this and bring up a family of his own!") Cathy was thrilled and gave me a warm, tearful hug. Dr. Padmanabh said, "Hear, hear!" And I prayed, to whatever entity that looked after me, to keep me on course.

<(··)>

The following spring, Marge and I got married in a chapel in Cambridge. It was a small ceremony, performed by a female Lutheran minister, famously one of the first in the country, and attended by a handful of our friends and acquaintances. My friends Russell, Bob, and Dick were present, the former acting as best man, the latter two having travelled long distances to be with me. Following the ceremony, they threw us a party at the local Howard Johnson, where we spent our first married night. The contrast of my nuptials to the village weddings of my childhood—colourful, noisy, and very public—couldn't have been greater. But I was now a private person. The vows we took we had composed ourselves. We gave the Padmanabhs the happy news after the event, thus avoiding a potential conflict with Cathy over the choice of church and ceremony. My father received the news by post, along with a photograph of myself with my bride, and he duly returned a note of congratulation, as did Mansoor. Marge and I agreed to a family reception in Winnipeg in the summer, and this was more of a celebratory occasion than the one in Cambridge, though not out of control. The Padmanabhs knew many people. Marge looked stunning in a red sari, this being the very first time that she wore one. Her grandparents from Iowa were present. The doctor read a moving poem to his daughter, in which he described her ragtag childhood camel, who had eventually come to life and carried her away. The oblique, humorous reference to her husband did not pass unnoticed.

When I finished my doctorate, I was fortunate in a job-scarce climate to find a teaching position at Prince Albert College in Burnaby, British Columbia. The fact that the English department of the college was run essentially by two counterculture radicals of the sixties worked in my favour, and it appeared that it was more my knowledge of Indian culture and mysticism than of Keats, Shelley, and Donne that had secured me the position. Here in an idyllic green suburb next to the ocean I became a beloved teacher of young people. I changed my name to Krishna Fazal, and I became the father of a boy, whom we named Julian. My happiness was complete.

32

British Columbia. 1980s.

My joy, my home.

I was determined to be happy. If there was the slightest shadow cast upon our home, it was this: that I would have liked to have fathered a brood, but we could have just this one child. He was the king of our world upon whom we doted; every moment of our lives was captive to our enormous devotion for him, this beautiful child-god, our offspring.

Marge had stayed home to care for Julian; on occasions when she had to be away by herself, he would accompany me to my office, and even to my classes, where he sat patiently at the back, his hands in his lap, staring with wide expressionless eyes at his father, and seemingly blind to the adoring eyes of the female students. In my small college department he was regarded as almost a member, and the library had assigned a special corner to him. Once, when he was still little, during a long afternoon seminar that seemed interminable even to me, he suddenly burst into tears. "Am I that bad today?" I asked the class with typical professorial humour. I knew the answer of course, which they all confirmed with something like, "Well, Professor, you haven't been all there!" I had had a quarrel with Marge that morning, which was why I was so distracted, had fumbled at reconciling greatness in art with bigotry—always a tricky subject when you judge the past by the standards of the present. It was when I uttered something like, "Were it not for Shakespeare we would not forgive Eliot," which did not sound quite right, that my little angel finally broke into tears of protest. And yet he had managed to save the day.

Our squabbles could be defused simply by referring to "him," the one irreducible between us. They were lovers' quarrels still, painful and debilitating and knotted up in egos, but there was this magician who watched over us, the child Julian. And so: "You want to hear what he did today?" Or, with the royal pronoun, "We had a tantrum today." "Yeah? What happened? Is he all right?" "Of course he's all right. Listen . . ." Without even noticing, we would be free of our misery and back in love.

I could go on and on, the unstoppable parent.

Fatherhood had rendered me a new man, infused in me an exuberant sense of purpose, conquered my shyness. I would stop on the sidewalks to admire a baby or pet a dog; quarrel with people and huff and puff over the rights and safety of my child; tour the neighbourhood in a Halloween costume. I even volunteered to be the Santa Claus at Julian's kindergarten. Add to all that a growing perversion, an uncontrollable tic: the habit of singing to my son—in the car, while walking together, when putting him to bed. How to explain this silly joyfulness? Only as that. I had not sung much as a child, except for Master-ji, who would tell me that I had a good voice. Singing was all around me as a child. Now from this child-crazy father lines and melodies would come pouring out, some of which I had not even known I had in me. Old English nursery rhymes, where would I have learned them? *A farmer went trotting upon his grey mare, bumpety-bumpety-bump*; half-remembered popular songs in English and Hindi and my mother's lullabies; I would recite Blake ("Tiger Tiger") and Eliot ("Macavity: The Mystery Cat") to this gifted child who was surely on his way to great things; but to my astonishment when I unthinkingly recited to Julian a few simple ditties of Pir Bawa, the boy began to sing them with unswaying vigour.

Anand anand kariyo rikhisaro . . . be happy, great souls, you have the guru. A lilting, happy melody that he could sing in a tremulous childish tone with a wonderful and sweet innocence to charm anyone in the vicinity. The ginans of my childhood, the happy ones at least, had become my son's nursery rhymes. Did this make me nervous, my darling child echoing the songs of Pirbaag? Sometimes. But I could take comfort in the fact that their words could not possibly mean anything to him; and of course they had lost their meaning for me. How far were we from ancient Pirbaag, what harm could they do in this unfettered, sunny existence . . .

the green mountains on one side of us, the blue sea on the other, the winding grey ribbon of road ahead, and that child's vibrato curling up from his throne at the back.

I never revealed to my own father the presence of this new fount of happiness in my life, his only grandson. I had considered a few times going back to Pirbaag to visit him. Marge was keen to come along and bring our son, and her parents encouraged us. It seemed so right. But every time, beyond the first suggestion of a brief return home, my legs would turn to jelly, my palms would sweat. I couldn't make myself go. I was jealous of my happiness; I was afraid for it. For even in the song lines that could go melodically and effortlessly through my head like a tape through a recorder, there were the rare but terrifying moments when I could sense their darker meanings—which I had thought were dead—reemerge, and Bapu-ji's message revive: I was living an illusion; Maya the wily sorceress of the material world had bewitched me; I had no right to be happy. But I had a right to my happiness, and I was determined to secure it. And I would not give my father my son even to contemplate as part of his pessimistic God-hood.

Was I afraid my son would grow up to reject me and the world I had given him—to turn towards his grandfather, return to those ancient roots?

I stopped writing to my father.

If Bapu-ji had been exiled to the farthest reach of my consciousness in this new world, the Padmanabhs were frequent visitors. I gradually began to appreciate the doctor's brand of the confessional poetry of wintry exile, in which elephants stomped unhappily on icy grounds and giraffes climbed ladders and Rama set off on his exile to the northern lands. He belonged to a growing literary movement in a new, multicultural Canada, and often I was invited to readings of poetry that contrasted images of the tropics with those of the winter to illustrate the clash of sensibilities. As an academic I was requested to bring legitimacy to this fringe-ish genre, and I obliged by interesting my students in it, organizing readings in my college, and publishing a couple of academic papers, albeit in small journals. I had come to a young country excited by its new identity, a condition which suited my own new existence very well.

The more intriguing aspect of the doctor's visits to us in Vancouver was when he set off on a Saturday afternoon with his saxophone case, wearing his typical light grey suit. There was a somewhat seedy-looking pub at a strip mall called Sammy's Café on Kingsway, owned by a fellow Indian, where he and a few old friends met and played to a very modest mixed crowd as a prelude to the main fixture later that evening. For this appearance the doctor would have neatly slicked his hair and worn a garish tie, this being his concession to show business. Thus transformed, he was Doctor Paddy the saxophone player. There would be his tiny flickering smile when he played; and when time came for his solo, I liked to imagine he was more absorbed in the piece than he could ever be in his Buddhist meditations.

We were more friends than in-laws. We spoke in English usually, but alone by ourselves, the two of us often broke off into Hindi. His family was from Banaras and had been Buddhists for a few generations, ever since a group of monks had come to the city and converted a locality there. He had been brought up with Hindu practices also, but had relinquished most of them as an adult. He had come as a medical intern to Iowa City, and there met Cathy—who, as the family joke went, had initially taken him for a Native Indian.

Late one afternoon I picked him up from his session at Sammy's, and the two of us emerged onto a wet pavement, for it had rained. We had had a couple of drinks with a snack earlier and were deep in conversation as we headed for the car. It was a few weeks after Indira Gandhi's assassination by her bodyguards, in 1984. Mrs. Gandhi had not been popular, especially after her emergency measures of a few years before; still, the murder was ghastly news. More ghastly were the reports of the bloodbath brought upon the Sikhs of Delhi as a consequence. Our homeland was far away but its news still had an effect upon our thoughts and feelings, if not so much on our lives. Such were the ancient animosities there, and in Sri Lanka, and in Pakistan, that I was only too happy to be away from all that. I asked my father-in-law what was the point of the wistful elephant-and-ice poetry if the elephant had turned mad in the meantime.

Arguing strongly about this—he called me naive—we passed an old church, a dirty-yellow brick fortress with a square crenellated tower; the board outside indicated a Korean denomination. Suddenly our attention was caught. From far inside the building came what sounded like the strains of a very untrained chorus. But the high notes and the unusual melody were strangely arresting so that, unconsciously, we had paused to listen.

"Strange singing," I observed.

"Doesn't it sound like what you sing sometimes?" Paddy asked.

He could have been joking, it was his turn to pick up our banter where we had last left off. But my sense of humour had vanished.

"No—really?" I quickly replied. But I wasn't so sure.

"Maybe we should inquire?"

"No, let's go," I told him. "I don't feel so good."

The doctor told me I should not have had that last beer and drove me home.

One used to hear stories of how an elephant never forgets, how a female cobra could cross the ocean to seek you out and wreak her revenge . . .

Was that a mere coincidence of sound and circumstance I had discerned outside the church? This was not unheard-of, surely. Two alien chants sounding alike.

Or was that my father reaching out yet again; was this Pirbaag's ancient magic working on me . . .

The following days I was taunted by a melody playing at the very back reaches of my head; not even a real melody, but a fleeting image or shadow of it, the mere threat of it. I could not suppress it.

The next Saturday, my in-laws back in Winnipeg, I was possessed by a burning temptation, almost gave in to it. Came afternoon, I picked up my car keys: perhaps I should walk past that church again, and listen; or even go inside and have a look, satisfy my curiosity: who were the singers? Presumably they gathered there every Saturday. They could not be . . . But suppose they were? I put the keys back. And the following Saturday the feeling returned, this tormenting serpent. I fought it off, only because had those singers been my people, I would have had to face my father, whose photo would surely have been there in a place of prominence.

My *former* people, I reminded myself, for I did not want or need them again. I had left them already.

"What's wrong with you these days?" Marge asked.

"Oh?"

My head on her lap, her hand through my hair; Julian playing nearby, though he would soon demand attention. My favourite scene at home, this, a faint odour of her warm womanhood wafting through her night-dress. We could have had many children. Initially she had wanted only this one child; finally, when she came around and desired a companion for Julian, a series of miscarriages destroyed our plans.

This was a pity, for motherhood became her, and she enjoyed looking after our home. Like other women in the area, she had postponed her career. I would sometimes muse about this, for I knew her to have been a brilliant science student. But family and home were all for now. Over the years she had softened, lost some of the snappiness that had so provoked me once. But if she was no longer the beautiful enigma who had bewitched me before, she was now the woman who tenderly cared about me, even loved me. Physically she had grown a little plumper (her Indian genes, she called this) and had cut her hair short, but she was still pretty, and her face had acquired a radiance that could only reflect her condition, make me proud that I was a decent father and husband.

"You've been distracted—something's been bothering you and you're not telling me."

"It's nothing."

She was not meant to accept this, of course, and I waited.

"Nothing?—like what?"

A ruffle through the hair, and I confessed.

"Just that I remembered my father."

A long intake of breath. Then: "Why don't you write to tell him that? If you don't write, perhaps I will."

"Please. In my own time."

She had accepted this before, and she accepted it now.

She had not wanted me complicated, and I had presented her with a simplified, new me; I did not even have any pictures from home, except that one of my mother. So she did not know what I had shrunk from, and that my father was not a normal person, he was a god, a role that I was sup-posed to take over. A fully Indian girl might have guessed, from whatever little I had revealed about myself; Paddy, I think, had an idea. My past, after all, reflected the hoariness and complicatedness of India.

"All right," she said.

With another ruffle through my hair, she withdrew her hand. And I wondered for the first time whether she understood more than she let on. If she did, I knew that she would still prefer me uncomplicated. She too had kept secrets from me. Teenage episodes I had only caught hints of, from her mother's mouth. Details of those wild years as an activist, from which she had sought out the safe haven of our relationship. It was what counted. We had a home and a child, and now we were no longer young.

It began to seem gradually over the days that I had simply conjured up my spectre from that unusual chanting outside the church and frightened myself like a child. With that observation, I was back on track, the serpent from across the seas vanquished.

Time passed. Julian went to grade school. From a stocky toddler with rubber cheeks he had grown into a tall boy with a fair complexion and brown eyes and hair. The facial lines were finer, ending in a tipped chin that was his mother's. The ears were a bit long, a reminder of my father that I had to live with; the hair was curly, surprisingly unlike that of anyone we knew in our families, and could not be parted. He played soccer, did not take to cricket. He played piano, did not take to tabla and spurned the sitar, and wished to play the sax one day like his grandfather. He liked to read and had his own bookshelf.

He could make you laugh. On the way home from school, holding hands:

—*Dad, what would you like to become?*

—*Become? I am a dad already, and a professor . . .*

—*But when you grow up!*

—*Granddad, perhaps? And you? What would you like to be?*

—*I would like to be a dad and a politician.*

—*A politician, Julian?*

—*I don't like to work hard, Dad.*

—*Well . . .*

—*Maybe I'll be a teacher too. I'll race you home!*

—*All right!*

Everything was done for our Julian, as it was for his friends in the neighbourhood; no doubt he would have grown up spoilt, but—we argued—our values and those of our neighbours were sure to keep a check on him. We would hold earnest discussions about him, plan his life in detail: what school—the farther private or the neighbourhood public; what second and third language; what university, ultimately? Everything had to be right. It was pure idolatry, this devoted care for a child, however reasoned and cautious. Punishment was as rare as it was painful. I recall every reprimand I gave him; I recall my own pain when I yelled at him and slapped him once above the wrist, and I would cut off my hand now to take that moment back.

Exaggeration, yes, but true in its way.

33

And the sorrow; the end of the illusion.

Saturday morning. It was junior league soccer at Forest Hill Park, Scotland were to play Brazil today. We dropped Julian off and rushed to the variety store for a water bottle, guilty and quarrelsome because had we brought it with us we would not miss the vital start of the game and be the only ones absent among the cheering parents. Raucous encouragement and coaching from parents, with a ready drink for the champion to replenish his liquids and salts, made all the difference to his performance.

"Couldn't you have gone yourself and let me stay—"

"Well, I thought if I waited in the car, you would run inside and get the water—what would you have looked like—no water for the child."

"I would have cheered, at least. Taken him to the fountain."

"You always—"

Not the best start to the day, then. And she was right, I should have let her go with Julian. But she could have insisted. Now the Saturday traffic snared us; looking for parking we went around in circles. We returned with a pack of the best bottled drink but too late, the forty-minute game was over. Blue-shirted Scotland were already emerging from the park, cheerful and flushed with exhaustion. And there stood Julian on the other side of the street, the anxiety on his face melting into a smile, and he waved happily at us. Scotland had beaten Brazil, a rare event anywhere. I slowed down at a hydrant, he started running towards us; didn't see the other car that we both saw as he crossed, and he went flying, our boy, our happiness.

⤜⤙⇌⤚⤛

Nothing you've imagined about your worst fear comes close. In the first place you don't believe it, for weeks on end, most of the time; you'll wake up from the nightmare, something tells you, nothing can be so bad. It is not meant to happen, it hasn't. Life is a happy, positive occurrence, a spontaneous and joyful assertion of "I Am!" released from the primal slime. This . . . this death . . . is death, is regress, is not natural. There is nothing to say to your partner in grief; a brooding choking silence now sits on your heart. You can't eat together. You will not be touched. You sleep in the same bed; you listen in the night to the sounds of her grief that you cannot, dare not try to comfort. It's hers, just as you have yours. She needs it; you need yours. What's left in you to give? You so much want to be alone in your sorrow, to be consumed by it until you are one with it and no more. This is not your world any more.

Once a grieving woman came to the Buddha carrying a bundle in her arms.

"How can I help you, Mother? Why do you weep?"

She laid her burden at his feet, a dead child.

"You are the holiest of holy, Gautama, you know the secret of life itself. Make him live again. Only you can do it, Lord . . . and I will serve you the rest of my life!"

"There is one remedy," the compassionate Buddha said, placing his ample hand on her head. "But I need a certain oil. It is not easy to obtain."

"I will search heaven and earth to find it, Lord!"

"Then go and look for the people in this world who have not yet encountered grief. From each of them beg a mustard seed. When you have collected enough such seeds, bring them to me, and I will prepare the oil to bring back your child."

She understood, bowed her head.

"Now go cremate your child and your grief."

.　.　.

And that song line that you felt only as a distant shadow on the mind, a fleeting impression you turned away from—it sounds loud and clear. *Haré fuliya sohi karamave . . .* and the flower too withers; O mind, you fool, you deluded butterfly . . .

A funeral ginan, a dirge of sorts. How could your elders, your father, teach you this—this pessimism, this assertion of grief as a remedy to grief?

But grief there is, and you must learn to live with it. Look at the bigger picture, look at the world around you. You are not alone. The "I Am!" of life is not a boast but a struggle to survive.

Finally you begin to talk to each other, try to pick up the pieces of your life together.

"Would you like an egg this morning?"

"Yes . . . I would love that actually. Scrambled, perhaps."

"Or you could make your Indian omelette . . ."

"Yes, I'll do that!"

The sound of a mother and child outside the window . . . you pretend not to notice, but you listen: there are two children actually, with the mother or nanny. And you think, If only she hadn't been so hotheaded; a brood would have glued us together . . . and perhaps she reads your mind as your eyes meet.

And thou—who tell'st me to forget, Thy looks are wan, thine eyes are wet.

This new vacuum in your life; how will you fill it?

You go out, you meet friends. The Padmanabhs come and go. What can they do for you; what can anybody do. Gautam-George flies in for a day to comfort his sister; missed the funeral. He is married in suburban Toronto with *three* children. In this day and age. Well, better three than zero with memories. Try as you might, your home is like a lovely garden on which a freezing heartless wind swept down one day; now there is only this barrenness to take in. You make efforts to revive, but each time your heart pulls you back into its dark depth.

One day you come home to a note on the dining table, placed with consideration under your coffee mug: "I have gone away." Just that. We had a life together, we had love and friendship and a child, we had some great times; but now there's nothing but pain and I have gone away. Hug and kiss also understood. We did love each other, with our own brand of passion. We laughed. But that last long cry killed us.

I had been punished for my arrogance; shown up. Fool, you thought you knew better. This was what God said to his favourite Azazel—and sent him straight to hell and damnation, because he had said no to the command, to the role He had envisioned for him. And the demon Ravana had his island-fortress Lanka set ablaze by a band of monkeys. Archangel and demon, they defied and tempted—and angered—their God. Their worlds came tumbling down. Azazel and his books; Ravana's worldly power and glory. And I—all my happiness founded on my sense of myself in a larger world, and my love for a woman, and finally our devotion to our child. How flimsy a construct, this happiness, how vain; how easily it tumbled down. Hadn't I always been taught, all is illusion, all will come to naught?

It was as if I had been allowed to run with my liberty and my own private happiness, all the while a trap having been laid for me on the road ahead to teach me just this lesson that the gurus could then preach in their sermons. I had nothing but contempt for myself, for my naivety and my illusions. What perfect, terrible karmic symmetry I had called upon myself. In my desperation to escape my father I had become my father, each of us clinging jealously to his child; just that should have warned me: tempt not the gods. What deity of irony or mischief could have restrained himself from gleefully hurling at me my father's fate with a vengeance?

34

British Columbia.

Years pass, a life detached.

Alone again, and lonely, after so many years; a deafening silence, my interminable evenings, the aftermath of an explosion; absolutely no one in the world to call upon.

The Padmanabhs had abandoned me. The few perfunctory telephone conversations I had with them after Marge's departure were indication enough. There was nothing to say, no relationship to keep. I would not have expected this of Paddy. But grief has its own strange ways with people.

Neighbours knew well enough to leave me alone; I needed no pity and no reminders of what had been; and I presumed they needed no token of tragedy on their doorstep. It was suggested at work that I move and make a new start, find a job elsewhere. I ignored it. I would overcome.

Do I believe in miracles? No, but . . . But what? This, that a number of random-seeming events can connect themselves into a sequence that leads you to a remarkable outcome. A miracle? Perhaps only miraculous. The sequence I have in mind started long ago in Worcester, Mass., I think. And it's brought me here, where I write.

One listless, drizzly Saturday I drove down Kingsway, parked my car, and ambled towards Sammy's Café, hoping perhaps on the off chance to see

Paddy performing with his band. The hope of desperation; how close we had become, Paddy and I, the two in-laws. I would look forward to each visit by him with Cathy. By ourselves together, all the way to and from Sammy's, we would be passionately discussing poetry, religion, politics, and India the homeland. We had never been angry with each other, and our disagreements seemed ultimately to have been rather superficial. To my surprise now, the dingy Sammy's had metamorphosed into a cheerful, brightly lit, Bollywood-postered Sammy's Paan and Vegetarian Thali, where they also rented videos, and where I had a meal. Walking back to the car, I passed the Korean church, sheathed in a misty darkness, where a few years before Paddy and I had stopped to listen to an odd-sounding chorus emanating from inside. Perhaps it was this distant memory which had brought me here. It had nagged for a time, then I had pushed it back like so much else. No sound came from the church at this moment, but there were two young Indian men chatting against the pipe fence next to the sidewalk; seeing me hesitate, they pointed to the stone-paved walkway leading off in the dark to the side of the church. I followed it, came to an entrance lit by a naked low-wattage bulb overhead. The street was behind me some distance away, all was quiet here. The heavy door slowly gave to my push, and I stepped inside; a dim stone staircase led from the tiny hallway down to an airy basement, from which there seemed to echo the faint sounds of people. Still uncertain of myself, I started walking down, when suddenly there came the opening salvo of a song or hymn, which then abruptly stopped; it sounded familiar. I held on firmly to the banister and steadied my pace in an effort to stay calm. I had committed myself to my curiosity, there was no going back. The singing resumed in a few moments, accompanied this time by a chorus. And I knew that it was definitely a ginan, song of my childhood, song of the Pir.

The basement was a large cavernous space, one side of it partitioned into two long adjoining rooms with panelled frosted-glass walls; one room had its door ajar, through which escaped a wedge of light and the sound of singing. I went towards it, slowly pulled open the door. The devotees were seated cross-legged in rows on the carpeted floor. All eyes turned briefly to size me up, as I made my way to the back of the last row and sat down by myself. When I looked up to face the front, my father was staring down at me from a large portrait stood up on a table. He looked much the same as he did when I last saw him, I noticed, and about the same age as I was now.

An upsurge of feeling came over me. But I held my composure; I knew he could not help me. I had chosen my life and its consequences.

After the singing, everybody stood up and queued to take the holy water of the Ganges, as it was deemed, and the prasad, the familiar sweet sooji halwa. Then they milled around.

They were modest people, mostly, holding modest jobs of various kinds. I introduced myself as Krishna Fazal, a local professor, which raised looks of approval. Their curiosity extended to making sure I was a devotee and not some intruder or spy; in that they were satisfied, for I knew the right words. How trusting they were, how easy it was to fit right in with them. They seemed the same to me as I had known them, it was I who had ineradicably altered, changed my colour. With this uneasy thought I turned to depart, when a vaguely familiar face caught my eye from a distance. The man hurried forward past a number of people to greet me. By now I had recalled him. He wore checkered pants as before, but looked more suave and composed; and of course, older. The man from Worcester, the man with the bag of apples—the fertility apples—which I had blessed a long time ago.

"Namasté, Karsan-ji," he said, speaking softly. "I am Dervesh, do you remember me? How are you?" He took my hand and kissed it.

"I am well, Dervesh-ji," I said, quickly withdrawing my hand, and asked politely about him and his family. They were well, he said, his face lighting up. He had three children, a boy and two girls. His wife was somewhere in the room—he cast an eye around and pointed to a group of women chatting together.

"You gave me my first child, Karsan-ji. You blessed our womb and our home. When I was in Pirbaag, I told Saheb about this, and he was proud. Proud, Karsan-ji," he said with emotion.

Did he know of my defection?

"And your first child—boy or girl?" I asked.

"My son, whom we named Karsan in your honour. He is in Atlanta. He has a job."

I had no choice but to tell him where I taught, and give him my work phone number. He wanted to tell me about his visit to Pirbaag, and about the Saheb, but I hurried out before I compromised myself further.

I never went back to that basement. But one more link had been added to a sequence, and the miracle, or miraculous, would be apparent later.

. . .

I recovered from my loss, slowly and partially; how could I look at a boy, any age, and not recall my own Julian. The possibilities. The innocence. The joy. Why should that be extinguished and cynical old age, failed adulthood, remain. An age-old question, a cliché, I know; but tell that to the sufferer. The key to survival now was a life of unattachment; as Gautama the Buddha had taught, after he saw a world full of suffering; as my father the Saheb of Pirbaag had always taught. And so many others. They were right. And so I closed my life to the possibility of relationships, and refused an offer of marriage. I kept busy with college administration; and I volunteered for local charities. More and more I lent my name to multicultural causes. Occasionally I dabbled with writing poetry and translating from my native Gujarati. In the summers I volunteered as an umpire and coach for local cricket teams and these were some of my happiest moments.

One spring I went to Winnipeg for a conference. Early the morning after my arrival, as I sat in the hotel restaurant with my breakfast, perusing my program, Paddy walked in the door looking for me. The same little smile flickering on his lips, though he seemed slighter, and the age lines on the face had cut deeper. I stood up and we embraced warmly. I told him I would have called, and he nodded.

"How are you coping?" he asked after a while, concern on his face.

"Fine, fine . . ."

"You didn't remarry or . . . ?"

I shook my head, surprised at the question. But there was a look in that face as he averted it, and so I asked,

"How is Marge? Do you hear from her?"

"We call," he said slowly. "She's well."

"And?"

"She lives on one of the islands now," he added, then blurted out, "She's remarried. He's an old friend—an American."

Past the initial shock, more acute because she lived so close to Vancouver, I knew that I was pleased for her. It was the right thing she had done for herself, find a companion to help her heal. I wondered who he was. Not Steve, surely? But there had been others we had not spoken of. In our grief we were useless for each other; and it was now useless to agonize over why this had been so, though I could hardly control the rush of thoughts that came to torment me. Had our love been so shallow? Had I been only a shelter for her to escape to, after her disappointments? Was the child our only real cement? I did not ask Paddy if she had any children. I imagined that he and Cathy must visit her sometimes; they would pass through Vancouver, where we had spent so many happy times together as a family. And I guessed, sitting there, watching me, he was reading my thoughts; he reached out for my hand and pressed it.

"Life must go on."

"Yes, it must," I said, because there was nothing else to say.

"And you? You've found someone?" he asked with concern.

"No, but I have survived. And how is Cathy?"

He nodded sagely. "Well. A bit more into the religious stuff, though . . . goes away on faith trips . . ."

We met once again before I left, and he promised to come visit me. I did not think he would. And I did not see Cathy.

35

British Columbia. February 2002.
The call of Pirbaag.
One day after a lecture that had ended at noon, as I was strolling over to the cafeteria for lunch, accompanied by a student, the department secretary came running after me waving an envelope. "Professor—a letter!" she panted. "Is it urgent?" I asked in surprise, taking it from her. Secretaries were more apt to bully you, not run outside after you on their high heels with your mail. "It is from India," she gasped. I had not received any mail from India at my department, and she must have concluded—or hoped, as her look seemed to indicate—that this one was something special. We went back a long way at the college. I smiled my thanks, then stared at the handwriting on the front, as familiar as an old photograph.

And so the miracle-miraculous was complete: he had finally found me, in his hour of need.

It was some time later, when the student had excused herself, that I had the chance to tear open the envelope. I had hardly touched my food.

"My dear son Karsan:

"May this letter find you in the best of health and circumstances. May Pir Bawa bless you.

"My son, until recently I did not know where you were. Some of my letters to you were returned from America, others were probably lost. But in my heart I knew that you were safe and doing well, and I prayed for you constantly. Recently, however, our Dervesh Bhai was on a visit from Canada and told me where you were; and also that at work you were known as Krishna Fazal. A good name, it pays appropriate tribute to our heritage. How is my daughter-in-law? Mira: a beautiful name also.

"My dear Karsan, I was deeply saddened to hear from Dervesh of your son's death. Julian: what does it mean? Something worthy, I have no doubt. It sounds beautiful, a lovely name. He would have been the new gaadi-varas. But we must believe that Julian's purpose in life was fulfilled; a great soul departed having paid its karmic debt. It has found its eternal resting place.

"I am aware that you have been loath to hear from your Bapu. I have dictated my will upon you; I placed an expectation on you that you had no desire to fulfill. I gave no thought to your own feelings and inclinations— at least, so you thought. But as Saheb I believed I knew better, and that I knew my own son, who was in line to a seat that has not lain vacant for seven hundred years.

"I have come to accept your wishes, my son. And since, spiritually, I have always believed I was in touch with you, I also came to accept that you would not write to me. But I am not young any more, and I desire to communicate with you as your father before my time comes. There are some matters that a father has to communicate to his son; there are some matters a Saheb has to tell his successor.

"Fortunately, through Pir Bawa's miracle, Dervesh came to town, bringing news of you, and sadly, also of your tragedy. Some time ago, during a previous visit, he had told me of the miracle you had performed for him.

"My son, I have this one wish of you: that you return to Pirbaag once and let your father set his eyes on you again. Will you come? Let me know. But right now is not a good time to come; we are going through bestial times yet again; demons are on the roam feeding on blood and the screams of the innocent. But here in Haripir and Pirbaag, we will manage, as we have always done; our people can be made to see reason. This madness will soon be over, and I will inform you when it is safe to return.

"Accept best wishes from

"Your father,

"who longs for you."

. . .

I was in tears.

I heard the voice of an old man, who had been my father, whom I had rejected and consciously kept away. I believed I had no choice, but there it was. And now he had come pleading.

I wrote to my father that I too wished dearly for a reunion. I would be able to come in the summer, by which time the violence in Gujarat would surely be over. And I would then be able to stay a few months with him. Meanwhile he should take care of himself.

I sent my best wishes to Mansoor, whom he had not mentioned at all. What could he be up to, now, near middle age? Was he close enough to be of assistance to Bapu-ji, should he need it?

At the last minute, suppressing my qualms, I inserted a short note to Mansoor.

The situation in Gujarat had been worrying since long before Bapu-ji's letter. News of the riots ravaging our state had been all over the Internet in recent months, on the websites of the Indian newspapers and elsewhere. In January a train full of Hindu pilgrims and activists was returning from contentious Ayodhya, where ten years before a fifteenth-century mosque had been destroyed by extremists claiming it to be the birthplace of the god Rama. A compartment of the train, the Sabarmati Express, was set on fire outside the town of Godhra, and some sixty people, including women and children, were trapped inside and burnt to death. Presumably Muslim extremists were responsible for this grisly deed, though no charges had been laid, and there were those who believed that the fire was started inside the compartment. Whatever the case, there followed an orgy of retaliation, a so-called riot, in which masses of extremists and their henchmen went about Muslim areas of Gujarat armed with swords, maces, knives, and petrol bombs, maiming, killing, raping, and burning people. In mixed areas they systematically picked out the Muslim households. In response to the situation, the populist chief minister of Gujarat had famously paraphrased Newton's third law of motion, to every action there is a reaction, thus apparently fuelling the carnage.

Our village of Haripir had been spared such violence in the past, because its shrine of Pirbaag lent it an aura of sanctity, having over the centuries drawn countless souls to its gate and comforted them, without regard to caste or creed; and if that sanctity were not enough, the Sahebs had been ready with words of wisdom and caution whenever conflagration threatened. During the time of India's Partition, my Dada had been the voice of reason, and we had been spared the bloodshed which had afflicted nearby towns. In my father's reign, however, there had been one terrifying day in my childhood when we had come to the brink of bloodshed, and the pushcart vendor Salim Buckle had paid a savage price for the peace that ultimately prevailed. That death had always troubled me, but I could never pick up the nerve to question Bapu-ji about it. It had affected him deeply, for he had been involved in negotiating the devil's bargain that maintained that peace. Still, he had preserved us.

And so I had little cause to doubt my father's certainty that Haripir would be preserved yet again from the madness. Of the inviolability of Pirbaag and its Saheb there was not even a question.

How wrong I was.

Six weeks after writing to my father, this telegram from India: "Bapu-ji dead. Come at once. Mansoor."

36

Postmaster Flat, Shimla.
Communal killings ("riots"); some thoughts on a concept hard to accept.

So troubling, so heartbreaking is this phenomenon we call the "riot" in India that I find myself caught up in a need to understand, to grasp and comprehend the pure hatred for a fellow human being that lies behind the quality of violence that is inflicted on the innocent each time. Perhaps there is no answer. We are too complex as a nation, too raw as a people, etc. But perhaps this madness to try to grasp the ungraspable is an affliction incurred from having lived away so long, in a culture where a rational answer is only a matter of effort. I have become naive, forgotten the skill of blinking at the right moment, letting the unspeakable pass away. Still, this is what I am.

One of the earliest recorded instances of communal violence is reported in the reign of Raja Jayasingh Siddhraj (1094–1143) of Gujarat. An altercation among Parsis, Muslims, and Hindus in the port city of Cambay apparently resulted in the destruction of a mosque; a complaint in the form of a long poem was brought to Gujarat's greatest king, who compensated the Muslims for the mosque.

In 1714, a bloody riot occurred in Ahmedabad during Holi celebrations; the city was under control of the Mogul dynasty of Delhi. There were subsequent riots in 1715, 1716, and 1750. The list goes on, through to the Partition of India, to the butchery in Ahmedabad in 1969 shortly after I left, about which I learned not from my family but from my friend Elias. I wonder if Mr. Hemani the bookseller perished in this last riot, for I never heard from him.

A depressing thought: are we doomed then to these perpetually recurring communal conflagrations we call "riots"?

The reasons given for them are varied: economical; the past atrocities of Muslim armies; manipulation and instigation by the colonizing power, Britain; ditto by cynical Indian politicians; etc. The riots have not been exclusively between Hindus and Muslims, but sometimes have involved Sikhs, Dalits, and Tamils. But how to explain slicing a child's body in two with a sword; inserting a rod up a woman's vagina; removing an eight-month foetus from a mother and killing it before her eyes; electrocuting an entire family inside a room?

Descriptions of the personal violence make the blood curdle, make one wonder what it means to be human after all. That the most ghastly violence imaginable, perpetrated on women and children, could occur in the state of Gandhi makes one wonder too how aberrant was the Mahatma; was he real, after all?

The "riot" is a euphemism for intercommunal murder; it allows the perpetrators to go free, for rioters need not be charged, murderers must. And so they are back again during the next conflict with their swords and their knives to feed once more on the blood of the innocents.

37

Postmaster Flat, Shimla.
Happily, he is not armed.

Is this the same brother who once quarrelled with me about wanting his turn to clean Rupa Devi's temple? Look at him now, praying to Allah, backside in the air, hands to his ears the way he would put them there to tease me and make me laugh and chase him—but now it is his seriousness behind the posture, the ritual, that teases and mocks me. We never prayed like that; we were never taught this Arabic prayer, this namaz; it was not our custom, it was not in our language.

But why does this abstract, geometric form of worship—this ballet on the floor—repel me so? Is it because it also is a part of me (Pir Bawa was a Muslim, wasn't he), and I fear it, fear that it will swallow me up, that I will be pushed and fall irrevocably on that other side, become them, become it—a Muslim—when Bapu-ji had always told me that our path was the middle one, between the two? Our path was spiritual; outward forms of prayers and rituals didn't matter. (Though we had a few of our own, they were only ceremony and tradition, reminders of our fraternity.) It always troubled me, this ideal of Pirbaag; it made us so different from the rest of the world, which required clean spiritual boundaries. But if you chose one or the other, you were compelled to lose something of yourself, let it go—those were the rules.

—*But we should choose, nai, Bapu-ji—between Hindu and Muslim? Everybody chooses.*

—*There's nothing to choose, Karsan, we have been shown our path, in which there is neither Hindu nor Muslim, nor Christian nor Sikh, just the One. Brahman, the Absolute. Ishvar. Allah. God.*

And Ogun, Adonai, Mungu, I know. Except that, dear Bapu-ji, we will not be left alone until we choose; the choice will be made for us—as it was, recently, wasn't it, Bapu-ji. A choice was made for us and we paid a price. You paid with your life. Now I sit here amidst the mountains recalling what I am and, if I can, what we were; and this fellow here who was our Mansoor is an angry, arrogant stranger called Omar, and denies you.

At least he did not bring a weapon; a belt of explosives.

Unless they are hidden somewhere.

⪡⟡⟢⪢

It was in Ahmedabad three months ago, as I was sitting by myself at the café of the graves, at the place that I had always preferred, beside the tiny grave of a child, that I saw Mansoor for the first time in thirty years.

I had already been to Pirbaag and seen its devastation, and had come to the city at the suggestion of Neeta Kapur after the remarkable coincidence of our meeting on the road outside the shrine. I had put up in a hotel in teeming Teen Darwaja, an area I had got to know well during my excursions there as a teenager. Right across from the three-storey Hotel Azure, next to an overly lit shop with a sleek mannequin in shades and a business suit standing outside its door, stood the desultory, boarded-up building that once was the Daya Punja Library, my window into the world. On the steps of this library George Elias and I had sat down with an over-sized, glossy-paged guide to American universities and picked the one that would suit me best. The area was at the edge of the old city, which had been savagely afflicted by the recent violence, and it was where I expected to find Mansoor. Neeta had dropped me off here with some qualms. Take care, she said, you can still smell the tension that's in the air. Her own suburban Ahmedabad was safely across the river, with its coffee bars and shopping strips. In my nostalgic meanderings I had already been to the site of the chemist shop which had belonged to Elias's family and saw that the building had been demolished, and in its place stood a small shopping complex; coincidentally or not, there was a chemist shop in it, but it was not owned by Jews. Across the street was the site of Mr. Hemani's used-book store; it was now occupied by a modern bookstore.

I had no idea what to do with Pirbaag. I could surrender it to the authorities, who would seal it off, and it would join the ranks of the ruins of bygone eras, an overgrown home to snakes, scorpions, and monkeys. But there were those people to consider for whom Pirbaag still meant something; among them, those from Haripir were already busy cleaning the shrine and restoring it. There were many such devotees in various other places, as I well knew. And there was Neeta who, in spite of her class and education, had drawn comfort from it; who had said, You can't abandon your heritage so easily. When I argued, she told me in a pert manner that I had no right. She spoke for them all now, who still found comfort in Pirbaag, and we had become familiar enough for her to make her point forcefully. Then what do you suggest, I asked in exasperation, to which she said nothing but gave me an odd, quizzical look. I did not even want to think about the implication.

As I sat in the chai shop now, beside the olive green grave of a child with a red flower on top, I noticed a fair-featured middle-aged man with a trim black beard sitting a few tables away: his hair thick and short, a cup of tea before him, next to a blue pamphlet. He wore a green and maroon vest open in front, in the pocket of which, I guessed, was a cellphone. He had been throwing me covert looks, a thin private smile flickering on his face, and it had just occurred to me that he must have passed me outside and followed me in. A wave of irritation hit me—here was another smooth customer hoping to touch an unwary visitor from abroad for a few hundred rupees—an immoderate reaction on my part perhaps—when I realized with a shock that I was staring straight at my brother. I had of course been expecting to run into him, having left a message for him at Pirbaag that I would be staying in Ahmedabad at Teen Darwaja.

My face had betrayed me, for at that moment he got up and came over. "How are you, Bhai?" he said.

"Mansoor—"

My voice came out hoarse, and there lay an uneasy instant before I stood up and we quickly embraced. He was shorter in stature than I but better proportioned and stronger; a good-looking man now, my brother.

We sat down, and he turned around to order another tea for himself, then faced me again.

"You recognized me."

"Yes—though for a moment there I didn't. You were only a little boy when I last saw you!"

A small-statured, thin-faced imp, and eleven years old, to be precise.

He nodded briefly in response to my inane, though heartfelt smile. "Now you see a man. And you saw what they did to Pirbaag."

The voice hard and clear, so certain of itself.

"Yes, but what happened, Mansoor, why did they attack us?"

"You've been away a long time, Bhai. You have a lot to learn."

"Yes. All right."

What had I expected from him? A welcome. A tender embrace. Some understanding. Not this cold carapace. We remained in awkward silence for some moments, occasionally stealing glances at each other, for it still had to sink in completely that we had finally met after so many years and were sitting across from each other. Physically I could not have changed as much as he had, I thought, but he was still the rebel. It would take some doing to get to know him.

"Well?" I ventured at length.

He met my look, and his face softened a whit as he said, "I have Bapu's ashes with me that I would like to give you. It's for you to decide what to do with them."

"They should be buried in Pirbaag," I told him.

"What's left of it."

He said he lived not far away, behind the great mosque on Gandhi Road, and so we paid and left. Outside the mosque, on the sidewalk, a perfumer had laid out his samples on a cart, in tiny coloured bottles; on the steps a man sat watching the footware placed in his care by the worshippers who had gone inside. We took ours in our hands and entered the vast courtyard with the washing pool in the centre. There were not many people about, it was not prayer time. This was where I had come a few times during my escapades long ago, and watched in bewilderment the people praying, and wondered how to relate to them. In silence we crossed the courtyard to the back gate, and thence went through a crowded shopping district to the run-down area of the Tomb of the Queen. Here, above a store selling modest kitchenware, was where he roomed with an old widow who kept the keys to the tomb, he told me, in case I cared to visit. He gave me water, and it was mostly he who talked.

There remained that edginess in him, and he had a look whenever he paused that made me nervous, as if I was being judged and dare not contradict him. He had become a proper Muslim, he said, and no longer was the half or hidden or confused Muslim of before. They—the Hindus— were out to exterminate the Muslims of India; none of them were to be trusted. Bapu would just not understand this; but Iqbal Uncle had been right to leave the superstitions and impure practices of Pirbaag behind and get away to Pakistan in time. And I was lucky to be living abroad. Did I bring any clothes for him?

"I brought two shirts," I said, taken completely by surprise.

"No jeans?"

"I'm sorry. I was in a desperate hurry."

Shopping had been the furthest thing from my mind; but perhaps I should have paid more thought to my brother. My luggage had been laughably paltry compared to the leviathan cargoes of my fellow passengers.

"And you didn't send anything in a long time. Forgot your little brother, eh—living in all that affluence?"

"But you wouldn't write to me!"

"We didn't know where you were," came the sharp retort. "Bapu tried desperately to find you. I wrote to you too. One of the letters came back, saying, 'Addressee Unknown.' " He announced those two words like a proclamation.

I didn't ask him if in that letter he had written more than his customary two lines to me. He was right, of course, in that I had ultimately escaped into a world of my making. And quietly closed the door behind me. But if he had responded to my pleas for friendship and fraternal love, I could hardly have abandoned him. I had often thought and worried about him. And now again I wanted desperately to reach out to him, but as always he remained insensitive. We met a couple of times more in Ahmedabad, once again in the chai shop and then in a restaurant. What had he been doing these many years? He had been to a college in Baroda, and married in Jamnagar, Ma's hometown, and lived there a few years. He was divorced now. He had travelled, but wouldn't give me the details. He had worked in

Master-ji's print shop in Haripir, but had fallen out with him. He had been a teacher for some time in Godhra. At the mention of this infamous town where the train compartment with all its passengers had been set on fire, I perked up; he eyed my unspoken response and said emphatically, "I taught there."

Before we parted the final time, promising to meet again soon, I asked him, "How did Ma die, Mansoor?"

"You mean to say Bapu didn't tell you?"

"No."

He didn't tell me either. He gave his tight smile and said, "The Saheb wasn't the saint you thought he was."

I asked if he wanted some money. "Yes, if you don't mind," he replied, and I gave him a wad of notes I had cashed that day for this purpose. Perhaps he would buy a pair of jeans from one of the many stores in the area.

I buried the earthen urn containing my father's ashes at Pirbaag, in the area where our ancestors were commemorated. The spot had been tidied, the marble plaques were in place and gleaming—though bearing the scars of damage and perhaps having lost their original arrangement—for which I was grateful. Neeta was with me; she must have known where the urn in my arms had come from but did not ask. I had become rather dependent on her. In my shocked disoriented state, it was convenient to be minded by a woman of means and influence, and an old friend, if I could call her that.

After a week's stay in Ahmedabad, during which I visited Pirbaag several times, still unsure of its fate, I departed for this stay in Shimla which she had arranged for me.

—◄—►—

We have an argument, my brother and I.

M: "Why don't you join me in prayer?"

K: "You go ahead, it's all right."

"Don't you pray? I have not seen you pray. Have you ever prayed?"

(Yes, I have; I once prayed to Pir Bawa for your life to be saved, and the prayer was answered.)

I tell him, "I don't pray formally."

"Do you believe in God?"

No reply. To which the believer's incredulous response: "Do you believe in anything? You must believe in something?"

I look away.

I could tell him that over the weeks I have resolved to remember, construct a shrine of my own out of the ashes of Pirbaag; a bookish shrine of songs and stories. This is my prayer, if you will, this is my fist in the air, my anger, so unlike his; it is my responsibility, my duty to my father and all the people who relied on us as the sufi's representatives and whose stories are intertwined with ours. I say nothing.

Two nights ago there came a rapid knock at the back door. It was not very loud but it was clear and discrete and in that cold dead stillness it could have been heard perhaps half a mile away. Why would Ajay bring tea from the kitchen this late, was my first thought. I hadn't ordered it anyway. Or was it some animal? A ghost? The whisky reverend, again?

"Kaun?" I said softly, ear cocked at the door.

"It's me, Karsan Bhai," came the reply. "Hurry!"

I opened, and Mansoor hustled in. He was wearing a bomber jacket, his arms folded, hands inside the armpits. A small pack on his back.

"Arré, it's cold, what a place you picked to hide."

"What—" I began. What was he doing here?

"I've come to hide—I hope you don't mind."

"You know I am being watched."

"Don't worry."

As a boy, I remembered, he would call and plead when he needed me to play with him; at other times he would play by himself or with his friends, among them the Muslim boys of the Balak Shah shrine. Karsan was there when needed; and Ma said, But you are the older one, you understand.

He sat down at my large, rarely used dining table. I boiled some tea for him. I brought out what little I had in dry food and placed it before him.

"What happened?" I asked him. "Have you left Delhi?"

"They were onto us—" He paused, watched my face, then changed tack and continued quietly, "We had to leave . . . we went our separate ways."

"Look, Mansoor—"

"Omar," he said, reminding me of his new name, and dunked a couple of biscuits into his tea. He looked up defiantly.

I felt a wave of annoyance rising up in me, yet I dared not reveal my feelings. Here we were, two bereaved brothers without a relation in the country, strangers to one another, yet hopelessly entangled with each other. He with his familiarity and antagonism towards me, and his easy dependence on me, and I with my guilty concern and fear for him. I did not believe he cared a whit for me; he assumed he knew me, and what he gave me of his life story was selected only to wound.

"Why don't you come clean," I ventured, not quite sure of myself; perhaps my voice gave me away. "I know you've not done anything dreadful . . . why don't you speak to the police? We'll get you a lawyer."

He opened his mouth, closed it. Then he said in a surprisingly even tone, "They don't want to talk—don't you understand that? They want bodies. The evidence they supply later—a packet of pistachios, a letter in Urdu found on your corpse—there, a manufactured Kashmiri terrorist killed in a so-called encounter!"

I stared at him in shock. What do you say to that? How far off he had gone on his own path. He was in another league altogether. He had been in Godhra, I knew that. And that made me scared for him.

He slept as soundly as a babe that night, the way he always did; like an angel, as Ma would say, standing and watching over him tenderly with a smile, before waking him up on Sundays.

And he is as reckless as ever, though now his attitude borders on arrogance. When Ajay came with a pot of wake-up tea the morning after his arrival, he showed himself and asked for another cup to be brought. At breakfast later in the dining room, Ajay asked me—in full hearing of everyone—if the other sah'b would be joining us. I said no, but now there is always the extra cup on the wake-up tray early in the morning. All I need is for Major Narang to show up and ask questions.

And so at my suggestive silence in response to his question, "Do you believe in anything?" he almost shouts at me:

"Then how can you be Saheb? What will you tell the people when they come to you for guidance? Nothing! You are a false Saheb. You forfeited your status of successor when you abandoned us!"

I do not tell him what he does not apparently know, that I had already in a letter to my father abdicated my successorship to the position of Saheb. Instead, I reply, surprising myself,

"But I am his successor, nevertheless! He gave me the succession and he gave me his bol."

"Bol. Hunh. Now you think of succession, when everything is gone. And what bol? Do you even remember it?"

"Yes, I do."

We glare at each other. Then quietly, defiantly, I pick up pen and paper from my desk and suppressing all thought from my mind unconsciously write down the syllables my father spoke to me, and made me repeat, at the moment of my departure. They come, flowing out of my pen, concrete and mysterious. I repeat the sounds to myself in silence, as my brother watches me from the sofa, incredulous. There, the precious bol of the Sahebs, handed down father to son. I take the piece of paper to the kitchen and burn it in the flame of the gas stove, for the bol must remain a secret; I pick up the ashes and crush them; still holding them in one hand, with the other I open the back door and walk out to the lawn. I throw the ashes out into the wind.

In the distance, the hundreds of pinprick lights of Shimla hug the dark hills; in the farther distance, the faint shapes of the mountains, guardians of our nation; above me, the galaxies and stars, the Milky Way casually shaded in . . .

There, Bapu-ji, I have recalled the bol. Now tell me what you wanted to say.

38

"You did not want to be God, you said," wrote my father.

"But who does? The call descends upon those who are chosen. It is a responsibility, it is not a status. In what manner one is God is not simple or to be ridiculed, Karsan. We are all God, parts of the One, and therefore the same as the One, as all the great mystics before us have said. *Tat tvam asi,* our ancient Upanishads have told us: you are That. The great Persian mystic Mansoor said, *An al haq:* I am the Truth. For this he was killed by the ignorant. You have been taught all this. Now for centuries the Sahebs of Pirbaag have been called upon to exercise that God within them, so they could assist the simple people to face the travails of their daily lives; and also, in order to teach the few among them how to reach beyond the mundane to the higher truth that is the One, Brahman. Not everyone wants to attain this nirvana, Karsan; for some, the daily roti or the relief of a child from disease is blessing enough. Whatever blessing they seek we cannot refuse them.

"The truth of our line is acknowledged in the bol of the Sahebs, passed from father to son, and accompanied always by the symbol of a kiss. This bol was the message whispered by Pir Bawa to his successor Ginanpal, the first Saheb, just before he breathed his last. In its syllables lay hidden the secret of his identity. You will remember that Pir Bawa had escaped from persecution and come to India. Were his identity to be revealed to all, calamity would have befallen us, his followers. The bol has remained secret ever since because the Sahebs saw that the world, and the community of Pirbaag, were not ready for its truth. Events have proved them right. If you, my son, have lost the bol and therefore do not come to read this last testament from your father, then let the secret of Nur Fazal the sufi die with me. Let his spirit be extinguished with mine. Let this be the end of Pirbaag."

"My dear Karsan: I too did not want to be God. (I prefer the more modest term avatar, because there are stages of God-hood; but I will indulge your mockery, my son.)

"I have a clear memory of my father on the empty ground beside the shrine where you used to play cricket, grappling and thrashing about with someone or the other in a bout of wrestling. His arms and legs and back would be covered in sand, while he himself would be in a state of half undress and grunting most unbecomingly. After a few tumbles amidst this mass of legs and arms, he would emerge on top of his opponent, a firm neckhold in place. Pehlwaan Saheb, he was called: Guru Champion. But even then, at the age of five, I knew they only let him win. The opponent, sometimes burlier, stronger than him, could easily have shaken him off.

"How could my father be the Saheb, the avatar of Pir Bawa, I would ask myself. How could this man covered in dirt and stinking sweat have special, spiritual powers?

"But the people knew better. They came in hordes to see him. Every Saturday and Thursday morning he would sit on the pavilion in his white dhoti, waiting for them; and they came, bringing all their troubles with them. Patiently and with good humour, he would hear them out and bless them, and ask them to go and pay homage to Pir Bawa in the mausoleum. They went away with promises of children; peace in their lives; sufficiency in their homes; cures for their diseases.

"Did I want this responsibility? I too wanted to play sports, and dress up as a dandy and visit the cinema, then stand outside and smoke cigarettes with my friends; to be part of the world and its thrills. You are surprised, you never thought of your Bapu in that light. Later, when I became serious about myself, in university I desired to be a scientist. And I'll tell you another secret. There was a certain girl in my college whom I liked; she was good in maths and wanted to be a teacher. I wanted to marry her. But I had been chosen, and I had to bow.

"This is how it happened. You will be surprised to learn that it had to do a little with Gandhi-ji. But the Mahatma was connected with the politics of those times, and these were beginning to affect us in Pirbaag, and so my father went to seek him. I went with him and met your mother. Everything is connected and has a purpose, there are no accidents."

"Why would the avatar of Pir Bawa, to whom multitudes came for advice and blessing, go to see Gandhi-ji? It was not an ordinary time. The independence of the country was near, and its fate was debated with passion everywhere. There were calls for partition and the formation of Pakistan. Rioting had begun in some regions. A certain Professor Ivanow and the collector of Ahmedabad, Mr. Ross, had come to see your Dada and advised him to throw in his lot with Mr. Jinnah of the Muslim League. 'Your Pir Bawa was a Muslim,' they told him; 'hidden in your ginans is the message of Islam.' Your Dada had no intention of throwing in his lot with anybody, Hindu, Muslim, Sikh, or Christian. But he had to reassure those devotees who were confused and doubtful and feared for the future. Agitators from outside would not spare even a small village such as Haripir, their aim only to divide the people and extinguish the flame of tolerance which had burned here for centuries.

"It happened that a certain devotee of Pirbaag was on a visit from Wardha district, where Gandhi-ji had his ashram. He told my father that the great man would be at the ashram in a few days and it would be possible to see him. Right then your Dada decided he would pay a visit to that area, and while there meet the Mahatma. Your uncle Rajpal refused to accompany him, he was very much in Jinnah's thrall, and so it fell upon me to go with my father. Two others came with us from Haripir, one of them Master-ji. The man from Wardha had gone ahead of us to advise his people of the Saheb's visit.

"Your Dada hardly travelled. When he did, it was a big event, the whole town came to see him off. Our journey began with the bus to Ahmedabad. It was crowded as usual, but ample space was made for us to sit in comfort at the back. Bhajans and ginans were sung on the way, while my father sat upright, smiled, occasionally closed his eyes. At every stop the new passengers would first come to touch his feet and receive his blessings. Before we knew it this bliss-filled bus had arrived in the great city.

From Ahmedabad we had to take a train to Poona. This was a long journey during which I had the chance to observe and learn much from my father; it was one of those rare moments when he spoke about his own youth, and about his own father and grandfather. What I learned I will impart to you at a later time. At Poona station we were greeted by a jubilant group of some fifty disciples, with garlands and all; we stayed a few days at the house of a merchant and the atmosphere was festive. From here we then departed by train for Wardha. We were to stay at the house of one Hirji Bhai, but as soon as we arrived we had to leave on a cart for Gandhi-ji's ashram in Sevagram, four miles away, for we were told that the Mahatma saw people briefly after one o'clock in the afternoon, and it was already close to that time.

"When we arrived at the ashram gate, there were two young men sitting outside who pointed casually to a clay pot and invited us to help ourselves to water. We were thirsty and were grateful for the water; when we had had our fill, our host told the two gatekeepers that the Saheb here had come to see Gandhi-ji.

" 'What business do you have with Gandhi-ji?' one of them said sternly. 'He is a busy man. He is still weak from his fasts. He has a cough and a cold. You should not bother him.' They took us for some local poor folk, perhaps, hence their tone. The other one spoke even more severely, 'The whole world wants to see Gandhi-ji; kings and queens come to see him. He has to go to America, to Delhi, to Madras. He has to meet Einstein and the viceroy. He is not well. He blesses you, now go, please.'

"My father was taken aback a little. He glared at these officious youngsters. Then he said, 'I am the Saheb of Pirbaag. I have come to discuss with the Mahatma my people's future.'

"They whispered to each other and to a young woman who had arrived. She hurried away to take this message to Gandhi-ji. She returned after a few minutes and said to us, 'Come.' On the way she added, 'Please don't take long. He will soon rest; and he starts on a journey tomorrow morning.' 'To where?' I asked. 'To Delhi,' she said, 'to see Nehru, Jinnah, and the viceroy. This is not a happy time for him.' Her desperate voice, I recall, rather surprised me. The memory of it doesn't, any more.

"We arrived at one of several cottages; the door was open; inside, where it was refreshingly cool, a small, wrinkled old man was sitting on the floor beside a small writing desk, on which were a bottle of ink and a pile of small sheets of paper. In his fingers, delicate like feathers, he held a pen. I could see that he had been writing letters. Two women were taking their leave of him, a European and a desi. Both wore white saris.

"It was hard to believe that this fragile little frame belonged to the man we had been reading about every day for these many years, for whom we worried and prayed whenever he fasted for some noble cause. Mohandas Gandhi of Porbandar, a bania lawyer and the soul of India. Our nation's fate rested on those frail shoulders. I could see every rib in his body, and perhaps even the beating of his heart. We had heard many stories about him on the way from Wardha; he woke up at four every morning and prayed from the Gita, he walked two miles every day, he worked in the kitchen and cleaned the toilets, and so on.

" 'Ao, béso,' Mahatma-ji said, his voice like the rustle of thin paper, and he paused to catch his breath. When we had sat down, my father across from the old man, and I near the open door so as not to seem intrusive, Gandhi-ji said to my father, mischievously, 'Saheb, *you* come to ask me the future?'

"He had heard of Pirbaag, you see, and the prestige of the Sahebs. Gandhi-ji is supposed to have known everything about every part of India.

"My father replied in equal measure: 'Even the Saheb needs blessings, Mahatma-ji.' And he added, chidingly, 'You big people are now in the process of carving up our land.'

"Gandhi-ji said, 'Saheb, I have said I would give my life to keep this motherland together. But if we do give up a part of it, I can assure you that what will remain will be God's country—but not the God of only the Hindu or only the Musalman or the Sikh or the Issai. For as you well know in your life and practices at Pirbaag, there is only the God. Bhagwan and Allah are the same; Rama and Rehman are the same.'

"Why do I tell you all this in detail, Karsan? Because it made such an impression on your young father. (Even though, when Gandhi-ji asked, 'How is the baba doing?' referring to me by the term for a small boy, I had been a little annoyed.) But Gandhi-ji the great Mahatma had affirmed what your Dada believed and taught. This impressed me considerably and brought me comfort even late in my life. Even now it brings me some hope.

"During this visit I met your mother.

"At Hirji Bhai's house a girl and her mother were visiting from Jamnagar. We had been told that the girl was disturbed, but we had caught only a glimpse of her—out in the yard sorting grains. It seemed that she suffered from fits. Now as we prepared to leave after two days in Wardha, Hirji Bhai begged my father to bless the girl. The family were all standing at the railway platform bidding us goodbye. The girl was brought forward from the back of the crowd, and gently nudged on, and my father—the train bogey was behind him, I recall, and it was time to board—reached out and caressed her face, saying, 'What a beautiful child. She should be well.'

"At that moment I saw a cloud of sadness lift off the girl's face. Her full cheeks lighted up, her eyes shone, and she smiled. It was a wonderful smile. I think everybody who was there saw this small miracle. Your Dada turned around and we boarded. 'Did you see that she was cured, Tejpal?' he asked me casually when we were seated. I replied, 'Yes, Bapu-ji, a cloud lifted from her face.' 'Taro mojijo,' he said. That was your presence.

"A few days after we returned, on the night of the full moon, standing before the mausoleum of Pir Bawa, my father recited the syllables of the bol to me; putting his hands against my head he kissed me on the mouth. 'You are my successor, Tejpal,' he said. 'Fulfill your responsibilities.' "

"My brother was slighted by my father's choice of me as his successor; and he continued to agitate for Pakistan, even though he knew now that our father would not take that side. When the Partition of India was announced, he left with his family for his new country.

"Soon after Rajpal, now calling himself Iqbal, left, I myself departed for Bombay to study at St. Xavier's College. This was the carefree period in my life, and I forgot all about my succession. It was too far away, I told myself, I would worry about it when the time came. I have memories of Bombay's Flora Fountain and Chowpati Beach, drinking cups and cups of tea at an Irani restaurant called Hafiz, and the learning that excited me. And that girl I dreamt of marrying. But one day the inevitable happened. A young man came from Haripir straight to my hostel late at night. The Saheb calls you, he said.

"Imagine my surprise when I stepped down from the bus outside Pirbaag. A welcome party was waiting for me. I was taken to the house to dress up, and then led to the pavilion where many people sat waiting. A girl sat with her face partly covered, and I was taken to sit beside her. It was the girl I had seen in Wardha, whom my father—and, according to him, I—had cured of her illness at the town's railway station. We were married by your Dada, and she became your mother."

39

And he throws off a clue.

I imagine Bapu-ji sitting on the floor in his beloved library, his writing table across his knees, addressing his apostate son, uncertain about his own life and fearful for the ancient shrine of which he is the spiritual lord. Extreme violence has spread across the state, narratives of the horror out there keep arriving with every fresh batch of devotees, and this time it looks impossible to stanch the flow outside the village, there seems to be an absolute intention to its fury and no force to counter it. The police are nowhere. I can't see his face: that old official photo won't do, and I don't have a recent picture in my mind to help me visualize him. He must have retained those outlines of his face that I always knew—though how much did that beatific smile shrink over the years? The elongated face I recall, and the large flat ears; the hair must have grown white and thin . . . There is no preaching in this letter, only a confession of sorts. Does this portend closeness or distance?

And sitting there he throws off casually the meaning of the secret bol. And goes on to narrate how he first met my mother.

The envelope he left me contained this one letter, seven sheets of it, unnumbered, and two manuscript pages, one in Arabic and another in a Nagari script, back to back and contained between plastic sheets to protect them, the way he would use glass sheets in the past. Is this all he could—or wished to—preserve? He could have slipped in an old coin or two, I suppose, the likes of which he had shown me once long ago; come to think of it, he could have packed a shoe box of papers and mementoes and shoved it into that recess for me. But what right do I have to ask for more, for anything? I had rejected it all. The meagreness of this treasure reflects perhaps the shred of his remaining faith in me. Everything about my life seems laden with symbolic meaning, so desperate have I become.

I don't read Arabic, of course; and the Nagari looks impossible, both the script and the language must be archaic. Why specifically these two pages for me? And my father's own hand—it seems erratic, at times clear and bold, then suddenly hurried and scrawly. He had not written his pages at one sitting, or even with the same pen. The order in which I read them is perhaps not the one in which he wrote.

The night is dark, thick with mist, and my feet crunch audibly upon the gravel. There is not another soul around in this loneliness. In the near distance lurks the gothic silhouette of the Institute, lit eerily by a few isolated lamps, reminding me of the ghosts of rulers past that are supposed to be resident there. I turn back, partly grope my way to the thick boundary wall of the grounds, and sit upon it, a faint shiver running down my neck. Within a few months of my Dada's and my father's visit to Gandhi at his ashram, the Mahatma had come here to this retreat, when it was still the viceroy's summer residence, to discuss with Nehru, Jinnah, and others the fate of this country. We now live with their compromises. Many have suffered and died because of them. Everything is connected, with a purpose, Bapu-ji writes in his letter. There are no accidents. I wish I could be as certain.

I hold in my mouth—through the agency of the bol—the secret of the identity of Nur Fazal. How portentous that sounds. But it's true, though only partly. I have little illusion that the bol—even if the story of its first utterance were true—sounds exactly as it did seven centuries ago. The syllables have rounded with wear, the consonants softened or scattered away, and what remains sounds like nothing but a secret mantra, which is how I received it from my father. But when it had literal meaning, what did it spell out? The sufis of the past identified themselves by their spiritual ancestry—the names of their masters and their schools—and this is perhaps what the bol spelled out. The only problem is that it cannot be read now. It's like a message in a foreign language with key sounds missing. But did my father know more, from his own father and all the knowledge contained in his library? Are the two manuscript pages he included with his letter further clues? Perhaps he intended to tell me more.

When I was young, we knew that the sufi came from somewhere in the north. And that was enough. People came to Pirbaag not for details of its history. They came for the sick child, the barren hearth, the crippling disease; or something more, for there was no end to wants, as Bapu-ji always taught; or, having realized this truth, they came to elevate their souls to that state in which physical needs are meaningless. No one came for history, except foreign scholars, and they had stopped coming a long time ago.

And yet the prospect of an actual historical connection I find enticing. Bapu-ji was suspicious of my intellectual meanderings at university, but his own first love had been science, synonymous with curiosity, a search for answers; and despite his spiritual message and disparagement of book learning, he had spent a good portion of his life preserving the records of the past. It is a record that he has left me.

Back in the flat, my brother lies stretched out on the sofa with a book. (He has had me borrow books about Islam, which he reads during all the time he has at his disposal.) Should I tell him what I have learned? I would have to utter the bol, which I cannot. But does that injunction hold any longer? In any case, he would not care. Meanwhile I have to worry about him. Besides the books, he pores over the newspapers. What is he up to, what does he want? Earlier today he had a narrow escape from the police, but looking at him, you would never guess.

⤛⤜⤙⤚

The game, it seemed, was up. Major Narang walked in through the back door, which I held open for him. No sooner was he inside than there came a knock at the front door and in walked two of his aides. A typical police approach, often seen in the movies. All of us in the living room now, the major sat down, stretched out his legs; glanced distastefully at the sofa seat. The furniture at this institute is half a century old and the sofa cover has the prickly texture of a jute mat. One of the major's aides also sat on the sofa, uncomfortably on the edge; the third fellow hung around; and I was on the armchair facing the major. My heart was in my mouth, as we say. If they had checked the bedrooms, they would have discovered their quarry and taken him away. If they had pondered long enough over the unusually high pile of newspapers at the side of the sofa, they might have become suspicious. They stayed for forty-five minutes, but they didn't find him because they didn't think to look inside. And Mansoor did not let out a squeak.

The major, as I have indicated, is a sociable fellow and always certain of himself. He had brought samosas and pakodas from the canteen, wrapped in a newspaper; the aide who was standing, called Jamal, went into my kitchen and made us all some tea.

"No news from your brother?"

I shook my head; I don't think I convinced him.

"Mansoor has been associating with elements of the Lashkar in Delhi, there is no doubt about that. We raided their hideout a few days ago. Your brother escaped, with two others, and two of them were shot in an exchange of fire. They were armed. One was from Kashmir—papers were found on him; and the other was from Gujarat, your state."

I tried to stay calm as I recalled Mukhtiar, son of Salim Buckle, looking out from his belt shop in Old Delhi as I ventured up the alley in quest of my brother. That was hardly three months ago.

"Had they done anything?" I asked quietly.

"Planning, dear chap, planning," he said. "There were maps and schedules in their flat. There was of course that bombing in Hauz Khas market two weeks ago."

"You have information about my brother?"

"We suspected he might head here, for the mountains. But no one has seen him. If he contacts you—"

"I should let you know."

"In everybody's interest."

We had tea, and then they left. As soon as the last footfall faded on the front steps, Mansoor emerged from inside, grabbed a samosa.

Contrary to what Major Narang believes, Mansoor has been seen here, because he has brashly walked around the grounds, identifying himself as

Professor Ashok Bhalla from Hyderabad; the fact that there is such a person has helped his cause. There is little risk of being found out, because not everybody knows everybody else by face, and the professor happens to be away. In keeping with his borrowed identity, my brother has even shaved off his beard. But how long will he be able to keep up his charade?

—‹‹••››—

In the midst of all the excitement, Bapu-ji's revelations in his letter and Mansoor's narrow escape from the major, Neeta's voice on the phone is water to a thirsty man.

"How wonderful to hear your voice," I can't help exclaiming, embarrassing myself. Since my arrival at the Institute this is the first time we've spoken.

There is a short pause to follow my greeting, then she says, "That's nice." And then, with a welcome concern: "You all right, Karsan?"

"Yes, a bit anxious, though. Major Narang's been nosing around . . ."

(A little dig at the major, whose man I know is listening in.)

"And? . . . You shouldn't let that bother you."

"I won't. But listen—"

I tell her about reading my father's letters.

"That's most touching," she says. "He knew you would read his letter."

"I had to recall the bol first—"

"Which you did. He knew you, Karsan. You were his son."

What if he hadn't found me, I think to myself. What if that accident hadn't happened, the impulsive visit to that church basement in Kingsway. I tell her,

"I picture him sitting on the floor writing this letter on his portable desk, knowing he would not see me again . . . What did he look like, Neeta—when you last saw him—do you recall his face?"

"Oh yes. It was over a year ago. It was a kind face, with a smile. He had to be helped up from his chair—he was arthritic—and he walked with a stick. He was completely bald. He had an abdominal problem, I think. But there were his disciples who attended to him."

I want to tell her what I have learned from my father, that the bol is a clue to Pir Bawa's secret identity. But this bit of news seems trivial and academic now.

The next morning, however, I take the Arabic and Nagari pages that Bapu-ji left me and show them to Professor Barua in his office. His face breaks into a grin of satisfaction as with eager eyes he looks first at one, then the other, through the protective plastic sheath that contains them back to back. His interest in the sufi's mysterious identity has been obsessive from the start. Rubbing his hands gleefully he calls his secretary in, and has copies made of the two specimens and sends them off to professional acquaintances for advice and possible translation. Of course I do not tell him about the bol.

40

"One day, my dear Karsan, your mother left," wrote my father.
"I write this as we reel from the news that a railway bogey in a train full of pilgrims returning from Ayodhya was set on fire outside Godhra. Those inside were trapped and all perished, including children. What a ghastly and thoughtless crime. Now blood will pay for blood, and all madness will be set loose upon this land. Here in Haripir we must struggle to maintain the peace as we have done during past troubles. Your brother Mansoor is nowhere to be found. This worries me. You know he is a hotheaded fellow.

"He has wandered about much since coming of age. But finally he returned and for the last two years it seemed that he had settled down with me. He has been helpful in managing our home and even the shrine. And for a moment I began to harbour the desire that he become the next Saheb, my successor, since you had rejected this calling. But I know he is not the one, he does not possess that kindness and composure you had. The people know this too. They remember you well, Karsan, even after these many years. They say that the gaadi-varas Karsan will return one day. This has made your brother resentful.

"One morning I saw him bowed in the posture of namaz in his room; this was the first I learned that he had become a Muslim. I realized there was a seriousness and a need in him that he had never revealed to me before. It pleases me, this spiritual commitment, and yet it worries me too, if it comes purely out of resentment of Hindus. I wish you were here so that you two brothers could talk with each other.

"I began to tell you about your mother, but this new madness in our country and my worry about your brother have waylaid me into quite another path . . ."

"You wondered why she did not write to you. The truth is that she could neither read nor write. Your mother was illiterate. She did not want you to know this, and so when you begged her to write to you, she was ashamed of herself and resolved to learn. Meanwhile I was not to tell you her secret.

"I was fond of your mother, just as I was fond of my sons. They meant much to me. But the Saheb is aware more than others about the transience of ordinary life, and its real purpose. Moreover he has a responsibility to all those who come seeking comfort at the shrine. He cannot be a normal father or husband. Even the conjugal life of a Saheb is not normal; this is not easy to accept for a young couple. Sufis of old tried many means to curb their desires. Some of them resorted to tying stones round their waists. Recall the story of how Pir Bawa, when he stayed amidst the opulence of Patan, fell to the wiles of a seductress. We have followed the ways of the sufis and married, because life's wants are not to be despised, youthful energies must be spent, and the Saheb-ship must be passed on. And yet we know that pleasure is an illusion that leads to attachment and distraction, and finally, unhappiness. It is another miracle at Pirbaag that a successor has always become a Saheb only after he has enjoyed the married life and moreover fathered one or two sons. After that, celibacy is the desired state. It is after all the spirit that counts, our worldly possessions and desires we must shed. Your mother found this hard to accept.

"It did not bother me that I had married a girl who could neither read nor write. Illiteracy is not unusual in our country; it is more the norm. But she came from a city and an established family, and all her brothers and sisters had gone to school. She missed out only because of her illness. And so she would pretend to read . . ."

"She loved to see films. Before your Dada died, we lived our blissful life of a young married couple; we went to the cinema and sometimes ate in the restaurants. But after I had become the Saheb, the pursuit of worldly enjoyment did not become us; more than that, it ceased to interest me, just as a child one day sets aside its toys to engage with the real world. But for your Ma, besides her two sons, the illusion of the cinema screen was everything. And so she started going to the cinema in secret, and I could only look the other way, for I knew she could not help herself.

"All that is beside the point now. After you left she never recovered. She became depressed and seemed to have reverted to the condition she was in when I first saw her in Wardha, when my father cured her. (He—and she—believed that it was I who had cured her.) In her condition she became intensely suspicious and imaginative, making accusations unbecoming to her status and her dignity. I will not repeat them to you. She hurt herself more than others. Under these circumstances, Shilpa, our volunteer and benefactor of long, had to go away . . ."

[The lithe and luscious Shilpa of jasmines and roses, the temptress devotee who would subtly tease me, then return to haunt my tumescent dreams. How Ma hated her. Surely, Bapu-ji, there was more in her sweet devotions to you? You would have known. That bliss on your face. Did the stone around your waist save you, then, Bapu-ji?]

"Finally, I asked her brothers to come and take her away for some time; perhaps a change of air and perspective would do her good. I advised her to use her time there to learn to read and write enough so she could write to you and be happy. But she never returned. News came that she had died and they had cremated her there. I was not told the cause. I missed her, just as I missed you . . ."

What Indian woman in those times returned home from her husband's to be welcomed and loved? Sisters-in-law lurked like sharks in those risky waters, the poor victim set foot inside at her own peril.

It was Bapu-ji who lived in toyland.

Did he believe in all he taught? He must have. Yet the sadness is palpable there in his words, at having to deprive his young wife of love, keep her only to keep his home, be mother to his successor.

Ma never mentioned the circumstance of their first meeting, when she was healed by the Saheb of Pirbaag, or perhaps by his young successor who became her husband. How easily she was given away by her family, like a reject, to a shrine and into a life she would never have dreamed of or desired; no wonder she rarely went back to her parents. And when she did go that last time, sick again, it was only to die of some unknown cause.

> You, up in a fortress high
> I, a fish in the moat
> pining for the look
> of your eyes, beloved . . .

Thus the sufi's allegory of spiritual desire, which Bapu-ji would teach. But how appropriate a description of my mother's real want, though she would have preferred some playback singer to express it. All the romance in her life came from the films.

I almost said "her empty life"; but she had Mansoor and me. We too failed her. I had loved her, but how little I knew about her. My freedom from Pirbaag meant more to me than my duty to her; and here I am, back, not sure ultimately what I gained from my escape. Bapu-ji can at least claim that victory—if the dead have victories—in the return of his renegade son. But Ma?

41

A fraternal walk up to the Hanuman temple.

We take a moderately brisk pace; andantino, as Julian's music teacher
would say, a flash of memory intrudes like lightning into my thoughts. If I
have given the impression that I have forgotten my son, it is not true; I
have simply muffled the pain, as I cope with a more immediate one. And so
Mansoor and I walk at a moderate pace, our mood light on this hilly path,
as it always is on the road to a shrine, a temple. Our destination is Jhakhu,
temple to Hanuman. Dozens of people around us. Some make this arduous
trek daily, others occasionally; there is a scholar at the Institute who jogs
up every morning for his devotions to this god of physical prowess, among
other things.

Inspired by Bapu's wish, expressed in his letter, that my brother and I
could have spent time together and talked, I had with some trepidation
suggested this challenging hike up to a Hindu shrine that is a must for all
visitors to Shimla. To my surprise Mansoor readily agreed; he had gone
with Ma to the Kali shrine in Pavagadh once, he said. It was a few months
after I had left. That too had been a long trek uphill. At the end of it, he
exults in telling me, atop the Kali temple was a sufi shrine. Explain that!—
he exclaims. The answer is simple. But I keep my wisdom and we walk on.

Halfway up, the famous monkeys appear. They are supposed to understand Pahadi, the local mountain dialect, but we speak to them in our
Gujarati Hindi. "We have nothing on us, go away. Jao! Bhaago!" But the
one who has picked us as victims or benefactors, a moderate-sized female
with expressive eyes and holding a baby, follows us, taking leaps at my

shoulder bag until finally I open the jhola for her to peer inside—"See, there's nothing"—and confirm for herself that truly there is nothing to eat there. She disappears into the shadows.

A little later the food stalls appear, lighted in the evening by wick lamps, and the first stalls selling sweets and flowers for the pilgrims to take to the temple. Our monkey has followed us; the first order of fresh pakodas from the wok therefore must go to this Hanuman's ambassador, and she goes away to sit at the roadside with her prize; we consume the second batch before climbing up the rest of the way.

There is a dharamshala and dining hall at the top of the mountain, and more flower and sweets stalls; facing these, the Hanuman temple with the ancient icon of the monkey god at the back. All is light and festive here. Loudspeakers blare out devotional songs. People stride out from the temple with beaming faces.

"You believe in this kind of God?" my brother asks in surprise as we stand outside the temple. "You consider this form of worship mysticism—bowing to the gaudy image of a monkey?"

"You had more respect for the gods before, Mansoor. And there can be a mystery to an icon—we bring to it what is inside us."

"Stop acting the Saheb," he grumbles, but he lets me push him gently forward. We join a queue of worshippers inside. When our turn arrives at the sanctum, I watch him put some bills in the money chest, join hands, bow to Hanuman; it is instinct. I do likewise, have the bag of sweets in my hands blessed by the priest, and together we come out.

Our faces must be beaming. I have not prayed this way for a long time, bowed formally to a mystery, an image of a mystery with humility and fellow feeling for other humans who also come in all humility. I glance with covert satisfaction at the priest's saffron daub on my brother's forehead: the mark of a worshipper. Surely a miracle, this? But I must give him his due, his new form of worship, the ballet on the ground (not without its image, though: the compass direction West serves as that) is surely also an equivalent, humble form of worship to a mystery called Allah.

And what must he think, I who would not admit to any belief, also branded as a worshipper by a priest? Perhaps it is he who has brought me here.

.   .   .

Going back downhill, the path is dark, lighted only by the lamps of the closing food stalls and the worshippers' restless flashlights; but the mood is festive. Pilgrims are still heading up, throwing soft greetings to those going down. The monkeys are in abeyance, mostly, though our cellophane bag of blessed sweets has long been snatched away.

"What happened to Ma, Mansoor?" I ask when we reach a quiet, flat patch of track at the bottom of the climb.

Bapu has spared me the more painful details in his letter; Mansoor will be merciless.

One Saturday morning, our mother came out to the shrine in the burqa, showing her face so she would be recognized; the crowd was the thickest at this time. Calmly, it appeared, she went about tending to the small chores of the shrine, oblivious to the uneasy stares and the silence around her. Bapu-ji, seated on the pavilion, remained totally composed, as though all were normal. Beside him was the teacher and printer Master-ji, and close by were some volunteer attendants. Later, as the crowd changed, it seemed that some normality had returned, the people now used to the woman in burqa and discreet about her identity if they knew it. Then Shilpa hurried in, beautiful, cheerful, having just arrived on the bus; she put away her handbag to one side and went and greeted Bapu-ji with "Namasté, Saheb." Having touched his feet, she stood up and then gently attempted to arrange the shawl on his shoulders. It was a quietly possessive gesture, well practised, and it chewed up Ma's insides as she stood observing, surrounded by a dense group of visitors. Unable to contain herself, Ma let out a sudden, piercing shriek and approached the pavilion, crying, "You, let go of my husband!" Turning around, she addressed, pleaded with her petrified audience: "That rundi is all over my husband! Do something, you people!" One arm stretched out, a finger pointing to Shilpa, whom she had just called a whore. And then, in the silence that greeted her, my poor mother, the Saheb's wife who had turned herself into a hysterical freak in a dishevelled burqa, broke down into sobs and allowed herself to be taken to the back of the compound and inside the house. It could be explained to the people that she was suffering from hallucinations; that she was possessed and the Saheb was treating her.

It all began with my departure. Ma would accuse Bapu-ji of having driven me off. "He did not want to be a Saheb-shaheb at all, why did you pressure him? The poor boy would come and cry to me. You wrenched him away from my breast! You haunted him!"

Bapu-ji was completely astonished. "*You* say this, Madhu?" he told her. "You know there is no choice in the matter. This is our parampara, it has been going on for centuries! . . . You would want me to stop it?"

"To hell with your parampara!"

Her mood improved with my first letters and as she started learning to read and write. But she simply didn't have the confidence to begin a letter to her learned son in America, even a small letter, while her husband could write reams expressing concern and advice. Meanwhile she accused Bapu-ji of making lustful eyes at Shilpa. And Shilpa of seducing her husband. Her language would turn vulgar. She would shriek when she became abusive. "And don't think you are above it all! I know what you are capable of!—couldn't keep his hands off me, the lecher—even after he was Saheb!"

As a remedy she began visiting a few holy places in the area, sometimes taking Mansoor with her, at other times travelling with groups of women pilgrims. Her condition improved, she became normal for a few weeks. And then would come the unbearable depression, and the weeping and the outbursts.

At about this time Bapu-ji tried to recall me. With a one-way ticket. He could not believe that I would refuse his call, or not return to see my sick mother, whatever the cost. I proved him wrong; but here I am.

One day a young man came with his mother to Pirbaag. The woman suffered from migraines, for which she had visited many holy men and paid homage at many shrines. She had heard of this one from her son, who was studying in America and had met the Saheb's son. He brought news from Karsan, who was doing very well but was worried about his mother. Ma was brought and met the woman and her son. They handed out the chocolates I had sent. And the woman went away happy and cured—as her son had informed me. It was a day when Ma was feeling especially well; the visitors had raised her spirits even more. And I, a world away, was satisfied there was nothing wrong with my mother.

But immediately after, she went into a depression. Then that final outburst took place, when she came out in her burqa to humiliate my father.

Shilpa left that day, never to be seen again. And about a week later, one of Ma's brothers came and took her away.

"We went through hell," Mansoor says. "All three of us. But then it was all due to our father, wasn't it? The repressive lifestyle. The ancient mumbo-jumbo. If he really had the powers, why couldn't he cure her? And with Shilpa—"

"There was something there, you think?"

He doesn't say anything. We are back in the flat sitting together, all stillness around us, absolute silence except our voices.

"Did you see anything, Mansoor—between them?"

"She had her claws on him. She had plans for herself."

"What do you mean? What plans?"

"You know something? She had the guest rooms redecorated. The one she always used was done up both outside and inside. I think she was poisoning Ma, putting something in her food, so she could take her place."

"You accused her of that?"

"Yes, I told her to stop poisoning my mother and to leave us."

He smiles, says, "You would never have believed Ma capable of such language as she used against Bapu-ji—raw desi stuff!" He allows a rare chuckle. "You should have seen Bapu-ji's face, the embarrassment . . . she exposed him as the lecherous man that he must have been once—all too human, no? I lost my respect for him."

Whatever you had of it, I can't help thinking. There is the edge back in him after this bitter revelation; the good humour, the warmth of the previous few hours now suddenly all vanished.

42

Pirbaag, the final days.

"Fear is all around us," wrote my father, "and wrath. And shameless encouragement of the mobs by our leaders. It is said that in the darkest times of the Kali Yuga, the ruler will betray his subjects. This is now a fact. There is violence to freeze the heart, but then we should be used to it, we who saw or heard about it during Partition and in the '69 riots and in the '93 riots . . ."

In Vancouver I had seen reports of the Gujarat violence on the Internet, and I had duly signed my name to electronic petitions of protest, those easy, no-cost salves to the conscience. For many Indians these outbreaks of mass murder and rape happen elsewhere, in certain neighbourhoods; and so the problem is someone else's, they only brought it upon themselves. There is also this old adage to scuttle behind as the killings continue: India is an ancient civilization, it has survived much in its long history, it always recovers. I took comfort in the knowledge that Haripir had not seen a riot in a long time, perhaps ever. My father was a respected, revered elder, and the guru of its ancient shrine. He had been confident in his letter that once more the village would not succumb to the calls for communal retribution and bloodshed. Yet here, in these candidly composed pages written only days later, he sounded terribly fearful and fragile; not like the Bapu-ji I had known. How I keep coming back to this refrain. But the father I had known I had lost long ago, and he was writing close to doomsday.

"Your brother Mansoor," he continued, "after a few days' absence has returned. I don't know what he has been up to and where, but he has me worried. He does not talk to me except to say 'You don't understand' when I try to advise him. With a few others, mainly from the Muslim community, he has organized a defence force in Haripir. This is not the answer, and Mansoor has been told that Pirbaag needs no such defence. But the Muslim community is vulnerable, and the police are of no use; in Ahmedabad they refused to give assistance when houses were torched and goondas awaited outside to slaughter the escaping occupants. Taking comfort behind the statement that we are neither Hindus nor Muslims, however, is not correct. And so I have let it be known that the shrine of Pir Bawa is open to all those who will come to seek refuge, Hindu, Muslim, Christian, or Sikh. This way their lives may be saved."

Later, he wrote down his final, tortured paragraph:

"My dear son Karsan, wherever you are. If you do not read this letter then perhaps, still, these thoughts will find you. Our beloved shrine, the house of Pir Bawa, is beginning to fill with people terrified of the news and rumours they have heard. There are reports of gangs approaching Haripir . . . And rumours that Pirbaag will not be spared, so what to tell the people who are coming here? Your brother is nowhere to be seen, he may be at the Balak Shah place . . . I will close this letter with a kiss, I say the bol as I write this; and I will place this letter at the foot of Jaffar Shah, the pir of the travellers, whom you loved so much. Later I will take some select books from our collection and visit all the personages buried in our shrine and ask them to safekeep them. If the worst happens, there will be something left for you. There is nothing else I can do. Your Bapu."

The question comes tearing into the mind, now that I try to imagine what transpired after he wrote down those last words: How exactly did my father die? No one has wanted to tell me that.

43

The major is angry.

He almost storms in when I open the back door, his favourite entry. The associate he brings with him quickly disappears to search my two bedrooms.

"It has come to light that a cheeky bugger who could well be your brother has been masquerading as that Hyderabadi Professor Bhalla in his absence," he declares, and watches me, awaiting my answer.

"My brother is not here," I tell him squarely, and the implication is clear.

"We will find him, whoever this person is. We will search the roads, the buses, the taxis. Roadblocks are in place all over."

"This for a man who is wanted only for questioning? Is there something about my brother you did not tell me?"

"He could lead us to others more dangerous," he says, and sits down on the sofa he dislikes so much. I take the matching armchair beside him. No tea, no snacks today, this is all business. He leans forward and adds in a quiet voice, "Tell me, Karsan Sah'b——"

"Yes?"

"What would you do if you found yourself harbouring someone close—a son, say, or a brother—who could be a terrorist? What would your moral principles tell you to do?"

"That's the quandary, isn't it?" I reply. "If I was sure of his guilt, I suppose I would turn him in—or at least throw him out. But if I wasn't sure . . ."

"Yes?"

"Well, Major, there have been far more dead suspects than live ones, haven't there?"

He sits back and eyes the assistant who has emerged from the bedrooms. The man shakes his head.

The major says, "Your brother was in Godhra, he could assist us in apprehending those who set fire to the train. You are telling me he wasn't here? He didn't come to see his brother? He must need money, surely?"

"My brother was here, Major Narang. And we spoke. He was in Godhra as a teacher for three years; and he had friends there, some of whom were killed. In his own words, he has not killed any Hindus. When the train was set on fire, he was in Haripir."

"Why doesn't he talk to us, then? You could come with him. And you have an influential friend in Mrs. Kapur. Nothing will happen to him, you have my assurance."

"Major, my brother and I barely got to know each other. I am a stranger to him, the one who got away. We don't agree on many things and he doesn't trust me. How could I convince him of anything? And let's be honest—the police would hardly be trusted by the likes of him. They did nothing to rescue victims during the riots; they have been accused of aiding the rioters, and shooting down Muslim men in so-called encounters. I couldn't convince Mansoor to talk to you—even though I trust and like you myself."

He pauses a moment, staring before him at the coffee table, then abruptly stands up, and to my great surprise shakes my hand and strides out.

Two nights ago we had sat together in the living room, I at my writing desk and Mansoor stretched full-length on the sofa with a book. Before he came, by myself I might have had the radio on but turned down extremely low while I worked, an old habit; I might have hummed a tune to myself or recited something to counter my loneliness. Instead, he had Nusrat Fateh Ali Khan and Co. vigorously belting out qawalis, though at a moderate volume, and I was quite enjoying them. For the first time since he arrived I appreciated my brother's company. He had said his prayers and we had had our tea.

And then out of a sudden, panicky curiosity, I turned around and asked him, "Mansoor—what did you do in Godhra?"

"I was a teacher there—at the Mirza Ghalib School. Why?" He sat up, put the book on the table before him. *The Secret Order of the Assassins,* by Hodgson; he watched me read the spine. I was only vaguely familiar with the subject, a Shia Muslim sect in medieval Persia with a knack for dramatic political assassinations. Not the sort of reading to find on your brother wanted for questioning regarding a terrorism act.

"I told you about it before, didn't I?" he said. "I told you I had been in Godhra."

"Not the details. You must have made friends there . . ."

"Yes, I had friends there, and some of them were killed in the riots," he said, his bile rising, and glared at me, and I felt rather like a caught-out police spy. I had only been trying to express my worry about him.

"It's just that . . . I hope you've not been up to anything silly—criminal . . ."

"What could I have done?" He was holding his temper. "And no, I did not kill any Hindus during the riots. You forget that my mother was one."

"Bapu-ji says that he was worried when you disappeared after the riots started. Where were you?"

"I went back to Godhra." He spoke quietly. "To help out if I could. That was a mistake, I narrowly escaped the swords. A teacher at the Methodist school who was with me at St. Arnold's took me in. I hid with him for a few days."

"And when you returned?"

"There were rumours that Haripir was on the rioters' list. And it was said that Pirbaag was a Muslim shrine and this time it would not be spared. But would Bapu-ji listen? Some of us therefore organized a defence force for the town, our own militia. But before we could even properly prepare ourselves, at ten o'clock one night a mob entered the village, chanting their murderous slogans. There were too many of them, our own village people among them. And you know the result."

"How did Bapu-ji die?"

He turned away. Then he picked up his book and went inside to his room.

A little later his mobile rang. He identified himself as Professor Bhalla and spoke for a good length of time and sounded cheered up when he finished.

Last night my favourite kitchen hand Ajay brought our dinner for us. Having put the tray down, he tarried to tell me that Professor Bhalla had arrived, and the police were all over the Institute asking about the man who had been posing as Professor Bhalla. There was the faintest smile on his face at the evident humour in the situation. I thanked him, more profusely than usual. He could so easily have reported on my brother. But ever since my first visit to his church, he has been my quiet guardian angel.

"It's time for me to leave, Bhai," said Mansoor as the door closed behind Ajay. "Now you will be rid of me."

He went inside to pack his things, and I heard him make two calls on his mobile.

"I'll miss you, Mansoor," I said to him with emotion when he came out. "We never got to know each other well." We never had time to laugh together, I've worried and you've been defensive.

He smiled. "Some other time."

"Where do you plan to go?"

"The less you know the better, Bhai," he said.

We embraced, and I opened the back door for him. He carried a tray with him so he could pass as a kitchen hand part of the way. I saw him walk nervously in the shadows, then disappear. His first stop, I knew, would be the church behind the Guest House. He would presumably change there and be off somewhere else. What was he up to, where was he headed? Who were those friends who could comfort him more than I could? How little I knew him. We had arrived at the verge of closeness, now I had the depressing feeling that I would never see him again.

I prayed he would not do anything foolhardy and risky, though I had long stopped asking myself what my sporadic prayers mean.

The next morning I collected the books I had borrowed for him to return to the library. They were all about Islam: its history and past glory, its meaning and philosophy, its great personalities. Again the unjacketed white hardback caught my eye: why would my brother want to read about the Assassins? And how ironical, wasn't one of Pir Bawa's many epithets

Kaatil, Killer—though his sword had been his acumen and use of words. It occurred to me that my father might have had a copy of the book on his top shelf.

And then something happened, I don't know exactly how, or exactly when. Absently flipping the pages of the book, reading bits, once putting it down and picking something else up, and later returning to it, and finally unable to let it go, staring at that single entry in one of the back pages, I realized that I had in my hands the answer to the secret of the bol. For there was this familiar name, extensively referenced, in the index of Hodgson's book: W. Ivanow.

Professor Ivanow's passion evidently was the study of the medieval, controversial Muslim sect of the Assassins, who had occupied a number of fortresses in western Persia. He had written books about them and visited the ruins of their castles. And this Russian during his researches had also come to Pirbaag to speak with my Dada and have a look at its ancient manuscripts. I recalled the faded snapshot of him in our family album, taken in our pavilion with Dada, Bapu-ji, and Mr. Ross, the remarkably tall collector of Ahmedabad who had brought him.

Nur Fazal the sufi, I concluded, had been an Assassin. Everything I read in the book in my hand seemed to confirm this.

Could it be so easy?

44

In that breeding ground of heresy . . . there remains not one stone of the foundations upon another. And in that flourishing abode of innovations the Artist of Eternity Past wrote with the pen of violence upon the portico of each one the verse: "These their houses are empty ruins". . . Their luckless womenfolk, like their empty religion, have been utterly destroyed. And the gold of those crazy, double-dealing counterfeiters which appeared to be unalloyed has proved to be base lead.

Ata-Malik Juvaini,
on the destruction of the Assassin
fortresses by the Mongols (1252–1260)

The secret of the bol. Massacre of the heretics.
The Assassins, also called the Ismailis, were a mystical Shia sect who disdained the outer forms of worship and the Muslim laws of Sharia for inner spiritual truths. They operated from well-defended, hard-to-access mountain fortresses in western Iran, and they were loathed for their heresy and feared for their penchant for murdering their enemies with impudent and terrifying facility, either as defence against persecution or to intimidate through terror, depending on your viewpoint. The great Saladin is said to have checked for hidden Assassins under his bed before lying down to sleep. They were secretive but had an extensive network of followers, and are believed to have sent their dais, or missionaries, all the way to India to teach their esoteric brand of the Islamic faith.

One of these spiritual teachers, the Russian professor must have concluded, as I am convinced now too, was Nur Fazal the Sufi.

It is as if pieces of the puzzle, lost among myriad childhood impressions floating like unwanted debris in the recesses of the mind, now begin to find themselves and collect and cohere to form the certainty of this knowledge.

From all the stories about him which I heard from my teacher Master-ji and my father, Nur Fazal was a Muslim mystic who had escaped persecution in a war-torn Near East and was given refuge by the Gujarati king Vishal Dev, whose reign coincided with the Mongol destruction of the Assassin strongholds. He invoked Indian gods and mystical ideas freely in his teachings, and according to legend he had once sided with Hindu Brahmins against orthodox Muslim mullahs during a debate at a royal court. Not one Arabic prayer had he prescribed for his followers. These ways could only characterize an extremely nonconforming Muslim sectarian, a heretic. An Assassin.

If only the bol in my mouth would confirm this. But it cannot, and I must imagine.

In 1256 the castles of the Assassins were overrun by the armies of the Mongol Hulagu Khan, after which followed a typical Mongol massacre, as described in detail by the much-biased Persian historian Juvaini, who took special satisfaction in the burning of the famous Assassin library. Shortly before this destruction, a prominent denizen of the Assassin strongholds, Nur Fazal, had arrived in the kingdom of Gujarat and was welcomed by its ruler, Vishal Dev. Nur became a legend for his knowledge and mystical powers and came to be called Sufi, Wanderer, Gardener, and Kaatil—Killer: an ancient stand-in, perhaps, for Assassin? But to his followers he was always the beloved Pir Bawa.

The sufi must have heard of the deluge in his home when he was in Gujarat. In my childhood, and especially in my teenage years, I had imagined from his pithy love poems that he had left a lover back home in "the north," or uttara khanda, as we called it. According to Bapu-ji's teachings this love was mystical, and the lover was the sufi's spiritual master. But I had preferred a woman in the picture: for whom else would he have written the words, *My body shudders out of desire for you?*

The historian Juvaini writes, further, of that destruction,

Today, thanks to the glorious fortune of the World-Illuminating King [Hulagu Khan], if an Assassin still lingers in a corner he plies a woman's trade; wherever there is a dai [a missionary] there is an announcer of death . . . The propagators of Ismailism have fallen victims to the swordsmen of Islam. Their maulana, to whom they addressed the words: "O God, our Protector"—dust in their mouths!—has become the serf of bastards . . . They have been degraded amongst mankind like the Jews and like the highways are level with the dust.

And now to the havocking of Nur's Indian garden, Pirbaag.

45

The attack on Pirbaag.

This is what I have gathered.

March 9, 2002. By sunset, some hundred souls and more had come through the gate of Pirbaag, seeking refuge. Huddled like ghosts among the graves, they could only pray that the rumours were false, that this fearful night would pass like others without incident. But they knew otherwise, which was why they had come. In the darkness they ate what they had brought, or were given, and water was passed around. Gradually they began to nod off; the children had settled down and silence fell. But then suddenly they were awake and there was the slow murmur of an approaching human swarm outside on the road, accompanied by an inexplicable background music, and the sounds of gears crunching. The smell of oily smoke. The air was warm. There came an enormous explosion, as a gas-tank bomb was hurled at the massive gate of the Balak Shah commune. This of course the refugees in Pirbaag could not see, but amidst their confusion and terror, they could hear the screams that pierced this now endless night, imagine tableaux of slaughter to rack the mind.

Still, Pirbaag would be safe, they hoped. And they beseeched its lord, Pray for us, Saheb; tell them we are not Muslims, Saheb.

With a few attendants the old Saheb stood some feet from the gate, prevented by his young devotees from stepping out further.

And then, inevitably, a phalanx of torches appeared outside the gate, yellow lights quivering in the night, radiating heat and menace, the promise of mayhem; the smell of burning, the screams in the background; and drunk faces gradually discernible in the warm smoky darkness . . .

Perhaps if the Saheb had stayed put, had not come out in all his outdated elderly and spiritual authority to plead with and cajole and scold the men drugged on blood and red wine and bhang all evening . . . all he did was feed their wrath. But it would have made little difference, the rioters had arrived with intent. This centuries-old neutral sanctuary had now been marked as a Muslim abode to wreak vengeance on.

It was typical of Bapu-ji that he came out with an assistant and started speaking. A thin young man of medium height, a red bandana tied rakishly across his forehead, growth of beard on his face, made as if to listen, his sword held up poised. "Let go this silliness, for Bhagwan's sake"— the Saheb began, when the thin, long sword flashed and went straight through him. He fell and they cut him. Details don't matter. And then the rampage began inside. Violence to curdle the blood, as Bapu-ji had already written.

This is all I can muster about the massacre. Accounts of such violence fill the newspapers every time, eventually make their way into the archives. India is an ancient country, we say. We recover. Do we.

⊰⟨⟨∙⟩⟩⊱

Two days after Mansoor left, a piece of unsettling news in the papers: two terrorists were killed in an encounter with police on the Kalka highway to Shimla. Letters (in Urdu) and maps were found on them; the two were apparently planning to bomb the Institute of Advanced Study, formerly the viceregal and presidential summer residence.

Neither of these two could have been my brother. Ajay has informed me that Mansoor had departed in the opposite direction, higher up in the mountains, made over as a Tibetan monk. But the comfort this information brings is only fragmentary. Only the flurry of questions remains, each one with a sting to its tail.

Did Mansoor know those two men? Could one of them be his old friend Mukhtiar? Was he, busy on his cellphone, the contact in Shimla? Was the police report of a plot against the Institute true, or could it be a fabrication of the sort he had once described so derisively? Was he capable of wanton destruction to a place that gave a home to his brother? How innocent, relaxed he had looked when he left me; how little I knew him.

◅◄◄••►►▻

Neeta Kapur is here. Imagine my pleasure when I see her at breakfast, busy over her puri and potato curry. "I've come to check on you," she says half facetiously, and adds, "It's so hot on the plains—I never got used to the heat after my time in Boston." She spends the day with Mrs. Barua, shopping at the Mall, but has dinner with me at the Guest House.

Later, we walk outside on the grounds. The night is clear, dark, deep; town lights flickering dimly behind us across the valley; a flashlight meandering by itself down a track towards the local shopping area and bus stand of Boileau Ganj, named after an official of the Raj.

She takes a deep breath beside me, and says, "I love this place. It brings me closer to God, and myself."

"Thank you for sending me here," I tell her, "it's also brought me closer to myself."

"And God?"

When I tell her about my eureka moment, the discovery of Nur Fazal's identity, her excitement cannot match mine, of course, and that's a sobering thought. What I could describe as the secret behind my historical existence is for most people another event in our already crowded past. We speak about Mansoor, my anxiety about him. I am reminded primly that my brother is a mature man, fully formed in his personality. She tells me about her son who died, and I tell her about mine. Then the inevitable long silence, during which thoughtlessly we walk down the steep driveway towards the main gate and guard house. The paving is loose and slippery, and we hold on to each other part of the way. Outside, past the radio station, we come to stand at the ridge, a sheer drop protected only by a pipe fencing, across from which the twinkling lights of Shimla reappear in all their glory, spread out on the hills. It's like suddenly coming close upon a galaxy, I think. "When the children were little," she tells me, "it would scare me when they ran around here." She has a daughter, I recall, living somewhere in the States.

"Oh, let's be cheerful," she says after we've stood there awhile in contemplation. "How did we get into this mood?"

"You brought up God, I think. Yes, let's be cheerful."

"I'm sorry I brought up God then."

We walk on towards the new hotel, not far away. All is dark and quiet outside, but surprisingly the bar is open, though also quiet, and we are brought coffee, in the western style, and apricot pies. Sitting across a low table we talk about all kinds of subjects, earnestly, like young people. And suddenly surprised at ourselves we are staring at each other, smiling, laughing. A gem of a moment.

And so finally we come to it, confront together that blind date in Cambridge, Mass., when she spent what seemed an innocent night in my room. An unthinkable act, sign of the times. What else? When we last met, in Ahmedabad, it had been an embarrassing thought, a weight on the mind for us both, I think, and we never brought it up.

"What would you have done if I—" I begin.

"If you had tried to seduce me that night?"

"I suppose that's what I mean."

She laughs. "I knew you would never do it. I felt perfectly safe."

"I was like a brother, then?"

"Not quite . . . but I felt safe. You were so transparent, so earnest."

"And naive."

"Oh, very."

The night had not been so innocent after all; it was the beginning of all the trauma that followed, for it was its wide-eyed boldness that goaded Russell and Bob and the others to play the prank, hang a brassiere on the back of my chair. The shock, the distaste on Premji's face when he saw it; to him I was a goner for sure. He reported to Bapu-ji, and the rest is history. And the bra—black and intriguing—perhaps belonged to the woman now walking next to me? That thought never occurred to me, until now. Silly old me.

"I remember the namkeens you sent afterwards—" I tell her, "at the end of that summer, when you returned from Delhi. I never thanked you."

"Did you like them?"

"Yes, I'm sure I did."

And then, after a long pause, she says what she has come here to say in the first place: "You can't hide here forever, Karsan. Or anywhere else. It's time to think of the future. It's time to go back home and claim what is yours. Your heritage."

"I don't have a home and I don't have a heritage any more . . . except perhaps what I have recalled and written down here, at the Institute."

"That's too easy, isn't it?"

"What do you mean? I haven't lived in Pirbaag for thirty years. I am a different person now."

"You have to decide what to do with it, then. But are you really so very different?"

Yes, yes. I am different. I took off, I escaped, and for years I have walked my own path, away from that ancient place.

If out of defiance at Mansoor I had not made myself recall the bol, I would not have connected so hard to Pirbaag. But who am I fooling. The connection and the defiance were already there when I stood outside the ruins of Pirbaag and resolved to construct something, my own memorial, out of the ashes. And it was there surely when I tried so intensely to break away, but looked back all the time in panic to see if I was being followed. Can you never escape your destiny? Am I too much of an Indian, despite my three decades spent in the west? Is that what Marge always knew?

"You have a people, and they are waiting for you," Neeta says. "They have nothing else." She puts a hand on my arm. "They have cleaned and rebuilt what they could, and they have prepared a surprise for you."

"As what shall I go to them?" I ask her desperately. "What can I offer them?"

I will not repeat what she says, for she flatters me.

46

Pirbaag, Gujarat. August 10, 2002.
The call of the shrine.

We had decided to bury Julian, instead of cremating him, this being Marge's desire. And so he lies, appropriately, in that generous, still untainted soil that gave him birth; but I have brought his teddy bear with me, the one he called Rough, and a lock of his soft brown hair that I have always carried in my wallet. These I now place beside the remains of my father in the soil of Pirbaag. Oh, but how this shrine looks like a bandaged old man who's had a terrible fall.

A cheeky phone call made to Neeta's mobile number: Mansoor is now in Pakistan, having reached there after a six-week journey. It's not clear who made the call and from where.

Do we always end up where we really belong?

Do I belong here?

When I returned to Pirbaag, in Neeta's Ambassador—she refused to let me take an auto, which would have been pretentiously modest, I admit—it seemed as if the entire population of Haripir (now Haripur) had lined up on the road to see me. Garland upon garland was thrown upon me, and I was visibly overcome with emotion. How unlike my father.

I chided Neeta for having announced my arrival.

"They have suffered," she said. "Now they need you."

The house has been done up and smells of paint. Typically (but I note this with affection) one of the new windows does not close; it will be fixed. The broken marble of the mausoleum will take substantial funds to replace. I have some of my own, and there is a donor ready with more; but better to let it stay there awhile with its wounds while other work gets done. Many of the graves are broken, though they have been cleaned. My first repair job, however, will be the ornately designed tomb of Deval Devi, the little princess of Gujarat, for which I always had a special fondness. She too had come to seek refuge at Pirbaag, but it couldn't save her.

I have already paid a visit next door to the new temple of Rupa Devi, Pir Bawa's bride, who for so long was deprived the bliss of the conjugal bed. It is truly impressive and—if one were inclined to think that way— she surely deserves the homage that comes her way. However, the stories the resident priests tell there are different from what I know: in them Rupa is the principal, and Nur Fazal a disciple; moreover, he was a Brahmin orphan brought up by an anonymous Muslim couple. The blatancy of these inventions is quite astounding, reflecting no doubt the political currency of the times. But I have reasserted the rights of Pirbaag to our front yard and the old gate, adjacent to the temple, which my father, perhaps to avoid conflict, had stopped using in favour of a new entrance.

I also paid a visit to my old friend Harish, at his thriving garage across the road. We had tea and chatted some, in between long uncomfortable silences. He lives in a new house up the road with his married son. I dared not ask him about the recent violence in the village, from which he has apparently come out quite unscathed. He is, I learned, a patron of the Rupa Devi temple. As also is, this he informed me proudly, Premji Chacha of America, whose guardianship I had once rejected.

Now my surprise. In the rebuilt Pirbaag library, on a table, a short row of tattered books, in various stages of damage, and some loose pages. That's all, though every page worth its weight in gold. After that night of terror, some of the survivors had gone around diligently collecting all the loose pages among the debris. And later, while cleaning the site, under some of the stones which had been loosened, they found books packed inside newsprint, hidden by my father. And in a corner of the ruined house they found a bundle of old newspapers from the sixties—Raja Singh's contribution to my education.

Before I left the Institute I had my final interview with the director, when I gave him my Assassin theory of the sufi. He was convinced I must be right but has undertaken more research on the subject. Meanwhile he had for me a provisional report on the two manuscript pages I had given him. The Nagari contains a love poem to Hari, a name for Krishna; the Arabic seems to be a fragment from a discussion on plane triangles. Both pages could be dated by their contents. But what did Bapu-ji expect me to make of them?

I have concluded that it is time to make every little item that has survived from the library open to the world. There will be no more secrets in Pirbaag.

It is an eerie feeling to be back. At the Postmaster Flat, I knew I was a guest; here, I now accept that I have come to stay.

Every once in a while I think about that other life that I left behind, the home I made and the happiness I enjoyed with my young family. Had it been a fool's world that I made? Had it been real at all? Ah yes; real as a baby's soft cheek, a woman's thrilling scent, young people's burst of laughter in a classroom. Perhaps I had never been equipped to handle that kind of engagement; how quickly it had unravelled. But now I don't have to choose any more.

The first few nights here I hardly slept, spent much of the time sitting out on the pavilion. Hearing and rehearing the echoes of the savagery that was let loose in this village. There are numerous stories of woe, from the survivors—if one can call them that—who come trickling back from the relief camps, and they don't sit easy on the heart. There is much to rebuild. Last night I slept, finally, as I should, and was awakened by the tinkle of a bell; then came the singing of ginans—sweet vindication, subtle welcome, for these songs ever held on to me.

But something was still missing. There was no prayer call from the mosque. It, with the entire Balak Shah settlement, was destroyed. To go there to look now is to feel sick to the stomach. I recall how Bapu-ji, Ma, and I had taken a comatose Mansoor to spend the night with the Child-imam at the mosque, and how old Sheikh-ji had brought my brother back the next morning, completely recovered. Happily a charitable foundation from Baroda has now surveyed the area and has undertaken to rebuild it.

I am the caretaker of Pirbaag. I do advise people on their worldly affairs when called upon and supervise some projects in the town. The local school needs revamping, working parents want a daycare, the potters need new tools, and so on. And the mausoleum remains a place for worship for those who need it. There are many who do, and they come in numbers on Saturday.

There are those who will touch my feet or my sleeves, ask for blessings. I flinch, internally, and try to cope without wounding. An old woman, bent almost double, came once and grabbed my hand, ran my fingers slowly all over her soft but spotted face, shocking me to the core. Did I know her? I could not quite tell. But as I attend to these people, unable to disappoint, to pull my hand or sleeve away, as I listen in sympathy and utter a blessing, a part of me detaches and stands away, observing. Asking, Are you real?

The answer is not simple.

But here I stop, to begin anew. For the call has come for me, again, and as Bapu-ji would say, this time I must bow.

Author's Note

The character of Nur Fazal in this novel is entirely fictitious, though undoubtedly inspired by the arrival in medieval India of Muslim mystics who gathered a following and came to be called pirs. I have quoted or adapted for my purposes several ginans, as the compositions of the Khoja Ismaili pirs, in old Gujarati and archaic mixtures of Indian languages, are called, and adopted the term *ginan;* however, the verses purporting to tell the story of Nur Fazal and appearing as epigraphs to certain of the chapters in this novel are pure inventions. Elements of the story of the arrival of Nur Fazal in Anularra (Anhilvad, Patan) were inspired by the story of Nur Satgur, who according to tradition arrived at the court of the great Jaisingh Siddhraj in the twelfth century, a hundred years before the arrival of the fictitious Nur Fazal to the court of Vishal Dev. I have used (and abused freely) the story from a translation from the Gujarati by Abualy A. Aziz. Nur Satgur is believed to be buried in Nawsari, and several of his descendants in Pirana and Champaner, all in Gujarat. I have had occasion to visit all of these shrines. It turned out that people of various beliefs and many of no single affiliation attended them, and some of the ginans I was familiar with were in fact common to several communities. The history of these traditions is complex and in a state of flux, with fundamentalisms of either stripe trying to claim them. But this is a work of fiction. The shrine of Pirbaag and the town of Haripir are inventions, as are all of the characters here. Unfortunately the mayhem unleashed in Gujarat was only too real.

Glossary

There used to be a time when non-English terms appearing in fiction were necessarily italicized to denote their foreignness, or adorned with a superscript to provide their meanings. Happily this is not the case any more, for the meaning of a term should be apparent in a novel or story wherever it occurs. However, to shun a glossary or even a hint of a meaning merely on principle risks becoming another orthodoxy, a posture which I would like to avoid. An explanation does not hurt if only to provide further context for a term. The reader is not obliged to consider it. I have resorted to italics where the narrator, Karsan Dargawalla, who writes in English, deems them necessary.

Atman	the true inner self or soul of a person or being
bhajan	a devotional song
bol	a secret mantra
Brahman	the Universal Soul that encompasses everything
brahmin	a member of the traditional priestly caste
chaddar	a coloured, decorated cloth, given as an offering at a shrine where it is used to drape a grave
dargah	a shrine where a Muslim holy man is buried
ginan	from the Sanskrit *gnan,* meaning "knowledge," here referring to a devotional song or hymn
Jain	a member of an Indian religious faith known especially for extreme aversion to killing all living forms

Glossary

Mahabharat	the great war of the Indian epic *Mahabharata*
namaz	the traditional Muslim prayer
pir	a Muslim holy man of saintly status
prasad	an offering received from a temple
puja	the act of devotion to a god
sufi	a Muslim mystic

Acknowledgements

Pankaj Singh, Arun Mukherjee, Alok Mukherjee, Marc Lizoain, for answering questions. Stella Sandahl, for reading the manuscript and catching a very Vedic error, besides providing the translation used. The New York Public Library and the Jawaharlal Nehru Library in Delhi, for their facilities. Rajkumar Hans, Muhammad Salat, Sudha Pandya, for their hospitality in Gujarat. Rikhav Desai and Sanjay Talreja, for their company on the roads of Gujarat. Professor Mrinal Miri and the staff of the Indian Institute of Advanced Studies, Shimla, for their generous hospitality; all my other hosts and friends in India: Charu Verma, Chandra Mohan, Om Juneja, Neerja Chand, Alka Kumar, Harish Narang. Abualy A. Aziz for generously making available manuscripts of his translations from Gujarati.

My family, as always, for their constant indulgence. And Nurjehan for her careful proofreading.

Maya Mavjee for her sensitivity and enthusiasm; Sonny Mehta, Bruce Westwood, Diya Kar Hazra, for their encouragement.

Charles Stuart for gently handling the text; Martha Leonard, Diana Coglianese, and Avanija Sundaramuti for constantly caring about the details.

Quotes were used from the following sources:

p. v. Don Paterson, "A God," *Orpheus: A Version of Rilke's* Die Sonnette an Orpheus (London: Faber and Faber Ltd., 2006).

p. 95. The Rig Veda 1.50.1.

pp. 231–32. Chapter 18, Verse 20, *The Bhagavad Gita*, trans. Swami Nikhi-lananda (New York: Ramakrishna-Vivekanada Center of New York, 2004).

p. 232. Lady Julian, quoted in Carolyn F. E. Spurgeon, *Mysticism in English Literature* (1913). The Project Gutenberg Ebook (#11935, 2004).

pp. 304–5. Ata-Malik Juvaini, *Genghis Khan: The History of the World Conqueror*, trans. J. A. Boyle (1958; rpt., Seattle: University of Washington Press, 1997).

The following publications, among many others, have been especially useful:

Attar, Farid al-Din. *Muslim Saints and Mystics.* Trans. A. J. Arberry. Arkana (Penguin), 1990.

Clements, A. L. *John Donne's Poetry,* Norton Critical Edition, 1966.

Commissariat, M. S. *A History of Gujarat,* 1938.

Forbes, Alexander Kinloch. *Ras Mala, Hindoo Annals of the Province of Gooʐerat in Western India.* 1924; rpt., Delhi: Low Price Publications, 1997.

Schimmel, Annemarie. *Mystical Dimensions of Islam.* Chapel Hill: University of North Carolina Press, 1975.

Complete Poems and Selected Letters of John Keats. The Modern Library, 2001.

Blake: Poems. Everyman's Library, 1994.

Byron: Poems. Everyman's Library, 1994.

PERMISSIONS CREDITS

Grateful acknowledgement is made to the following for permission to reprint previously published material:

Faber and Faber Ltd.: Excerpt from *Orpheus: A Version of Rilke's* Die Sonnette an Orpheus, translated by Don Paterson (London: Faber and Faber Ltd., 2006). Reprinted by permission of Faber and Faber Ltd.

Manchester University Press: Excerpt from *Genghis Khan: The History of the World Conqueror* by Ata-Malik Juvaini, translated from the text of Mirza Muhammad Qazvini by J. A. Boyle, translation copyright © 1958 by UNESCO (Manchester University Press, 1958). Reprinted by permission of Manchester University Press.

Ramakrishna-Vivekananda Center Publications: Excerpt from *The Bhagavad Gita*, translated by Swami Nikhilananda, copyright © 1944 by Swami Nikhilananda. Reprinted by permission of Ramakrishna-Vivekananda Center Publications.

A NOTE ABOUT THE AUTHOR

M. G. Vassanji was born in Kenya and raised in Tanzania. Before moving to Canada in 1978, he attended MIT, and later was writer-in-residence at the University of Iowa. Vassanji is the author of five acclaimed novels: *The Gunny Sack* (1989), which won a regional Commonwealth Prize; *No New Land* (1991); *The Book of Secrets* (1994), which won the very first Giller Prize and the Bressani Prize; *Amriika* (1999); and *The In-Between World of Vikram Lall* (2003), which also won the Giller Prize. In addition, he is the author of two collections of short stories, *Uhuru Street* (1992) and *When She Was Queen* (2005). He was awarded the Harbourfront Festival Prize in 1994 in recognition of his achievement in and contribution to the world of letters, and was in the same year chosen as one of twelve Canadians on Maclean's Honour Roll. Vassanji lives in Toronto with his wife and two sons.

A NOTE ON THE TYPE

Pierre Simon Fournier le jeune, who designed the type used in this book, was both an originator and a collector of types. His services to the art of printing were his design of letters, his creation of ornaments and initials, and his standardization of type sizes. His types are old style in character and sharply cut. In 1764 and 1766 he published his *Manuel typographique,* a treatise on the history of French types and printing, on typefounding in all its details, and on what many consider his most important contribution to typography—the measurement of type by the point system.

Composed by Creative Graphics, Allentown, Pennsylvania
Printed and bound by Berryville Graphics, Berryville, Virginia
Designed by Virginia Tan